Timar's Two Worlds

Mór Jókai

TIMAR'S TWO WORLDS

BOOK FIRST.—THE "ST. BARBARA."

1

CHAPTER I.
THE IRON GATE.

A mountain-chain, pierced through from base to summit—a gorge four miles in length, walled in by lofty precipices; between their dizzy heights the giant stream of the Old World, the Danube.

Did the pressure of this mass of water force a passage for itself, or was the rock riven by subterranean fire? Did Neptune or Vulcan, or both together, execute this supernatural work, which the iron-clad hand of man scarce can emulate in these days of competition with divine achievements?

Of the rule of the one deity traces are visible on the heights of Fruska Gora in the fossil sea-shells strewn around, and in Veterani's cave with its petrified relics of saurian monsters of the deep; of the other god, the basalt of Piatra Detonata bears witness. While the man of the iron hand is revealed by long galleries hewn in the rock, a vaulted road, the ruined piers of an immense bridge, the tablets sculptured in bas-relief on the face of the cliff, and by a channel two hundred feet wide, hollowed in the bed of the river, through which the largest ships may pass.

The Iron Gate has a history of two thousand years. Four nations—Romans, Turks, Roumanians and Hungarians, have each in turn given it a different name.

We seem to approach a temple built by giants, with rocky pillars, towering columns, and wonderful colossi on its lofty frieze, stretching out in a perspective of four miles, and, as it winds, discovering new domes with other groups of natural masonry, and other wondrous forms. One wall is smooth as polished granite, red and white veins zigzagging across it like mysterious characters in the handwriting of God. In another place the whole face is rusty brown, as if of solid iron. Here and there the oblique strata suggest the daring architecture of the Titans. At the next turn we are met by the portal of a Gothic cathedral, with its pointed gables, its clustered basaltic columns. Out of the dingy wall shines now and again a golden speck like a glimpse of the Ark of the Covenant—there sulphur blooms, the ore-flower. But living blossoms also deck the crags. From the crevices of the cornice

5

hang green festoons. These are great foliage-trees and pines, whose dark masses are interspersed with frost-flecked garlands of red and gold.

Now and then the mouth of some valley makes a break in the endless, dizzy precipice, and allows a peep into a hidden paradise untrodden by man.

Here between two cliffs lies a deep shadow, and into this twilight shines like a fairy world the picture of a sunny vale, with a forest of wild vines, whose small red clusters lend color to the trees, and whose bright leaves weave a carpet below. No human dwelling is visible; a clear stream winds along, from which deer drink fearlessly; then the brook throws its silver ribbon over the edge of the cliff. Thousands pass by the valley, and each one asks himself who lives there.

Then follows another temple more huge and awful than the first; the towering walls drawing closer by three hundred yards and soaring three thousand feet into the sky.

That projecting needle at the top is the "Gropa lui Petro," the grave of St. Peter; the two gigantic forms on either side are his apostolic companions; yonder monster opposite is the "Babile," and the one which closes the vista is the "Golumbaczka Mali" or Dove-rock; while the gray pinnacle which towers above is the high Robbers' Peak, "Rasbojnik Beliki."

Between these walls flows the Danube in its rocky bed. The mighty mother-stream, accustomed far above on the Hungarian plains to flow with majestic quiet in a bed three miles wide, to caress the overhanging willows, to look on blooming meadows and play with chattering mills, is here confined in a pass only a hundred and fifty fathoms in width.

With what rage it rushes through! He who traveled with it before recognizes it no longer; the grisly giant is rejuvenated into heroic youth. Its waves leap along the stony bed, from which sometimes a great bowlder projects like a witch's altar, the huge "Babagay," the crowned "Kassan." On this it bursts with majestic fury, roaring round it with swirls which hollow deep abysses in the bottom; thence it rushes, hissing and seething, across the slabs of rock which stretch obliquely from side to side of the channel. In many places it has already mastered the obstacles which barred its way, and flows foaming through the open breach. There, it has burrowed beneath the wall of the ravine, and by its continuous current has washed out a channel below the overhanging rock. Here, it has carved islands out of the stubborn granite, new creations, to be found on no chart, overgrown with wild bushes. They belong to no state—neither Hungary, Turkey, nor Servia; they are ownerless, nameless, subject to no tribute, outside the world. And there again it has carried away an island, with all its shrubs, trees, huts, and wiped it from the map.

The rock and islets divide the stream, which between Ogradina and Plesvissovicza has a speed of ten miles an hour, into many arms; and the sailor has need to study these intricate and narrow passages, for there is but one deep-water channel through the rocky bed—in-shore none but the smallest boats can float.

Among the small islands between the lesser branches of the Danube, singular constructions of human hands are mingled with the grand works of nature; double rows of palisades made of strong trunks of trees, which, joined in the form of a V, present their open side down stream. These are the sturgeon-traps. The marine visitors swim up stream into the snare, and on and on into the ever-narrowing trap—for it is not their custom to turn back—until they find themselves in the death-chamber from which there is no release.

The voices of this sublime region are superhuman. A perpetual universal tumult; so monotonous, so nearly akin to silence and yet so distinct—as if it uttered the name of God. How the great river dances over the granite shores, how it scourges the rocky walls, bounds against the island altars, dives rattling into the whirlpool, pervades the cataract with harmony!

The echo from the mighty cliffs raises this eternal voice of the waters into an unearthly melody, like organ notes and thunder dying away. Man is silent, as if afraid to hear his own language amidst this song of the Titans: sailors communicate by signs, and the fishermen's superstition forbids talking here under a penalty. The consciousness of danger impels all to silent prayer.

At any time the passage between these dark precipices, towering on either hand, might give the sensation of being ferried along under the walls of one's own tomb; but what must it be when that supreme terror of the sailor, the Bora, sweeps down! A continuous and ever-increasing gale, which at certain seasons makes the Iron Gate impassable.

If there were only one cliff it would be a protection from the wind; but the draught of air confined between the two is as capricious as the wind in the streets of a town; at each corner it takes a new departure, now it stops suddenly, then bursts out of a corner as from an ambush, seizes the ship, carries away the steering-gear, throws the whole towing-beam into the water, then shifts again, and drives the wooden vessel before it as though it were going down-stream—the water throwing up clouds of spray as blinding and fine as the sand of the desert in a simoom.

At such times the sighing church-music of the gale swells to the thunder of the Last Judgment, in which is mingled the death-cry of departing spirits.

At the time to which this history refers there were no steamers on the Danube. Between Galatz and the junction with the Main, over nine thousand horses were employed in towing ships up-stream; on the Turkish Danube sails were also used, but not on the Hungarian branch. Besides these a whole fleet of smugglers' boats traded between the two countries, propelled only by strong arms. Salt-smuggling was in full swing. On the Turkish side the same salt was sold for five gulden, which cost six and a half on the Hungarian shore. It was brought by contraband back from Turkey to Hungary, and sold here for five and a half gulden. So every one profited by this comfortable arrangement.

The only one not satisfied was the government, which for its own protection established custom-houses along the frontier, in which the male population of the neighboring villages had to keep guard armed with guns. Each village supplied watchmen, and each village had its own smugglers. While the young men of the place were on guard, the old ones carried the salt, and so both trades were kept in the family. But the government had another important object in its strict watch on the frontier—security from the plague.

The terrible Eastern plague!

In these days we know nothing of it, for it is a hundred and fifty years since a vain widow in Semlin brought an infected shawl, and fell dead as she went to church in it. But we have to thank the regulations which shut the

8

door against it for this immunity. For each contact with a new people has endowed us with a new disease. From China we received scarlet fever, from the Saracens small-pox, from Russia influenza, from South America yellow fever, and from the Hindoos cholera. But the plague comes from Turkey.

Therefore, along the whole bank, the opposite neighbors can only communicate with each other on condition of observing strict preventive measures, which must add considerable interest to their daily life.

If the plague breaks out in Brussa, everything living or dead is officially declared infected: whoever has been in contact with it comes under the same ban, and must be in quarantine for ten or twenty days. If the cable of a left-bank ship touches the cable of a right-bank vessel, the whole crew of the former is unclean, and she must lie for ten days in the middle of the stream; for the plague might pass along the ropes from one to the other, and be communicated to the whole crew.

And all this is carefully watched. On each ship sits an official called a "purifier." A terrible person, whose duty it is to keep an eye on every one, what he handles, what touches him; and if a passenger has been in contact with any person, or any material of hair, wool, or hemp on the Turkish side (for these substances carry infection), even with the hem of his garment, the health-officer must declare him under suspicion, and on arrival at Orsova must drag him from the arms of his family and deliver him over to quarantine.

Woe to the purifier if he should conceal a case! For the slightest neglect, fifteen years' imprisonment is the penalty.

It would appear, however, that smugglers are not liable to the plague, for they have no purifier on board, and if the disease should break out a hundred times over in Brussa, they would still ply day and night between the two banks. We must remember, however, that St. Procopius is their patron. Only the Bora disturbs their retail trade; for the swift current through the Iron Gate drives the rowing-boats toward the southern shore. Of course smuggling is done by tow-boats too, but that belongs to wholesale traffic, costs more than friendly business, and so is not for poor people: in them not only salt, but also tobacco and coffee are smuggled across the frontier.

The Bora has swept the Danube clear of vessels, and has thereby so raised public morality and obedience to law, that for the last few days there has been no occasion for forgiveness of sins. Every vessel has hastened into harbor, or cast anchor in mid-stream, and the watchmen can sleep in peace as long as this wind makes the joints of their wooden huts creak. No ship can travel now, and yet the corporal of the Ogradina watch-house has a fancy that ever since day-break, amidst the blustering wind and roaring waters, he can detect the peculiar signal tones which the speaking-trumpet sends for many miles, and which are not drowned even by the voice of the thunder; the haunting, mournful blasts which issue from the long wooden tube.

Is some vessel declaring its approach, so that no other ship may meet it in such weather in the narrow channel of the Iron Gate? Or is it in danger and calling for help?

This ship approaches.

It is an oaken vessel of ten to twelve thousand measures burden: deeply laden it would appear, for the waves wash over the bulwarks on each side.

The massive hull is painted black, with a white bow, which ends in a long upstanding spiral beak plated with shining tin. The upper deck is shaped like a roof, with narrow steps up to it, and a flat bridge leading from one side to the other. The forward part of the raised deck ends in a double cabin, containing two rooms, with doors to right and left. The third wall of the cabin shows two small windows with green painted shutters, and in the space between them the maidenly form of the martyred St. Barbara is painted on a gold ground, with a pink dress, light-blue mantle, red head-dress, and a white lily in her hand.

In the small space between the cabins and the thick coils of rope on the prow of the ship, stands a long green wooden trough filled with earth, in which lovely blooming carnations and stocks are planted. A three-foot iron railing shuts in the little garden, and on its spikes hang garlands of wild flowers. In the middle burns a lamp in a red glass globe, near to which is a bundle of dried rosemary and consecrated willow-catkins.

On the forepart of the vessel stands the mast, to whose center rings the tow-rope is attached; a three-inch cable, by which thirty-two horses on the bank are trying to move the heavy ship up-stream. At other times sixteen

10

horses would have sufficed here, and on the upper reaches twelve would be enough, but in this part and against such a wind even the thirty-two find it hard work. The horn signals are for the leader of the team-drivers; the human voice would be powerless here: even if the call reached the shore, no one could understand it amidst the confused echoes.

But the language of the horn is intelligible even to horses; from its now drawling, now abrupt, warning, or encouraging tones, man and beast understand when to hasten or slacken their speed, or when to stop altogether.

For in this narrow ravine the lot of the vessel is very uncertain; it has to struggle with gusts of furious wind, variable currents, its own weight, and the rocks and whirlpool which must be avoided. Its fate lies in the hands of two men. One is the pilot who steers; the other is the captain, who amidst the roar of the elements signals his orders to the towing-team by blasts on the horn. If the signal is misunderstood the ship either runs on to a rock, glides into the rapids, goes to pieces on the southern shore, or strands on some newly formed sand-bank, and sinks with every soul on board.

The steersman is a six-foot weather-beaten sailor with a very red face, whose color on both cheeks comes from a network of veins with which the white of the eye is also transfused. He is always hoarse, and his voice knows only two variations, either a loud bellow or a low growl. Probably this is what obliges him to take double care of his throat. Prevention by means of a red comforter tightly wound round his neck, and cure by means of a brandy-flask occupying a permanent position in his coat pocket.

The captain is a man of about thirty, with fair hair, dreamy blue eyes, and a long mustache, the rest of his face clean shaven. He is of middle height, and gives an idea of delicacy; with this impression his voice accords, for when he speaks softly it is like a woman's.

The steersman is called Johann Fabula; the name of the captain is Michael Timar.

The official "purifier" sits on the edge of the rudder bench; he has drawn a hood over his head, so that only his nose and mustache appear: both are red. History has not recorded his name. At present he is chewing tobacco.

One of the ship's boats, manned by six rowers, has taken out a line from the bow, and the united efforts of the oarsmen materially assist the

11

towing of the vessel.

At the door of the double cabin sits a man of fifty, smoking a Turkish chibouque. His features are Oriental, with more of the Turkish than the Greek type; his dress, with the striped kaftan and red fez, is like that of a Servian or Greek. It will not escape an attentive observer that the shaven part of his face is light in contrast to the rest, which is the case with a person who has lately removed a thick beard. This is Euthemio Trikaliss, under which name he appears in the way-book. He is the owner of the cargo, but the ship itself belongs to a merchant of Komorn called Athanasius Brazovics.

Out of one of the cabin windows looks the face of a young girl, and so becomes a neighbor of St. Barbara. One might fancy it was another sacred picture. The face is not pale but white—the inherent whiteness of marble or natural crystal. As an Abyssinian is born black, and a Malay yellow, so is this girl born white. No other tint disturbs the delicate snow; on this face neither the breath of the wind nor the eye of man calls up a blush. She is certainly only a child, hardly more than thirteen; but her figure is tall and slender, her face calm as if hewn out of alabaster, with severely antique lines, as if her mother had looked always at the Venus of Milo. Her thick black hair has a metallic gleam like the plumage of the black swan; but her eyes are dark-blue. The long delicate eyebrows almost meet over the brow, which gives her face a curious charm; it is as if these arching brows formed a black aureole round the brow of a saint.

The girl's name is Timéa.

These are the passengers of the "St. Barbara."

When the captain lays his speaking-trumpet aside, and has tried with the lead what water the ship has under her, he has time to chat with the girl as he leans against the iron railing round the picture.

Timéa understands only modern Greek, which the captain can speak fluently. He points out to her the beauties of the scenery, its grim, cruel beauties: the white face, the dark-blue eyes, remain unchanged, and yet the girl listens with fixed attention.

But it seems to the captain as if these eyes gave their thoughts not so much to him as to the stocks which grow at St. Barbara's feet. He breaks off one and gives it to the child, that she may listen to what the flowers tell.

The steersman sees this, away there by the tiller, and it displeases him. "You would do better," he growls in a voice like the rasping of a file, "instead of plucking the saint's flowers for that child, to burn a holy willow-wand at the lamp, for if the Lord drives us on to these stone monsters, even His own Son won't save us. Help, Jesu!"

This aspiration would have been uttered by Johann Fabula, even if he were alone; but as the purifier sat close by, there followed this dialogue:

"Why must the gentry pass the Iron Gate in such a storm?"

"Why?" answered Johann Fabula, who did not forget his laudable habit of aiding the collection of his thoughts by a gulp out of the wicker brandy-flask. "Why? For no other reason but being in a hurry. Ten thousand measures of wheat are in our hold. In the Banat the crops failed; in Wallachia there was a good harvest. This is Michaelmas; if we don't make haste, November will be upon us, and we shall be frozen in."

"And why do you think the Danube will freeze in November?"

"I don't think—I know. The Komorn calendar says so. Look in my berth, it hangs by my bed."

The purifier buried his nose in his hood, and spat his tobacco juice into the Danube.

"Don't spit into the water in such weather as this—the Danube won't bear it. But what the Komorn calendar says is as true as Gospel. Ten years ago it prophesied that frost would set in in November; so I started at once to get home with my ship—then too I was in the 'St. Barbara'—the others laughed at me. But on the 23d of November cold set in, and half the vessels were frozen in, some at Apathin, and others at Foldvar. Then it was my turn to laugh. Help, Jesu! Hard over, he—e—e—!!"

The wind was now dead ahead. Thick drops of sweat ran down the steersman's cheeks while he struggled to get the tiller over, but he asked for no help. Then he rewarded himself with a pull at his bottle, after which his eyes looked redder than ever.

"Now if the Lord will only help us to pass that stone pier," groaned he in the midst of his exertions. "Pull away, you fellows there! If only we can get by this point!"

"There's another beyond."

13

"Yes, and then a third, and a thirteenth, and we must keep our mass-money ready in our mouths, for we are walking over our open coffins all the time."

"Hark ye, my good friend," said the purifier, taking his plug out of his mouth, "I fancy your ship carries something besides wheat."

Master Fabula looked askance at the purifier under his hood, and shrugged his shoulders. "What's that to me? If there's contraband on the ship, at any rate we sha'n't stop in quarantine, and we shall get on pretty quick."

"How so?"

The steersman made a circle with his thumb behind his back, on which the health-officer burst out laughing. Could he possibly have understood this pantomime?

"Now, look you," said Johann Fabula, "since I was here last, the course of the river has altered; if I don't let her go a bit free we shall get into the new eddy which has formed under the 'Lovers' Rock.' Do you see that devilish monster which keeps swimming close to us? That's an old sturgeon—he must be at least five hundred-weight. If this beast keeps up with us, he'll bring us ill-luck. Help, Lord! If only he would come near enough for me to get the grappling-iron into him! The skipper is always sneaking up to the Greek girl instead of blowing his horn to the riders. She brings us misfortune—since she has been on board, we've had nothing but north wind; there's something wrong about her—she's as white as a ghost, and her eyebrows grow together like a witch's. Herr Timar, blow to the teamsmen, ho—ho—ho!"

But Timar did not touch the horn, and went on telling legends of the rocks and water-falls to the white maiden.

Beginning from the Iron Gate up to Clissera, each valley, each cave on both banks, every cliff, island, and every eddy in the stream has its history: a fairy tale, a legend, or an adventure with brigands, of which books, or sculptured inscriptions, or national songs, or fisherfolks' tradition tell the story. It is a library in stone, the names of the rocks are the lettered back of the volumes, and he who knows how to open them may read a romance therein.

14

Michael Timar had long been at home in this library. With the vessel committed to his charge he had often made the passage of the Iron Gate, and every stone and island was familiar to him.

Possibly he had another object with his legends and anecdotes besides the satisfaction of the girl's curiosity. When a highly strung creature has to pass through a great danger, which makes even a strong man's heart quake, then those who know the danger try to turn the attention of the ignorant person into the kingdom of marvels. Was it perhaps thus?

Timéa listened to the story of the hero Mirko with his beloved, the faithful Milieva; how they fled to the peaks of the Linbigaja Rock out in the Danube; how there he alone defended the precipitous approach to his refuge, against all the soldiers of his pursuer Hassan; how they lived on the kids brought by the eagles to their nest on the cliff, cared not for the roar of the breakers round the base of their island, and felt no fear of the white surges thrown up by the compressed force of the narrowed current. Mariners call these woolly wave-crests the "Lovers' Goats."

"It would be better to look ahead than astern," growled the steersman, and then exerted his voice in a loud call, "Haha! ho! skipper, what's that coming down on us?"

The captain looked round, and saw the object pointed out by the pilot. The ship was now entering the Tatalia Pass, where the Danube is only two hundred fathoms wide, and has a rapid incline. It looks like a mountain torrent, only that this torrent is the Danube. And besides, the stream is here divided in two by a mass of rock whose top is covered with bushes. The water forks in two arms on the western side, of which one shoots under the steep precipice of the Servian bank, while the other discharges through an artificial channel a hundred yards wide, by which the large vessels pass up and down. In this part it is far from desirable that two ships should meet, for there is barely room for them to pass in safety. To the northward lie hidden rocks where a ship might strike, and to the southward is the great whirlpool formed by the junction of the two branches; if this should seize a vessel, no human power could save her.

So that the danger which the steersman had announced by his question was a very real one.

15

Two ships meeting in the Tatalia Pass with the river so high and under such a pressure of wind!

Michael Timar asked for his telescope, which he had lent to Timéa to look at the place where Mirko had defended the beautiful Milieva.

At the western curve of the river a dark mass was visible in the stream.

Michael looked through his glass, and then called to the steersman, "A mill!"

"Holy Father! then we are lost."

A water-mill was driving down on them; probably the storm had loosened its chains from the bank. Obviously it was without pilot or oarsman, who must have fled to the shore; so it drifted blindly on, sweeping away the mills it met on its way, and sinking any cargo-boats which could not get out of its road.

How could they escape between Scylla and Charybdis?

Timar said not a word of this to Timéa, but gave her back the glass, and told her where to look for the eagles' nest whose ancestors had fed the lovers. Then he threw off his coat hastily, sprung into the barge where the rowers were, and made five of them get into the small boat with him; they were to bring the light anchor and thin cable with them, and cast off.

Trikaliss and Timéa did not understand his orders, as he spoke Hungarian, which neither of them knew.

The captain shouted to the steersman, "Keep her steady; go ahead!" In a few moments Trikaliss also could see what was the danger. The drifting mill came floating swiftly down the brawling stream, and one could see with the naked eye the clattering paddle-wheel, whose width occupied the whole fairway of the channel. If it touched the laden ship both must go down.

The boat with the six men still struggled up against the current. Four of them rowed, one steered, and Timar stood in the bow with folded arms.

What was their insane design? What could they do in a little boat against a great mill? What are human mind and muscles against stream and storm?

If each were a Samson, the laws of hydrostatics would set at naught their strength. The shock with which they touch the mill will recoil on the

16

skiff; if they grapple it they will be dragged away by it. It is as if a spider would catch a cockchafer in its web.

The boat, however, did not keep in the center, but tried to reach the southern point of the island.

So high were the waves that the five men disappeared again and again in the hollows between, then the next moment they danced on the foamy crest, tossed hither and thither by the willful torrent, seething under them like boiling water.

CHAPTER II.
THE WHITE CAT.

The oarsmen consulted in the boat what was to be done.

One advised cutting through the side of the mill below the water-line with an ax, so as to sink it: but that would do no good; the current would drive the wreck down on to the ship.

A second thought they ought to grapple the mill with hooks, and give it a list away, so as to direct it toward the whirlpool: but this counsel was also rejected, for the eddies would drag the boat down too.

Timar ordered the man at the tiller to keep straight for the point of the island where the Lovers' Rock lies.

When they approached the rapids he lifted the heavy anchor and swung it into the water without shaking the boat, which showed what muscular strength the delicate frame contained. The anchor took out a long coil of rope with it, for the water is deep there. Then Timar made them row as quickly as possible toward the approaching mill. Now they guessed his design—he meant to anchor the mill. Bad idea, said the sailors; the great mass will lie across the fairway, and stop the ship; besides, the cable is so long and slight that the heavy fabric will part it easily.

When Euthemio Trikaliss saw from the vessel Timar's intention, he dropped his chibouque in a panic, ran along the deck and cried to the steersman to cut the tow-rope, and let the ship drift down-stream.

The pilot did not understand Greek, but guessed from the old man's gestures what he wanted.

With perfect calmness he answered as he leaned against the rudder, "There's nothing to grumble at; Timar knows what to do." With the courage of despair Trikaliss drew his dagger out of his girdle in order to cut the rope himself; but the steersman pointed toward the stern, and what Trikaliss saw there altered his mind.

From the Lower Danube came a vessel toward them: an accustomed eye can distinguish it from afar. It has a mast whose sails are furled, a high poop, and twenty-four rowers.

18

It is a Turkish brigantine.

As soon as he caught sight of it, Trikaliss put his dagger back in his sash; if he had turned purple at what he saw ahead, now he was livid. He hastened to Timéa, who was looking through the glass at the peaks of Perigrada. "Give me the telescope!" he exclaimed in a hoarse voice.

"Oh, how pretty that is!" said Timéa, as she gave up the glass.

"What?"

"On the cliffs there are little marmots playing together like monkeys."

Euthemio directed the telescope toward the approaching vessel, and his brows contracted; his face was pale as death.

Timéa took the glass from his hand and looked again for the marmots on the rocks. Euthemio kept his arm round her waist.

"How they jump and dance and chase each other; how amusing!" and Timéa little knew how near she was to being lifted by the arm that held her, and plunged over the bulwarks into the foaming flood.

But what Euthemio saw on the other side brought back into his face the color it had lost.

When Timar arrived within a cast of the mill, he took a coil of the anchor-rope in his right hand; a hook was fastened to its end. The rudderless mass came quickly nearer, like some drifting antediluvian monster—blind chance guided it; its paddle-wheel turned swiftly with the motion of the water, and under the empty out-shoot the mill-stone revolved over the flour-bin as if it was working hard.

In this fabric devoted to certain destruction, there was no living thing except a white cat, which sat on the red-painted shingle roof and mewed piteously.

When he got close to the mill, Timar swung the rope and hook suddenly round his head, and aimed it at the paddle-wheel.

As soon as the grappling-iron had caught one of the floats, the wheel, driven by water-power, began to wind up the rope gently, and so give the mill a gradual turn toward the Perigrada Island; completing by its own machinery the suicidal work of casting itself on the rocks.

"Didn't I say Timar knew what he was about?" growled Johann Fabula; while Euthemio in joyful excitement exclaimed, "Bravo! my son," and pressed Timéa's hand so hard that she was frightened and even forgot the marmots.

"There, look!"

And now Timéa also noticed the mill. She required no telescope, for it and the ship were so near together that in the narrow channel they were only separated by about sixty feet.

Just enough to let the diabolical machine get safely past.

Timéa thought neither of the danger nor of the deliverance, only of the forsaken cat.

When the poor animal saw the floating house and its inhabitants so near to it, it leaped up and began running up and down the roof-ridge, and to measure with its eye the distance between the mill and the ship, whether it dared jump.

"Oh, the poor little cat!" cried Timéa, anxiously, "if we could only get near enough for it to come over to us."

But from this misfortune the ship was preserved by its patron saint, and by the anchor-rope, which, wound up by the paddle-wheel, got shorter and shorter, and drew the wreck nearer the island and further from the vessel.

"Oh, the poor pretty white cat!"

"Don't be afraid," Euthemio tried to console her; "when it passes the rock the cat will spring ashore, and be very happy living with the marmots."

Only unluckily the cat, keeping on the hither side of the roof, could not see the island.

When the "St. Barbara" had got safely past the enchanted mill, Timéa waved her handkerchief to the cat, and called out first in Greek, and then in the universal cat's language, "Quick, look, jump off, puss-s-s-s;" but the animal, frantic with terror, paid no heed.

At the very moment when the stern of the ship had passed the mill, the latter was suddenly caught by the current, swung round so that the grappled wheel broke, and the liberated mass shot like an arrow down the stream. The white cat sprung up to the ridge.

"Ah!"

But the mill rushed on its fate.

20

Below the island is the great whirlpool.

It is one of the most remarkable eddies ever formed by the river giants—on every map it is marked by two arrows meeting in a corner. Woe to the boat which is swept in the direction of either arrow! Round the great funnel the water boils and rages as in a seething caldron, and in the middle of the circle yawns the bare abyss below. This whirlpool has worn a hole in the rock a hundred and twenty feet deep, and what it takes with it into this tomb, no one ever sees again: if it should be a man, he had better look out for the resurrection. And into this place the current carried the mill. Before it reached there it sprung a leak and got a list over; the axle of the wheel stood straight on end; the white cat ran along to the highest point and stood there humping its back; the eddy caught the wooden fabric, carried it round in wide circles four or five times, turning on its own axis, creaking and groaning, and then it disappeared under the water. With it the white cat.

Timéa shuddered and hid her face in her shawl.

But the "St. Barbara" was saved.

Euthemio pressed the hands of the returning oarsmen—Timar he embraced. Timar might have expected that Timéa would say a friendly word; but she only asked, pointing to the gulf with a disturbed face, "What is become of the mill?"

"Chips and splinters!"

"And the poor cat?" The girl's lips trembled, and tears stood in her eyes.

"It's all up with her."

"But the mill and the cat belonged to some poor man?" said Timéa.

"Yes; but we had to save our ship and our lives, or else we should have been wrecked, and the whirlpool would have drawn us into the abyss, and only thrown up our bones on the shore."

Timéa looked at the man who said this, through the prism of tear-filled eyes.

It was a strange world into which she gazed through these tears. That it should be permissible to destroy a poor man's mill in order to save one's own ship, that you should drown a cat so as not to get into the water yourself!—she could not understand it. From this moment she listened no more to his fairy stories, but avoided him as much as possible.

CHAPTER III.
A DANGEROUS LEAP WITH A MAMMOTH.

Indeed Timar had but little time for story-telling; for he had hardly got his breath after the exertions of his perilous achievement, before Euthemio gave him the glass and pointed where he was to look.

"Gunboat—twenty-four oars—brigantine from Salonica."

Timar did not put down the telescope till the other vessel was hidden from him behind the point of the Perigrada Island.

Then suddenly he let it fall, and, putting the horn to his lips, blew first three, then six sharp blasts, at which the drivers whipped up their horses.

The rocky island of Perigrada is surrounded by two branches of the Danube. The one on the Servian side is that by which cargo-ships pass up; it is safer and cheaper, for half the number of horses suffice. By the Roumanian shore there is also a narrow channel, with just room for one vessel, but here you must use oxen, of which often a hundred and twenty are harnessed. The other arm of the river is again narrowed by the little Reskival Island, lying across the stream. (Now this island has been blown up in part, but at the time of our story the whole still existed.) Through the narrows between the two islands the river shoots like an arrow; but above, it lies between its rocky walls like a great lake. Only this lake has no smooth surface, for it is always in motion, and never freezes in the very hardest winter. Its bottom is thickly sown with rocks; some are under water, while other uncouth monsters project many feet above it.

This is the most dangerous part of the whole voyage. To this day, experienced seamen, English, Turks, Italians, at home on all seas, adventure themselves with much anxiety in this rock-strewn channel. Here the majority of shipwrecks occur. Here in the Crimean War the splendid Turkish man-of-war "Silistria" was lost. She had been ordered to Belgrade, and might have given a new turn to affairs if she had not received a thrust in the ribs from one of the Reskival rocks, so enthusiastic in their peace policy that they obliged her to stay where she was.

Yet this lake, with its dangerous bottom, has a passage through it which but few ships know, and still fewer care to use.

This short cut enables mariners to cross from the channel on the Servian side to the Roumanian shore. The latter channel is divided by a ledge of rock from the Upper Danube, and you can only enter it at Szvinicza, and come out at Szkela-Gladova.

This is the dangerous leap with a floating mammoth.

The captain blows first three, and then six blasts on his horn; the drivers know at once what it means, the leader of the team has dismounted—with good reason too—and they all begin with cries and blows to hurry on the horses. The vessel goes swiftly against the stream.

The horn blows nine times.

The drivers flog the horses furiously: the poor beasts understand the call and the blows, and tug till the rope is nearly strained to breaking. Five minutes of such effort are more exhausting than a whole day's labor.

Now twelve blasts of the horn sound in rapid succession. Men and horses collect the last remnant of their strength. Every moment one fancies they must break down. The towing-rope, a three-inch cable, is as taut as a bow-string, and the iron bolt round which the rope is wound is burning hot with the friction. The captain stands by with a sharp ax in his hand.

When the vessel gained its greatest impetus, with a single blow he severed the cable at the bow.

The tense rope flew whistling like a giant fiddle-string into the air; the horses of the towing-team fell down in a heap, and the leader broke its neck—his rider had wisely dismounted. The ship, relieved of the strain, altered its course suddenly, and began, with its bow to the northern shore, to cut obliquely across the river.

Sailors call this bold maneuver the "Cross-cut."

The heavy bulk is now propelled neither by stream nor oars; even the current is against it. Merely the after effect of the shock it has received drives it over to the other bank.

The calculation of this impulse, with the distance to be traversed and the resistance which lessens the speed, would be a credit to any practical engineer. Common sailors have learned it by rule of thumb.

From the moment when Timar cut the tow-rope, the lives of all on board were in the hands of the steersman.

Johann Fabula showed now what he could do. "Help, Lord Christ!" he muttered, but he did not keep his hands in his lap. Before him the ship rushed with winged speed into the lake formed by the Danube. Two men were now required at the tiller, and even these could hardly bridle the monster in its course.

Timar stood on the prow and sounded with the lead, in one hand holding the line; the other he stretched up, and showed the pilot with his fingers what water they had.

The steersman knew the rocks they were passing over just as well as he could have told exactly how much the river had risen in the last few weeks. In his hands the helm was safe; if he had made a single false movement, if only by an inch, the vessel would have received a shock which would stop her for a moment, and then she and all on board would have been driven head over heels into the Perigrada whirlpool, where the ship and the beautiful white girl would have joined the mill and the beautiful white cat.

Safely past the shallows of the Reskival rapids! Yet this is a bad place. The speed is less, the effect of the motive power already paralyzed by the force of the stream, and the bottom sown with sharp rocks.

Timéa leaned over the bulwarks and looked down into the water. Through the transparent waves, the bright-colored rocks, a huge mosaic of green and yellow and red, looked quite close. Between them shot silvery fishes with red fins. She was fascinated.

Deep silence fell over the scene; each knew that he passed over his grave, and would owe it to God's mercy if he did not find his monument down below. Only the girl felt no emotion of fear.

The vessel had arrived in a bay of rocks. Sailors have given them the name of "gun-stones"; perhaps because the sound of the breakers reminds one of the cracking of musketry fire.

Here the principal branch of the Danube concentrates itself in a deep bed. The sunken rocks are too far under water to be dangerous. Below, in the dark-green depths, one may see the slow and indolent forms of the dwellers of the sea—the great sturgeon and the hundred-pound pike, at whose approach the bright shoals of small fish scatter in haste.

Timéa gazed at the play of the aquatic population; it was like a bird's-eye view of an amphitheater.

Suddenly she felt her arm seized by Timar, who dragged her from the bulwarks, pushed her into the cabin, and shut the door violently.

"Look out! Halloo!" shouted the crew as with one voice.

Timéa could not imagine what was happening that she should be so roughly treated, and ran to look out of the cabin window.

It was only that the ship had passed safely through the "gun-rocks," and was about to enter the Roumanian channel; but from the little bay the water rushes so furiously into the canal that a regular water-fall is formed, and this is the dangerous moment of the "Leap."

When Timéa looked out of the cabin window, she only saw that Timar stood at the bow with a grappler in his hand. Then suddenly a deafening noise arose, a huge foam-crowned mountain of water struck the fore part of the vessel, splashed its spray right against the window, and blinded Timéa for a moment. When she looked out again, the captain was no longer to be seen.

There were great cries outside. She rushed out of the door and met her father. "Are we sinking?" she cried.

Timéa had seen that: the big wave had washed him away before her eyes. But her heart beat no faster when she heard it.

Curious! When she saw the white cat drowned, she was in despair, and could not refrain from tears, and now when the water had swallowed up the captain, she did not even say "Poor fellow!"

Yes, but the cat had cried so pitifully, and this man defies the whole world; the cat was a dear little animal, the captain only a great rough man. And then the cat could not help itself; but he is strong and clever, and can certainly save himself. That's the only good of a man.

After the last leap the ship was safe, and swam in the smooth water of the canal. The sailors ran with grappling-irons to the boat to seek the captain. Euthemio held a purse up as a prize for the rescue of Timar. "A hundred ducats for him who rescues the captain!"

"Keep your hundred ducats, good sir!" cried the voice of the man in question from the other end of the ship. "I'm coming."

Then they saw him climbing up the stern by the rudder-chains. No fear of his being lost!

As if nothing had happened, he began giving orders. "Let go!"

The three hundred-weight anchor was thrown over, and the ship brought up in the middle of the channel, so as to be hidden by the cliffs from the upper reaches of the river.

"And now ashore with the boat," Timar ordered three oarsmen.

"Change your clothes," advised Euthemio.

"Waste of time," answered Timar. "I shall soon be wet again; now I am thoroughly soaked. We have no time to spare."

The last words he whispered into Euthemio's ear.

The man's eyes glittered as he agreed. The captain sprung into the boat and rowed himself, so as to get quicker to the post-house on the bank, where towing-teams could be engaged. He collected hastily eighty oxen. Meanwhile, a new towing-rope was attached to the vessel, the oxen harnessed, and before half an hour had passed, the "St. Barbara" was on her way again through the Iron Gate, and on the opposite side of the stream.

When Timar returned on board, his exertions had dried his clothes.

The ship was saved, perhaps doubly saved, and with it the cargo, Euthemio, and Timéa.

But what are they to him that he should work so hard? He is only the captain and supercargo, and receives a scanty salary as such. It can not matter to him whether the vessel's hold is full of wheat or contraband tobacco or real pearls; his wages remain the same.

So also thought the "purifier," who, when they reached the Roumanian canal, resumed his interrupted conversation with the steersman.

"You'll allow, neighbor, that we were never nearer all going to destruction together than we were to-day."

"There's some truth in that," answered Fabula.

"But why should we try the experiment whether we could get drowned on St. Michael's day?"

"H'm!" said Johann, and took a short pull at his brandy-flask. "What salary do you get, sir?"

"Twenty kreutzers a day," answered the purifier.

"Why the devil do you come here to venture your life for twenty kreutzers a day? I didn't send for you. I get a gulden and my food; so I have forty kreutzers more reason to venture my life than you. What does it matter to you?"

The health-officer shook his head, and threw back his hood, so as to be more easily heard.

"Listen," he said; "it strikes me the brigantine is chasing you, and the 'St. Barbara' is trying to escape."

"H'm!" coughed the steersman, clearing his throat, and becoming suddenly too hoarse to make a sound.

"Well, it doesn't matter to me," said the purifier, with a shrug. "I'm Austrian born, and I don't like the Turks. But I know what I know."

"Well, then, will the gentleman listen to what he doesn't know?" said Fabula, who had suddenly recovered his voice. "Certainly the gunboat is chasing us, and that's why we are showing him our heels. For, look you, they wanted to take the white-faced maiden into the sultan's harem, but her father would not consent; he preferred to escape with her from Turkey, and now the object is to reach Hungarian territory as quickly as possible—there the sultan can't touch her. Now that's all about it, so no more questions, but go to St. Barbara's picture, and light the lamp again if the water has extinguished it; and don't forget to burn three consecrated willow-twigs, if you're a good Christian."

The purifier drew himself up slowly, and looked for his tinderbox, and then he growled in his beard—

"*If* I am an orthodox Catholic? But they say you are only a Papist on board, and a Calvinist directly you set foot on shore; that you pray in the ship, and can hardly wait for dry land before you begin cursing and swearing. And they say too that your name is Fabula, and that Fabula means just the same as a pocketful of lies. But of course I believe all you have told me, so you need not be angry."

"You're quite right there; but now you be off, and don't you come back till I call you."

The twenty-four rowers in the gunboat required three hours to get from the point where first the "St. Barbara" was seen to the Perigrada Island, where the Danube divides into two arms. The cliffs of the island masked the whole bend, and on board the brigantine nothing of what had passed behind them could be seen.

Even below the island the gunboat had met with floating wreckage, which the eddy had thrown to the surface. This was part of the sunken mill, but could not be distinguished from the remains of a vessel. When the brigantine had passed the island a reach of a mile and a half lay open before her; neither in the stream nor by the bank was any large craft to be seen; near the shore were only barges and rowing-boats.

The man-of-war went a little higher, cruised about in the river, and then returned to the shore. There the Turkish first-lieutenant inquired of the watchmen about a cargo-vessel passing by. They had seen nothing, for the ship had not got so far. Presently the brigantine overtook the "St. Barbara's" towing-team, and of them also questions were asked. They were all good Servians, and explained to the Turks where they could find the "St. Barbara."

"She has gone down at the Perigrada Island with her cargo of fruit and all her crew; you can see here how the tow-rope parted."

The Turkish brigantine left the Servian drivers, who were all lamenting because no one was left to pay their wages. (In Orsova they know full well they will come up with their ship and tow her on.) But the commander, being a Turk, of course turned about and went down-stream.

When the brigantine got back to the island the sailors saw a board dancing on the water which did not float away. They fished it out: a rope was fastened to it by an iron hook, for the board was a float from the mill-wheel. Then they heaved up the rope, which had an anchor at its other end. This also was got in, and on its cross-piece, painted in great letters, there was the name "St. Barbara."

Now the whole catastrophe was quite clear. Her towing-rope had broken, she cast her anchor, but it could not hold her, she drifted into the whirlpool, and now her timbers float on the surface, but her crew rests below in the deep pool.

Mashallah! We can not follow her there.

CHAPTER IV.
A STRICT SEARCH.

The "St. Barbara" had escaped two dangers—the rocks of the Iron Gate and the Turkish brigantine; two remained, the Bora and the quarantine in Orsova.

Above the bay of the Iron Gate, the powerful stream is confined by its steep banks in a chasm only a hundred fathoms wide, through which the pent-up current forces its way, in parts with a fall of twenty-eight feet.

Up above the mountain peaks, three thousand feet in air, the eagles circle in majestic flight across the narrow strip of sky visible, whose pure azure, seen from the awful depths below, looks like a glass vault, and further yet rise more and higher peaks.

It is a sight, I trow, to call up spirits from hell. The impotent vessel, which has neither hands nor feet, nor yet fins, which, like an overladen nutshell, floats upward in this narrow channel against wind and stream; and in it a handful of men, trusting in their intelligence and their strength. Here, too, even the Bora can not harm them, for the double range of cliffs keeps off the wind. The steersman and the towing-team have easier work now.

But the Bora was not asleep. It was already afternoon. The chief steersman had given over the tiller to his deputy, and had gone to the galley, which was in the stern. There he was busy preparing a "thieves' roast," of which the recipe is to spit on a long skewer a piece of beef, a piece of ham, and a piece of pork alternately, and then turn the skewer above an open fire till the meat is cooked.

All at once the narrow strip of sky visible between the almost touching cliffs grew dark. The Bora will not be defied.

Suddenly it drives down before it a storm which overcasts the blue sky, so that it is pitch dark in the valley. Up above masses of cloud; dark rocks on either hand. Now and then a dazzling flash darts through the heights, followed by a short abrupt thunderclap, as if the narrow gorge could only contain one chord of the awful concert; then again the lightning shoots into the Danube just in front of the ship, and by its fiery rays for an instant

30

the whole rocky cathedral looks like the flaming gulf of hell, and the thunder rolls, with a crash as of a world destroyed, from one end of the resounding Titan's hall to the other. Rain falls in torrents, but the vessel must go on.

It must get on, that it may have left Orsova before night.

They can only see by the flicker of the lightning. Even with the horn they dare not signal, for it might be heard on the Roumanian side. But inventive man has found a way out of this difficulty.

The captain goes into the bow, gets out his flint and steel, and begins to strike out sparks. This fire can not be extinguished by rain; it can be seen by the drivers through the darkness, and as often as the steel strikes a spark they know at once what to do; they also make signals from the bank by sparks. This is the secret telegraph of sailors and smugglers at the Iron Gate. And this silent language has been brought to perfection by the shore population on each side of the river.

Timéa liked the tempest. She had drawn her Turkish hood over her head, and looked out of the cabin window. "Are we in a cavern?" she asked the captain.

"No," answered Timar, "but at the door of a tomb. That high peak, which glows in the lightning flashes like a mountain of fire, is the grave of St. Peter, the 'Gropa lui Petro.' And the two other monsters near it are the 'Two Old Women.'"

"What old women?"

"According to the legend, a Hungarian and a Wallachian woman quarreled as to which of their two countries could claim the tomb of St. Peter. The apostle could not sleep in his grave for their squabbling, and in his anger he turned them into stone."

Timéa did not smile at the grotesque legend. She did not see anything ridiculous in it. "And how do they know that this is the grave of an apostle?" asked she.

"Because here many healing herbs grow, which they collect to cure all sorts of diseases, and send them great distances."

"So they call him an apostle, who even in his grave does good to others?" Timéa questioned.

"Timéa!" sounded from the cabin the imperious call of Euthemio.

31

The girl drew back her head from the window, and closed the circular shutter. When Timar looked round again, he saw only the saint's picture.

The vessel continued her course in spite of the storm.

Suddenly the dark ravine was left behind, and as the two rock walls trended further apart the gloomy vault overhead disappeared. Just as rapidly as the Bora had brought up the black thunderclouds, so quickly had it swept away the storm; and, all at once, the travelers saw stretched before them the lovely Cserna valley.

The cliffs on both shores were covered to their summits with vineyards and fruit orchards; the landscape glittered in the glow of the evening sun; out of the green distance shone while houses, slender spires, and red roofs, and through the crystal rain-beads gleamed a gorgeous rainbow.

The Danube had lost its uncanny aspect. In its wider bed it could spread itself out comfortably; and on the western reaches of its sea-green mirror the travelers saw the reflection of Orsova on its island—for them the fourth, and greatest, bugbear.

The day had already sunk into twilight when the "St. Barbara" arrived at Orsova.

"More wind to-morrow than even to-day," grumbled the steersman, looking at the red sky.

There the evening clouds were piled like an avalanche, in all shades of fiery and blood red, and if the glowing mist-veil parted through the rent, the sky was not blue but emerald-green. Below, mountain and valley, forest and field, gleamed in the sunset reflex with radiance which hurt the eye, unable to find a shady point of rest. The Danube rushing on beneath, like a fiery Phlegethon, and in its midst an island with towers and massive buildings, all glowing as if part of a huge furnace, through which every creature, coming from the pestilential east to the frontier of the healthy west, must pass as through purgatory.

But what most fixed the attention of the crew under this stormy sunset was a black-and-yellow striped boat, which was being rowed from the shore to the ship.

The Szkela is the double gate through which the neighboring inhabitants of both sides of the Danube speak, bargain, and do business together.

The "St. Barbara" had cast anchor before the island, and awaited the approaching boat, in which were three armed men—two with muskets and bayonets—besides two rowers and the steersman.

Euthemio paced anxiously up and down the small space in front of the cabin. Timar approached him and whispered, "The searcher is coming."

Trikaliss drew from his leathern pouch a silk purse, and took out two *rouleaux*, which he pressed into Timar's hand. In each were a hundred ducats.

Before long the boat was alongside, and the three armed men came on board. One is the overseer of taxes, the inspector, whose office it is to search the cargo for anything contraband or a prohibited importation of arms; the other two are custom-house officials, who render armed assistance, and serve as a check on the inspector to see if he carries out the search properly.

The purifier is the official spy, who reports whether the two officers have properly controlled the inspector. Then the latter three form a tribunal, which takes the evidence of the purifier as to whether he has detected the passengers in any infectious communication. This is all very systematically arranged, so that one organ should control the other, and each be mutually under inspection.

As a legal fee for these functions the chief has to receive a hundred kreutzers, each of the customs officials fifty, and the purifier also fifty—which certainly is a moderate fee enough.

As soon as the inspector reaches the deck, the purifier comes toward him: the former scratches his ear and the latter his nose. No contact takes place.

Then the inspector turns to the captain, and both the other officials ground their arms. Still three paces apart! One can't tell whether the man has not got the plague.

The examination begins.

"Where from?"

"Galatz."

"Name of ship's owner?"

"Athan Brazovics."

"Owner of cargo?"

"Euthemio Trikaliss."

"Where are the ship's papers?"

The reception of these is carefully arranged. A pan of live coals is brought, and strewn with juniper-berries and wormwood: the aforesaid papers are held over it and well smoked, then taken by the inspector with a pair of tongs, read from as great a distance as possible, and afterward returned. Nothing wrong, apparently, with the ship's papers.

The pan is carried away, and in its place a jug of water is brought. It is a capacious earthenware pot, with a mouth through which the largest fist can pass. It serves to facilitate the transmission of the tax. As the oriental plague is more easily communicated by coins than by anything else, the sailors coming from the Levant must throw the money into a jug of water, in order that the western health-officer may take it out cleansed: just as at the Szkela every one must fish the money he receives out of a basin.

Timar thrust his clinched fist into the water, and brought it out open.

Then the inspector puts his hand in, draws it out as a clinched fist, and transfers it to his pocket. He does not need to look at it by the sunset light to see what manner of money it is. He knows it by the size and weight. Even a blind man knows the feel of ducats. He does not change a muscle.

After him come the custom-house officials. These also with serious faces fish up their fee from the bottom of the jug.

Now for the turn of the purifier. His countenance is stern and forbidding. It hangs on a single word from his lips, whether the ship may have to lie ten or twenty days in quarantine with all her passengers. There are cold-blooded men like that who have only an eye to duty.

The inspector demands, in a surly, dictatorial tone, that the entrance to the lower deck be opened. His desire is obeyed. They all three go down; but none of the crew may follow them. When they are alone, the three strict

34

servants of the law grin at each other. The purifier remains on deck, and only laughs in his sleeve.

They unfasten one of the many sacks, in which certainly there is only wheat. "Well, I hope it's moldy enough," remarks the inspector. "Probably there is only wheat in the other sacks, and very likely even more worm-eaten."

A document is now drawn up describing the search: one of the armed officials has the writing materials, and the other the form to be filled in. All is accurately set down. Then the inspector writes something on a bit of paper, which he folds and seals with a wafer, on which he presses the official seal. He writes no address on the note.

Then, after they have rummaged in every hole and corner where nothing suspicious is hidden, the three searchers rise to the light of day once more. At least to moonlight; for the sun has set, and through the hurrying clouds the moon ever and anon peeps down, and then vanishing, plays hide-and-seek with the world.

The inspector calls for the captain and gives him to understand—still in a severe official manner—that nothing suspicious has been found on board: then he requires the purifier, in the same manner, to declare the condition of the ship's health.

With an appeal to his oath of fidelity, the purifier bears witness that every person on board, as well as the cargo, is free from infection.

A certificate that the papers are in order is prepared, and the receipts for the fees are handed over. A hundred kreutzers to the inspector, two fifties to the customs officers, and fifty to the health-officer. Not a kreutzer is wanting. These receipts are delivered to the owner of the cargo, who has never left his cabin the whole time—he is at supper. He also must countersign the receipts. From these signatures and indorsements, the shipowner and the honorable officials in question mutually learn that the captain gave away as many kreutzers as he received, and that not one remained sticking to his fingers.

Kreutzers! Well, yes; but about the gold?

The thought may well have passed through Timar's head, how would it be if of the fifty ducats which this dirty lot were to fish out of the jug he

35

were only to put in forty (a fabulous sum to such fellows)? No creature would know that he had kept back ten. Indeed he might easily retain half of the whole sum, for who is there to control it? Those for whom the money is intended are quite enough rewarded with half.

Another thought possibly answered thus. "What you are doing is without doubt bribery. You don't corrupt them with your own money, but Trikaliss gives it because his interests imperatively require it. You hand over the gold, and are as innocent of the bribery as the water-jug. Why he wants to bribe the inspector you do not know. Whether the ship carries contraband goods, whether he is a political refugee, or the persecuted hero of a romantic adventure, who in order to assist his escape strews gold in handfuls, what does it matter to you? But if one single gold piece sticks to your fingers, you become an accomplice in all which burdens another's conscience. Keep none of it."

The inspector gave permission for the vessel to proceed, in token of which a red-and-white flag with a black eagle on it was hoisted to the masthead. Then, after thus officially certifying that the ship from the Levant was quite free of infection, the inspector, without any previous ordeal by water, pressed the captain's hand and said to him: "You come from Komorn? Then you know Herr Katschuka, chief of the commissariat department? Be good enough to give him this note when you get home. There is no address on it—not necessary, you won't forget his name; it sounds like a Spanish dance. Take him the letter as soon as ever you get there. You won't be sorry."

Then he clapped the captain most graciously on the shoulder, as if to make him his debtor for life, and the whole four left the ship and returned to Szkela in their black-and-yellow boat.

The "St. Barbara" could now continue her voyage, and if all her sacks from the keel to the deck had been filled with salt or Turkish tobacco, and all her passengers covered with small-pox or leprosy from top to toe, no one could stop her any more on the Danube.

Now, however, there was on board neither contraband goods nor contagion, but—something else. Timar put the unaddressed note into his pocket-book and wondered what it contained.

This was what was written—

36

"Brother-in-law,—I recommend to you the bearer of this letter. He is a man of sterling worth."

CHAPTER V.
THE OWNERLESS ISLAND.

The towing-team left behind on the Servian bank crossed over the same night in ferry-boats to the Hungarian side with their severed hawser, spreading everywhere the news that the tow-rope had parted of itself at the dangerous Perigrada Island, and the ship had gone down with every soul on board. In the morning there was no longer a sign of the "St. Barbara" in the harbor of Orsova. If by chance the commandant of the Turkish brigantine had had an idea of rowing up the channel from the Iron Gate to Orsova, he would not have found what he sought; and above, as far as Belgrade, only half the Danube belonged to him: on the Hungarian side he had no jurisdiction, but the fortress at New Orsova belonged to him.

At two o'clock in the morning the "St. Barbara" left Orsova. After midnight the north wind generally stops; the favorable time must be utilized, and the crew had received a double ration of brandy to keep them in a good humor.

The departure was quite silent: from the walls of the New Orsova fort sounded the long call of the Turkish sentries. The horn gave no signal till the Allion point had disappeared behind the new mountain-chain.

At the first blast Timéa came from her cabin, where she had slept for a few hours, and went, wrapped in her white burnoose, to the bow to look for Euthemio, who had never lain down all night, nor entered his cabin, nor even—which was more remarkable—smoked at all. He was not allowed to light any fire on board the ship, so as to avoid attracting attention to the vessel at the Orsova fortress.

Perhaps Timéa felt that she had to make up for a fault, for she addressed Timar, and asked him about the wonders of both shores.

The instinct of her childish heart whispered to her that she owed this man a debt of gratitude.

Dawn found the ship near Ogradina. The captain drew Timéa's attention to a monument eighteen hundred years old. This was "Trajan's Tablet," hewn in the precipitous cliff, held by two winged genii and

38

surrounded by dolphins. On the tablet is the inscription which commemorates the achievements of the godlike emperor. If the peaks of the great "Sterberg" have vanished from the Servian shore, there follows a fresh rock corridor, which confines the Danube in a ravine five hundred fathoms wide. This mountain hall goes by the name of "Kassan." Cliffs of two to three thousand feet high rise right and left, their curves lost in opal-colored mist. From one precipice a stream falls a thousand feet out of a cave, like a delicate silver streak, dissolved in spray before it reaches the river. The two rock faces run on unbroken, only in one part the mountain is split, and through the rift laughs the blooming landscape of an alpine valley, with a white tower in the background. It is the tower of Dubova: there is Hungary.

Timéa never turned her gaze from this spectacle until the ship had passed, and the mountains had closed over the exquisite scene, hiding the deep chasm in their shadows.

"I feel," she said, "as if we were going through a long, long prison, into a land from which there is no return."

The precipices grow higher, the surface of the Danube darker, and, to complete the wild and romantic panorama, there is visible on the northern face a cave whose mouth is surrounded by an earthquake with embrasures for cannon.

"That is Veterani's Cavern," said the captain. "There, more than a century ago, three hundred men and five cannon held out for forty days against a whole Turkish army." Timéa shook her head. But the skipper knew more still about the cavern.

"Forty years ago our people defended that cave in a bloody struggle against the Turks; the Osmanli lost over two thousand men among the rocks."

Timéa drew together her delicate eyebrows and threw the narrator an icy-cold glance, so that all his eloquence died in his throat. She hid her mouth with her burnoose, turned from Timar, went into the cabin, and did not reappear till evening. She only looked through the little window at the toppling crags on the bank, the massive watch-towers now deserted, the wooded cliffs of the Klissura valley, and the rock-colossi projecting from the stream, as they swept by her. She did not even ask for the history of the octagonal castle-donjon, with three small ones beside it inside a bastion. And yet she would have heard the fate of the lovely Cecilia Rozgonyi, the danger of King Sigismund, and the defeat of the Hungarians. This ruin is the Galamboczer Tower.

From first to last this double shore is a petrified history of two nations, mutually shadowed by a mad vagary of fate with the lust of conquest, which makes them fly at each other's throats directly a war begins.

It is a long crypt containing the bones of many a hundred thousand heroes.

Timéa did not come out that day or the next. She sketched little views in her book, which she could hold quite steady on the smoothly gliding vessel.

Three days passed before the "St. Barbara" arrived where the Morava falls into the Danube.

At the junction lies Semendria. On the thirty-six towers of this fortress have waved the banners sometimes of the Blessed Virgin and anon of the Crescent, and their circular brown walls are sprinkled with the blood of many nations. On the other shore of the Morava stand only the bare walls of the forsaken "Veste Kulics," and beyond the Ostrovaer Island frown down from a peak the ruins of the castle of Rama, now only a monument.

But this is not the moment to stand gazing at them—no one is inclined to indulge in melancholy reflections on the vanished greatness of fallen nations, for there is more pressing work on hand.

As soon as the Hungarian plains open out, the north wind storms down on the ship with such force that the towing-horses can not make head against it, and the wind drives the vessel toward the opposite shore.

"We can get no further," is the general opinion.

Trikaliss exchanges a few private words with Timar, who goes to the pilot. Master Fabula makes the tiller fast and leaves it. Then he calls the rowers on board, and signs to the shore to stop the team. Here neither oars nor towing are of use. The ship is above the Orsova Island, which stretches a long pointed tongue into the stream: its northern side is steep and rugged, overgrown with old willows.

The task now is to get over to the south of the island, where the "St.

Barbara" can lie in a harbor protected from the north wind, as well as from the curious eyes of men; for the wider stream which circles round the island toward Servia is not used by sailors, being full of sand-banks and fords.

It is a work of skill to approach: cutting the cable is no use, for the ship could not carry any way against such a wind. The only solution is hauling to the anchor.

The vessel casts anchor in mid-stream: the towing-rope is brought on board; to its end a second anchor is attached and placed in the boat. The rowers go toward the island till the whole length of the cable is out, then cast anchor and return to the ship. Now they weigh the first anchor, and four men haul on the cable made fast to the windlass. Heavy work!

When the vessel is close up to the anchor, they put the other in the boat, row forward, cast anchor again, and haul up as before. So by the sweat of their brow they made their way up-stream step by step. It took them half a day of hard labor to work the heavy cargo-ship from the middle of the Danube to the point of the great island. A fatiguing day for those who had to work, and wearier still to look on at. The vessel had left the frequented branch, where, at any rate, one saw ruins from time to time, where one met other ships, or floated by long lines of clattering mills: it now passed through the unfrequented channel, where the view was hidden on the right by a long ugly island, on which only poplars and willows seemed to grow, nowhere a human habitation to be seen, and on the left the water was covered by a thick sea of reeds, among which the only sign of *terra firma* was a group of slender, silver-leaved poplars.

In this quiet uninhabited spot the "St. Barbara" was brought up. And now appeared a new calamity—the food was exhausted. When leaving Galatz, they had reckoned on the usual halt at Orsova for the purpose of shipping provisions; but after starting so suddenly at night, they found there was nothing on board when they reached the island of Orsova but a little coffee and sugar, and in Timéa's possession a box of Turkish sweets and preserved fruits, which, however, she would not open, because it was intended as a present.

"Never mind," said Timar; "somebody must live on one shore or the other. There are lambs and kids everywhere, and one can get anything for

41

money."

Another misfortune set in. The anchored ship was so rolled about by the wind-driven waves of the river, that Timéa got seasick and frightened.

Perhaps there was some house where she and her father could spend the night.

Timar's sharp eyes discovered that above the tops of the poplars rising from the reeds a faint smoke hovered in the air. "There must be a house there. I will go and see who lives in it."

There was a small skiff on board, which the captain used on sporting expeditions, at times when the ship was delayed by foul winds, and he had leisure for wildfowl-shooting. He lowered it into the water, took his gun, his game-bag, and a landing-net—one never knows what may come in one's way, a bird or a fish—and went toward the bed of rushes, rowing and steering with one and the same oar. Being an experienced marsh-sportsman, he soon found the one opening in the reeds through which it was possible to penetrate, and recognized by the vegetation the depth of the channel.

Where the great leaves and snowy cups of the water-lily float on the surface, there is deep water which scours the weeds and mud away; in other places duckweed forms a green carpet on the top, and on this floating velvet cowers the poisonous water-fungus in the form of a turnip-radish, blue and round, and swelled like a puff ball—deadly poison to every living thing. When Timar's oar struck one of these polyp-like fungi, the venomous dust shot out like a blue flame. The roots of this plant live in a fetid slime which would suffocate man or beast who should fall into it; nature has given this vegetable murderer a habitat where it is least accessible. But where the cardinal-flower spreads its clubbed suckers, and where the beautiful bells of the water-violet sway among the rushes, there is gravel, which is not always under water. And where the manna tendrils begin to form a thicket, in pressing through which the sailor finds the brim of his hat full of little seeds—the food of the poor, manna of the wilderness—there must be higher ground, so that only the root of the plant is submerged.

The boatman who does not know these vegetable guides might lose himself in the reed-beds, and not get out all day.

When Timar had worked his way through the brake, which formed a labyrinth of flesh-colored flower-clusters, he saw before him what he sought—an island.

No doubt this was a new alluvial formation, of which no trace was to be found on the latest maps.

In the bed of the right arm of the Danube lay long ago a great bowlder, at whose base the sluggish current had deposited a sand-bank.

During some winter flood, the ice-floes tore from the Ostrova Island a spit of land bearing earth, stones, and a small wood. This mingled deluge of ice, gravel, and trees flung itself on the sand-bank near the bowlder. Repeated inundations spread over it year by year layers of mud, and enlarged its circumference by fresh deposits of pebbles: from the moldering tree-trunks sprung a luxuriant vegetation as quickly as the natural creations of the New World; and so arose a nameless island, of which no one had taken possession, over which was no landlord, no king, no authority, and no church—which belonged to no country and no diocese. In Turco-Servian territory there are many such paradises, neither plowed nor sown, not even used for pasture. They are the home of wild flowers and wild beasts, and God knows what besides.

The northern shore plainly proclaims its genesis. The gravel moraine is heaped there like a barricade, often in pieces larger than a man's head; between are tufts of rushes and rotten branches; the shallows are covered with green and brown river-shells; on the marshy parts round holes are washed out, in which, at the sound of approaching footsteps, hundreds of crabs rush to hide. The shore is covered along its whole length with prickly willow, which the ice-floes shave off every winter close to the root.

Here Timar drew his boat ashore and tied it to a tree. Pressing forward, he had to push his way through a thicket of huge willows and poplars—overthrown in many places by repeated storms—and there the fruitful bramble forms a thorny undergrowth, and tall valerian, shooting upward from the weather-beaten soil, mixes its aromatic scent with the wholesome smell of the poplar.

On a level depression where are neither trees nor bushes, luxuriant umbelliferous plants rise amid the grass over a swamp—hemlock and "Sison Amonum," smelling of cinnamon. In an isolated tuft like a vegetable

43

aristocrat glitter the fiery blossoms of the veratrum; among the grass the forget-me-not spreads rankly, and the medicinal comfrey with red flowers full of honey. No wonder if in the hollows of the old trees there are so many wild bees' nests. And among the flowers rise curious green, brown and red capsules, the ripe seed-vessels of bulbous plants which bloom in spring.

On this flowery region follows more forest; but here the willows and poplar are mixed with wild apple-trees, and white-thorn forms the underwood. The island is higher here.

Timar stopped and listened. No sound. There can be no wild beasts on this island. The floods have exterminated them, and the place is only inhabited by birds.

Even among birds the lark and the wood-pigeon do not come here: it is no dwelling for them. They seek places where men live and sow and cultivate grain. But two creatures live here which betray the presence of man—the wasp and the blackbird; both of which come after the ripe fruit which they passionately love. Where the great wasps' nests hang from the trees, and where the blackbird's alluring whistle sounds in the hedges, there must be fruit. Timar followed the blackbird. After he had pushed through the prickly whitethorn and the privet-bushes which tore his clothes, he stood transfixed with admiration.

What he saw before him was a paradise.

A cultivated garden of five or six acres, with fruit-trees, not planted in rows, but in picturesquely scattered groups, whose boughs were weighed down by their sweet burden. Apple and pear-trees covered with glittering red and yellow fruit, plums of all colors looking as if the shining crop were turned to roses and lilies, the fallen surplus lying unnoticed on the ground. Beneath, a regular plantation formed of raspberry, currant, and gooseberry bushes, with their red, yellow, and green berries; and the spaces between the large trees filled by the hanging branches of the Sidonian apple or quince.

There was no path through this labyrinth of fruit-trees—the ground underneath was covered with grass.

But where you can see through, a flower-garden beckons you on. It is also a collection of wonderful field blossoms not to be found in an ordinary garden: the roots of blue campanula, swallow-wort, with its fleecy

44

seed-vessels from which a sort of silk is collected, the spotted turban-lily, alkermes, with its scarlet berries, the splendid butterfly orchis—all of these raised to the rank of garden-flowers, bear witness to the presence of man. And this is further betrayed by the dwelling from which the smoke comes.

It also is a fantastic little refuge. Behind it stands a great rock, in which is an excavation, where the hearth must be, and another hole for the cellar. At the top is a chimney, from which a blue cloud arises. A building of stone and clay tiles is stuck on to the cliff; it has two rooms, each with a window. One window is smaller, and one room lower than the other; both are roofed with rushes; each has a wooden porch, forming a veranda, with fanciful ornaments made of little bits of wood.

Neither stone, clay, nor wood-work can be distinguished, so thickly is it covered on the south side with vines, out of whose frost-bitten leaves thousands of red and gold bunches peep out. On the northern side it is overgrown with hops, whose ripe clusters hide even the pinnacle of the great rock with their greenish gold; and on its highest point tufts of house-leek are planted, so that no spot may remain which is not green.

Here women live.

CHAPTER VI.
ALMIRA AND NARCISSA.

Timar turned his steps toward the creeper-covered cottage. Through the flower-garden a path led to the house, but so covered with grass that his steps were not heard, and he could thus get as far as the little veranda quite noiselessly. Neither far nor near was a human being visible.

Before the veranda lay a large black dog—one of the noble race of Newfoundland, generally so sensible and dignified as to forbid undue familiarity on the part of strangers. The aforesaid quadruped was one of the finest of the race—a colossal beast, and occupied the whole width of the door-way.

The sable guardian appeared to be asleep, and took no notice of the approaching stranger, nor of another creature which left no fool-hardy impertinence untried in order to tax the patience of the huge animal. This was a white cat, which was shameless enough to turn somersaults back and forward over the dog's recumbent form, to strike it on the nose with her paw, and at last to lay herself before it on her back, and take one of its webbed paws between her four soft feet and play with it like a kitten. When the great black porter found its foot tickled, it drew it back and gave the cat the other paw to play with.

Timar did not think to himself—"Suppose this black colossus seizes me by the collar, it will go hard with me;" but he thought, "Oh! how delighted Timéa will be when she sees this white cat."

You could not pass the dog and get in—it barred the whole entrance. Timar coughed, to announce that some one was there. Then the great dog raised its head and looked at the new-comer with its wise nut-brown eyes, which, like the human eye, can weep and laugh, scold and flatter. Then it laid its head down again, as much as to say, "Only one man; it's not worth while to get up."

But Timar decided that where a chimney smokes, there's a fire in the kitchen; so he began from outside to wish this invisible some one "Good-morning," alternately in three languages—Hungarian, Servian and

Roumanian. Suddenly a female voice answered in Hungarian from within, "Good-day. Come in then. Who is it?"

"I should like to come in, but the dog's in the way."

"Step over it."

"Won't it bite?"

"She never hurts good people."

Timar took courage and stepped across the powerful animal, which did not move, but raised its tail as if to wag him a welcome.

Going into the veranda, Timar saw two doors before him: the first one led to the stone building, the other to the grotto hollowed in the rock. The latter was the kitchen. There he observed a woman busy at the hearth.

Timar saw at a glance that she was not preparing a magic potion of witch's cookery, but simply roasting Indian-corn.

The woman thus occupied was a thin but strong and sinewy figure, with a dark skin; in her compressed lips lay something severe, though her eye was soft and inspired confidence. Her sunburned face betokened her age as not much over thirty. She was not dressed like the peasants of the district; her clothes were not bright in color, but yet not suited to towns.

"Now, come nearer and sit down," said the woman, in a singularly hard voice, which, however, was perfectly quiet; and then she shook the floury snow-white Indian-corn into a plaited rush-basket, and offered it to him. Afterward she fetched a jug which stood on the floor, and gave him elder-wine, this also just freshly made.

Timar sat down on the stool offered him, which was skillfully woven of various osiers, and of a curious shape. Then the Newfoundland, rising, approached the guest and lay down in front of him.

The woman threw the dog a handful of the white confectionery, which it at once began to crack in the proper way. The white cat attempted to do the same, but the first cracked kernel of the maize stuck in her teeth, and she did not try it again. She shook the paw with which she had touched it, and sprung up to the hearth, where she blinked with much interest at an unglazed pot which was simmering by the fire, and probably held something more to her taste.

"A magnificent beast," said Timar, looking at the dog. "I wonder it is so gentle; it has not even growled at me."

"She never hurts good people, sir. If a stranger comes who is honest, she knows it directly, and is as quiet as a lamb—doesn't even bark; but if a thief tries to get in, she rages at him as soon as he sets foot on the island, and woe to him if she gets her teeth in. She is a formidable creature! Last winter a large wolf came over the ice after our goats—look, there is his skin on the floor of the room. In a moment the dog had throttled him. An honest man can sit on her back, she won't touch him."

Timar was quite satisfied to have such excellent evidence of his honesty. Who knows, perhaps, if some of those ducats had lost their road in his pocket, he might have been differently received by the great dog?

"Now, sir, where do you come from, and what do you want of me?"

"First, I must beg you to excuse my having pushed through the thorns and bushes into your garden. The storm has driven my vessel over to this bank, so I was obliged to run for shelter under the Ostrova Island."

"Indeed, yes; I can hear by the rustle of the branches that a strong wind is blowing."

This place was so completely sheltered by the virgin forest, that one could feel no wind, and only knew by the sound when it blew.

"We must wait for a change of wind before the storm blows over. But our provisions have run out, so I was forced to seek the nearest house from which I saw smoke rising, to ask the housewife whether for money and fair words we could get food for the crew."

"Yes, you can have what you want, and I don't mind being paid for it, for that's what I live on. We can serve you with kids, maize-flour, cheese, and fruit; choose what you want. This is the trade which keeps us; the market-women round about fetch away our wares in boats: we are gardeners."

Till now Timar had seen no human being except this woman; but as she spoke in the plural, there must be others besides herself.

"I thank you beforehand, and will take some of everything. I will send the steersman from the ship to fetch the things; but tell me, my good lady, what's to pay? I want food for my seven men for three days."

"You need not fetch out your purse; I don't receive payment in

48

money. What should I do with it, here on this lonely island? At best thieves would be sure to get in and kill me to get hold of it; but now every one knows there is no money on the island, and therefore we can sleep in peace. I only barter. I give fruit, wax, honey, and simples, and people bring me in exchange grain, salt, clothes, and hardware."

"As they do on the Australian islands?"

"Just the same."

"All right, good lady; we have grain on board, and salt too. I will reckon up the value of your wares, and bring an equal value in exchange. Rely upon it, you sha'n't be the loser."

"I don't doubt it, sir."

"But I have another favor to ask. On board my vessel there is a grand gentleman and his young daughter. The young lady is not accustomed to the motion, and feels unwell. Could you not give my passengers shelter till the storm is over?"

"Well, that I can do too, sir. Look, here are two small bed-rooms. We will retire into one, and in the other any honest man who wants shelter can have it—rest, if not comfort. If you also would like to stay, you will have to be contented with the little garret, as both the rooms will have women in them. There is new hay there, and sailors are not particular."

Timar puzzled his head as to the position of this woman, who chose her words so well and expressed herself so sensibly. He could not reconcile it with this hut, which was more like a cave, and with the residence on this lonely island in the midst of a wilderness. "Many thanks, good lady; I'll hurry back and bring up my passengers."

"All right; only don't go back to your boat the same way you came. You can't bring a lady through those marshes and briers. There's a tolerable path all along the bank, rather overgrown with grass, it is true, for it is very little trodden, and turf grows quickly here; but you shall be conducted to where your boat lies; then when you come back in a larger one, you can land rather nearer. I will give you a guide now. Almira!"

Timar looked round, to see from what corner of the house or from what bush this Almira would appear who was to show him the way. But the great black Newfoundland rose and began to wag her tail, whose strokes made a noise on the door-post as if an old drum was touched.

"Off, Almira; take the gentleman to the shore," said the woman; on which the creature growled something to Timar in dog's language, and taking the edge of his cloak in her teeth, pulled at it, as if to say, Come along.

"So this is Almira, who is to conduct me. I am much indebted to you, Miss Almira," Timar said smiling, and took his gun and hat; then saluted his hostess and followed the dog. Almira led the guest steadily in all friendship by the hem of his cloak. The way lay through the orchard, where one had to tread carefully so as not to crush the plums which covered the ground. The white cat, too, had not remained behind; she wanted to know where Almira was conducting the stranger, and leaped here and there in the soft grass.

When they arrived at the edge of the orchard, somewhere above was heard the call of a musical voice, "Narcissa!"

It was a girl's voice, in which some reproach, but much love and maidenly shyness, were blended—a sympathetic voice. Timar looked round: he wanted to know, first, where it came from, and then to whom it belonged.

He soon discovered who was called, for at the sound the white cat sprung quickly to one side, and, curling her tail, climbed zigzag up a gnarled pear-tree, through whose thick foliage Timar saw something like a white dress glimmering. He had no time for further research, for Almira gave a few deep sounds which, in quadruped's language, probably meant, "What business have you to spy about?" and so he was obliged to follow his leader, if he did not desire to leave a piece of his cloak in her teeth.

Almira led Timar by a soft turf path along the bank to the place where his boat was made fast. At this moment a couple of snipe rose with their shrill cry close to the island. Timar's first thought was of the savory dish they would make for Timéa's supper. In an instant he had shouldered his gun, and with a well-aimed right and left brought down both snipe.

But the next moment he was himself on the ground. As soon as he had fired, Almira seized him by the collar, and like lightning pulled him down. He tried to rise, but soon felt that he had to do with an overpowering adversary who was not to be trifled with. Not that Almira had hurt him, but she held him by the collar, and would not allow of his getting up.

Timar tried every conceivable means to soften her, called her Miss

50

Almira, his dear friend, and explained to her sport and its usages; where the devil had she heard of a dog that retrieves a sportsman? she should rather go after the snipe in the rushes: but he talked to deaf ears.

He was at last relieved from this dangerous situation by the woman of the island, who had run up at the report of the gun, and called Almira by name from afar, on which the dog let go her hold.

"Oh, my God!" she lamented, hastening over the stones to the point of danger. "I forgot to tell you not to shoot, because Almira was sure to attack you. She gets in a fury when a shot is fired. Well, I was stupid not to tell you."

"Never mind, good woman," said Timar, laughing. "Almira would really make a capital gamekeeper. But look, I have shot a couple of snipe; I thought they would be a help toward the supper that you will set before your guests."

"I will fetch them; get into your boat, and when you come back, just leave your gun at home, for, believe me, if the dog sees you with a gun on your arm, she will take it away from you. You can't joke with her."

"So I find. A powerful, grand animal that! Before I had time to defend myself, I was on the ground: I can only thank Heaven that she did not bite my head off."

"Oh, she never bites any one; but if you defend yourself, she seizes your arm in her teeth, as if it were in irons, and then holds you fast till we come and call her off. *Auf Weidersehen!*"

In less than an hour the larger boat had landed its passengers safely at the island. All the way from the vessel to the shore, Timar talked to Timéa of Almira and Narcissa, to make the poor child forget her sickness and her fear of the water. As soon as she set foot on shore, her seasickness vanished.

Timar went on in front to show the way; Timéa followed, leaning on Euthemio's arm; and two sailors and the steersman carried behind them on a stretcher the equivalent of the barter in sacks. Almira's bark was heard a long way off. These were the sounds of welcome by which the dog acknowledged the approach of good friends. Almira came half-way, barked at the whole party, then had a little talk to the sailors, the steersman, and Timar; then trotting to Timéa, tried to kiss her hand. But when the dog came to

51

Euthemio, it was quiet, and began to sniff at him from the soles of his feet upward, never leaving his heels. It snuffed continually, and shook its head violently, rattling its ears till they cracked. It had its own opinion on this subject.

The mistress of the island settlement awaited the strangers at the door, and as soon as they appeared between the trees, called in a loud voice, "Noémi!"

At this summons some one appeared from inside the garden. Between two tall thick raspberry hedges, which, like green walls, almost closed in an arch at the top, came a young girl. Face and form those of a child just beginning to develop, dressed in a white chemise and petticoat, and carrying in her upturned overskirt fruit freshly plucked.

The figure coming out of the green grove is idyllic. The delicate tints of her face seem to have been borrowed from the complexion of the white rose when she is grave, and take that of the red rose when she blushes, and that up to the brow. The expression of the clear-arched brow is personified sweet temper, in complete accord with the innocent look of the expressive blue eyes; on the tender lips lies a mixture of devoted regard and modest shyness. The rich and luxuriant golden-brown hair seems to be curled by nature's hand; a lock thrust back gives a view of an exquisite little ear. Over the whole face gentle softness is spread. It is possible that a sculptor might not take each feature as a model, and perhaps if the face were hewn in marble one might not think it beautiful; but the head and the whole figure, just as they are, shine with a loveliness which charms at the first glance, and inthralls more every moment.

From one shoulder the chemise has dropped, but, that it may not remain uncovered, there sits a white cat, rubbing her head against the girl's cheek. The delicate feet of the maiden are naked—why should she not go barefoot? She walks on a carpet of richest velvet. The spring turf is interspersed with blue veronica and red geranium.

Euthemio, his daughter, and Timar, stopped at the entrance of the raspberry arcade to await the approaching figure.

The child knew of no more friendly reception to give the guests than to offer them the fruit she had in her lap. They were beautiful red-streaked

Bergamot pears. She turned first to Timar. He chose the best, and gave it to Timéa.

Both girls shrugged their shoulders impatiently. Timéa because she envied the other one the white cat on her shoulder, but Noémi because Timar had given the fruit to Timéa.

"Oh, you rude thing!" cried the mistress to her from the cottage; "could you not put the fruit in a basket, instead of offering it in your apron? Is that the proper way?"

The little thing grew red as fire, and ran to her mother; the latter whispered a few words into her ear, so that the others might not overhear, then kissed the child on the forehead, and said aloud, "Now go and take from the sailors what they have brought, carry it into the store-room, and fill the sacks with corn-flour, the pots with honey, and the baskets with ripe fruit: of the kids, you can choose two for them."

"I can't choose any," whispered the girl; "they must do it themselves."

"Foolish child!" said the woman with a kind reproof; "if it were left to you, you would keep all the kids and never let one be killed. Very well, let them choose for themselves, then no one can complain. I will look after the cooking."

Noémi called the sailors, and opened the food and fruit stores, which were each in a different cave and shut off by a door. The rock which formed the summit of the island was one of those wandering blocks, called "erratic" by geologists—an isolated bowlder, a monolith, which must once have been detached from a distant mountain, some limestone formation from the Dolomites, out of a moraine. It was full of large and small caves, which the first person who took possession of it had adapted to his own purposes: the largest with the natural chimney for the kitchen, the highest, as a dove-cote, the others for summer and winter storehouses. He had settled on the heaven-sent rock, and, like the wild birds, built his nest there.

The child managed the barter with the crew well and honestly. Then she gave each his glass of elder-wine to wet the bargain, begged for their custom when they passed again, and went back to the kitchen.

Here she did not wait to be told to lay the table. She spread a fine rush mat on the small table in the veranda, and placed on it four plates, with knives and forks and pewter spoons. And the fifth person?

She will sit at the cat's table. Near the steps to the veranda stands a small wooden bench; in the center is placed an earthenware plate with a miniature knife and fork and spoon, and at each end a wooden platter, one for Almira, the other for Narcissa. They require no *couvert*. When the three guests and the mistress of the house have sat down and helped themselves from the dish, it goes to the cat's table, where Noémi serves her friends. She conducts the division with great fairness—the soft pieces to Narcissa, the bones to Almira—and helps herself last. They must not touch their food till she has cooled it for them, however much Almira may cock her ears, and the cat snuggle up to her mistress's shoulder. They must obey the girl.

The island woman wished, according to the good or bad Hungarian custom, to show off before her guests, and especially to prove to Timar that her larder was independent of his game. She had cooked the two snipe with oatmeal, but whispered to Timar that that was only food for ladies; for the gentlemen she had some good fried pork. Timar attacked it bravely, but Euthemio touched none of it, saying he had no appetite, and Timéa rose suddenly from the table. But that was natural: she had already cast many inquisitive glances toward the party at the other table; there was nothing remarkable in her rising suddenly and going over to sit by Noémi. Young girls soon make friends. Timéa did not know Hungarian, nor Noémi Greek; but between them was Narcissa, to whom both languages were the same.

The white cat seemed to understand perfectly when Timéa said "Horaion galion" to it, and stroked its back with a soft white hand: then it crept from Noémi's lap to Timéa's, raised its head to her face and gently rubbed its white head against her white cheeks, opened its red mouth, showed its sharp teeth, and blinked at her with cunning eyes; then sprung on her shoulder, crawled round her neck, and clambered to Noémi and back again.

Noémi was pleased that the strange young lady liked her favorite so much, but bitterness mingled with her pleasure when she saw how much the stranger had fallen in love with the cat, kept and kissed it; and still more painful was it to realize how easily Narcissa became untrue to her, how willingly it accepted and replied to the caresses of its new friend, and took no notice when Noémi called it by name to come back to her. "Horaion galion" (pretty pussy) pleased it better. Noémi grew angry with Narcissa, and seized her by the tail to draw her back. Narcissa took offense, turned her claws on her mistress, and scratched her hand.

Timéa wore on her wrist a blue enameled bracelet in the form of a serpent. When Narcissa scratched her mistress, Timéa drew off the elastic bracelet, and wanted to put it on Noémi's arm, obviously with the intention of comforting her in her pain; but Noémi misunderstood, and thought the stranger wanted to buy Narcissa with it. But she was not for sale.

"I don't want the bracelet! I won't sell Narcissa! Keep the bracelet! Narcissa is mine. Come here, Narcissa!" and as Narcissa would not come, Noémi gave her a little box on the ear, on which the frightened animal made a jump over the bench, puffing and spitting, climbed up a nut-tree, and looked angrily down from thence.

As Timéa and Noémi at this moment looked into each other's eyes, each read there a dreamy presentiment. They felt like a person who shuts his eyes for a moment, and in that short time dreams whole years away; yet, when he awakes, has forgotten it all, and only remembers that the dream was very long. The two girls felt in that meeting of looks that they would some day mutually encroach on each other's rights, that they would have something in common—a grief or a joy—and that, perhaps, like a forgotten dream, they would only know that each owed this grief or joy to the other.

Timéa sprung up from beside Noémi and gave the bracelet to the housewife: then she sat down by Euthemio and leaned her head on his shoulder.

Timar interpreted the gift. "The young lady gives it to the little girl as a remembrance—it is gold."

As soon as he said that it was of gold, the woman threw it, frightened, from her hand, as if it were a real snake. She looked anxiously at Noémi, and was not even able to articulate "Thank you."

Then Almira suddenly drew attention to herself. The dog had sprung quickly from its bed, had uttered a low howl with its head up, and now began to bark with deafening noise. In the sound lay something of the lion's roar; it was a vehement, defiant tone, as if calling to the attack, and the dog did not run forward, but remained by the porch, planted its paws on the ground, and then threw up the earth with its hind feet.

The woman turned pale. A figure appeared between the trees on the footpath.

"The dog only barks in that way at one man," she murmured. "There he comes. It is he!"

CHAPTER VII.
THE VOICES OF THE NIGHT.

The new arrival is a man of youthful appearance; he wears a blouse and trousers, round his neck a red cotton handkerchief, and on his head a Turkish fez.

He has a handsome face. If he sat quietly to an artist, every one would say of his portrait that it was the ideal of a hero; but when he is in motion, the first thought must be—that is a spy. His features are regular, the thick hair curly, the lips finely chiseled, the eyes deeply black; but the wrinkles round them and their restless fire, the upturned corners of the mouth, and the ever-twitching brows, betray the soul of a slave to his own appetites.

Almira barked furiously at the new-comer, who came swinging along with defiant nonchalance, like one who knows that it is other people's duty to protect him. Noémi told the dog to lie down, but it gave no heed; she caught the creature's ears in both hands and drew it back: the dog whined and growled at the discomfort, but did not cease barking. At last Noémi put her foot on its head and pressed it to the ground. Then Almira gave in, lay down growling, and let the girl's foot lie on her great black head, as if that were a burden she could not shake off.

The stranger came whistling and humming up to them. From afar he called out—"Ah! you have still got that confounded big brute; you haven't had her poisoned? I shall have to get rid of her in the end. The stupid beast!" When the young man got near Noémi, he stretched out his hand with a familiar smile toward the girl's face, as if he would have pinched her cheek; but she drew her face quickly away.

"Well, my dear little *fiancée*, are you still so shy? How you have grown since I saw you!"

Noémi looked at the speaker with her head thrown back. She wrinkled her forehead, curled her lips, and threw a defiantly penetrating glance at him; even her complexion changed, the rose tint on her cheeks turned livid. Evidently she could look odious if she chose.

The new-comer, however, quite unabashed, continued, "How pretty you have grown!"

Instead of answering she said to the dog, "Down, Almira!"

The stranger behaved as though he were quite at home under the veranda, where his first act was to kiss the hand of the woman of the house. He greeted Timar with friendly condescension, made a polite bow to Euthemio and Timéa, and then opened the flood-gates of his eloquence. "Good-evening, dear mother-in-law! Your obedient servant, captain! Sir and mademoiselle, you are welcome. My name is Theodor Krisstyan; I am chevalier and captain, the future son-in-law of this worthy lady. Our fathers were bosom friends, and betrothed Noémi to me in their life-time, so I come every year to see my sweetheart in her summer abode, in order to judge how my bride is growing. Uncommonly delighted to find you here: you, sir—if I am not mistaken, your name is Timar—I have had the pleasure of meeting before? The other gentleman, I fancy—"

"Understands nothing but Greek," interrupted Timar, thrusting his hands well into his pockets, as if he wanted to make it impossible for the stranger to shake hands over the joy of meeting. He, who from his calling was always traveling, might very likely have met him before.

Theodor Krisstyan did not feel inclined to occupy himself any more with Timar, but looked at life from the practical side. "It is just as if you had expected me; a beautiful supper, an unused place, pork, just my weak point. Thanks, dear mamma, thanks, gentlemen and young lady; I will pay my respects to the supper—so many thanks!"

Not that a single person of those addressed had asked him to sit down and partake; but as though accepting their invitation, he seated himself in Timéa's empty place and began to enjoy the pork; offering it repeatedly to Euthemio, and seeming much astonished that any Christian should neglect such a delicious dish.

Timar rose from the table and said to the hostess, "The gentleman-passenger and the young lady are tired. They want rest more than food. Would you be so good as to show them their beds?"

"That shall be done at once," said the woman. "Noémi, go and help the young lady to undress."

Noémi rose and followed her mother and the two guests into the

58

back-room. Timar also left the table, at which the new-comer remained alone, and gobbled down with wolfish hunger every eatable left: meanwhile, he talked over his shoulder to Timar, and threw to Almira the bare bones with his fork.

"You must have had a devilish bad journey, sir, with this wind. I can't think how you got through Denin Kafoin and the Tatalia Pass. Catch, Almira! and don't be cross with me any more, stupid brute! Do you remember, sir, how we once met in Galatz?—there, that's for you too, you black beast!"

When he looked round, he found that neither Timar nor Almira was there. Timar had gone to the attic to sleep, where he soon made himself a couch of fragrant hay, while Almira had crept into some cranny in the great mass of rock.

He turned his chair round, but not till he had drained the last drop from the wine-jug and the glasses of the other guests. Then he cut a splinter from the chair he was sitting on, and picked his teeth with it, like a person who has thoroughly deserved his supper.

Night had set in; travelers weary of knocking about want no rocking. Timar had stretched himself on the soft sweet hay very comfortably, and thought that to-night he would sleep like a king. But he deceived himself. It is not easy to fall asleep after hard work, which has been mingled with varied emotions. Successive shapes besieged his bed like a chaotic panorama: a confusion of pursuing forms, threatening rocks, water-falls, ruined castles, strange women, black dogs, white cats; and amid it all a howling tempest, blasts of the horn, cracking of whips, showers of gold, laughing, whispering, and screaming human voices.

And all at once people began to speak in the room below. He recognized the voices, the hostess and the last comer talking together. The garret was separated from the other room only by a thin floor, and every word was audible, as if it had been whispered in the listener's ear. They spoke in suppressed tones, only now and then the man raised his voice.

"Well, Mother Therese, have you much money?" began the man.

"You know very well that I have none. Don't you know that I only barter and never take money?"

"That's very stupid. I don't like it. And what's more, I don't believe it."

"It is as I say. Whoever comes to buy my fruit brings me something for my own use. What should I do here with money?"

"I know what you could do, you could give it to me. You never think of me. When I marry Noémi you can't give her dried plums for a dowry; but you don't care about your daughter's happiness. You ought to help me, that I may get a good situation. I have just received my nomination as first dragoman at the embassy; but I have no money to get there, for my purse has been stolen, and now I shall lose my situation."

The woman answered in a calm tone, "That any one has given you any place that you could lose I don't believe; but I do believe you have a place you can't lose. That you have no money, I believe that; but that it was stolen from you I don't believe."

"Well, don't then. And I don't believe you have no money; you must have some. Smugglers land here sometimes, and they always pay well."

"Speak loud, of course! Yes, it is true, smugglers often land on the island; but they don't come near my hut, or if they do, they buy fruit and give me salt in exchange. Will you have some salt?"

"You are laughing at me. Well, and such visitors as you have to-night?"

"I don't know whether they are rich or not."

"Ask them for money! Demand it! Don't make a solemn face! You must get money somehow; don't try to take me in with this ridiculous Australian barter. Get ducats if you want to keep the peace with me; you know if I say a single word at the right place it's all up with you."

"Softly, you wretched man!"

"Ay! now you want me to whisper. Well, shut my mouth then, be kind to me, Therese—let me have a little money."

"But I tell you there is none in the house! Don't worry me! I have not a farthing, and don't want any; there is a curse on anything which is gold. There, all my chests and boxes are here; look through them, and if you find anything, take it."

It appeared that the man was not slow to take advantage of this permission, for soon he was heard to exclaim, "Ah! What is this? A gold bracelet."

"Yes; the strange lady gave it to Noémi. If you can make use of it, take it."

"It's worth some ten ducats—well, that's better than nothing. Don't be angry, Noémi; when you are my wife I will buy you two bracelets, each thirty ducats in weight, and with a sapphire in the middle—no, an emerald. Which do you prefer, a sapphire or an emerald?" He laughed at his sally, and as no one answered his question, he continued, "But now, Mother Therese, prepare a bed for your future son-in-law, your dear Theodor, so that he may dream sweetly of his beloved Noémi!"

"I can not give you a bed. In the next room and in the garret are our guests; you can't sleep here in our room, that would not be proper—Noémi is no longer a child. Go out and lie down on the bench."

"Oh, you hard-hearted, cruel Therese. You send me to the hard bench—me, your beloved future son-in-law!"

"Noémi, give your pillow—there, take it! And here's my coverlet. Good-night."

"Yes, if there were not that accursed great dog out there—the fierce brute will devour me."

"Don't be afraid, I will chain her up. Poor beast! she is never tied up except when you are on the island."

Frau Therese had some trouble to entice Almira out of her hole; the poor dog knew well enough what awaited her in these circumstances, and that she would now be chained up, but she was used to obedience, and allowed her mistress to fasten the chain.

But this made her all the more furious against him who was the cause of her confinement. As soon as Therese had gone back to her room, and Theodor remained alone outside, the dog began to bark madly, and danced about on the small space left free to her by the chain, now and then making a spring, to see whether she could succeed in breaking the collar or the chain, or rooting up the tree-trunk to which the chain was fastened.

But Theodor teased her again. He thought it amusing to enrage an animal which could not reach him, and foamed with fury at its impotence. He went closer, leaving only a step between himself and the point the chain

61

permitted the dog to reach; then he began to creep toward her on all fours and make faces at her. He brayed at her like a donkey, put his tongue out, spat in her face, and imitated the dog's bark. "Bow-wow! You would like to eat me, wouldn't you? Bow-wow! There's my nose; bite it off if you can. You're a lovely dog—you horrid beast! Bow-wow! Break your chain and come wrestle with me; snap at my finger, there it is before your nose; only don't you wish you may get it?"

At the moment of her greatest fury, Almira suddenly stopped. She barked no more; she understood. It is the wise one that gives in, thought she. She stretched her head up as if to look down on that other four-legged beast in front of her, then turned and scratched as dogs do, backward, with her hind feet, whirling up dust and sand, so that the other brute got his eyes and mouth full of it, which made him beat a retreat, breaking out in the human bark—curses, to wit. But Almira retired with her chain into the hole near the elder-tree and came out no more; she ceased to bark, but a hot panting could be heard for a long time.

Timar heard it too. He could not sleep; he had left the trap-door open to get some light. The moon shone, and when the dog was silenced, deep stillness lay over the scene; a wonderful calm, rendered more fantastic by the isolated voices of the night and the solitude. The rattle of carriages, the clatter of mills, human voices—none of these struck the ear. This is the kingdom of swamps, islets, and shallows. From time to time a deep note sounds through the night—the boom of the bittern, that hermit of the marsh. Flights of night-birds strike long-drawn chords in the air, and the breathing wind stirs in the poplars, as it sighs through their quivering leaves. The seal cries in the reeds like the voice of a weeping child, and the cockchafer buzzes on the white wall of the hut. All around lies the dark brake, in which fairies seem to hold a torch-light dance; under the decayed trees will-o'-the-wisps wander, pursuing each other. But the flower-garden is flooded by the full radiance of the moon, and night-moths hover on silvery peacock wings round the tall mallows. How exquisite, how divine is this solitude! the whole soul is absorbed in its contemplation.

If only no human tones were mingled with these voices of the night!

But there below in the two little divisions of the hut lie other sleepless

62

people, whom some evil spirit has robbed of their slumber, and who add their deep sighs to the other voices. From one room Timar heard the sigh, "Oh, thou dear Christ!" while from the other "Oh, Allah!" resounded.

They can not sleep; what is there down below which keeps people awake?

While Timar tried to collect his thoughts, an idea flashed through his mind which induced him to leave his couch, throw on the coat he had had over him, and descend the ladder to the ground.

At the same moment, some one in one of the rooms below had had the same thought. And when Timar, standing at the corner of the house, uttered the name of "Almira" under his breath, another voice from the door opening into the veranda called Almira's name too, as if one were the ghostly echo of the other.

The speakers approached each other with surprise.

The other person was Therese. "You have come down from your bed?" she asked.

"Yes; I could not sleep."

"And what did you want with Almira?"

"I will tell you the truth. The thought struck me, whether that . . . man had poisoned the dog, because she became so suddenly silent."

"Just my idea. Almira!" At the call the dog came out of the hole and wagged her tail.

"No; it's all right," said Therese. "His bed on the veranda is undisturbed. Come, Almira, I will set you free."

The great creature laid her head on her mistress's lap, and allowed her to take off the leather collar, sprung round her, licked her cheeks, and then turned to Timar, raised one of the shaggy paws, and placed it as a proof of doggish respect in his open hand. Then the dog shook herself, stretched herself out, and, after a roll on both sides, lay quiet on the soft grass. She barked no more; they could be thoroughly satisfied that that man no longer remained on the island.

Therese came nearer to Timar. "Do you know this man?"

"I once met him in Galatz. He came on board and behaved so that I could not make up my mind whether he was a spy or a smuggler. At last I got rid of him, and that concluded our acquaintance."

"And how came you by the notion that he might have poisoned Almira?"

"To tell you the truth, every word spoken down below is audible in the garret, and as I had lain down I was forced to hear all the conversation between you."

"Did you hear how he threatened me? If I could not satisfy him, it would only cost him a single word, and we should be ruined?"

"Yes; I heard that."

"And what do you think about us? You believe that some great, nameless crime has banished us to this island outside the world? that we drive some dubious trade, of which one can not speak? or that we are the homeless heirs of some dishonored name, who must hide from the sight of the authorities? Say, what do you think?"

"Nothing, my dear lady; I don't trouble my head about it. You have given me hospitable shelter for a night, and I am grateful. The storm is over; to-morrow I shall go on my way, and think no more of what I saw and heard on this island."

"I do not want you to leave us so. Without your desire you have heard things which must be explained to you. I do not know why, but from the first moment when I saw you, you inspired me with confidence, and the thought troubles me that you should leave us with suspicion and contempt: that suspicion would prevent both you and me from sleeping under this roof. The night is quiet, and suitable to the story of the secrets of a hard life. You shall form your own judgment about us; I will conceal nothing, and tell you the whole truth, and when you have heard the history of this lonely island and this clay hut, you won't say, 'To-morrow I go away and think no more of it,' but you will come back year by year, when your business brings you near us, and rest for a night under this peaceful roof. Sit down by me on the doorstep, and listen to the story of our house."

CHAPTER VIII.
THE HISTORY OF THE ISLANDERS.

"Twelve years ago we lived in Pancsova, where my husband held a municipal office. His name was Bellovary; he was young, handsome, and honest, and we loved each other dearly. I was then two-and-twenty and he was thirty.

"I bore him a daughter, whom we called Noémi. We were not rich, but well off; he had his post, a pretty house, and a splendid orchard and meadow. I was an orphan when we married, and brought him some money; we were able to live respectably.

"My husband had a friend, Maxim Krisstyan, of whom he was very fond. The man who has just been here is his son, who was then thirteen, a dear, handsome, clever boy. When my little daughter was still a baby, the fathers already began to say they would make a pair, and I was glad when the boy took the little thing's hand and asked her, 'Will you be my wife?' at which the child laughed merrily.

"Krisstyan was a grain dealer without having ever learned regular business, but was like the speculators in a small way, who catch hold of a rope behind the great wholesale dealers, and go blindly in their wake. If the speculation succeeds, well and good; if not, they are ruined. As he always won, he thought there was nothing easier than mercantile transactions. In the spring he went round to see the crops, and made contracts with the large dealers for the grain to be delivered to them after the harvest. He had a regular customer in the wholesale merchant of Komorn, Athanasius Brazovics, who made large advances to him every spring for grain which he was to deliver in autumn at the price settled in advance, on board ship. This was a lucrative affair for Krisstyan; but I have often thought since that it was not so much trade as a game of chance, when one sells what does not yet exist. Brazovics advanced large sums to Krisstyan, and as the latter had no real property, security was required of him. My husband went surety for him gladly—was he not a landowner and Krisstyan's friend? Krisstyan led an easy life; while my good man sat for hours bent over his desk, the other was at the

65

café, smoking his pipe and chatting with tradespeople of his own sort. But at last God's scourge alighted on him. The year 1819 was a terrible year; in the spring the crops looked splendid over the whole country, and every one expected cheap prices. In the Banat a merchant was lucky if he could make a contract for delivery of grain at four gulden a measure. Then came a wet summer—for sixteen weeks it rained every day; the corn rotted on its stem. In places reputed as a second Canaan, famine set in, and in autumn the price of grain rose to twenty gulden a measure: and even so there was none to be had, for the landowners kept it for seed."

"I remember it well," Timar interrupted. "I was then just beginning my career as a ship's captain."

"Well, in that year, it happened that Maxim could not fulfill the contract he had concluded with Athanasius Brazovics; the difference he had to cover made an enormous sum. What did he do then? He collected his outstanding debts, got loans from several credulous people, and disappeared in the night from Pancsova, taking his money with him, and leaving his son behind.

"He could easily do it; his whole property consisted of money, and he left nothing for which he cared. But what is the good of all the money in the world if it can make a man so bad as to care for nothing else? His debts and liabilities rested on the shoulders of those who had been his good friends, and stood security for him, and among these was my husband.

"Then came Athanas Brazovics, and required from the sureties the fulfillment of the contract. It was true that he had advanced money to the absconding debtor, and we offered to pay it back: we could have sold half our property, and so met the obligation. But he would not hear of it, and insisted on the fulfillment of the contract; it was not how much money he had lost, but what sums we were bound to pay him. Thus he made five-fold profits; his contract gave him the right to do so. We begged and entreated him to be content with smaller gain—for it was only a question of more or less gain, not of loss—but he was inflexible; he required from the sureties the satisfaction of his claims in full. What is the use, say I, of faith and religion, and all Christian and Jewish churches, if it is permitted to make such a demand?

"The affair came before the court; the judge gave sentence that our house, our fields, our last farthing, should be distrained, sealed and put up to auction.

"But what is the use of the law, a human institution, if it can be possible that people should be brought to beggary by a debt of which they have never had a groschen, and fall into misery for the benefit of a third, who rises laughing from the ground?

"We tried everything to save ourselves from utter ruin. My husband went to Ofen and Vienna to beg an audience. We knew the artful deceiver who had escaped with his money was living in Turkey, and begged for his extradition, that he might be brought here to satisfy those who had presented claims against him; but we were told that there was no power to do so. Then what is the use of the emperor, the ministers, the authorities, if they are not in a position to extend protection to their subjects in distress? After this fearful blow, which brought us all to beggary, my poor husband one night sent a bullet through his head. He would not look on the misery of his family, the tears of his wife, the pale, starved face of his child, and fled from us into the grave.

"But what is a husband good for, if, when he falls into misfortune, he knows no other outlet than to quit the world himself, and leave wife and child alone behind?

"But the horrors were not yet at an end. I was a beggar and homeless; now they tried to make me an infidel. The wife of the suicide begged her pastors in vain to bury the unhappy man. The dean was a strict and holy man, for whom the laws of the Church were the first thought. He denied my husband a decent burial, and I had to look on while the dear form of my adored one was carried by the knacker's cart to be hastily buried in a corner of a church-yard. What are the clergy for, if they can not relieve us of such misery as that? What is the whole world about?

"Only one thing was left; they drove me to kill myself and my child, both at once. I wrapped a shawl round the child at my breast, and went with it to the river bank.

"I was alone. Three times I went up and down to see where the water was deepest. Then something plucked my dress and drew me back. I looked round. Who was it? The dog here—of all living beings the only friend left to me.

"It was on the shore of the Ogradina Island that this happened. On this island we had a beautiful fruit-garden and a little summer-house; but there too the official seal had been affixed to every door, and I could only go through the kitchen and out under the trees. Then I sat down by the Danube and began to reflect. What, am I, I, a human being, a woman, to be worse than an animal! Did one ever see a dog drown its young and then kill itself? No, I will not kill either myself or my child; I will live and bring it up. But how? Like the wolves or the gypsy woman, who have no home and no food. I will beg—beg of the ground, the waters, the wilderness of the forest; only not of men—never!

"My poor husband had told me of a little island which had been formed some fifty years ago in the reed-beds near Ogradina; he often went shooting there in autumn, and spoke much of a hollow rock in which he had sought shelter from bad weather. He said, 'The island has no master; the Danube built it up for no one; the soil, the trees, the grass which grow on it belong to no one.' If it is ownerless, this island, why should not I take possession of it? I ask it of God, I ask it of the Danube. Why should they refuse it? I will raise fruit there. How? and what fruit? I do not know, but necessity will teach me.

"A boat remained to me which the officer had not noticed, and which, therefore, had not been seized. Noémi, Almira and I got into it, and I rowed myself over to the ownerless island. I had never used an oar before, but necessity taught me.

"When I touched this piece of ground, a wonderful feeling took possession of me: it was as if I had forgotten what had happened to me out in the world. I was surrounded by a pleasant silence and rest, which softened my heart.

"After I had explored pasture, grove, and meadow, I knew what I should do here. In the field bees were humming, in the woods hazel-nuts were hanging, and on the surface of the river floated water-chestnuts. Crabs basked on the shore, edible snails crept up the trees, and in the marshy thickets manna was ripening. Kind Providence, Thou hast spread a table before me! The grove was full of wild fruit—seedlings; the blackbirds had brought seeds from the neighboring island, and already the wild apples grew rosy on the trees, and the raspberry bushes bore a few belated berries.

"Yes, I knew what I would do on the island. I alone would make of it a Garden of Eden. The work to be done here could be managed by a single person, one woman, and then we should live here like the first man in Paradise.

"I had found the rock with its natural grottoes, in the largest of which a layer of hay was spread, which must have served as a bed to my poor husband. I had a widow's right to it; it was my legacy. I hushed my child to sleep there, made it a couch in the hay, and covered it with my large shawl. Then I told Almira to stay there and watch over Noémi till I came back, and rowed across to the large island again. On the veranda of my old summer-house there was an awning spread out, which I took down; it would serve as a tent or roof, and perhaps later on be used for winter clothing. I packed in it what food and vegetables I could see, and made a bundle as large as I could carry on my back. I had come to the house in a four-horse wagon richly laden; with a bundle on my back I left it; and yet I had been neither wicked nor a spendthrift. But what if even that bundle were stolen goods? It is true that the contents were my own; but that I should carry them off, was it not theft? I hardly knew: notions of right and wrong, the legal or the illegal, were confused in my head. I fled with the bundle like a thief out of my own home. On my way through the garden I took a cutting of each of my beautiful fruit-trees, and shoots from the figs and bushes, picked up some seeds from the ground and put them in my apron; then I kissed the drooping branches of the weeping willow under which I had so often dozed and dreamed. Those happy dreams were gone forever. I never went back there. The boat took me safely along the Danube.

"While I rowed back two things fretted me. One was that there were noxious inhabitants on the island—snakes; probably some in that grotto: the thought filled me with horror and alarm for Noémi. The other anxiety was this. I can live for years on wild honey, water-nuts, and manna fruit; my child lives on her mother's breast; but how shall I feed Almira? The faithful creature can not live on what nourishes me; and yet I must keep her, for

69

without Almira as a protector I should die of fright in this solitude. When I had dragged my bundle to the grotto, I saw before me the still quivering tail of a large snake, and not far off lay its head, bitten off; Almira had eaten what lay between the head and tail. The clever beast lay before the child, wagging her tail and licking her lips, as if to say, I have made a good meal. Thenceforward she made war on snakes; they were her daily food. In the winter she scratched them out of their holes. My friend—for so I grew to call the dog—had found her own livelihood, and freed me from the objects of my dread.

"Oh, sir, it was an indescribable feeling, our first night alone here—no one near but my God, my child, and my dog. I can not call it painful—it was almost bliss. I spread the linen awning over us all three, and we were only awoke by the twitter of the birds. Now began my work—savages' work, for before sunrise I must collect manna, called by Hungarians 'Dew-millet.' Poor women go out into the swamp, where this bush with its sweet seeds luxuriates; they hold up their dress in both hands, shake the bush, and the ripe seeds fall into their lap. That is the bread from heaven for those whom no one feeds. Sir, I lived two whole years on that bread, and thanked daily on my knees Him who cares for the birds of the air. Wild fruit, honey, nuts, crabs, wild fowls' eggs, water-chestnuts preserved for winter use, land snails, dried mushrooms, formed my food. Praised be the Lord who so richly provides the table of His poor! And during the whole time I labored for the object I had set before me. I grafted the wild stocks with the cuttings I had brought, and planted in the cultivated soil fruit-trees, vines, and walnut-seeds. On the south side I sowed cotton-plant and silky swallow-wort, whose products I wove on a loom made of willow-wood, and made clothes for us. From rushes and reeds I made hives, in which I housed swarms of wild bees, and even in the first year I could begin a trade in wax and honey. Millers and smugglers often came here; they helped me with the hard labor, and never did me any harm. They paid me for provisions by their work; they knew already that I never took money. When the fruit-trees began to bear, then I lived in luxury, for in this alluvial soil all trees flourish, to that it is a pleasure to see them. I have pears which ripen their fruit twice in a year; all the young ones make fresh shoots at St. John's day, and the others bear every year. I have learned their secrets, and know that in the hands of a good gardener there should be no failure nor over-crop. Animals understand the language of man, and I believe that trees too have ears and eyes for those who tend them kindly and listen to their private wishes; and they are proud to give them pleasure in return. Oh, trees are very sensible! a soul dwells in them. I consider that man a murderer who cuts down a noble tree.

"These are my friends. I love them, and live in and by them. What they yield me year by year is fetched away by the people of the villages and mills round, who give me in exchange what I need for my housekeeping. I have no use for money, I have a horror of it—the accursed money, which drove me out of the world and my husband out of life: I don't want ever to see it again.

"But I am not so foolish as to be unprepared for some years of failure, which make vain the work of man. There might be late frosts or hail-storms, which would destroy the blessings of the season; but I am prepared for such bad times. In the cellar of my rock and in its airy crevices I store away whatever durable wares I possess—wine in casks, honey in pots, wool and cotton in bales, in sufficient quantity to keep us from want for two years. You see I have some savings, though not in money; I may call myself rich, and yet for twelve years not a single coin has passed through my hands. For I have lived on this island twelve years, sir, with the other two, for I count Almira as a person. Noémi declares we are four; she counts Narcissa, too—silly child!

"Many people know of our existence, but treachery is unknown here. The artificial barrier which exists between the frontiers of the two countries has made the people about here very reserved. No one meddles in a stranger's affairs, and every one instinctively keeps secret what he knows. No intelligence from here ever reaches Vienna, Ofen, or Stamboul. And why should they inform against me? I am in nobody's way, and do no harm; I grow fruit on my bit of desert land, which has no master. God the Lord and the royal Danube gave it to me, and I thank them for it daily. I thank Thee, my God! I thank Thee, my King!

"I hardly know if I have any religion; it is twelve years since I saw a priest or a church. Noémi knows nothing about it. I have taught her to read

71

and write: I tell her of God, and Jesus, and Moses, as I knew them. Of the good, all-merciful, omnipresent God—of Jesus, sublime in His sufferings, and divine in His humanity—and of Moses, that leader of a people to liberty, who preferred to wander hungry and thirsty in the wilderness rather than exchange freedom for the flesh-pots of slavery—Moses who preached goodness and brotherly love—of these as I picture them to myself. But of the relentless God of vengeance, the God of the chosen people—a God calling for sacrifices, and dwelling in temples—of that privileged Christ asking for blind faith, laying heavy burdens on our shoulders, followed by a crowd of worshipers—and of the avaricious, revengeful, selfish Moses of whom books and preachers tell—of these she knows nothing.

"Now you know who we are, and what we are doing here, you shall learn with what we are threatened by this man.

"He is the son of the man for whom my husband stood surety, who drove him to suicide, on whose account we have fled from human society into the desert. He was a boy of thirteen when we lost our all, and the blow fell on him also, for his father had forsaken him.

"Indeed, I do not wonder that the son has turned out such a wretch. Abandoned by his own father, thrust out like a beggar into the world, cast on the compassion of strangers, deceived and robbed by the one on whom his childish trust was placed, branded in his earliest youth as the son of a rogue, is it surprising if he was forced to become what he is?

"And yet I hardly know what to think of him; but what I do know is enough. The people who come to the island can tell a great deal about him. Not long after his father had escaped, he also started from Turkey, saying he was going to look for his father. Some maintained that he had found him, others that he had never been able to trace him. According to one report he robbed his own father and squandered the money he stole, but no one knows for certain. From him nothing can be learned, for he tells nothing but lies. As to where he has been, and what he has done, he relates romances, in whose invention he is so well versed, and which he presents so skillfully, that he staggers even those who have actual knowledge of the facts, and makes them doubt the testimony of their own eyes. You see him here to-day and there to-morrow. In Turkey, Wallachia, Poland, and Hungary he has been met. In all these countries he is by way of knowing every person of distinction. Whomsoever he meets he takes in, and whoever has once been deceived by him may be sure it will happen again. He speaks ten languages, and whatever countryman he pretends to be, he is accepted as such. He appears now as a merchant, then a soldier, again as a seafaring man; to-day a Turk, to-morrow a Greek. He once came out as a Polish count, then as the betrothed of a Russian princess, and again as a quack doctor, who cured all maladies with his pills. What his real profession may be no one knows. But one thing is certain, he is a paid spy. Whether in the service of the Turks, Austrians, or Russians, who can tell? Perhaps he is in the pay of all three and more besides—he serves each, and betrays all. Every year he comes several times to this island. He comes in a boat from the Turkish shore, and goes in the same boat from here to the Hungarian bank. Of what he does there I have no idea; but I am inclined to believe that he inflicts the torture of his presence on me for his own amusement. I know, too, that he is an epicure and a sensualist: he finds good food here, and a blooming young girl whom he loves to tease by calling her his bride. Noémi hates him; she has no idea how well founded is her abhorrence.

"Yet I do not think that Theodor Krisstyan visits this island only for these reasons; it must have other secrets unknown to me. He is a paid spy, and has a bad heart besides; he is rotten to the core, and ripe for any villainy. He knows that I and my daughter have only usurped the island, and that by law I have no claim to it, and by the possession of this secret he lays us under contribution, vexes and torments us both.

"He threatens that if we do not give him what he wants, he will inform against us both in Austria and Turkey, and as soon as these governments know that a new piece of land has been formed in the midst of the Danube, which is not included in any treaty, a dispute about its jurisdiction will commence between the countries, and until its conclusion all the inhabitants will be warned off, as happened in the case of Allion Castle and the Cserna River.

"It would only cost this man a word to annihilate all that I have brought to perfection by my twelve years' labor; to turn this Eden, where we are so happy, back into a wilderness, and thrust us out anew, homeless, into the world. Yes, and more still. We have not only to fear discovery by the imperial officials, but discovery by the priest. If the archbishops, the patriarchs, archimandrite, and deans learned that a girl is growing up here who has never seen a church since she was baptized, they would take her away by force and put her in a convent. Now, sir, do you understand those sighs which kept you awake?"

Timar gazed at the full disk of the moon, which was beginning to sink behind the poplars. "Why," thought he to himself, "am I not a man of influence?"

"So this wretch," continued Therese, "can throw us into poverty any day. He need only give information in Vienna or Stamboul that here on the Danube a new territory exists, and we should be ruined. No one here would betray us—he alone is capable of it. But I am prepared for the worst. The whole foundation of this island is solely and entirely formed by the rock: it alone stems the force of the Danube current. In the year when Milos made war against the Serbs, some Servian smugglers hid three barrels of blasting powder in the bushes near here, and no one has ever fetched them away. Perhaps those who hid them were taken prisoners by the Turks, or killed. I found them, and have concealed them in the deepest cavity of this great rock. Sir, if they try to drive me from this island, now ownerless, I shall thrust a burning match into the powder, and the rock and all upon it will be blown into the air. In the next spring, after the ice has melted, no one would find a trace of the island. And now you know why you could not sleep well here."

Timar leaned his head on his hand and looked away.

"There is one more thing I ought to say," said Frau Therese, bending close to Timar, that he might hear her low whisper—"I fancy this man had another reason for coming here and vanishing again, besides his having gambled away his money in some low pot-house, and wanting to get more out of me. His visit was either on your account, or that of the other gentleman. Be on your guard, if either of you dreads the discovery of a secret."

The moon disappeared behind the poplars, and it began to dawn in the east. Blackbirds commenced their song; it was morning. From the Morova Island long-drawn trumpet-calls sounded, to awake the seafaring folk. Steps were audible in the sand; a sailor came from the landing-place with the news that the vessel was ready for departure, the wind had gone down, and they could proceed. The guests came out of the little dwelling: Euthemio Trikaliss and his daughter, the beautiful Timéa, with her dazzling pale face.

Noémi also was up and boiling fresh goat's milk for breakfast, with roasted maize instead of coffee, and honey for sugar. Timéa took none, but let Narcissa drink the milk instead, who did not despise the stranger's offer, to Noémi's great vexation.

Trikaliss asked Timar where the stranger had gone who came last evening? Timar told him he had left in the night. At this intelligence his face fell.

Then they all took leave of their hostess. Timéa was out of sorts, and still complained of feeling unwell. Timar remained behind, and gave Therese a bright Turkish silk scarf as a present for Noémi; she thanked him, and said the child should wear it. Then they took the path leading to the boat, and Therese and Almira accompanied them to the shore. But Noémi went up to the top of the rock: there, sitting on soft moss and stonecrop, she watched the boat away.

Narcissa crept after her, cowered in her lap, and crept with bending neck into her bosom. "Be off, faithless one! that is how you love me. You leave me in the lurch, and make up to the other girl, just because she is pretty and I am not. Go! I don't love you any longer!" and then she caught the coaxing cat with both hands to her breast, pressed her smooth chin on the white head of the little flatterer, and gazed after the boat. In her eye glittered a tear.

CHAPTER IX.
ALI TSCHORBADSCHI.

The following day the "St. Barbara" continued her voyage with a fair wind up the Hungarian Danube. Until evening nothing remarkable occurred, and all went to bed early; they agreed that the previous night no one had been able to sleep. But this night also was to be a wakeful one for Timar. All was quiet on board the ship, which lay at anchor—only the monotonous splash of the wavelets against the vessel broke the stillness; but amidst the silence it seemed to him as if his neighbor was busy with important and mysterious affairs. From the neighboring cabin, which was only divided from his by a wooden partition, came all sorts of sounds; the clank of money, a noise as of drawing a cork and stirring with a spoon, as of one clasping his hands and performing his ablutions in the darkness, and then again those sighs, as in the previous night, "Oh, Allah!"

At last there was a gentle knocking at the partition. Trikaliss called—"Come to me here, sir."

Timar dressed quickly and hastened into the cabin. There were two beds, and between them a table. The curtains were closed in front of one, and on the other lay Euthemio. On the table stood a casket and two small glasses. "What are your orders, sir?" asked Timar.

"I have no orders—I entreat."

"You want something?"

"I shall not want anything long. I am dying; I want to die—I have taken poison. Don't give the alarm—sit down and listen to what I have to tell you. Timéa will not wake. I have given her opium to send her into a deep sleep, for she must not wake up now. Don't interrupt; what you would say is useless, but I have much to tell you, and only one short hour left, for the poison acts quickly. Make no vain attempts to save me. I hold the antidote in my hand—if I repented of my deed it rests with me to undo it. But I will not—and I am right—so sit down and listen.

"My true name is not Euthemio Trikaliss but Ali Tschorbadschi. I was once governor of Candia, and then treasurer in Stamboul. You know

76

what is passing in Turkey now. The Ulemas and governors are rising against the sultan, because he is making innovations. At such times men's lives are of little value. One party murders by thousands those who are not its allies, and the other party burns by thousands the houses of those in power. No one is high enough to be safe from his rulers or his slaves. The Kaimakan of Stamboul had at least six hundred respectable Turks strangled there, and then was stabbed by his own slave in the Mosque of St. Sophia. Every change cost human blood. When the sultan went to Edren, twenty-six important men were arrested, and twenty of them beheaded, while the other six were stretched on the rack. After they had made false accusations against the great men of the country in order to save themselves, they were strangled; then those were arrested against whom they had borne witness, and these suspected nobles disappeared without being heard of again. The sultan's secretary, Waffat Effendi, was sent to Syria, and murdered by the Druses. The Pasha Pertao was invited to dinner by the governor of Edren, Emin Pasha: when the meal was over, black coffee was brought, and he was told that the sultan commanded him to take poison in it. Pertao only asked that he might be allowed to mix the poison he had with him in the coffee, as it was more certain; then he blessed the sultan, performed his ablutions, prayed and died. Even in these days every Turkish noble carries poison in his signet-ring, to have it at hand when his turn comes.

"I knew in good time when my turn was coming. Not that I was a conspirator, but for two reasons I was ripe for the sickle; these reasons were my money and my daughter.

"The treasury wanted my treasures and the seraglio my daughter. Death is easy, and I am ready for it; but I will not let my daughter go into the harem, nor myself be made a beggar. I determined to upset the calculations of my enemies and fly with my daughter and my property; but I could not go by sea, for the new galleys would have overtaken me. I had kept a passport for Hungary in readiness for a long time; I disguised myself as a Greek merchant, shaved off my long beard, and reached Galatz by by-roads. From there I could go no further by land; I therefore hired a vessel and loaded it with grain which I bought: in this way I could best save my wealth. When you told me the name of the ship's owner I was very glad, for Athanas Brazovics is a connection of mine; Timéa's mother was a Greek of his family. I have often shown kindness to this man, and he can return it now. Allah is great and wise—no man can escape his fate. You guessed I was a fugitive, even if you were not clear whether you had a criminal or a political refugee on board—still you thought it your duty as commander of the vessel to help the passenger intrusted to you in his speedy escape. By a miracle we traversed safely the rocks and whirlpools of the Iron Gate; by fool-hardy audacity we eluded the pursuit of the Turkish brigantine; by lucky chance we escaped quarantine and the search at the custom-house—and after we had left every bugbear behind, I stumbled over a straw under my feet into my grave.

"That man who followed us last evening to the unknown island was a spy of the Turkish Government. I know him, and he certainly recognized me; no one could have traced me except himself. He has hurried on in front, and at Pancsova they are ready to receive me. Don't speak—I know what you mean; you think it is Hungarian territory, and that governments grant no extradition of political refugees.

"But they would not pursue me as a political criminal, but as a thief—unjustly—for what I took was my own, and if the State has claims on me, there are my twenty-seven houses in Galatz, by which they can be satisfied; but in spite of that they will cry after me 'Catch thief!'

"I pass for one who has robbed the treasury, and Austria gives up escaped thieves to Turkey if the Turkish spies succeed in tracing them. This man has recognized me and sealed my fate."

Heavy drops of perspiration stood on the speaker's brow. His face had turned as yellow as wax.

"Give me a drink of water that I may go on, for I have still much to tell you. I can not save myself, but by dying I can save my daughter and her property. Allah wills it, and who can flee from His presence? So swear to me by your faith and your honor that you will carry out my instructions. First, when I am dead, do not bury me on shore—a Mussulman does not require Christian burial, so bury me like a sailor; sew me up in a piece of sail-cloth, fasten at my head and feet a heavy stone, then sink me where the Danube is deepest. Do this, my son, and when it is done, steer steadily for Komorn, and take care of Timéa!

"Here in this casket is money—about a thousand ducats; the rest of my property is in the sacks packed as grain. I leave on my table a note which you must keep. I declare therein that I have contracted dysentery by immoderate enjoyment of melons, and am dying of it; further, that my whole possessions were only these thousand ducats. This will serve you as a security that no one may accuse you of having caused my death or embezzled my money. I give you nothing; what you do is of your own kind heart, and God will reward you: He is the best creditor you can have. And then take Timéa to Athanas Brazovics and beg him to adopt my daughter. He has a daughter himself who may be a sister to her. Give him the money—he must spend it on the education of the child; and give over to him also the cargo, and beg him to be present himself when the sacks are emptied. There is good grain in them, and it might be changed. You understand?"

The dying man looked in Timar's face, and struggled for breath. "For—" Again speech failed him. "Did I say anything? I had more to say—but my thoughts grow confused. How red the night is! How red the moon is in the sky! Yes; the Red Crescent—" A deep groan from Timéa's bed attracted his attention and gave another turn to his thoughts. He raised himself anxiously in his bed, and sought with a trembling hand for something under his pillow, his eyes starting from their sockets. "Ah, I had almost forgotten—Timéa! I gave her a sleeping-draught—if you do not wake her up in time she will sleep forever. Here in this bottle is an antidote. As soon as I am dead, take it and rub her brow, temples, and chest, until she awakes. Ah! how nearly I had taken her with me! but no, she must live. Must she not? You vow to me by all you hold sacred, that you will wake her, and bring her back to life—that you will not let her slumber on into eternity?"

The dying man pressed Timar's hand convulsively to his breast: on his distorted features was already imprinted the last death-struggle. "What was I talking of? What had I to tell you? What was my last word? Yes; right—the Red Crescent!"

Through the open window the half-circle of the waning moon shone blood-red, rising from the nocturnal mists. Was the dying man in his delirium thinking of this? Or did it remind him of something?

"Yes—the Red Crescent," he stammered once more; then the

death-throes closed his lips—one short struggle, and he was a corpse.

CHAPTER X.
THE LIVING STATUE.

Timar remained alone with the dead body, with a person sunk in a death-like stupor, and with a buried secret. The silent night covered them, and the shades whispered to him, "See! if you do not do what has been committed to you—if you throw the corpse into the Danube, and do not wake the slumberer, but let her sleep on quietly into the other world—what would happen then? The spy will have already given evidence in Pancsova against the fugitive Tschorbadschi; but if you anticipate him and the land at Belgrade instead, and lay information there, then, according to Turkish law, a third of the refugee's property would fall to you; otherwise it would belong to no one. The father is dead, the girl, if you do not rouse her, will never wake again; thus you would become at one stroke a rich man. Only rich people are worth anything in this world—poor devils are only fit for clerks."

Timar answered the spirits of the night—"Well, then, I will always remain a clerk;" and, in order to silence these murmuring shadows, he closed the shutters. A secret anxiety beset him when he saw the red moon outside; it seemed as if all these bad suggestions came from it, as well as an explanation of the last words of the dying man about the Red Crescent.

He drew back the curtain from Timéa's berth.

The girl lay like a living statue; her bosom rose and fell with her slow breathing—the lips were half open, the eyes shut; her face wore an expression of unearthly solemnity. One hand was raised to her loosened hair, the other held the folds of her white dress together on her breast.

Timar approached her as if she were an enchanted fairy whose touch might cause deadly heart-sickness to a poor mortal. He began to rub the temples of the sleeper with the fluid from the bottle. In doing so, he looked continually in her face, and thought to himself, "What, should I let you die, you angelic creature? If the whole ship were filled with real pearls, which would be mine after your death, I could not let you sleep away your life. There is no diamond in the world, however precious, that I should prefer to your eyes when you open them."

The lovely face remained unchanged, in spite of the friction on brow and temples; the delicate meeting eyebrows did not contract when touched by a strange man's hand. The directions were that also over the heart the antidote must be applied. Timar was obliged to take the girl's hand, in order to draw it away from her breast: the hand made no smallest resistance; it was stiff and cold, as cold as the whole form—beautiful and icy as marble.

The shadows whispered—"Behold this exquisite form! a lovelier has never been touched by mortal lips; no one would know if you kissed her."

But Timar answered himself in the darkness, "No—you have never stolen anything of another's in your life. This kiss would be a theft." And then he spread the Persian quilt, which the girl had thrown off in her sleep, over her whole person up to her neck, and rubbed above the heart of the sleeper with wetted fingers, while, in order to resist temptation, he kept his eyes fixed on the maiden's face. It was to him like an altar-picture—so cold, yet so serene.

At last the lids unclosed, and he met the gaze of her dark but dull eyes. She breathed more easily, and Timar felt her heart beat stronger under his hand; he drew it away. Then he held the bottle with the strong essence for her to smell. Timéa awoke, for she turned her head away from it, and drew her brows together. Timar called her gently by name.

The girl started up, and with the cry "Father!" sat up on her bed, gazing out with staring eyes. The Persian quilt fell down from her lap, the night-dress slipped from her shoulders. She looked more like a Greek marble than a sentient being.

"Timéa!" and as he spoke he drew the fine linen over her bare shoulders. She did not answer. "Timéa!" cried Timar, "your father is dead." But neither face nor form moved, nor did she notice that her night-dress had left her bosom uncovered. She seemed totally unconscious.

Timar rushed into the other cabin, returned with a coffee-pot, and began in feverish haste, and not without burning his fingers, to heat some coffee. When it was ready, he went to Timéa, took her head on his arm and pressed it to him, opened her mouth with his fingers, and poured some coffee in. Hitherto he had only had to contend with passive resistance; but as soon as Timéa had swallowed the hot and bitter decoction of Mocha, she pushed Timar's hand with such strength that the cup fell; then she drew the quilt over her, and her teeth began to chatter.

"Thank God! she lives; for she is in a high fever," sighed Timar, "And now for a sailor's funeral."

CHAPTER XI.
A BURIAL AT SEA.

On the ocean this is managed very easily: the body is sewed up in a piece of sail-cloth, and a cannon-ball is suspended to the feet, which sinks the corpse in the sea. Corals soon grow over the grave. But on a Danube craft, to throw a dead person into the river is a great responsibility. There are shores, and on the shores villages and towns, with church bells and priests, to give the corpse his funeral-toll and his rest in consecrated ground. It won't do to pitch him into the water, without a "By your leave," just because the dead man wished it.

But Timar knew well enough that this must be done, and it caused him no anxiety. Before the vessel had weighed anchor, he said to his pilot that there was a corpse on board—Trikaliss was dead.

"I knew for certain," said Johann Fabula, "that there was bad luck on the way when the sturgeon ran races with the ship—that always betokens a death."

"We must moor over there by the village," answered Timar, "and seek out the minister to bury him. We can not carry the body on in the vessel—we should be under suspicion as infected with plague."

Herr Fabula cleared his throat violently, and said, "We can but try."

The village of Plesscovacz, which was nearest at hand, is a wealthy settlement; it has a dean, and a fine church with two towers. The dean was a tall, handsome man, with a long curling beard, eyebrows as broad as one's finger, and a fine sonorous voice. He happened to know Timar, who had often bought grain from him, as the dean had much produce to sell.

"Well, my son," cried the dean, as soon as he saw him in the court-yard, "you might have chosen your time better. The church harvest was bad, and I have sold my crops long ago." (And yet there was threshing going on in yard and barn.)

"But this time it is I who bring a crop to market," Timar answered. "We have a dead man on board, and I have come to beg your reverence to go over there, and bury the corpse with the usual ceremonies."

"Oh, but my son, that's not so easy. Did this Christian confess? Has he received the last sacraments? Are you certain that he was not a heretic? For if not, I can not consent to bury him."

"I know nothing about it. We don't carry a father-confessor on board, and the poor soul left the world without any priestly assistance—that is the lot of sailors. But if your reverence can not grant him a consecrated grave, give me at any rate a written certificate that I may have some excuse to his friends why I was not in a position to show him the last honors; then we will bury him ourselves somewhere on the shore."

The dean gave him a certificate of the refusal of burial; but then the peasant threshers began to make a fuss. "What! bury a corpse within our boundaries which has not been blessed? Why, then, as certain as the Amen to the Pater Noster, the hail would destroy our crops. And you need not try to bestow him on any other village. Wherever he came from, nobody wants him, for he's sure to bring a hail-storm this season before the vintage is over—the farmer's last hope; and then next year a vampire will rise from a corpse so buried, which will suck up all the rain and the dew!"

They threatened to kill Timar if he brought the body ashore. And in order that he might not bury it secretly on the bank, they chose four stout fellows, who were to go on board the ship and remain there till it had passed the village boundaries, and then he could do what he liked with the dead man.

Timar pretended to be very angry, but allowed the four men to go on board. Meanwhile, the crew had made a coffin and laid the body in it: there was nothing more to do but to nail the lid down.

The first thing that the captain did was to go and see how Timéa was. The fever had reached its highest point; her forehead was burning, but her face still dazzling white. She was unconscious, and knew nothing of the preparations for the burial.

"Yes, that will do," said Timar, and fetched a paint-pot and busied himself in marking Euthemio Trikaliss's name and date of death in beautiful Greek letters on the coffin-lid. The four Servian peasants stood behind and spelled out what he wrote.

"Now, then, you paint a letter or two while I see to my work," said

85

Timar to one of the gazers, and handed him the brush. The man took it and painted on the board an X, which the Servians use like S, to show his skill.

"See what an artist you are!" Timar said, admiringly, and got him to draw another letter. "You are a clever fellow. What is your name?"

"Joso Berkics."

"And yours?"

"Mirko Jakerics."

"Well, God bless you! Let us drink a glass of Slivovitz." They had nothing against the proposition. "I am called Michael; my surname is Timar—a good name, and sounds just the same in Hungarian, Turkish, or Greek—call me Michael."

"Egbogom Michael."

Michael ran constantly into the cabin to see after Timéa. She was still very feverish, and knew no one. But that did not discourage Timar: his idea was that whoever travels on the Danube has a whole chemist's shop at hand, for cold water cures all maladies. His whole system consisted in putting cold compresses on head and feet, and renewing them as soon as they got hot. Sailors had already learned this secret before Priessnitz the hydropath. The "St. Barbara" floated quietly all day up-stream along the Hungarian bank. The Servians soon made friends with the crew, helped them to row, and in return had a thieves' roast offered them from the galley.

The dead man lay out on the upper deck; they had spread a white sheet over him—that was his shroud. Toward evening Michael told his men that he would go and lie down for a spell—he had had no sleep for two nights; but that the vessel might as well go on being towed till it was quite dark, and then they could anchor. He had no sleep that night either. Instead of going into his own cabin, he stole quietly into Timéa's, placed the night-lamp in a box, that its light might not disturb her, and sat the whole time by the sick girl's bed listening to her delirious fancies and renewing her compresses. He never shut his eyes. He heard plainly when the anchor went down and the ship was brought up; and then how the waves began to plash against the sides! The sailors tramped about the deck for some time, then one by one they turned in. But at midnight he heard a dull knocking. That sounds, thought he, like hammering in nails whose heads have been covered with cloth to muffle the sound. Before long he heard a noise like the fall of some heavy object into the water, then all was still.

Michael remained awake, and waited till it was light and the vessel had started again. When they had been an hour on their way, he came out of the cabin. The girl slept quietly, the fever had ceased.

"Where is the coffin?" was the first question.

The Servians came up with a defiant air. "We loaded it with stones and threw it into the water, so that you might not bury it anywhere ashore and bring bad luck on us."

"Rash men! what have you done? Do you know that I shall be arrested and have to render an account of my vanished passenger? They will accuse me of having put him out of the way. You must give me a certificate in which you acknowledge what you did. Which of you can write?"

Naturally, not one of them knew how to write.

"What! You, Berkics, and you, Jakerics, did you not help me to paint the letters on the coffin?"

Then they came out with a confession that each only knew how to write the one letter which he had painted on the lid, and that, only with the brush and not with a pen.

"Very well; then I shall take you on to Pancsova. There you can give evidence verbally to the colonel in my favor; he will find your tongues for you."

At this threat suddenly every one of them had learned to write; not only those two, but the others as well. They said they would rather give a certificate at once than be taken on to Pancsova. Michael fetched ink, pen, and paper, made one of these skillful scribes lie on his stomach on the deck, and dictated to him the deposition in which they all declared that, out of fear of hail-storms, they had thrown the body of Euthemio Trikaliss into the Danube while the crew slept, and without their knowledge or aid.

"Now, sign your names to it, and where each of you lives, so that you may be easily found if a commission of inquiry is sent to make a report."

One of the witnesses signed himself "Ira Karakassalovics," living at "Gunerovacz," and the other "Nyegro Stiriapicz," living at "Medvelincz."

And now they took leave of each other with the most serious faces in the world, without either Michael or the four others allowing it to be seen what trouble it cost them not to laugh in each other's faces.

Michael then put them all ashore.

Ali Tschorbadschi lay at the bottom of the Danube, where he had wished to be.

CHAPTER XII.
AN EXCELLENT JOKE.

In the morning when Timéa awoke she felt no more of her illness; the strength of youth had won the victory. She dressed and came out of the cabin. When she saw Timar forward she went to him and asked, "Where is my father?"

"Fraülein, your father is dead."

Timéa gazed at him with her great melancholy eyes; her face could hardly become paler than it was already. "And where have they put him?"

"Fraülein, your father rests at the bottom of the Danube."

Timéa sat down by the bulwarks and looked silently into the water. She did not speak or weep; she only looked fixedly into the river.

Timar thought it would lighten her heart if he spoke words of consolation to her. "Fraülein, while you were ill and unconscious, God called your father suddenly to himself. I was beside him in his last hour. He spoke of you, and commissioned me to give you his last blessing. By his wish I am to take you to an old friend of his, with whom you are connected through your mother, who will adopt you and be a father to you. He has a pretty young daughter, a little older than you, who will be your sister. And all that is on board this vessel belongs to you by inheritance, left to you by your father. You will be rich; and think gratefully of the loving father who has cared for you so kindly."

Timar's throat swelled as he thought, "And who died to secure your liberty, and killed himself in order to endow you with the joys of life."

And then he looked with surprise into the girl's face. Timéa had not changed a feature while he spoke, and no tear had fallen. Michael thought she was ashamed to cry before a stranger, and withdrew; but the maiden did not weep even when alone. Curious! when she saw the white cat drowned, how her tears flowed! and now, when told that her father lies below the water, not a drop falls.

Perhaps those who break out in tears at some small emotion brood silently over a deep grief?

It may be so. Timar had other things to do than to puzzle his head over psychological problems. The towers of Pancsova began to rise in the north, and down the stream came an imperial barge, straight for the "St. Barbara," with eight armed Tschaikists, their captain, and a provost. When they arrived they made fast to the side without waiting for permission, and sprung on deck. The captain approached Timar, who was waiting for him at the door of the cabin. "Are you in command of this vessel?"

"At your service."

"On board this ship, under the false name of Euthemio Trikaliss, there is a fugitive treasurer from Turkey—a pasha with stolen treasures."

"On board this vessel travels a Greek corn-merchant, of the name of Euthemio Trikaliss, not with stolen treasures but with purchased grain. The vessel was searched at Orsova, and here are the certificates. This is the first; be so good as to read it, and see if all is not as I say. I know nothing of any Turkish pasha."

"Where is he?"

"If he was a Greek, with Abraham; if a Turk, with Mohammed."

"What! is he dead, then?"

"Certainly he is. Here is the second paper, containing his will. He died of dysentery."

The officer read the document, and threw side glances at Timéa, who still sat in the place where she had heard of her father's death. She understood nothing; the language was strange to her.

"My six sailors and the steersman are witnesses of his death."

"Well, that is unlucky for him, but not for us; if he is dead he must be buried. You will tell us where, and we shall have the body exhumed; we have a man who can recognize it, and prove the identity of Trikaliss with Ali Tschorbadschi, and then we can at any rate lay an embargo on the stolen property. Where is he buried?"

"At the bottom of the Danube."

"Oh! this is too much. Why there?"

"Gently now. Here is the third paper, prepared by the Dean of Plesscovacz, in whose parish the decease of Trikaliss took place, and who not only refused him a consecrated burial, but forbid me to bring the body

90

ashore; the people insisted on our throwing it overboard."

The captain clinched his hand angrily on the hilt of his sword. "The devil! these confounded priests! Always the most trouble with them. But at any rate you can tell me where he was thrown into the river?"

"Let me tell you everything in proper order, Herr Captain. The Plesscovaer sent four watchmen on board, who were to prevent our landing the corpse; in the night, when we were all asleep, they threw the coffin, which they had loaded with stones, into the Danube without the knowledge of the crew. Here is the certificate delivered to me by the culprits; take it, search them out, take their evidence, and then let each have his well-merited punishment."

The captain stamped with his foot, and burst into angry laughter.

"Well, that is a fine story. The discovered fugitive dies, and can not be made responsible; the priest won't bury him, the peasants shove him into the water, and hand in a certificate signed with two names which no man ever possessed, and two places which never existed in this world. The refugee disappears under the water of the Danube, and I can neither drag the whole Danube from Pancsova to Szendre, nor get hold of the two rogues, by name Karakassalovics and Stiriapicz. If the identity of the fugitive is not proved, I can not confiscate the cargo. You have done that very cleverly, skipper. Cleverly planned indeed! And everything in writing. One, two, three, four documents. I bet if I wanted the baptismal certificate of that lady there, you would produce it."

"At your orders." That Timar certainly could not produce, but he could put on such an innocent, sheepish face, that the captain shook with laughter and clapped him on the shoulder.

"You are a splendid fellow, skipper. You have saved the young lady's property for her; for without her father I can do nothing to either her or her money. You can proceed, you clever fellow!"

With that he turned on his heel, and the last Tschaikiss, who had not swung round quick enough, got such a box on the ear that the poor devil all but fell into the water; and then he gave the word for departure.

When he was down below in the boat, he cast one searching look back; but the skipper was still looking after him with the same sheepish face.

The cargo of the "St. Barbara" was saved.

CHAPTER XIII.
THE FATE OF THE "ST. BARBARA."

The "St. Barbara" could now pursue her way unmolested; and Timar had no worse misfortunes than the daily disputes with the leader of the towing-team. On the great Hungarian plains the voyage up the Danube becomes extremely wearisome; there are no rocks, no water-falls or old ruins, nothing but willows and poplars, which border both sides of the river. Of these there is nothing interesting to relate.

Timéa frequently did not come out of her cabin during a whole day, and not a word did her lips utter. She sat alone, and often the food they set before her was brought out again untouched. The days grew shorter, and the bright autumn weather turned to rain; Timéa now shut herself entirely into her cabin, and Michael heard nothing of her except the deep sighs which at night penetrated to his ear through the thin partition. But she was never heard to weep; the heavy blow which had fallen on her had perhaps covered her heart with an impenetrable layer of ice. How glowing must that love be which could melt it!

Ah, my poor friend, how came you by that thought? Why do you dream waking and sleeping of this pale face? Even if she were not so beautiful, she is so rich, and you are only a poor devil of a fellow. What is the good of a pauper like you filling all his thoughts with the image of such a rich girl? If only it were the other way, and you were the rich one and she poor! And how rich is Timéa? Timar began to reckon, in order to drive himself to despair, and turn these idle dreams out of his head. Her father left her a thousand ducats in gold and the cargo, which, according to the present market prices, must be worth, say, ten thousand ducats—perhaps she has ornaments and jewels besides—and might be counted in Austrian paper-money of that date as worth a hundred thousand gulden; that in a Hungarian provincial town is a very rich heiress. And then Timar asked himself a riddle whose solution he could not guess.

If Ali Tschorbadschi had a fortune of eleven thousand ducats, that would not weigh more than sixteen pounds; of all metals, gold has the smallest volume in proportion to its weight. Sixteen pounds of ducats could be packed in a knapsack, which a man could carry on his back a long way, even on foot. Why was the Turk obliged to change it into grain and load a cargo-ship with it, which would take a month and a half for its voyage, and have to struggle with storms, eddies, rocks, and shallows—which might be delayed by quarantine and custom-houses—when he could have carried his treasure with him in his knapsack, and by making his way cautiously on foot over mountain and river, could have reached Hungary safely in a couple of weeks?

The key to this problem was not to be found.

And another riddle was connected with this one. If Ali's treasure (whether honestly come by or not) only consists of eleven or twelve thousand ducats altogether, why does the Turkish Government institute a pursuit on such a large scale, sending a brigantine with four-and-twenty rowers, and spies and couriers after him? What would be a heap of money for a poor supercargo is for his highness the Padischa only a trifle; and even if it had been possible to lay an embargo on the whole cargo, representing a value of ten or twelve thousand ducats, by the time it had passed through the fingers of all the informers, tax-collectors, and other official cut-purses, there would be hardly enough left for the sultan to fill his pipe with.

Was it not ridiculous to set such great machinery in motion in order to secure so small a prize?

Or was it not so much the money as Timéa that was the object? Timar had enough romance about him to find this a plausible assumption, however little it agreed with a supercargo's one-times-one multiplication table.

One evening the wind dispersed the clouds, and when Timar looked out of his cabin window he saw on the western horizon the crescent moon.

The "red moon!"

The glowing sickle seemed to touch the glassy surface of the Danube. It looked to Timar as if it really had a human face, as it is depicted in the almanacs, and as if it said something to him with its crooked mouth. Only that he could not always understand—it is a strange language.

Moonstruck people perhaps comprehend it, for they follow it; only they, as well as the sleep-walkers, remember nothing of what was said when they awake. It was as if the moon answered Timar's questions. Which? All. And the beating of his heart? or his calculations? All.

Only that he could not put these answers into words.

The red crescent dipped slowly toward the water, and sent its reflected rays along the waves as far as the ship's bows, as if to say, "Don't you understand now?" At last it drew its horns gently below the surface, saying plainly, "I shall return to-morrow, and then you will know."

The pilot was in favor of making the most of the light of the after-glow to go on further, until it grew dark. They were already above Almas, and not far from Komorn; in those parts he knew the channel so well that he could have steered the vessel safely with his eyes shut. As far up as the Raab Danube, there was no more danger to fear.

And yet there was something! Off Fuzito a soft, dull thud was heard; but at this thud the steersman cried "Halt!" in a fright, to the towing-team.

Timar also grew pale, and stood petrified for a moment. For the first time during the whole voyage dismay was depicted in his features. "We have struck a snag!" he cried to the steersman.

And that great strong man entirely lost his head, left the rudder, and ran crying like a little child across the deck to the cabin.

We have touched a snag! Yes, that was so. When the Danube is in flood it makes breaches in the bank, the uprooted trees fall into the current, and are carried to the bottom by the weight of the soil clinging to their roots; if a cargo-ship drawn by horses touches such a tree-trunk, it pierces the hull. From shallows and rocks the steersman can guard his vessel, but against a tree-trunk lying in ambush under water, neither knowledge, experience nor skill is of any avail. Most of the shipwrecks on the Danube are from this cause.

"It is all up with us!" howled the pilot and the sailors. Every one left his post and ran for his bundle and his chest, to get them into the boat.

The vessel swung across the stream, and the forepart began to sink. It was useless to think of saving it—absolutely impossible. The hold was filled with sacks of grain; before they could shift these in order to get at the leak and stop it, the vessel would long ago have gone down.

Timar broke in the door of Timéa's cabin.

"Fraülein, put on your cloak quickly, and take the casket which stands on the table; our ship is sinking, we must save ourselves." As he spoke he helped her into her warm kaftan, and gave her directions to get into the boat; the pilot would help her. He himself ran back into his cabin to get the box which held the ship's papers and cash. But Johann Fabula was not thinking of helping Timéa; he flew into a rage when he saw the girl. "Didn't I say this milk-face, this witch with the meeting eyebrows, would bring us all to destruction? We ought to have thrown her overboard."

Timéa did not understand what he said, but she shrunk from his bloodshot eyes, and preferred to go back to her cabin, where she lay down, and saw the water rush through the door and mount gradually to the level of the edge of her bed. She thought to herself that if the water washed her away, it would carry her down-stream, to where her father was lying at the bottom of the Danube, and then they would again be united.

Timar was wading up to his knees in water before he had collected all he wanted from his cabin and packed them in a box, which he took on his shoulder and then hurried to the boat.

"And where is Timéa?" he cried, not seeing her there.

"The devil knows!" growled the pilot. "I wish she had never been born." Timar flew back into Timéa's cabin, now up to his waist in water, and took her in his arms. "Have you the casket?"

"Yes," whispered the girl.

He asked no more, but hurried with her on deck, and carried her in his arms into the boat, where he put her on the middle seat. The fate of the "St. Barbara" was being decided with awful rapidity. The ship was going down stern first, and in a few minutes only the upper deck and the mast, with the dangling tow-rope, were visible above water.

"Shove off!" Timar said to the rowers, and the boat moved toward the shore.

"Where is the casket?" Timar asked the girl, when they had already gone some distance.

"Here it is," answered Timéa, showing him what she had brought away.

96

"Miserable girl! that is the box of sweetmeats, not the casket." In fact, Timéa had brought the box of Turkish sweets, meant as a present to her new sister, and had totally forgotten the casket which held her whole fortune. That was left behind in the submerged cabin. "Back to the ship!" Timar cried to the pilot.

"Surely nobody has got such a mad notion as to look for anything in a sunken ship," grumbled Fabula.

"Back!—no words—I insist!"

The boat returned to the vessel. Timar asked no one's help, but sprung himself to the deck and down the steps to the cabin.

Timéa looked after him with her great dark eyes as he vanished under the surface, as if to say—"And you too go before me into the watery grave."

Timar reached the bulwarks, but had to be very careful, because the vessel had a list toward the side where Timéa's cabin door was. He had to hold on by the timbers of the roof, so as not to slip altogether under water. He found the door, luckily, not shut by the waves; for it would have been a long job to get it open. It was quite dark inside, the water had filled it almost to the ceiling; he groped to the table, the casket was not there; perhaps she had left it on the bed. The water had floated the bed to the roof, and he had to draw it down; but the casket was not there either. Perhaps it had been knocked over by the rush of water. He felt about vainly with his hands, stooping under water. His feet were more fortunate, for he stumbled over the object sought for; the casket had fallen to the ground. He lifted it, and tried while holding it to climb up to the other side, where he need not hold on with both hands.

The minute that Timar was under water seemed to Timéa an eternity.

He was a full minute under water. He had held his breath the whole time, as if to try an experiment how long a man could do without breathing.

When Michael's head appeared above the water she heaved a deep sigh, and her face beamed when Timar gave her the rescued casket, but not on its account.

"Well, captain!" exclaimed the steersman, as he helped Timar into the boat, "that's thrice you've got soaked for the love of these eyebrows. Thrice!"

Timéa asked Michael in a whisper, "What is the Greek for the word

97

thrice?" Michael translated it. Then Timéa looked at him long, and repeated to herself in a low voice "Thrice."

The boat approached the shore in the direction of Almas.

Against the steely mirror in the twilight a long line was visible, like a distressful note of exclamation or a pause in life. It was the topmast of the "St. Barbara."

CHAPTER XIV.
THE GUARDIAN.

At six in the evening the ship's crew had left the sunken craft, and by half past seven Timar with Timéa was in Komorn. The post-cart driver knew Brazovics' house very well, and galloped his four bell-decked horses with unmerciful cracks of the whip through the little streets up to the square, as he had been promised a good *trinkgeld* if he brought his passengers quickly to their destination.

Michael lifted Timéa from the country wagon and told her she was now at home. Then he took the casket under his cloak and led the girl up the steps.

The house of Athanas Brazovics was of two stories—a rarity in Komorn; for in remembrance of the destructive earthquakes by which the town had been visited in the last century, people usually only built on the ground-floor. The lower story was occupied by a large café, which served the resident tradespeople as a casino; the whole upper floor was inhabited by the family of the merchant. It had two entrances from the street, and a third through the kitchen.

The owner was generally not at home at this hour, as Timar knew; he therefore led Timéa straight to the door through which the women's rooms were reached. In these reigned fashionable luxury, and in the anteroom lounged a man-servant. Timar asked him to fetch his master from the café, and meanwhile led Timéa to the ladies.

He was certainly hardly got up for company, as may be imagined when one remembers what he had gone through, and the number of times he had been soaked; but he was one of those who belonged to the house, who could come in at any time and in any dress: they looked upon him as "one of our people." In such a case one gets over the strict rules of etiquette.

The announcement revives the old habit of the mistress, as soon as the door of the anteroom is open, of putting her head through the parlor door to see who is coming. Frau Sophie has kept this habit ever since her maid-servant days. (Pardon, that slipped out by accident.) Well, yes, Herr

Athanas raised her from a low station; it was a love-match, so no one has a right to reproach her.

It is therefore not as idle gossip, but only as a characteristic touch, that I mention that Frau Sophie even as "gracious lady" could not get rid of her early habit. Her clothes always fitted her as if they had been given to her by her mistress. From her coiffure an obstinate lock of hair would always stick out either in the front or at the back; even her most gorgeous costumes always looked tumbled and creased; and if nothing else went wrong, there would be invariably a pair of trodden-down shoes with which she could indulge in her old propensity. Curiosity and tattle were the ingredients of her conversation, in which she generally introduced such extraordinary expressions that when she began to scatter them in a mixed party, the guests (that is, those who were seated) almost fell off their chairs with laughter. Then, too, she had the agreeable custom of never speaking low; her voice was a continuous scream, as if she were being stabbed and wished to call for assistance.

"Oh, good Lord, it's Michael!" she cried, as soon as she got her head through the door-way. "And where did you get the pretty fräulein? What is the casket you have under your arm? Come into the parlor! Look, look, Athalie, what Timar has brought!"

Michael let Timéa pass, then he entered and politely wished the company good-evening. Timéa looked round with the shyness of a first meeting. Besides the mistress of the house there were a girl and a man in the room. The girl was a fully developed and conscious beauty, who, in spite of her naturally small waist, did not disdain tight stays; her high heels and piles of hair made her appear taller than she was; she wore mittens, and her nails were long and pointed. Her expression was of artificial amiability; she had somewhat arrogant and pouting lips, a rosy complexion, and two rows of dazzling white teeth, which she did not mind showing; when she laughed, dimples formed on chin and cheek, dark brows arched over the bright black eyes, whose brilliancy was increased by their aggressive prominence. With her head up and bust thrown forward, the beautiful creature knew how to make an imposing appearance. This was Fräulein Athalie.

The man was a young officer, verging on thirty, with a cheerful open

100

face and fiery black eyes. According to the military regulations of the period, he had a clean-shaven face, with the exception of a small crescent-shaped whisker. This warrior wore a violet tunic, with collar and cuffs of pink velvet, the uniform of the engineers. Timar knew him too. It was Herr Katschuka, first lieutenant at the fort, and also a commissariat officer—rather a hybrid position, but so it was.

The lieutenant has the pleasure of taking a portrait of the young lady before him in chalks; he has already finished one by daylight, and is trying one by lamplight. The entrance of Timéa disturbs him in this artistic occupation.

The whole appearance of the slender delicate girl was something spiritual at this moment—it was as if a ghost, a phantom, had stepped out of the dusk.

When Herr Katschuka looked up from his easel, his dark-red chalk drew such a streak across the portrait's brow, that it would be hard for bread-crumbs to get it out, and he rose involuntarily from his seat before Timéa.

Every one rose at the sight of the girl, even Athalie. Who can she be?

Timar whispered to Timéa in Greek, on which she hastened to Frau Sophie and kissed her hand, while the girl herself received a kiss on her cheek.

Again Timar whispered to her. The girl went with shy obedience to Athalie, and looked steadily in her face. Shall she kiss her, or fall on the neck of her new sister? Athalie seemed to raise her head higher still. Timéa bent to her hand and kissed it—or rather not her hand, but the kid mitten. Athalie allowed it, her eyes cast a flaming glance on Timéa's face, and another on the officer, and she curled her lips yet more.

Herr Katschuka was completely lost in admiration of Timéa.

But neither his nor Athalie's fiery looks called up any emotion on Timéa's face, which remained as white as if she were a spirit.

Timar himself was not a little confused. How was he to introduce the girl and relate how he had come by her, before this officer?

Herr Brazovics helped him out of his difficulty. With a great bustle he burst in at the door. He had just now in the café—to the surprise of all the

101

regular customers—read aloud from the Augsburg *Gazette* that the escaped pasha and treasurer, Ali Tschorbadschi and his daughter, had fled on board the "St. Barbara," evaded the watchfulness of the Turkish authorities, and reached Hungary in safety. The "St. Barbara" is his ship. Tschorbadschi is a good friend of his—even a connection by the mother's side. An extraordinary event! One can fancy how Herr Athanas threw his chair back when the servant brought him the news that Herr Timar had just arrived with a beautiful young lady, and under his arm a gilt casket.

"So it is actually true!" cried Herr Athanas, and rushed up to his own apartments, not without upsetting a few of the card-players on his way.

Brazovics was a man of enormous corpulence. His stomach was always half a step in front of him. His face was copper-colored at its palest, and violet when he ought to have been rosy: even when he shaved in the morning his chin was all bristles by the evening, his scrubby mustache perfumed with smoke, snuff, and various spirits; his eyebrows formed a bushy wall over his prominent and bloodshot eyes. (A fearful thought, that the eyes of the lovely Athalie, when she grows old, will resemble her father's!)

When Herr Brazovics opens his mouth, one understands why Frau Sophie always screams; her husband, too, can only speak in shouts, but with the difference that he has a deep bass voice like a hippopotamus.

Naturally Frau Sophie, when she wants to overpower his voice with her own, raises it to a yell. It was as if they had a wager which could bring on the other a lung disease or a stroke of apoplexy. It is doubtful who will win; but Brazovics always stops his ears with wool, and Frau Sophie invariably has a comforter round her throat.

Athanas rushed, panting with haste, into the ladies' room, where his voice of thunder had already preceded him. "Is Michael there with the young lady? Where is the fraülein? Where is Michael?"

Timar hastened to catch him at the door. He might have succeeded in keeping back the man himself, but the weight of his approaching paunch, when once set in motion, bore down all obstacles.

Michael made a sign to him that a visitor was present. "Ah, that doesn't matter! You can speak openly before him. We are *en famille*; the Herr Lieutenant belongs to the family. Ha! ha! don't get cross, Athalie; every one knows it. You can speak freely, Michael; it is all in the papers."

"What is in the papers?" exclaimed Athalie, angrily.

"Well, well, not you; but that my friend Ali Tschorbadschi, my own cousin, the treasurer, has fled to Hungary with his daughter and his property on board my ship the 'St. Barbara;' and this is the daughter, isn't she? The dear little thing!" And with that Herr Brazovics suddenly fell upon her, took her in his arms, and pressed two kisses on her pale face—two loud, wet, malodorous kisses, so that the girl was quite confused.

"You are a good fellow, Michael, to have brought her here so quickly. Have you given him a glass of wine? Go, Sophie—quick! A glass of wine!"

Frau Sophie pretended not to hear; but Herr Brazovics threw himself into an arm-chair, drew Timéa between his knees, and stroked her hair with his fat palms. "And where is my worthy friend, the governor of the treasury? Where is he?"

"He died on the journey," answered Timar in a low voice.

"What a fatality!" said Brazovics, trying to give an angular form to his round face, and taking his hand from the girl's head. "But no accident happened to him?"

A curious question. But Timar understood it.

"He intrusted his property to my care, to deliver it over to you with his daughter. You were to be her adopted father and the guardian of her property."

At these words Herr Brazovics grew sentimental again; he took Timéa's head between his two hands, and pressed it to his breast.

"As if she were my own child. I will regard her as my daughter;" and then again smack! smack! one kiss after another on brow and cheek of the poor victim. "And what is in this casket?"

"The gold I was to deliver to you."

"Very good, Michael. How much is there?"

"A thousand ducats."

"What!" cried Brazovics, and pushed Timéa off his knee; "only a thousand ducats? Michael, you have stolen the rest!"

Something stirred in Timar's face. "Here is the autograph will of the deceased. He declares therein that he has given over to me a thousand ducats

103

in gold, and his remaining property is contained in the cargo, which consists of ten thousand measures of wheat."

"That's something more like. Ten thousand measures of wheat, at twelve gulden fifty a measure in paper money, that makes a hundred and twenty-five thousand gulden, or fifty thousand gulden silver. Come here, little treasure, and sit on my knee; you're tired, aren't you? And did my dear never-to-be-forgotten friend send me any other directions?"

"He told me to tell you that you must be present in person when the sacks are emptied, lest they should exchange the grain, for he had bought a very good quality."

"Naturally I shall be there in person. How should I not be? And where is the ship with the grain?"

"Below Almas, at the bottom of the Danube."

But now Athanas thrust Timéa right away, and sprung up in a rage. "What! my fine vessel gone down, as well as the ten thousand measures of wheat! Oh, you gallows-bird! you rascal! You were all drunk, for certain. I'll put you all in jail; the pilot shall be in irons; and I shall not pay one of you. You forfeit your ten thousand gulden caution-money: you shall never see that again. Go and sue me if you like!"

"Your vessel was not worth more than six thousand gulden, and is insured for its full value at the Komorn Marine Insurance Office. You have come to no harm."

"If that were true a hundred times over, I should still require compensation from you, on account of the *lucrum cessans*. Do you know what that means? If you do, you can understand that your ten thousand gulden will go to the last kreutzer."

"So be it," answered Timar, quietly. "We will speak of that another time; there's time enough. But what we have to do now is to decide what is to happen to the sunken cargo, for the longer it remains under water, the more it will be spoiled."

"What does it matter to me what happens to it?"

"So you will not take it over? You will not be personally present at the discharge of cargo?"

"The devil I will! What should I do with ten thousand measures of

104

soaked grain? I am not going to make starch of ten thousand measures of corn; or shall I make paste of it? The devil may take it if he wants it!"

"Hardly; but the stuff must be sold. The millers, factors, cattle-dealers, will offer something for it, and the peasants too, who want seed-corn; and the vessel must be emptied. In that way some money may be got out of it."

"Money!" (This word could always penetrate into the cotton-stuffed ears of the merchant.) "Good. I will give you a permit to-morrow to empty the vessel and get rid of the cargo in bulk."

"I want the permit to-day. Before morning everything will be ruined."

"To-day! You know I never touch a pen at night; it is against my habits."

"I thought of that beforehand, and brought the permit with me. You have only to sign your name to it. Here are pen and ink."

But now Frau Sophie interrupted with a scream. "Here in my parlor I do not allow writing to be done! That's the only thing wanting—that my new carpet should be all spotted with ink. Go to your room if you want to write. And I won't have this squabbling with your people here in my rooms!"

"I should like to know if it isn't my house," growled the great man.

"And it's my sitting-room!"

"I am master here!"

"And I am mistress here!"

The screeching and growling had the good result for Timar that Herr Brazovics flew into a rage, and in order to show that he was master in his own house, seized the pen and signed the power of attorney. But when he had given it, both fell on Timar, and overwhelmed him with such a flood of reproaches and invective, that he would willingly have taken yet another bath in the Danube to wash them away. Frau Sophie only scolded Timar indirectly, as she abused her husband for giving such a ragged, dirty fellow, such a tipsy, beggarly scoundrel, a warrant like that.

Why had he not given it to any other supercargo than Timar, who would run away with the money, and drink and gamble till it was gone.

Timar stood the whole time with the same immovable calm in the midst of this tumult as that with which he had defied storm and waves at the

105

Iron Gate. At last he broke silence: "Will you take charge of the money which belongs to the orphan, or shall I give it over to the City Orphanage?" (At this last question Brazovics got a great fright.) "Now, then, if you please, come with me into the office and we will settle the affair at once, for I don't like servants' squabbles."

With this hundred-pound insult he succeeded in suddenly silencing both master and mistress. Against such scolds and blusterers, a good round impertinence is the best remedy. Brazovics took the light and said, "All right; bring the money along." Frau Sophie appeared all at once to be in the best of tempers, and asked Timar if he would not have a glass of wine first.

Timéa was quite stunned; of what passed in a foreign language she understood not a word, and the gestures and looks which accompanied it were not calculated to enlighten her. Why should her guardian now kiss and hug her, the orphan, and the next moment push her from him? Why did he again take her on his lap, only to thrust her away once more? Why did both of them scream at this man, who remained as calm as she had seen him in the tempest, until he spoke a few words, quietly, without anger or excitement, and thereby instantly silenced and overpowered the two who had been like mad people the minute before, so that they could prevail as little against him as the rocks and whirlpools and the armed men. Of all that went on around her, she had not understood one word; and now the man who had been hitherto her faithful companion, who had gone "thrice" into the water for her sake, with whom alone she could speak in Greek, was going away—forever, no doubt—and she would never hear his voice again.

Yet no; once again it sounds in her ear. Before he stepped over the threshold Timar turned to her and said in Greek, "Fraülein Timéa, there is what you brought away with you."

And with that he took the box of sweets from under his cloak. Timéa ran to him, took the box, and hastened to Athalie, in order to present to her, with the sweetest smile, the gift she had brought from far away. Athalie opened the box.

"*Fi donc!*" she exclaimed, "it smells of rose-water, just like the pocket-handkerchiefs the maid-servants take to church."

Timéa did not understand the words, but from the pouting lips and

106

turned-up nose she could easily guess their meaning, and that made her very sad.

She made another attempt, and offered the Turkish sweetmeats to Frau Sophie, who declined with the remark that her teeth were bad, and she could not eat sweets. Quite cast down, she now offered them to the lieutenant. He found them excellent, and swallowed three lumps in three mouthfuls, for which Timéa smiled at him gratefully.

Timar stood at the door and saw Timéa smile. Suddenly it occurred to her that she must offer him some of the Turkish delight. But it was already too late, for Timar no longer stood there. Soon after, the lieutenant took leave and departed. Being a man of breeding, he bowed to Timéa also, which pleased her greatly.

After a time Herr Brazovics returned to the room, and they were now just the four alone.

Brazovics and Frau Sophie began to talk in a gibberish which was intended for Greek.

Timéa understood a word here and there, but the sense seemed to her more strange than those languages which were altogether unknown to her.

They were consulting what to do with this girl whom they had been saddled with. Her whole property consists of twelve thousand paper gulden. Even if it were likely that the soaked grain should bring in a little more, that would not suffice to educate her like a lady, like Athalie.

Frau Sophie thought she must be treated as a servant, and get used to cook and sweep, to wash and iron—that would be some use. With so little money no one would marry her except some clerk or ship's captain, and then it would have been better for her to be brought up as a servant and not a lady.

But Athanas would not hear of it; what would people say? At last they agree on a middle course; Timéa is not to be treated like a regular servant, but take the position of an adopted child. She will take her meals with the family, but help to wait. She shall not stand at the wash-tub, but must get up her own and Athalie's fine things. She must sew what is wanted for the house, not in the maid's room but in the gentlefolks' apartments; of course she will help Athalie to dress, that will only be a pleasure to her, and she need not sleep with the maids but in the same room as Athalie; the latter wants some one to keep her company and be at her service. In return, Athalie can give her the old clothes she no longer requires.

A girl who has only twelve thousand gulden can thank Heaven that such a fate should fall to her share.

And Timéa was satisfied with her lot. After the great and incomprehensible catastrophe which had thrown her on the world, the lonely creature clung to every being she came near. She was gentle and obliging. This is the way of Turkish girls. It pleased her to be allowed to sit by Athalie at supper, and it was not necessary to remind her: she rose of her own accord to change the plates and wash the spoons, and did it with cheerful looks and kind attention. She feared to annoy her guardians if she looked sad, and yet she had cause enough. Especially she busied herself in trying to help Athalie. Whenever she looked at her, her face showed the open admiration which young girls feel for a grown-up beauty; she forgot herself in gazing at the rosy cheeks and bright eyes of the other. Those innocent minds think any one so lovely must be very good.

She did not understand what Athalie said, for she did not even speak bad Greek, like her parents; but she tried to guess by her eyes and hands what was wanted. After supper, at which Timéa only ate fruit and bread, not being used to rich dishes, they went into the salon.

There Athalie sat down to the piano. Timéa crouched near her on the footstool and looked with admiration at her rapid execution. Then Athalie showed her the portrait which the lieutenant had executed, and Timéa clasped her hands in astonishment.

"You never saw anything like it?"

"Where should she have seen such things?" answered the father. "If is forbidden to the Turks to take a likeness of any one. That is why there is a revolution just now—because the sultan has had his picture painted and hung up over the divan. Ali Tschorbadschi was mixed up in the movement, and was forced to fly. You poor old Tschorbadschi, to have been such a fool!"

When Timéa heard her father's name, she kissed the hand of Brazovics. She supposed he had sent some pious blessing after the dead man.

Athalie went to bed, and Timéa carried the light for her. Athalie

108

seated herself at her dressing-table, looked in the glass, sighed deeply, and then sunk back in her chair tired and cross, with a gloomy countenance. Timéa would have liked to know why this lovely face had suddenly grown so sad.

She took the comb from Athalie's hair and loosened the plaits with a skillful hand, and then again dressed the richly flowing chestnut locks for the night in a simple coil.

She took out the earrings, and her head came so near to Athalie's that the latter could not help seeing the two contrasting faces in the mirror.

One so radiant, rosy, and fascinating, the other so pale and soft; and yet Athalie sprung up angrily and pushed away the glass. "Let us go to sleep." The white face had thrown hers into the shade. Timéa collected the scattered clothes and folded them neatly together by instinct.

Then she knelt before Athalie and took off her stockings. Athalie permitted it.

And after Timéa had drawn them off, and held the snow-white foot, more perfect than a sculptor's ideal, in her lap, she bent and pressed a kiss on it. Athalie permitted that too.

BOOK SECOND.—TIMÉA.

CHAPTER I.
GOOD ADVICE.

Lieutenant Katschuka went through the café and found Timar there gulping down a cup of black coffee. "I am soaked and frozen, and have a great deal still to do to-day," he said to the officer, who hastened to press his hand.

"Come and have a glass of punch with me."

"Many thanks, but I have no time now; I must go this instant to the insurance company, that they may help me with the salvage of the cargo; for the longer it remains under water the greater the damage. From there I must run to the magistrate, that he may be in time to send some one to Almas to receive the power of attorney; then I must go round to the cattle-dealers and carriers, to induce them to come to the auction; and later on I must go by the stage to Iotis to find out the starch manufacturers there: they can make the best use of the wet grain. Perhaps in this way some of the poor child's property may be saved. But I have a letter to deliver to you which was given me in Orsova."

Katschuka read the letter, and then said to Timar, "Very good, my friend. Do your business in the town, but afterward come to me for half an hour; I live near the Anglia—over the door hangs a shield with a large double eagle. While the diligence baits we will drink a glass of punch and have a sensible talk; be sure you come."

Timar consented, and went off to look after his business. It might be about eleven o'clock when he entered the door under the double eagle, which was near the promenade called in Komorn the Anglia. Katschuka's private servant waited for him there, and led him up to his master's room. "Well, I expected," began Timar, "you would have been already married to Athalie long before I came up from yonder."

"Yes, comrade, but the affair doesn't get on well; it is delayed by first one thing and then another. It seems to me as if one of us is not keen about it."

"Oh! you may be sure Athalie is keen enough."

111

"In this world you can't be sure of anything, least of all a heart. I only say one thing, long engagements are bad. Instead of getting nearer to each other people only get further apart, and learn to know each other's failings and weaknesses. If this occurs after marriage one thinks, in God's name, we can not go back. Let me advise you, comrade, if you wish to marry and have fallen in love, don't wait long to think about it; for if you begin to calculate it will only end in a breach."

"With you I should fancy there is no danger in calculations about a girl who is so rich."

"Riches are relative, my friend. Believe me, every woman knows how to get rid of the interest of her dowry; and then no one exactly knows the financial position of Herr Brazovics. A heap of money goes through his hands, but he does not like striking a proper business-like balance, so as to show what he has gained or lost by his dealings."

"For my part I think he is very well off. And Athalie is a very pretty and clever young lady."

"Yes, yes; but you need not praise Athalie to me like a horse you take to market. Let us rather talk of your affairs."

If Katschuka had been able to look into Timar's heart he would have found that what they had been talking of *was* his friend's affair. Timar had turned the conversation to Athalie because—because he envied the officer the smile of Timéa's face. It was as if he had said, "You have no right to Timéa's smile—you are engaged; marry Athalie!"

"Now, let us talk of serious matters. My friend in Orsova writes me that I am to befriend you. Good; I will try. You are in a position anything but pleasant: the ship intrusted to you is wrecked. It is not your fault, but a great misfortune for you, for every one will now fear to intrust you with a vessel. Your principal seizes your caution-money, and who knows whether you can recover it by law. You would like to help the poor orphan—I see it in your eyes; that she should lose such a pretty fortune affects you more than any one else. How can we get out of this with one *coup*?"

"I know no way out of it."

"But I do. Listen to me; next week the annual concentration of troops begins round Komorn. Twenty thousand of them will be maneuvering here for three weeks. A contract for the bread supply is on hand; large sums will be paid, and he who goes about it wisely will make a good haul. All the tenders go through my hands, and I can say beforehand who will get the contract, for it depends more on what is not contained in the offer than on what is. Till now Brazovics' tender is the lowest. He is prepared to undertake the contract at 140,000 gulden, and promises 'the officials concerned' 20,000 gulden."

"What do you mean?—the officials concerned?"

"Don't be so stupid. It is the usual thing that whoever receives such a large contract should give a present to those who get it for him. It has always been so since the world began. What else do we live on? You know that well enough."

"Certainly; but I never tried it in my own person."

"Very foolish of you. You burn your fingers for other people, while you might get the chestnuts out of the fire for yourself, if you knew how to do it. Send in a tender to undertake the contract at 130,000 gulden, and promise 30,000 commission."

"I can not do that for several reasons. First, I have not got the deposit, which must accompany the tender; then I have not the capital requisite to buy such quantities of grain and flour; next, I greatly object to bribery; and lastly, I am not such a bad reckoner as to persuade myself of the possibility of undertaking with only 130,000 gulden to complete the contract as well as pay the friendly commission."

Katschuka laughed at him. "Oh, my dear Michael, you will never be a man of business. In our line that is always the way. Only to make a groschen on a gulden is peddler's trade. The chief thing is to have interest, and you don't want for that; that's what I am good for. We have been good friends ever since our school days: rely on me. How do you mean you have no money to deposit? Hand over the receipt for your caution-money of 10,000 gulden which you left with Brazovics—it will be regarded as a sufficient security—and then I will tell you what to do next; go quickly to Almas, and bid yourself for the sunken cargo. The grain, which represents a value of 100,000 gulden, will certainly be knocked down to you for 10,000. Then you will possess 10,000 measures of corn. You will promise all the millers in

Almas, Fuzito, and Izsaer double pay if they will grind your corn at once. Meanwhile you build ovens, in which the corn is immediately baked into bread. Within three weeks it will all be consumed, and if a bad part slips in, it will be the business of your 'good friends' to hush it up. At the end of three weeks you will have a clear gain of at least 70,000 gulden. Believe me, if I were to take such an affair to your principal, he would seize it with both hands. I wonder at your slowness."

Timar thought it over. It was indeed a tempting offer. To make in three weeks 60,000 or 70,000 gulden—and without much trouble, in complete security. The first week the ration-bread would be rather sweeter than usual, the second week rather bitterer, and the third week rather musty. But soldiers do not look narrowly at such things; they are used to it.

But yet Timar turned with disgust from this bitter cup. "Oh, Emerich!" he said, laying his hand on his former schoolmate's shoulder, "where have you learned such things?"

"Why," answered the other, with a gloomy face, "there where they are taught. When I entered on the military career, I was full of romantic illusions. They are all in ashes now. Then I thought this was the school of chivalry, the heroic career, and my heart beat high at the thought: now I know that all in this world is speculation, and that public concerns are governed by private interests. In the engineers I had completed my studies, with remarkable, I may say distinguished results. When I was sent to Komorn, the prospect filled me with pride, at the opportunity I should have for the development of my capacities in military engineering. The first plan for the fortifications submitted by me was declared to be a masterpiece by good judges; but do not imagine that it was accepted: on the contrary, I received orders to prepare another, which was more costly, and involved the expropriation of whole streets in the town. Well, I prepared that too. You will remember that part of the town which is now an open space—this change cost half a million. Your principal had some ruinous houses there which he sold at the price of palaces. And they call that fortification! And for that I had studied engineering. Well, a man falls by degrees and finds his level. Perhaps you have heard the anecdote—it is in every mouth—how the Crown-Prince Ferdinand, when he visited us last year, said to the commandant of the fortress, 'I thought this fortress was black?' 'Why should it be black, your imperial highness?' 'Because in the fortification accounts there are every year 10,000 gulden put down for ink. I thought the walls must be dyed with ink.' Every one laughed, and that was the end of it. If nothing comes out, nothing is said; and if everything comes out, it only raises a laugh. You had better laugh too! Or will it please you better to be shoved out into the world from the threshold of the corn-dealer, and sell matches with two kreutzers profit a day? I have already come down from the ethereal regions. Off, my friend, to Almas, and buy the sunken wheat. Till ten to-morrow night you will have time to send in your tender. Listen, there is the diligence—be off, and see that you get back quickly."

"I will think it over," said Timar, slowly.

"Remember that you will do the poor orphan a good turn, if you give 10,000 gulden for her lost property. Otherwise she won't have as many hundred when the salvage is paid."

Those words rang in Timar's ears. An invisible hand drove him on. "*Fata nolentem trahunt!*" says St. Augustine. Soon after, Timar sat again in the diligence, which galloped away with its four Neudorf horses. In the town every one slept. Only at the station-house sounded the night watchman's call. No one has written on his brow what the next day will bring to him; but from the walls the sentries, wet through with the autumn rain, challenged in turn "Who goes there?"—"Patrol"—"Pass."

What sort of bread have these fellows had?

CHAPTER II.
THE RED CRESCENT.

On the following day, Timar did actually bid for the sunken grain in company with brokers and millers, who made trifling bids, a few groschen a measure. Timar got tired of this groschen business, and suddenly cried, "I will give ten thousand gulden for the whole cargo." When the bidders heard this they ran away, and it would have been in vain to run after them. The official auctioneer accepted Timar's offer, and gave over the whole cargo to him as his property. Every one thought him mad. What could he do with such a mass of soaked grain? What he did was this.

He lashed two lighters together, fastened them with iron clamps to the deck of the sunken ship, and made arrangements to get up the cargo. There was a change since yesterday in the position of the vessel, for the stern had sunk so that now the forepart stood out of water, and one of the two cabins was quite dry. Timar installed himself here, and then began the hard work. He tore up the deck, and with the help of a crane drew up one sack after the other. They were first piled near the cabin, that the water might drain away; then they were transferred to a raft, and taken ashore: there straw mats were laid, on which the grain was shaken and spread out. Timar bargained meanwhile with the millers for immediate grinding of the corn. The weather was favorable, there was a strong wind, and the corn dried fast.

If only the work would go on quickly!

He began to calculate. The little ready money he had would all go to the payment of the work-people; if the undertaking failed he would be a beggar. Johann Fabula told him beforehand, that after this senseless purchase nothing would be left him but to hang the last sack round his neck, and throw himself into the Danube. A thousand disquieting thoughts passed through Timar's head, without beginning or end. He looked on till night-fall, while one sack after the other was propped against the cabin wall. The sacks all had the same mark—a five-spoked wheel printed in black on the sacking. In truth, that poor fugitive pasha had been wiser, if, instead of buying so much grain, he had just put his money in his knapsack. And to think of

116

pursuing him so obstinately only for this stuff! Was it worth while to flee only for this, and then actually to poison himself? Till late evening the work continued, and still only about three thousand measures were spread out to dry. Timar promised the laborers double pay if they would work a few hours longer. The grain which lies a second night under water will hardly make bread. The sack-carriers worked on cheerfully.

The wind had dispersed the clouds, and the moon appeared again in the sunset sky. Heavens and moon were red.

"How ghostly it looks!" said Timar, and turned his back on the moon, so as not to see it.

But even as he stood there, and counted the sacks as they were drawn up, the red moon rose again before him. This time it was painted on a sack. In the place where the other sacks bore a wheel of five spokes, here above the trade-mark a crescent was painted in vermilion.

A cold shiver ran through Timar. Here was the answer to the riddle! This was what the dying man meant by his last words. But either his confidence was not strong enough, or else time had failed him to finish his phrase. When the laborers turned away Timar took the sack and carried it into the cabin; no one noticed it, and then he locked the door behind him.

The work-people went on for two hours more; but at last they were so tired, wet, and stiff with water and wind, that they were not in a condition to go on any longer: the rest of the cargo must wait till the morrow. The wearied folk hurried to the nearest alehouse to warm themselves with food and drink. Timar remained alone on board: he said he wished to count the unloaded sacks, and would row himself ashore in the little boat. The moon had reached the water with its lower horn, and seemed to look in at the cabin window. Timar's hand trembled as if with ague. When he opened the blade of his knife, he cut his hand, and the drops of blood painted stars on the sack by the side of the red crescent. He cut the rope with which the sack was tied, and put his hand in; what he brought out was beautiful white wheat. Then he cut the lower end of the sack; here too only grain came out. He now slit the whole sack up, and with the scattered corn, a long leathern bag fell at his feet. The bag had a lock. He broke it open.

And then he shook the contents out on to the bed—the same bed

117

where once the living marble statue had lain.

What a sight was presented to him in the moonlight! Long rows of rings strung together—brilliant, sapphire, and emerald rings; armlets of opals and huge turquoises; pearl bracelets, each bead as large as a hazel-nut; a necklace of magnificent brilliants of the finest water; an agate box, from which when he opened it a whole heap of unset diamonds flashed upon him; at the bottom of the bag a number of agraffes and girdles, all set with rubies, and four rouleaux, each containing five hundred louis d'or. Here was an enormous treasure, at least a million gulden.

Now one can understand the man fleeing even to the bottom of the Danube, that this treasure might not fall into the hands of his pursuers. For this, it was worth while to send a gunboat and spies after the fugitive. For this, it was worth while to cut the tow-rope in the midst of a storm at the Iron Gate.

The "St. Barbara" had carried a million on board! that is no child's play, no dream—it is reality. Ali Tschorbadschi's treasures lie there on the wet quilt with which Timéa had once covered herself. Whoever knows the value of pearls and precious stones, can understand that it was not for nothing that Ali Tschorbadschi had been Governor of Candia and guardian of the treasury.

Timar sat in silent stupefaction on the edge of the bed, and held in his trembling hands the agate box, whose diamonds sparkled in the moonlight. He looked away through the window at the moon shining in. Again the moon seemed to have eyes and mouth, as it is depicted in the almanac, and to be entering into conversation with the poor mortal.

"To whom do these treasures belong?"

"Why, whom should they belong to but you? You bought the sunken cargo, just as it is, with the sacks and the grain. You were liable to the danger that it might remain on your hands as spoiled waste, as stinking rubbish. Now it has turned into gold and jewels. It is true that the dying man said something about the Red Crescent, and you puzzled your head as to what he could have meant; you wondered how it was possible that the refugee should have no more property than was visible. Now you see clearly how it all hung together; but then, when you bought the cargo, you did not know—you bought this mass of wet grain for quite another purpose. You wanted to make sweet and bitter bread out of it for the poor soldiers. Fate willed otherwise. Do you not see that this is a sign from Heaven? It would not permit you to make a shameful profit at the expense of twenty thousand poor soldiers—it has provided for you otherwise. As Providence has prevented something wicked, that which happened by its direction must without doubt be good."

"Besides, to whom should these treasures belong?"

"The sultan must have stolen them in his victorious campaigns; the treasurer most probably stole them from the sultan. Both were robbed of them by the Danube: now they have no owner—they belong to you. You possess them at any rate with just as much right as the sultan, the treasurer, and the Danube."

"And Timéa?"

At this question a long narrow black cloud rose before the moon's face.

Timar remained long in thought. The moon appeared again.

"So much the better for you. You know best how the world treats a poor devil like you. They scold him when he has done his duty; they call him a knave when a misfortune overtakes him; they allow him to hang himself on the nearest tree when he has nothing more to live on; for his love-sorrows pretty girls have no balm. A poor man remains always only a clerk. Then see how the world honors the rich man—how people seek for his friendship, ask his advice, and trust him with the fate of the nation; and women, how they fall in love with him! Did you ever get even a friendly word of thanks from their lips? What would you get if you took the treasure you have found and laid it at her feet with the words, 'There, take what is yours—I saved it for you from the depths?' In the first place, she would not know how to use it. She can hardly distinguish the value of a box of diamonds from that of a box of sweets; she is only a child; and then it would never reach her hands, for her adopted papa would absorb it and get rid of nine tenths of it. Who can prevent him from taking one gem at a time and turning it into money? But granted that Timéa gets it, what would be the result? She would be a rich lady, who would not cast a look at you from her height; and you would

119

remain a miserable supercargo, in whom it would be madness even to dream of her. Now, however, things are the other way—you will be a rich man and she a poor girl. Is not that exactly what you desired of fate? Well, that is what has happened. Did you put that log in the way of the ship which stove her in? Do you mean badly by Timéa? No; you do not want to keep for yourself the treasures you have found; you will invest them profitably, increase them, and when you have earned with the first million a second and a third, then you will go to the poor girl and say, 'There, take it—it is all yours; and take me too.' Do you wish to do anything wrong with it? You only wish to become rich in order to make her happy. You can sleep with a good conscience, having such designs."

The moon was already half hidden in the Danube; only the tip of one horn rose from the water like a light-house; its reflection in the waves reached to the ship's bow; and every ray and every wave spoke to Timar. And they all said, "You have fortune in your hand; hold it fast—you risk nothing. The only one who knew of the treasure lies below the Danube."

Timar heard what was whispered to him, and also the secret voice in his own breast, and cold drops stood on his brow. The moon's fiery tip vanished beneath the surface of the water, and cried to him with its last ray, "You are rich—you are a made man!"

But when it was dark, the inward voice whispered in the silent night, "You are a thief!"

An hour afterward a four-horse post-chaise was rushing along the Szönyer road at a gallop, and as the tower clock of St. Andrew's Church in Komorn struck eleven, the carriage stood at the door in the Anglia under the double eagle. Timar sprung quickly out and hurried in. He was expected.

CHAPTER III.
THE GOLD MINE.

After the concentration of troops in Komorn, Timar had suddenly become a wealthy man. He had bought a house in the Servian Street, the "City" of the Komorn merchants. No one was surprised. The phrase once uttered by the Emperor Francis I. to a contractor who had remained poor, was, "The ox stood at the manger, why did he not eat?" These golden words have, I fancy, been written by every contractor in his memorandum-book.

How much Timar made by his bread contract it is impossible to say; but that he has suddenly become a great personage it is easy to see. He is always on the spot when there is a large undertaking on hand, and has money in abundance. This is not surprising to merchants or speculators; the first stage is the difficult one. If once the first hundred thousand gulden are made, the rest follows of itself—he has credit.

On one point Herr Brazovics had no doubt whatever. He guessed rightly that Timar had offered the officials a larger commission than he himself usually did, and that he had thus obtained the profitable bread contract by which Brazovics usually enriched himself. But that he should have made so large a profit out of it—on that point he shook his head incredulously. Since Timar had risen in the world, and become his own master, Brazovics cultivated the friendship of his former supercargo, and invited him to his evening receptions, which Timar accepted willingly enough. He met Timéa there very often, who had already learned a little colloquial Hungarian.

Timar was now welcome even to Sophie, who once half whispered and half screamed to Athalie that it would do no harm if she was rather more friendly to him, for he was now a rich man, a far from despicable *parti*, worth more than three officers put together, who have nothing but their smart uniform and their debts. To which Fraülein Athalie replied, "It does not follow that I should take my father's servant for a husband." Frau Sophie could finish the sentence for herself—"Because my papa married his maid-servant"—in which lay a well-earned reproach to Frau Sophie. How could she have dared to intrude herself in the capacity of mother upon such a grand young lady!

Toward the end of supper one evening, as the two sat alone at table, Herr Brazovics began to incite Timar to drink, by repeatedly taking wine with him. His own head was pretty strong from constant practice, but this poor devil could never have been used to the bottle.

When they were well on the road, he cunningly brought up the subject. "You, Michael, out with the truth now—how did you contrive to profit so much by the commissariat contract? I have tried it myself, and I know what can be got out of it. I also have mixed feldspar, bran, and millers' dust with the dough; I understand how to get acorns ground instead of corn, and know the difference between rye and wheat flour; but to make such a *coup* as you have done has never happened to me. Confess now! What trick were you up to? You are already wealthy—you have found a gold mine."

Timar put on the look of a tipsy man who required six horse-power to raise his eyelids, and began with drunken fluency and a stammering tongue to explain. "Well, you must know, sir—"

"No sir to me! How often have I told you! Call me by my name."

"Well, then, you must know, Nazi, it was no trick. You remember that I bought in the soaked grain-cargo of the 'St. Barbara' at a nominal price, a gulden a measure. I did not get rid of it, as people fancied, to the millers and farmers, with a profit of a couple of groschen; but I had it baked into bread at once, which did not cost me half so much as if I had bought the very cheapest flour."

"Oh, you prodigy! I ought to go to school to you in my old age. You arch-rascal! Was the ration-bread very bad, then?"

Michael laughed so that the wine almost ran out of his mouth again. "I should just think it was bad—bad beyond words."

"And were no complaints laid before the commissariat committee?"

"What use would that have been, when I had the whole lot of them in my pocket?"

"But the commandant of the fortress, the inspector of ordnance?"

"I squared them too," cried Michael, proudly, striking his pocket, in which so many great men had found room. The eyes of Herr Brazovics shone in a curious way, as if they were even redder than usual. "And did you give the bread made of soaked wheat to the soldiers to eat?"

"Why not? Bread once swallowed tells no tales."

"Quite true, Michael, quite true; but you be careful not to tell any one yourself. You can tell me, of course—I am your true friend; but if one of your enemies got wind of it, it might go badly with you. Your house in the Servian Street might go too. Hold your tongue before other people."

On this Timar began, like one who has suddenly come to his senses, to entreat Herr Brazovics not to betray his secret and make him miserable; he even kissed his hands. Brazovics pacified him, he need not be uneasy about him, he must not let out his secret to others. Then he called the servant and ordered him to take a lantern and go home with Herr Timar, and take good care of him that he should come to no harm, and if he were unable to walk, to take his arm. When the servant returned, he related what trouble it had cost him to get Timar home; he had not known his own door, and had begun to sing in the street. They had at last got him to bed, and there the good gentleman had instantly gone to sleep. But when Brazovics' servant had gone, Timar left his bed, and wrote letters until morning.

He had not been in the least tipsy. Timar was as certain that his dear friend would at once give information of the whole affair as that Monday comes after Sunday; and he also knew to whom.

It was therefore no surprise to him that, a few days later, after an evening spent with Brazovics, he was cited to appear at the fortress, where a gentleman entitled "Financial Privy Counselor" gave him to understand that he was to remain for the present under strict observation, and demanded his keys, in order to lay an embargo on his books and papers.

This will be a big thing. Timar's secret had been denounced to the general chamber of finance, which was in rivalry with the leaders of the council of war. Here was an opportunity to reveal in the most conspicuous way the scandals which took place in the bosom of this community, and to remove from it the control of the commissariat. The accusation was supported by the three high courts—only the police department was on the side of the council of war. At last the chamber gave its decision, and a commission was appointed, with strict injunctions to spare no one, to suspend the whole department of supply, to request the commandant to arrest the contractor, commence a criminal suit, and discover everything. If one morsel of musty bread should appear against Timar, woe to him!

But nothing of the sort was found. For eight days the commission worked day and night. They heard witnesses, took oaths, inquired, had the provost up—all in vain, no one could say anything against Timar. From the whole inquiry it was proved that he had divided the spoiled cargo among millers, country people, and manufacturers; that not one single handful had been mixed with the bread baked for the troops. They had even the soldiers up to give evidence. They said they had never eaten better bread than during the two weeks when it was provided by Timar. No complaint, no adverse witness appeared against him, much less could the officials be accused of corruption; they had given the contract to him who offered the best and lowest terms. At last they boiled over; they felt insulted by the inquiry, stormed and rattled their swords; the commission, driven into a corner, got alarmed, revoked, rehabilitated, and tried to get away from Komorn as quickly as possible. Timar was set free with many excuses, and with the assurance that he was a thoroughly honest man.

At his acquittal Herr Katschuka was the first who hastened to congratulate him, and shook his hand demonstratively in public. "My friend, you must not put up with this quietly; you must have satisfaction for it. Just fancy, they suspected *me* of being bribed! Go to Vienna and demand reparation; the informer must have an exemplary punishment. And in future," he added aside, "you may be sure no one will ever get us out of the saddle. Strike while the iron is hot."

Timar promised to do so, and mentioned his intention to Brazovics when he next met him. The latter seemed furious at the ill-treatment his friend Michael had received. Who could the scoundrel be who had so libeled him?

"Whoever it may be," Timar declared, "shall rue it dearly; and if he has a house in Komorn, I'll lay my head that this joke will cost him his home. I am going to-morrow morning to Vienna, to demand satisfaction from the treasury."

"Yes, do so, by all means," said Brazovics; and thought to himself,

"Just as well that I know it; I shall be there too."

And he happened to get there a day sooner than Timar. There, with the assistance of his old connections, he so prepared the way (which cost him a mint of money) that if once Timar set his foot in this labyrinth, he would never get out again. From the treasury he will be sent to the high court; there the affair will be given over to the judicial office, thence to the superintendent of police, and from there to the secret department of finance.

The unfortunate plaintiff at last loses patience, gets angry, and says a few impudent words—even possibly gets them printed. Then the censor gets hold of him, and at last he begs to be let go, and swears never again to pull the bell at any public office. He will be a fool for his pains if he tries to get justice. But Timar was not a fool; he was far cleverer than either of his advisers—than both put together. He had grown cunning from the time when he let himself be persuaded to take the first wrong step: he knew already that you should never tell any one the real thing you are going to do. At Pancsova, when he snapped his fingers at the authorities, he had shown what talents lay undiscovered in him. Then he had done in another's interest what could be of no use to himself: he did what he was told to do, and humbugged the pursuers; now he was doing it in his own interest. Being in possession of the treasure-trove, he must find some excuse for appearing as a rich man before the public. He must pretend to be a speculator who had been lucky in his business. In his very first affair he must be reputed to have made large sums. If people imagined he had made his money by corrupt means, that was the lesser evil; and it could not be proved, for it was not true. He had been put to such great expense by the contract, that hardly any profit was left; but he was in a position to buy houses and ships, and pay in gold, and every one thought the money at his disposal came from his successful tender. He required a pretext, a title, a visible ground, in order to go quietly forward with the help of Tschorbadschi's wealth.

What, then, did he do in Vienna?

He must ask for compensation from the exchequer, and could reckon on the support of the war department. From his friends at Komorn he had received letters of recommendation to the most influential officials. He left all these letters at the bottom of his trunk, and went direct to the chancellor

125

himself, of whom he requested an audience. The minister was pleased that this man did not try to get in by backstairs influence, but came direct by the front entrance. He admitted him. The minister was a tall man with a clean-shaven face, an imposing double chin, severe brows, and very bald. On his breast shone numerous orders. He had stuck both hands under his coat-tails when this poor individual with the big mustache was shown in. Timar wore a simple black Hungarian costume.

The first question of his excellency to Timar was, "Why do you not wear a sword when you come to an audience?"

"I am not a noble, gracious sir."

"Indeed! I suppose you have come to me to ask for compensation for your arrest and the injury which was inflicted on you?"

"Far from it," answered Timar. "The government only did its duty in proceeding against greater men than I, as well as myself, on the ground of apparently well-founded information. As I am not of nobility, it is of no consequence to me to lay damages on account of my injured honor. Indeed, I owe gratitude to the informer as well as to the court, for having by their strict inquiry made it perfectly clear that my hands were clean all through my contract."

"Oh, then, you have no intention of demanding satisfaction from the informer?"

"On the contrary, I should think it unadvisable to do so, for many an honest man might be prevented from revealing real abuses. My honor is established: it is not my nature to revenge myself. Besides, I have neither time nor desire for it. Forgive and forget."

While Timar spoke, his excellency had already taken one hand from under his coat-tails in order to clap Timar on the shoulder.

"That is a very practical way of looking at it. You can do better than losing time by running about after vengeance. A very sensible idea. What brings you, then, to me?"

"A tender for which I need your excellency's protection."

The excellency stuck his hand behind him again.

"The crown has a property on the frontier, in Levetincz."

"H'm!" grumbled the great man, and frowned. "What do you want with it?"

"In my business as a wholesale dealer, I have often been there, and know the local circumstances. The crown lands extend to thirty thousand acres, and are let to Silbermann, the Vienna banker, at forty kreutzers an acre. The conclusion of this contract lies within the province of the treasury; but the disposal of the income belongs to the military department. This income amounts to a hundred thousand gulden. Silbermann divided the estate into three parts, and let to subtenants at a gulden an acre."

"Of course he wanted to make something out of it."

"Naturally. The subtenants let the land in smaller parcels to the peasantry for a certain percentage of the crops. But now, after two bad harvests, the land in the Banat has not even grown enough for seed-corn. The peasants got nothing, and could not give any percentage to the subtenants, who paid nothing to the crown lessee; and he, in order to get rid of his contract, went bankrupt, and paid no rent to the government."

Now both hands of the great official came out and began to gesticulate. "Yes; because he lived in princely luxury, the rascal! Just imagine, he kept horses which cost eight thousand gulden, and drove them about. Now they are up for sale. I am an 'excellency,' but I am not in a position to keep such costly horses as those."

Timar took no notice, and continued his remarks: "The treasury now is defrauded of its rent, for there is nothing to seize. The tenant and the subtenants are married; their whole property belongs to their wives under the name of dowry. The hundred thousand gulden are lost to the military department, which, I have been told, will claim the sum from the exchequer."

The chancellor opened his snuff-box, and while he put his two fingers in for a pinch, he threw an inquiring look on the speaker with one eye.

"My humble offer therefore is," continued Timar, laying a folded paper on the table, "to rent the Levetincz estate for ten years at the price paid by the sub-lessees—namely, a gulden an acre."

"Very good."

"The new tenant will already have lost a year, for it is November, and all the fields are lying fallow. But in spite of that, I offer not only to include the past year in the term, but also to be responsible for the irrecoverable rent."

His excellency tapped twice on the lid of his gold snuff-box, and pursed his lips together. Well, thought he, this is a man of gold. He is not such a fool as he looks. He guesses that the treasury would like to take the commissariat out of the hands of the war office, and that all this was mixed up with the inquiry at Komorn. Then, after that horrible fiasco, the clattering swords are at the top of the tree, and would be very glad to get the manipulation of the lands on the military frontier into their own hands. They think it would be a good milch-cow, and the deficit caused by the bankruptcy of the Levetincz tenant gives them a pretext. And now this fellow does not combine with the enemies of the treasury which persecuted him, but comes over to us, and will improve our position and help us out of our difficulty. A man of gold indeed, and to be properly appreciated! "Good!" said his excellency; "I see you are an honest man. You had some cause to complain of us, but abstained: you will see that this is the right way for a good citizen to act. Just to show you that the state knows how to reward patriotic subjects, I guarantee you the acceptance of your offer. Come to my office to-night. I pledge you my word as to the result."

Timar presented his offer in writing, and took leave with low bows. His excellency was pleased with this man. In the first place, he is wise enough to look over the injustice done to him, which if he had followed it up would have brought unpleasant scandal on the department. Secondly, he offers the government an advantageous rent, fifty per cent higher than the last. Thirdly, he comes to the aid of the exchequer with a generous offer, and enables them victoriously to repel the attack of the war department. He is a threefold man of gold—no, fourfold—but of that his excellency knows nothing as yet. He was to learn it for the first time when he went home to dinner at his palace, and his stud-groom informed him that the gentleman from Hungary who had been commissioned by his excellency to bid for the eight thousand gulden horses had brought them home, and would personally report particulars of their price to his excellency.

A four-fold treasure!

When Timar visited the great man in his office that evening, he saw on every face a polite smile—the reflection of gold. His excellency met him at

128

the door, and led him to the table. There lay the contract outspread; complete with all signatures, with the greater and lesser seals affixed. "Read—I hope you will be satisfied."

The first thing which surprised Timar was that the lease ran for twenty years instead of ten.

"Well, are you satisfied with the term."

Was he satisfied! The second surprising thing was his own name, "Michael Timar, Baron von Levetinczy."

"Do you like your title?"

CHAPTER IV.
MICHAEL TIMAR, BARON VON LEVETINCZY.

"The diploma of nobility shall be sent to you," said the great man with a gracious smile.

Timar signed his name, with the addition of his new title, to the contract.

"Do not be in a hurry," said his excellency, "I have something more to say. It is a duty of the government to distinguish those who have deserved it by their services to the nation. Especially in regard to such as have won universal recognition in the regions of commerce and political economy. Could you name any one whom I could recommend in the highest quarters for the decoration of the Iron Crown?"

His excellency was quite prepared to receive for answer—"Here is my own button-hole, sir; you can find no better place for your order of merit. If you only want an honest man, here am I." And the offer was made with this idea.

So much the greater was the astonishment of the minister when Michael Timar-Levetinczy after a brief pause replied—"Yes, sir, I will make so free as to point out a person who has long enjoyed universal respect, who has secretly been the benefactor of the district where he lives; it is no other than the Dean of Plesscovacz, Cyril Sandorovics, who deserves this distinction in an imminent degree."

The minister started back. An individual had never before come under his notice who, on being asked—"To whom shall I give this order," had not turned to the mirror, and pointing to himself, replied—"Give it to this worthy man!" but who instead of that had indicated with his finger the furthest limit of the national map, and there seeking out a country priest, not his brother-in-law or godfather, not even a priest of his own church, had said—"This is a better man than I." Indeed this is a man of pure gold. A gold worker would have to mix at least three carats of silver with him before he would be malleable. But as the question has been asked, it must be seriously considered. "Good, good," replied the great man, "but the bestowal of an order involves certain formalities. The sovereign can not contemplate the eventuality of a refusal: the person to whom such a distinction falls must go through the form of personally applying for it."

"His reverence is a very modest man, and would only, if I know him, decide on such a step on receiving an invitation from high quarters."

"Indeed? I understand. A line from my hand would suffice? Good. As it is recommended by you, it shall be done. Yes; the state must reward modest merit."

And the great man wrote with his own hand a few lines to the Rev. Dean Cyril Sandorovics, with the assurance that, if he desired it, he should receive the decoration of the Iron Crown in return for services. Timar thanked his excellency warmly for this favor, and was assured of his high protection for all future time. And, further, Timar had the pleasure of finding that in the whole office, where one generally has to go through every kind of tiresome formality, here every one was at his service, so that he only required an hour to get through his business, while it would have taken any one else weeks before he could get out of this official labyrinth. The water-jug of the Orsova purifier was there in an invisible shape!

It was night before he had packed all the documents relative to his completed contract in his portmanteau. And now for speed! He neither supped nor slept, but hastened to the Golden Lamb, where the mail-cart put up. In the bar he bought a roll and a smoked sausage, which he put in his pocket; he could eat them on the journey. Then he called to the driver, "We must be off at once—spare neither whip nor horses. I will give you a gulden an hour for yourself, and pay double price for my place." It was needless to say more.

Two minutes later the mail-cart was dashing through the streets of Vienna with great cracking of whips, the police in vain calling out that it was forbidden in Vienna. The courier-posts, which at that time took the place of railways, formed one connected chain between Vienna and Semlin. The horses stood harnessed day and night, and as soon the crack of the whip at one end of the village announced the approach of the post, the postmaster brought out the new team from the stable, and in two minutes the cart with the fresh horses rolled away over hill and dale at a gallop. If two post-carts

131

met on the road they changed horses and drivers, who then had only half the distance to go back. The speed of the journey was regulated by the amount of the pay.

Timar sat in the cart two days and nights without getting down for a meal, let alone a night's rest. He was quite used to sleeping in the carriage, in spite of shaking and rolling and knocking about.

On the evening of the second day he was in Semlin, whence he drove all night to the first village on the Levetinczy estate.

It was fine mild weather for the first of December. He drove to the little town hall, and sent for the village judge; he told him he was the new tenant of the estate, and requested him to make known to the farmers that they could rent the land in shares as in former years. During the two last years the fields which bore no fruit had lain as good as fallow, so that there would be a prospect of a rich harvest for the next season. The weather was favorable, the autumn lasting long; by setting to work at once there was still time to plow and sow.

That was all very well, they replied; plowing could be managed if the principal thing, seed-corn, were not wanting. It was not to be got for love or money. The landowners had only with the greatest difficulty secured any for themselves; poor people would have to live on maize all the winter.

Timar gave the consoling assurance that he would take care that they did not want for seed-corn, and so he went through the other villages whose inhabitants farmed as subtenants, and who, on his permission, got out their plows and went to turn over the fields which had been allowed to lie fallow a whole year. But where was the seed to come from? It was too late to get grain from Wallachia, and there was none in the neighborhood. But Timar knew where to get it. On the 2d December he reached Plesscovacz, whence a short time before he had almost been driven by force, and sought out his reverence, Cyril Sandorovics, who had then turned him out of his house.

"Aha! my son, are you here again?" This was his reception by the venerable gentleman, that friend and benefactor of the people who ought long ago to have received the order of the Iron Crown if he had not been so retiring. "What do you want now? To buy grain? I told you two months ago I had none, and could not sell any. It is no use talking! You will lie in vain, for I don't believe a word you say. You have a Greek name and a long mustache. I don't trust your face."

Timar smiled. "Well, this time nothing but truth shall pass my lips."

"Tell that to the other people. You dealers from the upper country are always deceiving us. You pretend there was a poor harvest in your parts and drive our prices down. When you wanted to buy hay from us, you spread the report that the government was going to sell all its horses. You are a rascally lot."

"But now I tell you the truth. I am here with a commission from the government to beg your reverence in their name to open your granaries. The government having heard that the people are in need of seed-corn, wishes to divide among them some supplies of grain. This is a sacred purpose, a great benefit to be conferred on the people, and whoever assists them in this renders them a great service. I am not to receive the grain, but it is to be delivered to the farmers, who will use it for seed-corn."

"My son, that is all very true, and I am very sorry for the poor people, but I have no grain. Where should I get it? I had no harvest. There is my great stupid barn, but all three floors are empty."

"It is not empty, reverend sir. I know very well that three years' harvest is stored away there: I could get at least ten thousand measures out of it."

"You would get trash. Spare yourself the trouble. I would not sell for five gulden a measure; in the spring it will be seven gulden, and then I will sell. You lie in your throat when you say the government sends you; you only want to make your own profit, and not a grain will you get from me. Much the government knows about you and me; we might as well be in the moon for all it cares!"

Till now the fortress had held out bravely against small arms. But Timar put his hand in his pocket and brought out a four-and-twenty pounder, the minister's letter. When the reverend gentleman had read it he could hardly believe his own eyes.

The great seal on the envelope with the imperial double eagle, the stamp of the exchequer on the paper, left no room for doubt. It was no deception but the absolute truth.

To wear that brilliant cross upon his breast had long been the *ne plus ultra* of his dreams. Timar knew of this weakness of the dean's, who often, as they sat over their wine, had bitterly complained of the injustice of the government in heaping decorations on the patriarch at Carlovitz. Why give all to one and send the other empty away? Now he had attained his greatest desire—how the peasants will gape at him when he has attached this order to his breast, and how the Tschaikiss captain will envy him, having none of his own! Even the patriarch will be a degree more condescending in future. Meanwhile, his own manner to Timar had suddenly undergone a great change.

"Sit down, little brother!" (until now he had not even offered a seat)—"tell me, how did you get to know their excellencies? Why did they intrust the letter to you?"

Timar told him some story or other, and lied like print. He had given up his post under Brazovics and taken service under government. He had great influence with the minister, and it was he who had recommended his reverence for this distinction, as a good old friend of his own.

"I knew you were not such a fool as you look; that's why I have always liked you so much. Now, my son, because you have such a beautiful Greek name, and such an honest face, you shall have the grain. How much do you want? Ten, twelve thousand measures? I will sell you all I have. Not to please the minister, no, indeed! but for the sake of your own honest face, and to do good to the poor people. What price did I say? Five gulden? I will tell you what, I will give it to *you* for four gulden nineteen kreutzers. You pay cash down? Or shall I get the money in Vienna? I shall be going there, and can do it at the same time. I must thank his excellency in person for this honor. You will come and introduce me? Or if you want to have nothing to do with it, tell me at any rate what sort of a man he is. Is he big or little, friendly or haughty? Will he give me the cross himself? Does he like good

Carlovitz and Vermuth? Now then, you shall taste some yourself."

In vain Timar assured him he must go back that night to Levetinczy, to give orders to the steward to send the tenants for the seed-corn. The friendly host would not part with his guest, but placed the servant at his disposal, who could ride to Levetinczy and deliver the instructions. Michael must remain overnight with him. The reverend gentleman had glasses with rounded bottoms, which when they were filled could not be laid down till they were empty. He gave one to Timar, took another himself, and so they caroused till morning. And Timar showed no signs of drink; he had lived in that district and had got used to it. Early in the morning the farmers came with their wagons to the dean's court-yard. When they saw that the doors of the three-storied granary were really open, they said to Timar he was the right sort of saint and could work miracles. In the barn were supplies for three years, more than was required for all their winter seed.

Timar never left the estate he had rented until the winter frosts set in, which stopped field-work for the season. But it was enough for the present. The remaining acres would do for spring-sowing, or as fallows, or for pasture. On the whole estate of thirty thousand acres there were only a few hundred acres of meadow-land, all the rest was arable and of the first class. If the next year should be favorable, the harvest would be superabundant.

It was sown at exactly the right time. October remained dry and windy to the end. Those who had sown before that might be sure of a bad crop, for the legions of marmots had scratched out the seed before it sprung up. Those who sowed during the wet November were no better off, for it had snowed early, and in the warm ground, under the snow-covering, the seed rotted; but when the snow had melted, a long mild spell set in which lasted till Christmas. Whoever had sown then could congratulate himself; the marmots were gone; frost now came before snow, and under the beautiful white covering the treasure intrusted to the soil lay safely hidden till spring. Farming is a game of chance. Six or nothing! Timar threw six.

Then followed such a fruitful year that whoever had profited by the favorable season in Banat received twenty-fold in crops.

In this year Timar brought thirty cargoes of the finest wheat to Komorn and Raab, and these thirty had cost him no more than three to

135

another person. It depended on himself whether to make half a million of profit or a hundred thousand more or less—either to make poor people's bread cheaper, or to hold a knife to the throat of his competitors.

It lay with him to drive prices down as low as he chose. In Brazovics' café there was angry talk every evening among the assembled corn-dealers. He scatters money like chaff, and squanders his goods as if they were stolen. If only he would come among them they would get him by the throat!

But he does not come; he goes nowhere and seeks no acquaintances. He takes care to tell no one what he is going to do, and all he undertakes turns into gold. Many new industries are called into being by him, which might have occurred to anyone else: they lay, so to speak, in the street, and only wanted picking up; but they were only noticed by others when this man had already got hold of them. He is always in movement, traveling here and there, and people wonder why he goes on living in this town; why he does not move to Vienna; why he, who is so rich, has his headquarters in Komorn, though it was certainly then an important commercial center.

Timar knows what keeps him there. He knows why he lives in a town where all his mercantile colleagues are his sworn enemies, where the people sitting before Brazovics' café send a curse after him every time he passes. That house too he means to get into his clutches, with all that therein is. This it was which kept him in Komorn, when already he was the owner of a million and a half; he remained where they still called him Timar, and had not got used to his noble title of Levetinczy.

Yet he knew how to suit noble deeds to his noble name. He founded an hospital for the poor of the town, he endowed the Protestant schools; even the chalice turned to gold in his hands. Instead of the silver one he presented a golden one to the church. His door was always open to the poor, and every Friday a long line of beggars went through the streets to his house, where each received a piece of money, the largest copper coin in existence, the so-called "schuster-thaler." People said that when a sailor was drowned, Timar maintained his orphans and gave a pension to his widow. A heart of gold indeed! A man of gold!

But in his heart a voice continually whispered, "It is not true! It is all false!"

CHAPTER V.
A GIRL'S HEART.

Herr Brazovics usually drank coffee after dinner, and had it served in the ladies' sitting-room, which he filled unmercifully with clouds of Latakia tobacco.

Katschuka sat whispering with Athalie at a little table, at the corner of which Frau Sophie pretended to be busy sewing. (For years this table had been ostentatiously spread with needle-work and knitting, so that visitors might imagine they were occupied with the trousseau.)

Herr Katschuka almost lived in the house; he came in the forenoon, was pressed to stay to dinner, and only found his way home late in the evening.

It would appear that the fortifications of Komorn were complete, as the engineer officer had the whole day to spend with Fraülein Athalie. But the fortifications of Herr Katschuka's own fortress could not hold out any longer—the time was come for his marriage. He resisted like a second Zriny. When driven from the outworks, he retreated to the citadel. He always had some plausible pretext for delaying the marriage. Now, however, the last mine had been exploded. His deposit was indorsed by the Brazovics firm, and the council of war had accepted their receipt instead of money down; a house had been found for the young couple, and besides all this Katschuka had received his promotion to the rank of captain. This removed his last excuse; the last cartridge of the besieged had been expended, and nothing remained but to capitulate, and take the rich and beautiful girl home.

Herr Brazovics became more and more venomous every day when he drank his coffee with the ladies; and the man by whom his coffee was poisoned was always Timar.

This was his daily *delenda est Carthago*.

"What confounded tricks that fellow is up to! While other honest dealers are glad to rest in winter from their labors, he is busy with things that no cat would think of. He has hired the Platten-See now, and fishes under the ice: a little while ago his people caught three hundredweight of fish in one haul. It is a theft! Before the spring comes he will have cleared the Platten-See, so that not a single perch, not a shad nor a roach, not a garfish, let alone a fogasch,1 will be left in it. And he sends them all to Vienna. As if that was what fogasch swam in the Balaton lake for—that those Germans might eat them! The damned scoundrel! The government ought to set a price on his head. Sooner or later I will get rid of him, that's certain. When he goes over the bridge I will get a couple of fishermen to throw him into the Danube; I will pay a sentry a couple of gulden to shoot him by accident when he passes in the dark; I'll turn a mad dog into his yard, that it may bite him when he comes out in the morning. They ought to hang the rascal! I'll set his house on fire, that he may burn with it! And they ennoble such a fellow! In the town council they make him assessor, and the good-for-nothing sits at the green table with me. I, whose grandfather was of ancient Hungarian nobility, must suffer him near me, this runaway rogue!

[1] Leucia perca.

"But just let him attempt to come near this café. I'll set a band upon him who will throw him out of the window and break his neck! If ever I sat down to table with him I would season his soup so that he would soon be on his back like a dead fish! And this vagabond pays visits to ladies! This Timar, this former supercargo, who used to be a mud-lark! If he happened to be in the company of a brave officer who would call him out, and spit him like a frog—so!"

Herr Brazovics threw a meaning glance on Herr Katschuka, who seemed as if he had heard nothing. He had heard well enough; but what had principally struck him in the monologue of his future father-in-law was that the new millionaire must have made a great breach in the riches of Herr Brazovics, and that this rage was caused by the threatened ruin of the firm. A thought not calculated to increase the officer's joy at the approaching wedding-day.

"No; I will not wait for some one else to get rid of him!" said Brazovics at last, and stood up, laid aside his chibouque, and fetched his bamboo cane from its corner. "I have a dagger. I bought it since the fellow settled here, on purpose for him" (and that he might be believed he drew the sharp blade out of his sword-stick). "There it is! The first time we meet alone,

I will stick it into him and nail him to the wall like a bat. And that I swear!"

And he tried by rolling his bloodshot eyes to give emphasis to his threat. He drank the rest of his coffee standing, drew on his overcoat, and said he was going to business.

He would come home early (that is, early in the morning). Every one was glad when he went.

Just as Herr Brazovics went carefully down the steps to the street—for his corpulence prevented his running down-stairs—who should come to meet him but—Timar!

Now is his chance; at striking distance, and in a dark place where no one can see them. We know by history that most murders are committed on the stairs. Timar had no weapon with him, not even a walking-stick; but Herr Athanas had a stiletto two feet long.

When he saw Timar, he put his sword-stick under his arm, and cried aloud as he took off his hat, "Your obedient servant! good-day to you, Herr von Levetinczy!"

Timar answered with a "Servant, Nazi—off to business again?"

"He! he! he!" laughed Herr Brazovics jovially, like a boy who is caught in a bit of mischief. "Now then, Michael, won't you keep us company?"

"Shouldn't think of it. If you want to win a couple of hundred gulden from me, I had better pay them now; but to sit the whole night gambling and drinking, no, thank you."

"He! he! he! Well, go up to the ladies then; they are upstairs. A pleasant evening to you. I sha'n't see you again to-day."

And they parted with a hearty shake of the hand, for Herr Athanas does not mean anything by his threats. No one is afraid of him, in spite of his frightful voice and imposing appearance, not even his wife—especially his wife. He knows well enough that Timar goes regularly to his house, and arranges to be away when he comes. Frau Sophie has not concealed her opinion that the visits are doubtless owing to the fine eyes of Athalie. Well, that is Katschuka's affair: if he does not spit his rival like a frog it is his own fault; he has been warned. But he does not seem inclined to do it, though Timar and Athalie are often together.

And why the devil should the captain challenge Timar? They are as good friends as ever they were.

Herr Brazovics guessed—indeed he had means of knowing—that it was no other than Captain Katschuka who had opened the door through which Timar had attained his riches. Why he had done so was easy to imagine. He wanted to get rid of Athalie, and it would suit him very well if Brazovics intervened and forbid him the house.

But that was just what he did not do, but overflowed with tenderness for the captain—his son-in-law. There was no way out of it: he must marry Athalie. The captain has long been betrothed to Athalie, to whom a dangerous rival pays daily court—a rich man whom he ought to hate, because he left him in the lurch in the quarrel between the treasury and the war office, and yet the captain is so fond of his old friend that he is capable of forgiving him if he ran away with his bride.

Athalie despises Timar, once her father's clerk, but treats him nevertheless in a friendly way. She is passionately in love with the captain, but pays attention to Timar in his presence to make him jealous.

Sophie hates Timar, but receives him with honeyed words, as if it were her dearest wish to have him for her son-in-law, and live under the same roof with him.

Timar, on the other hand, means to ruin the whole of them—the master, the mistress, the young lady, and the bridegroom; all of them he would like to turn into the street, and yet he visits at the house, kisses the ladies' hands, and endeavors to make himself agreeable.

They are all civil to him. Athalie plays the piano to him. Frau Sophie keeps him to supper, and offers him coffee and preserved fruits. Timar drinks the coffee with the thought that perhaps there is rat-poison in it.

When the supper-table is brought, Timéa appears, and helps to lay it. Then Timar hears no more of Athalie's words or music; he has eyes only for Timéa. It was a pleasure to see the pretty creature. She was fifteen and already almost a woman, but her expression and naïve awkwardness were those of a child. She could speak Hungarian, though with a curious accent, and sometimes with a wrong word or phrase—ridiculous, of course, but not wholly unknown even in Parliament, and during the most serious debates.

Athalie had made an acquisition in Timéa: she had now some one to

140

make fun of. The poor child served her as a toy. She gave her old clothes to wear which had been fashionable years ago. At one time people wore a high comb turned backward, over which the hair was drawn, and on the top rose a gigantic bow of colored ribbon. They wore crinoline round their shoulders instead of their waists, having huge sleeves stuffed and padded. This dress looked well when in fashion; but a few years after the vogue had passed, its revival suggested a masquerade.

Athalie found it amusing to dress up Timéa thus. In taste the poor child, never having seen European fashions, stood on a par with a wild Indian: the more remarkable the dress the better she liked it. She was charmed when Athalie dressed her in the queer old silk gowns, and struck the high comb and bright ribbon in her hair. She thought she looked lovely, and took the smiles of the people whom she met in the street for admiration, hastening on so as not to be stared at. In the town she was always called "the mad Turkish girl."

And it was easy to make fun of her without her taking it ill. Athalie took special delight in making the poor child an object of ridicule before gentlemen. If young men were present, she encouraged them to pay court to Timéa, and it amused her highly when she saw that Timéa accepted these attentions seriously; how pleased she was to be treated like a grown-up lady, to be asked to dance at balls, or when some pretended admirer offered her a faded bouquet, and extracted some quaint expression of thanks in reply, which caused the company to burst into fits of laughter. How Athalie's laugh resounded on these occasions!

Frau Sophie took a more serious view of Timéa. She scolded her continually; all she did was wrong. Adopted children are often awkward, and the more Timéa was scolded the more awkward she became. Then Fraülein Athalie defended her. "But, mamma, don't be always scolding the girl! You treat her like a servant. Timéa is not a servant, and I won't have you always going on at her!"

Timéa kissed Sophie's hand that she might cease to be angry, and Athalie's out of gratitude for taking her part, and then the hands of both that they might not quarrel. She was an humble, thankful creature. Frau Sophie only waited till she had left the room to say to her daughter what was on the

141

tip of her tongue, in order that the other guests, Timar and Katschuka, might hear. "We ought to get her used to being a servant. You know her misfortune: the money which Timar—I mean Herr von Levetinczy—saved for her was invested in an insurance company. It has failed and the money is gone. She has nothing but what she stands up in."

(So they have already brought her to beggary, thought Timar, and felt his heart lighter, like a student who is let off a year before his time.)

"It annoys me," said Athalie, "that she is so unimpressionable. You may scold her or laugh at her, it is all the same. She never blushes."

"That is a peculiarity of the Greek race," remarked Timar.

"Nonsense!" said Athalie, contemptuously. "It is a sign of sickliness. That artificial white complexion could be attained by any school-girl who chose to eat chalk and burned coffee-berries."

She spoke to Timar, but looked toward Herr Katschuka. He, however, was glancing at the large mirror in which one could see when Timéa came back. Athalie saw it, and it did not escape Timar's notice.

Timéa now came in, carrying a large tray of clinking glasses, her whole attention concentrated on preventing one from falling.

When Frau Sophie shrieked at her, "Take care not to drop them!" she did let the whole tray fall. Fortunately the glasses fell on the soft carpet, and did not break, but rolled about.

The mistress would have burst out in a storm, but Athalie silenced her with the words, "That was your fault; why did you scream at her? Remain here with me, Timéa; the servant shall bring the coffee."

That made Sophie angry, and she went out and brought it all in herself. But at the instant when Timéa let the glasses fall, Katschuka, with military promptitude, sprung up, collected the glasses, and put them all on the tray, still held by Timéa's trembling fingers. The girl cast a grateful look on him out of her large dark eyes, which was seen by both Athalie and Timar.

"Captain Katschuka," whispered Athalie to her *fiancé*, "just for a joke make the little thing fall in love with you; pretend to pay court to her; it will be great fun. Timéa, you sup with us to-night; come and sit down here by the captain."

This might be a cruel joke, or perhaps scornful raillery; or was it an ironical outbreak of awakened jealousy, or was it pure wickedness? We shall see what comes of it.

With feverish excitement and ill-concealed delight, the girl sat down opposite Athalie secure in conquering charms, who, while encouraging her *fiancé* to pay compliments to Timéa, did it like a queen who throws a gold piece to a beggar. The child is made happy by the gift for a day, and she herself does not feel its loss.

The captain offered the sugar-basin to Timéa; she could not manage the tongs.

"Take the sugar with your pretty little white hand," said he to the girl, who was so confused that she put the lump into the tumbler instead of the coffee cup. No one had ever told her that she had a pretty white hand. These words remained on her mind, and she looked often privately at her hands to see if they were really white and pretty. Athalie could hardly suppress a smile. She found it amusing to carry on the jest—"Timéa, offer the cakes to the captain."

The girl lifted the glass dish from its silver stand, and handed it to Katschuka.

"Now then, choose one for him."

By accident she chose one in the shape of a heart. She certainly did not know that it represented a heart, nor what it meant.

"Oh, that is too much for me!" laughed the captain; "I can only take it, if pretty Miss Timéa divides it with me." And with that he broke the heart in two and gave part to Timéa.

The girl left it on her plate; she would not have eaten it for the world. Jealously guarding it with her eyes, she did not wait till Frau Sophie or the servant should change the plates, but hastened to remove the dish of cakes herself and to vanish with them from the room. No doubt she will keep this half-heart, and it will be found in her possession. That will be droll! There is nothing easier than to turn the head of a girl of fifteen, who takes everything in earnest and believes the first man who tells her that she has pretty hands.

And Herr Katschuka was just the man not to forgive himself if he came near a pretty girl without paying her attention. He paid court even to older women; that he could do without scruple. But even to the house-maid, when she lighted him to the door, he could not resist paying compliments. His ambition was to make every girl's heart beat higher at the sight of his blue uniform.

Still Athalie was certain that she was the ruling planet. But it was, of course, worth his while to take a little trouble for Timéa. She was only a child; but one could see she would be a beauty. Then she was an orphan, and a Turkish girl, not baptized, and not quite right in her head—all reasons for flattering her without compunction. Herr Katschuka let no chance escape him, and thereby gave great amusement to his bride.

One evening Athalie said to Timéa, as she was going to bed, "I say, Timéa, the captain has proposed for you. Will you accept him?"

The child looked at Athalie quite frightened, ran to her couch, and drew the covering over her head, so that no one should see her.

Athalie was highly entertained that the girl could not sleep on account of these words—that she should toss restlessly on her bed, and sigh wakefully all night. The delicate jest had succeeded.

The next day Timéa was unusually quiet. She laid aside her childish manner; thoughtful melancholy lay on her features; and she became monosyllabic. The philter had done its work.

Athalie let the whole household into the secret. They were to treat Timéa henceforward as a future bride—as the betrothed of Herr Katschuka. The servants, the mistress, all took part in the comedy.

Let no one say this was a heathenish jest; on the contrary, it was a Christian one.

Athalie said to Timéa:

"Here, see, the captain has sent you an engagement-ring; but you must not put it on your finger as long as you are a heretic. You must first become a Christian. Will you be baptized?"

Timéa crossed her hands on her breast and bowed her head.

"Then you shall be baptized first. That this may be done, you must learn the articles of faith, the catechism, the Bible history, psalms, and prayers; you must go to the priest and to the schoolmaster to be instructed. Will you do that?"

Timéa only nodded. And now she went every day to be taught, with

144

her books under her arm like a little school-girl; and late at night, when the rest were in bed, she went to the empty sitting-room, and sat half the night learning by heart the ten plagues of Egypt, and the highly moral histories of Samson and Delilah, Joseph and Potiphar's wife. Learning was difficult to her, as she was not used to it. But what would she not have done to be baptized?

"You see," said Athalie, often in Timar's presence, "without this hope in her mind we should never have induced her to be converted and to study in order to be baptized."

So it was quite a pious work to turn the child's head, and make her fancy she was already betrothed. And Timar must look on at the cruel trick played on the girl without moving a finger to prevent it. What could he say? She would never understand. And his coming to the house made it worse, for it justified the fable in her eyes. She was often told that the rich Herr von Levetinczy visited them on Athalie's account, which seemed to her quite natural. The rich man woos a rich girl. They suit each other. Who should suit the poor Hungarian officer better than the poor daughter of a Turkish officer? Nothing more natural. She studied day and night, and when she had finished with the catechism and the psalter, they found a new trick to play upon her. They said the wedding-day was fixed, but there was still much to be done to the trousseau. On account of the dresses, linen, and other details, the day could not be a very early one. And then her wedding-dress! That the bride herself must embroider. This is also a Turkish custom and suited Timéa, who knew how to work beautifully in gold and silver, for the harems are all instructed in that art.

She was given Athalie's dress, in order to execute upon it the beautiful designs which had been taught her at home. Of course they told her it was her own. Timéa drew lovely arabesques upon it, and began to embroider them. A perfect masterpiece grew under her fingers; she worked at it from early morning till late evening, and did not even lay it aside when visitors came, with whom she conversed without looking up, and that was fortunate, as then she could not see how they made fun of her. Timar, who had to look on at all this, often left the house with such bitterness in his heart that he struck the two marble pillars at the door with all his force. He would have liked to do as Samson did, and pull the house of the Philistines down on his head.

How long will he allow it to stand?

The day to which Timéa looked forward with secret alarm was really fixed for Herr Katschuka's marriage—but with Fraülein Athalie. Only that various hinderances stood in the way of its arrival. Not in the stars, nor in the hearts of the lovers, but in the financial position of Herr Brazovics.

When the captain asked Athanas for his daughter's hand, he told him plainly that he could only marry if the wife's dowry was sufficient to keep house upon.

Herr Brazovics made no objection. He was not going to be stingy about it: he meant to give his daughter a hundred thousand gulden on her wedding-day, and they could do as they liked with it. And at the time when he made this promise, he was in a position to carry it out. But since then Timar had put a spoke in his wheel. He had in many ways thrown Herr Brazovics' speculations into confusion, upset his safest combination, run him up in the corn-market, outbid him in contracts, and barred his road to influential quarters where before he had had interest, so that it was no longer possible to pay the dowry down. It was well known that his affairs were in confusion, and whoever had a claim to his money would be wise to ask for it to-day rather than to-morrow.

And Herr Katschuka was a wise man.

His future father-in-law tried to persuade him that it would be much better to leave the money at interest with him; but the engineer would not allow his last redoubt to be taken. He charged the mines, and threatened to blow the whole marriage citadel into the air if he did not have the money down before the wedding-day.

Then a brilliant idea shot into the head of Athanas. Why not marry Athalie to Timar? The exchange would not be a bad one. It is true that he hated him and would like to poison him in a spoonful of soup. But if he married Athalie his opposition would cease, he would be a member of the firm and have its interests at heart.

Timar comes to the house regularly—if only he were not so modest! He must be helped.

One afternoon Herr Athanas poured a double dose of anisette into his black coffee (a capital way of encouraging one's self), and had it brought into his office, giving orders that if Timar came, the ladies were to send him into his room.

There he lighted his chibouque, and surrounded himself with such an atmosphere of smoke, that as he walked up and down he appeared and disappeared alternately, with his great starting, bloodshot eyes, like a huge cuttle-fish lying in wait for its prey.

The prey did not keep him waiting long.

As soon as Timar heard from Frau Sophie that Athanas wished to speak to him, he hastened to his room. The great cuttle-fish swam toward him through the smoke, with his horrible fishy eyes fixed upon him, and fell upon him just like the sea-monster, while he cried, "Listen to me, sir; what is the meaning of your visits to this house? What are your intentions with regard to my daughter?"

That is the best way to bring these poltroons to their senses; they get startled, their head swims, and before they can turn round they fall into the net of holy matrimony. It is no joke to answer such a question as that.

The first thing Timar remarked from the speech of Herr Athanas was that he had again taken too much anisette. Thence this courage.

"Sir," he replied, quietly, "I have no intentions whatever with regard to your daughter. So much the less because your daughter is engaged, and the bridegroom is a good old friend of mine. I will tell you why I come to your house. If you had not asked me, I should have kept silence longer, but as you inquire I will tell you. I visit your house because I swore to your dead friend and kinsman, who came to such a dreadful end, that I would look after his orphan child. I come here to see how the orphan committed to your care was treated. She is shamefully treated, Herr Brazovics, disgracefully! I say it to your face in your own house. You have made away with the whole of the girl's property—defrauded her; yes, that is the word. And your whole family carries on a shameful game with the poor child. Her mind is being poisoned for her whole life. May God's curse light on you for it! And now, Herr Brazovics, we two have met for the last time in your house, and you had better pray that you may never see the day when I come into it again."

147

Timar turned on his heel and slammed the door behind him. The cuttle-fish drew back into the dusky depths of its smoky lair, poured down another glass of anisette, and considered that some answer ought to have been given. But what?

For my own part I don't know what he could have said.

Timar went back to the reception-room, not only to get his hat, which he had left there, but for something else.

In the room there was no one but Timéa; Athalie and her *fiancé* were in the next room.

In Timar's face, flushed with anger, Timéa saw a great change. His generally soft and gentle countenance looked proud, and was roused into emotion which made it beautiful. Many faces are beautified by passion's flame.

He went straight to Timéa, who was working golden roses and silver leaves on the bridal dress.

"Fraülein Timéa," he said to her in deeply moved tones, "I come to take leave of you. Be happy, remain a child for a long time; but if ever an hour comes in which you are unhappy, do not forget that there is some one who would—for you—"

He could not speak, his voice failed, his heart contracted. Timéa completed the interrupted phrase—"Thrice!"

He pressed her hand and stammered brokenly, "Always."

Then he bowed and went, without troubling those in the next room.

No "God be with you!" came from his lips. At this moment he was only conscious of the wish that God would withdraw His hand from this house.

Timéa let the work fall, and gazed before her, sighing again, "Thrice!"

The gold thread slipped out of the needle's eye.

As Timar went down the path, he came once more to the two marble pillars which supported the veranda. With what rage he struck them! Did those above feel the shock! Did not the tottering walls warn them to pray, because the roof was falling in on them?

But they were laughing at the mystified child, who worked so diligently at her wedding-dress.

148

CHAPTER VI.
ANOTHER JEST.

The newly ennobled Herr von Levetinczy was already, not only in Hungary but in Vienna, a famous person. He was said to be a "golden man." Everything he touched turned to gold, all he undertook became a gold mine; and this is the real gold mine.

The science of the gold digger consists in finding out earlier than his rivals what large affairs are in contemplation by the government; and in this art Timar was a past master. If he took up any speculation, a whole swarm of speculators threw themselves upon it, for they knew money was to be had there for the picking up.

But it was not only on that account that Timar was called a "golden man," but also for quite another reason.

He never swindled or defrauded any one.

He made large profits, for he undertook large concerns, but he was never tempted to steal or lie, for he never risked anything. He shared the profit with those on whom it depended whether he received a contract on reasonable terms, and in this way kept the source always open.

Once he began to buy up vineyards on the Monostor, the highest point of Komorn. It is a sandhill lying above Uj-Szöny, and its wines are very poor. But notwithstanding this, Timar bought ten acres of vine-growing land there.

This excited attention in the commercial world. What could he want with it? There must be some sort of gold mine there.

Herr Brazovics thought he was on the right track, and attacked Katschuka on his own ground. "Now, my dear son, tell me the truth; I swear by my soul and my honor that I will not betray it to a creature. Confess now, the government is going to build fortifications on the Monostor? That fellow Timar is buying up all the land: don't let us leave him the whole mouthful. It is so, isn't it—they are going to build a fort there?"

The captain allowed the acknowledgment to be got out of him that there might be something in it. The council of war had decided to extend the fortifications of Komorn in that direction. There could be no better news for Athanas. How many hundred thousand gulden had he made in similar circumstances by buying hovels before the expropriation, and selling them afterward to the government at the price of palaces? Only he would certainly like to have seen the plans, and begged his future son-in-law as prettily as possible to let him have just one peep at them.

Katschuka did him that favor too, and thus Athanas learned what portion would be bought by government. And that wretch of a Timar had really pitched on the place where the fort was to be built.

"And what are to be the terms of the expropriation?"

That was the question, and that the captain could not reveal without committing a capital crime. But he did it. The terms were, that the government would pay double the last purchase money.

"Now I know enough," cried Herr Athanas, embracing his son-in-law; "the rest is my affair. On your wedding-day the hundred thousand gulden will be on your table."

But he was wrong in thinking that he knew enough. He would have done well to ask one more question. Herr Katschuka, after saying so much, would have told him that too. But Katschuka no longer cared much about the hundred thousand gulden, nor yet about what depended on them. It he gets them, all right; if not, his hair will not turn gray for lack of them.

Brazovics hurried off to Uj-Szöny, and went to all the vine-growers to ask who had a vineyard to sell. He paid whatever was asked, and if any one refused to sell, he offered treble the price. The more he paid the better for him. Naturally this attracted the attention of other speculators, who arrived in troops and ran up the prices, so that the poor "Hönigler" and "Schafschwanz" wines of Monostor could not understand why they had suddenly turned into "Grands Crûs," to be bought up even before the vintage.

The price of vineyards ran so high, that the land for which the government would have had to pay, before the plans were betrayed, at most one hundred thousand gulden, now could not be bought under five hundred thousand.

150

Brazovics had himself bought a fifth of them, though he had the greatest difficulty in getting the money together. He got rid of his stock of grain, sold his ships, borrowed from the usurers, and made use of trust-money committed to his care. This time he was safe! Timar was in the swim. He was the worst off, for he had bought cheap and would make a very small profit.

But this, too, was perfidy on Timar's part. It was a *coup* aimed at the head of Herr Brazovics. He had learned from Katschuka the one thing Athanas had omitted to ask. It was true that the government would this year greatly enlarge the fortifications; but the question was, Where would they begin? For the work would extend over thirty years.

Here again Timar had done his rivals a bad turn, which would bring their maledictions down on him. As a good business man, he took care, whenever he had undertaken anything which would bring him curses, to set something else to work for which many more would bless him. So that between blessing and cursing he might keep a good balance on the credit side.

He sent for Johann Fabula and said to him, "Johann, you are getting old; many hardships have aged you. Would it not be better to look out for some employment which will allow you to rest?"

Fabula was already hoarse, and when he spoke it sounded as if he was whispering to the actors from the prompter's box.

"Yes, sir; I have often thought of leaving the sea and looking out for work on shore; my eyes are weak. I wish you would give me a stewardship on your land."

"I know of something better than that. You would never get on with the Rascians; you are too much used to the white bread at Komorn. Much better turn farmer."

"I should like it well enough; but there are two things wanting—the land and the stock."

"Both will come in time. I have an idea: the old pastures by the river are for sale—go to the auction and buy them all."

"Oh," said Fabula, with a hoarse laugh, "I should be a fool indeed! It is a waste where nothing grows but camomile. Shall I sell it to the chemists?

And it's a large piece of land; one would want several thousand gulden."

"Don't argue, but do as I tell you. Just you go there. Here are the two thousand gulden for the deposit, which you must hand in at the auction. Then bid till it is knocked down to you, and take it all at the price agreed on. Share with no one, whoever offers to go into partnership with you. I will lend you the money to pay for it, and you shall repay me when you are able. I ask no interest, and you need not give me a receipt. The whole bargain shall be a verbal one. There now, shake hands on it!"

Johann Fabula shook his head thoughtfully. "No interest, no writing, a lump of money, and bad waste land! The end of it will be, that I shall be arrested and stripped to my shirt."

"No scruples, my friend; you have it for a year, and whatever you get off it meanwhile will be entirely yours."

"But what shall I plow and sow with?"

"You will neither plow nor sow. But go and do what I told you—the harvest will not be wanting; but do not tell any one."

Fabula was in the habit of looking on all that Timar did or said as folly *à priori*; but nevertheless he acted with absolute obedience on his orders, for *à posteriori* he had been forced to acknowledge that these unheard-of follies had the same result as if they had been wisdom personified. So he did as Timar had advised.

And now we will let the reader into the secret of these singular proceedings. The plan for the fortification did really exist. But it had been suggested to the council by some busybody that it was not necessary to execute all the sections at once, and that it would be sufficient for the present to expropriate the land lying between the two arms of the river, while the portion covered by the Monostor vineyards could wait twenty years. Now the speculators who got wind of the new plans had all thrown themselves on the sandhill, and no one thought of the shore between the two river branches. Herr Fabula got it for twenty thousand gulden. The land on the Monostor would not be wanted for twenty years to come, and during that time the money invested in the unproductive vineyards would all be eaten up by the interest. This was a trick played by Timar especially for the benefit of Herr Athanas Brazovics; and as soon as he had bought the Monostor vineyards,

Timar set every lever in motion to prevent the council of war from beginning the fortifications on all points at the same time.

Affairs were in this position three days before the time fixed for Athalie's wedding.

Two days before it Johann Fabula came flying into Timar's house. Yes, flying—his floating cloak represented the wings.

"Ten thousand! Twenty thousand! Forty thousand! Commission paid! The emperor! The king! Pasture! The crop!" He gasped out disconnected words, which Timar at last put together.

"All right, Johann; I know what you mean. The commission has come to settle the value of the land wanted for the new works. Your fields, bought for twenty thousand, will be sold by you for forty thousand: the surplus is your profit; that is the crop—did not I tell you?"

"Yes, sir; and they were words like those of the golden-mouthed St. John. I see very clearly that you told me the truth, and I see that I get the twenty thousand gulden for nothing. Never in my life did I earn so much money by the hardest work. My senses are going. Do let me turn a somersault!"

Timar had no objection. Johann Fabula turned not one but three somersaults all across the floor, and then three back again; and then stood straight on his legs again before Timar.

"There! now I am all right again. All that money belongs to me."

He came six times that day to pay a visit to Timar. First he brought his wife, then his younger daughter, then his married daughter, afterward his son who had left college, and the fifth time the little boy who was still at school. His wife brought Timar a splendid Komorn loaf of white bread with a brown glazed crust; the married daughter a dish of beautiful Indian-corn cakes; the unmarried one a plate of red eggs, gilt nuts, and honey-cakes decorated with colored paper like a wedding present; the big boy, who was a noted bird-catcher, brought a cage full of linnets and robins; and the school-boy declaimed a rhymed ode. The whole day they overwhelmed him with gratitude, and the sixth time they all came together late in the evening and sung in his honor a song of praise out of the hymn-book.

But what will his competitors, and especially Herr Brazovics, bring

153

and sing to him when they learn how he has entrapped them about the purchase of the Monostor?

CHAPTER VII.
THE WEDDING-DRESS.

The wedding was to be in three days' time.

On Sunday afternoon Athalie went to pay visits in turn to all her school friends. It is one of the bride's privileges to pay these visits without her mother; they have so much to say to each other the last time in all their girlhood.

Frau Sophie was delighted to be allowed to stay at home one day in the year, and neither pay nor receive calls—not to act as chaperon to her daughter and listen to conversation in German, of which she did not understand a word. She could remain at home and think of her happy parlor-maid times—the days when on an idle Sunday like this she could fill her apron with ears of Indian corn, and sit down on the bench before the door picking out the grains one by one and cracking them, while she chatted and gossiped with her companions. To-day the leisure time and the boiled ears of maize were at hand, but the friends and the gossip on the bench were wanting. Frau Sophie had allowed the maid-servants and the cook to go out, that she might have the kitchen to herself; for you can not eat corn in the parlor on account of the husks which get strewn about. In the end she found suitable company. Timéa came creeping up to her. She also had no work to do. The embroidery was finished, and the dress had gone to the needle-woman, who would send it home at the last moment. Timéa was quite suited to the kitchen bench beside Frau Sophie. They were both only on sufferance in the house. The difference was that Timéa felt herself a lady, though every one looked on her as a servant; while all the world knew that Frau Sophie was the mistress of the house, and yet she felt like a servant. So Timéa perched herself on the little bench near Frau Sophie, as the nursery-maid and the cook do after quarreling all the week, when they make it up on Sunday and have a chat together.

Only three days and then the marriage!

Timéa looked cautiously round to see if any listeners were near to overhear, and then in a low voice asked, "Mamma Sophie, do tell me what is a wedding like?"

Frau Sophie drew her shoulders up and shook like a person who laughs internally, looking with half-shut eyes at the inquiring child. With the malicious delight old servants take in deceiving young ones, she encouraged the laughable simplicity of the girl. "Yes, Timéa," in the important tone of a story-teller, "that is a wonderful sight. You will see it."

"I tried once to listen at the church door," confessed Timéa, frankly; "I had crept in when a wedding was going on, but all I could see was that the bride and bridegroom stood before a lovely golden shrine."

"That was the altar."

"Then a naughty boy saw me and drove me away, calling out, 'Be off, you Turkish brat!' Then I ran away."

"You must know," began Sophie, while she took out a grain at a time and put them in her mouth, "that then comes the venerable pope, with a golden cap on his head, on his shoulders a robe of rustling silk worked with gold, and carrying a great book with clasps in his hand. He reads and sings most beautifully, and then the bridal pair kneel on the steps of the altar. The pope asks them both whether they love each other."

"And are they obliged to answer?"

"Of course, silly; and not only that, but the priest reads out of the big book an oath to the bridegroom and then afterward to the bride, that they will love and keep to each other till death divides them. They swear it by the Holy Trinity and the Blessed Virgin and all the saints, forever and ever, Amen; and the whole choir repeats the Amen. Then the priest takes the two rings from a silver dish and puts one on each of their third fingers, makes them clasp hands and winds a golden girdle round them, while the precentor and the choir sing to the organ 'Gospodi Pomiluj.'"2

[2] Lord have mercy on us.

The melancholy sound of the words "Gospodi Pomiluj" pleased Timéa. That must be some magic blessing.

"Then they cover the bridegroom and also the bride with a flowered-silk veil from head to foot, and while the pope blesses them the two witnesses hold a silver crown over each."

"Ah!"

When Frau Sophie noticed the deep interest of the girl she got warmer and warmer, and tried to inflame her fancy with the splendors of the Greek ritual. "The choir goes on singing, and the pope takes one crown and makes the bridegroom kiss it, then places it on his head and says, 'I crown thee as servant of God and husband of this handmaid of the Lord.' Then he takes the other crown, gives it to the bride to kiss, and says to her, 'I crown thee as handmaid of the Lord, and wife of this servant of God.' The deacon begins to pray for the young pair, and meanwhile the priest leads them three times round the altar, and the witnesses take off the veil which covered them. The church is full of people, who all look and whisper, 'That is a bride to be kissed. What a beautiful pair!'"

Timéa nodded her head with girlish delight, as if to say, "That is delightful; it must be lovely."

"Then the pope brings out a golden cup of wine, and the bride and bridegroom drink from it."

"Is there really wine in it?" asked Timéa in alarm. Her fear of wine came partly from the recollection of the prohibition in the Koran.

"Of course there is—real wine. Then the bride-maids and groomsmen throw maize baked in honey over them; that brings luck. It is lovely, I can tell you."

Timéa's eyes shone with the prophetic fire of a magnetic dream. She pictured these mysterious proceedings to herself as partly a rite, partly an enigma of the heart, and trembled all over. Sophie laughed in her sleeve and found this most amusing; a pity she should be disturbed in it. Manly steps approached the kitchen door, and some one came in.

What a surprise! it was Herr Katschuka.

The mistress of the house was horrified, for she had only slippers on,

157

and her apron full of maize. Which should she hide first? But Timéa was more frightened, though she had nothing to hide.

"Excuse me," said Katschuka, with familiar ease; "I found the doors all shut on the other side, so I came round by the kitchen."

"You see," screeched Frau Sophie, "my daughter has gone to visit her friends. I sent the maids to church, and we two are the only ones at home; so we just sat down in the kitchen. Pray excuse our *négligée*, Herr Captain."

"Don't disturb yourself, I will remain here with you."

"Oh, no, I could not allow it. Here in the kitchen! We have not even a chair for the captain."

But Herr Katschuka knew what to do in any emergency. "Don't make a stranger of me, Mamma Sophie. Here, this can will do for a seat," and he sat down opposite Timéa on a pail, and even set the hostess at ease with respect to the ears of maize. "That is excellent for dessert; give me a handful in my cap. I like it very much."

Frau Sophie was on the broad grin when she saw that the captain did not disdain to take the vulgar sweets in his military cap, and eat a quantity without even shelling them. It made him very popular with his mother-in-law. "I was in the midst of an interesting conversation with Timéa," began Sophie; "she was asking me about—a baptism."

Timéa was on the point of rushing away, if Frau Sophie had told the truth; but she would not have been the mother of a marriageable daughter if she had not possessed the art of turning the conversation at the entrance of an unexpected visitor.

"I was describing a baptism to her. She is quite frightened at it. Just look how she is trembling; for I was telling her that she would have to be wrapped up like a baby and carried in arms, and that she must cry like one. Don't be alarmed, you little fool. It is not true; I was only joking. Her greatest trouble is that her hair will be all spoiled."

This requires explanation. Timéa had splendid long, thick hair. Athalie amused herself by making the hairdresser execute on it the most surprising coiffures. Sometimes all the hair was combed up and built into a tower, again it was frizzed into wings on each side over the ear; in short, the girl had to appear in the most ridiculous head-dresses, such as no one had

158

ever worn, and which required unsparing use of tongs, pincers, brushes, and pomade. Athalie pretended to do this out of affection for her cousin, and the poor child had no idea how she was disfigured by it.

Herr Katschuka undeceived her. "Fraülein Timéa, you need not regret this coiffure. It would suit you much better if you wore your hair quite plain; you have such lovely hair, that it is a sin to burn it with irons and smear it with pomade. Do not allow it; it is a shame to lose any of your magnificent hair, and it is soon ruined by the ill-treatment which ladies call hairdressing—it loses its brilliancy, splits at the points, breaks easily, and falls early. You do not require all that artificial structure. Your hair is so beautiful that you need only plait it plainly, to possess the finest of all coiffures." It is possible that Herr Katschuka only said this out of a humane sympathy with the ill-treated head of hair, and meant merely to free it from the tortures inflicted on it. But his words had a deeper effect than he expected: From that moment Timéa had a feeling as if the comb in her hair was splitting her head, and could hardly bear it till the captain had gone. He did not stay long, for he took pity on Frau Sophie, who was struggling continually to hide her feet in their torn and down-trodden slippers. Herr Katschuka promised to look in again in the evening, and took his leave. He kissed Frau Sophie's hand, but made a low bow to Timéa.

Hardly was he out of the door before Timéa snatched the large comb from her hair, tore down the heaped-up plaits, destroyed the whole edifice, then went to the basin and began to wash her hair and her whole head.

"What are you doing there, girl?" said Frau Sophie, angrily. "Will you leave off this moment! Let your hair alone. Athalie will be fine and angry when she comes home and sees you."

"Let her be angry, for all I care," replied the girl, defiantly; and she wrung her locks out, sat down behind Frau Sophie, and began to put up her loosened hair into a simple threefold plait. Pride was awakened in her heart; she began to be less timid; the word of the captain infused courage into her—his wish, his taste, were laws to her. She coiled the plait simply into a knot, and wound it round her head as he had suggested. The mistress laughed to herself: this child has been made a fool of certainly!

While Timéa was plaiting her hair, Sophie came nearer and tried to wheedle her again.

"Let me tell you more about the wedding. Where did that stupid Katschuka interrupt us? If he had only known what we were talking about! Yes, I stopped where the bride and bridegroom drink from the cup, the choir and the deacon sing 'Gospodi Pomiluj.' Then the pope reads the Gospel, and the witnesses hold the crowns over the heads of the couple. The pope receives them back, lays them on the silver dish, and says to the bridegroom, 'Be praised like Abraham, and blessed like Isaac, and increase like unto Jacob;' and to the bride, 'Be praised like Sara, happy like Rebecca, and increase like Rachel'—and after this blessing the bride and bridegroom kiss each other three times before the altar and before the wedding-guests."

Timéa shut her eyes at the thought of the scene.

Athalie was not a little surprised when she came home and saw Timéa with plaited hair.

"Who allowed you to turn up your hair? Where is your giraffe comb and your bow? Put it on at once."

Timéa pressed her lips together and shook her head.

"Will you do what I tell you instantly?"

"No."

Athalie was staggered at this resistance. It was unheard of that any one should contradict her. And this from an adopted child, who ate the bread of charity, who had always been so submissive, and once even kissed her foot. "No!" said she, going toward Timéa, and bringing her face, red with anger, as close to the other's alabaster cheek as if she would set it on fire.

Frau Sophie looked on with malicious joy from her corner, and said, "Didn't I say you would catch it when Athalie returned?"

But Timéa looked straight into Athalie's flaming eyes, and repeated her "No!"

"And why not?" screamed Athalie, whose voice was now like her mother's, while her eyes were exactly like her father's.

"Because I am prettier thus," answered Timéa.

"Who told you that?"

"He."

Athalie crooked her fingers like eagles' claws, and her teeth shone

160

clinched between her red lips. It was as if she would tear the girl in pieces. Then her unbridled rage suddenly turned into scornful laughter. She left Timéa and went to her room.

Herr Katschuka paid another visit the same evening. At table Athalie overwhelmed Timéa with unwonted kindness.

"Do you not think, Herr Captain, that Timéa is much prettier with her hair dressed in this simple way?"

The captain assented. Athalie smiled. Now it was no longer a joke, but a punishment which was to be inflicted on the girl.

Only two days to the marriage. During that time Athalie overflowed with attention and tenderness to Timéa. She must not go out to the kitchen, and the servants were told to kiss her hand on entering the room. Frau Sophie often called her "little lady." The dress had come home finished, and what child-like delight it gave Timéa! She danced round it and clapped her hands.

"Come and try on your wedding costume," said Athalie, with a cruel smile.

Timéa let them put on the splendid dress she had herself embroidered. She wore no stays, and was already well formed for her age, and the dress fitted her very fairly. With what shy pleasure she looked at herself in the great mirror! Ah! how lovely she will be in her wedding finery! Perhaps she thought, too, that she would inspire love! Perhaps she felt her heart beat; and possibly a flame was already alight there which would cause her grief and pain.

But that was no matter to those who were carrying on the shameful jest. The maid who dressed her bit her lips so as not to laugh aloud. Athalie brought out the bridal wreath, and tried it on Timéa's head. The myrtle and the white jasmine became her well.

"Oh, how beautiful you will be to-morrow!"

Then they took the dress off Timéa; and Athalie said, "Now I will try it on; I should like to see how it would suit me."

She required the help of the stays to squeeze her waist into the dress, which gave her splendid figure an even more magnificent "contour." She also put on the wreath and looked at herself in the glass. Timéa sighed deeply, and whispered to Athalie, in tones of undisguised admiration, "How lovely, how lovely you are!"

It might, perhaps, have been time now to make an end of this deception. But no—she must drain the cup. First, because she is so forward; and then, because she is so stupid. She must be punished. So the contemptuous farce was carried on the whole day by all the household. The poor child's head swam with all the congratulations. She listened for Herr Katschuka, and ran away when she saw him coming.

Did he know what was going on? Quite possibly. Did it vex him? Perhaps it did not even vex him. Very likely he knew things of which the laughers did not dream, and awaited the important day with perfect indifference.

On the last morning before the marriage, Athalie said to Timéa, "To-day you must fast entirely. To-morrow is a very solemn day for you. You will be led to the altar, and there first baptized and then married; so you must fast the whole of the day before, in order to go purified to the altar."

Timéa obeyed this direction, and ate not a morsel for the entire day.

It is well known that all these adopted children have excellent appetites. Nature demands its rights; and the love of good things is the only desire which they have a chance of satisfying. But Timéa conquered that appetite. She sat at dinner and supper without touching anything, and yet they had purposely prepared her favorite dishes.

In the anteroom the maids and the cook tried to persuade her to eat secretly the delicacies which they had put aside for her, telling her she might break her fast if no one knew it. She would not be persuaded, and controlled her hunger. She helped to prepare the tarts and jellies for the wedding feast; a mass of tempting and luscious cakes lay before her, but she never touched one. And yet Athalie's example, who also was busy with the preparations for the next day, showed her that it is quite permissible to take a taste when one has a chance. She must keep her fast. She went early to bed, saying she felt chilly. And so she was, and trembled with cold even under her quilt and could not sleep. Athalie heard her teeth chattering, and was cruel enough to whisper in her ear, "To-morrow at this time where will you be?"

How should the poor child sleep, when all the slumbering feeling

162

which at this age lie in the chrysalis stage were being prematurely scared into life?

Timéa lay till dawn in a fever, and slumber never closed her eyes. Toward day-break she slept heavily; a leaden hand lay on her limbs, and even the noise which went on around her in the morning did not rouse her.

And this was the marriage-day!

Athalie ordered the servants to let Timéa sleep on; she herself let down the window curtains that the room might be dark: Timéa was only to be awakened when Athalie was already dressed in all her bridal array. That required much time, for she wished to appear to-day in the whole panoply of her beauty. From far and near numerous relations and friends had arrived to assist at the marriage of the rich Brazovics' only daughter, the prettiest girl for seven parishes round.

The guests were already beginning to assemble in the house of the bride. Her mother, Frau Sophie, had been squeezed into her new dress, and into her even more uncomfortable new shoes, by which her desire to get the day over was much increased.

The bridegroom had also arrived, with a beaming countenance, and polite as usual; but this cheerful aspect did not mean much—it was only part of his gala uniform. He had brought the bouquet for the bride. At that time camellias were unknown; the bouquet was composed of various colored roses. Herr Katschuka said as he presented it that he offered roses to the rose. As a reward, he received a proud smile from the radiant face.

Only two were wanting—Timéa and Herr Brazovics.

Timéa was not missed; no one asked after her. But every one waited most impatiently for Herr Brazovics. It was said that he had gone very early to the castle to see the governor, and his return was impatiently expected. Even the bride went several times to the window and looked out for papa's carriage.

Only the bridegroom showed no anxiety. But where could Herr Brazovics be? Yesterday evening he had been in a very good temper. He had been amusing himself with his friends, and invited all his acquaintances to the wedding. Late in the night he had knocked at Herr Katschuka's window, and called to him, instead of "Good-night," "The hundred thousand gulden will be all ready to-morrow." And he had good reason to be in such a merry mood. The governor of the fortress had informed him that the plans had been accepted to their full extent by the war department: the expropriation was arranged. Even the money had been paid for that part which lay on the ground between the two river branches; and the others concerned had received notice that this very night they would obtain the signature of the minister. It was as good as having the money in one's pocket. The next morning, Herr Brazovics could hardly await the usual hour of reception, and arrived so early in the ante-chamber of the governor, that no one else was there. The governor did not keep him waiting, but called him in at once.

"A little misfortune," said he.

"Well, if it is not a great one—"

"Have you ever heard of the privy council?"

"Never."

"Nor I. For fifteen years I never heard it spoken of. But it does exist, and has just given a sign of life. As I told you, the minister had agreed to the execution of the fortifications and the necessary purchase of land. Then from some unknown source evidence was brought forward by which many disadvantageous circumstances were discovered. It would not do to compromise the minister, so they called the council together, which had not been heard of for fifteen years, except when its members drew their salary and had their band to play. The council, when this questionable affair was submitted to it, found a wise solution: it agreed to the decision in principle, but divided its execution into two parts. The fortifications on the river-side are to be provided for at once, but the Monostor section is only to be begun when the other is finished. So the owners of the Monostor land will have the pleasure of waiting eighteen or twenty years for their money. Good-morning, Herr Brazovics."

Herr Athanas could not utter a syllable. There was no help for it. The profit so certainly counted on was gone—gone also those other hundred thousand gulden which were buried in vineyards of no value, which are now worthless. He saw all his castles in the air destroyed: his beautiful house, his cargo-ships on the Danube, the lighted church with the brilliant company, they were only a *fata morgana*, blown away with the mirage of the Monostor

164

forts by the first puff of wind—melted into nothing, like the light cloud which obscures the sun.

Ah! here comes Timéa!

At last she had had her sleep out. In the twilight of the curtained room it had taken her long to rouse herself; she dressed like one in a feverish dream, and groped sleepily through the adjoining rooms, all empty, till she came to the one where Athalie had dressed. When she entered the bright room full of flowers and presents, she remembered for the first time that this was her wedding-day.

When she saw Herr Katschuka with the bouquet in his hand, the thought shot across her that this was the bridegroom; and when she cast a glance on Athalie she thought, "That is my wedding-dress." As she stood there in her astonishment, with wide eyes and open mouth, she was a sight for laughing and weeping.

The servants, the guests, Frau Sophie, could not contain their merriment.

But Athalie stepped forward majestically, took hold of the little thing's delicate chin with her white-gloved hand, and said, smiling, "To-day, my little treasure, you must allow me to be the one to go to the altar. You, my child, must go to school and wait five years before you are married, if indeed any one proposes to you."

Timéa stood as if petrified, and let her folded hands fall into her lap. She did not blush or become paler. There was no name for what she felt.

Perhaps Athalie knew that this cruel jest was not calculated to enhance her charms, and tried to lessen its effect. "Come, Timéa," she said; "I only waited for you. Come and put on my veil."

The bridal veil!

Timéa took the veil with stiffened fingers, and went toward Athalie. It was to be fastened to her hair with a golden arrow.

Timéa's hand trembled, and the arrow was heavy: it would not go through the thick hair. At an impatient movement of Athalie's its blunt point pricked the lovely bride's head slightly.

"You are too stupid for anything!" cried Athalie, angrily, and struck Timéa on the hand. Her eyebrows contracted. Scolded, struck, on such a day, and in the presence of that man! Two heavy drops formed in her eyes and rolled down her white cheek. I trow those two drops turned the scale held by the Great Judge's hand, from which happiness and misery are measured out to man.

Athalie tried to excuse her hastiness by her feverish excitement. A bride may be pardoned if she is nervous and irritable at the last moment. The witnesses, the bride-maids, are ready, and the bride's father has not yet arrived.

Every one was uneasy; only the bridegroom was quite composed.

A message had come from the church that the pope was ready and waiting for the bridal pair. Already the bells are ringing, as is the custom at grand weddings. Athalie's heart beats high with vexation that her father does not come. One messenger after another is sent for him. At last his glass coach is seen approaching. Here he is at last!

The bride steps up to the mirror once more, to see if her veil falls in the right folds. She puts her bracelets and necklace straight.

Meanwhile, a curious sound is heard below, as if many people were rushing upstairs together. Mysterious noises and smothered exclamations are heard in the next room; every one presses thither; the bride-maids and friends run out to see what it is; but it is remarkable that none of them return.

Athalie hears her mother scream. Well, she generally screams even when she is talking quietly.

"Do see what has happened," says Athalie to her bridegroom.

The captain goes out, and Athalie remains alone with Timéa, the suppressed whispering grows louder. At last even Athalie becomes uneasy.

The bridegroom returns. He remains standing at the open door, and says thence to his bride, "Herr Brazovics is dead."

The bride throws her arms into the air and falls swooning backward. If Timéa had not caught her in her arms, she would have struck her head on the marble table behind her. The lovely, haughty face of the bride is whiter even than Timéa's; and Timéa, while she holds Athalie's head on her breast, thinks, "See how the beautiful wedding-dress lies in the dust!"

The bridegroom stands at the door and looks at Timéa, then turning away suddenly, he leaves the house amid the universal confusion.

He does not even take the trouble to lift his bride from the ground.

CHAPTER VIII.
TIMÉA.

"How the beautiful dress lies in the dust!"

Instead of the wedding feast there followed the funeral banquet, and in the place of the embroidered robe came the mourning garments.

Black! The color which makes rich and poor alike.

Athalie and Timéa were dressed alike in black. And if the mourning had consisted only in the wearing of its outward garb! But with the sudden death of Herr Athanas, all the birds of ill omen had collected, as the ravens come and sit in long lines on the roof before a great storm.

The first croak was, that the bridegroom sent back his engagement-ring. He did not appear at the funeral to lend his bride a supporting arm as she followed the coffin half fainting; for in this little town it was the custom that the mourners, whether gentle or simple, should follow their dead on foot and with bare heads to the burial-ground.

There were some who blamed this course of action in Katschuka, and did not consider it an excuse that, as Herr Brazovics had not kept to the condition of handing over the dowry beforehand, the bridegroom was justified in considering himself freed from his obligations. There are a few narrow-minded people who can find no excuse for such a withdrawal. Then came the ravens and sat on the roof. One creditor after another appeared and demanded his money. And then the whole house of cards collapsed.

The first who spoke of a suit at law blew the concern into the air. When once the avalanche begins to roll, it never stops till it gets to the foot of the hill.

It was soon ascertained that the fears of the bridegroom, who had got safely away, were only too well founded. In the affairs of Herr Brazovics there figured so many investments apparently sound but really unprofitable, such false calculations, unsecured debts, and imaginary securities, that when order was brought into this chaos, the whole property did not suffice to satisfy the creditors. Besides, it came to light that he had used moneys intrusted to his honor: orphans' capital, church endowments, hospital funds, the deposits of his ship captains. The floods rose over the roof of the house, and these floods brought mire and dirt with them; and what they left behind was—shame.

Timéa too lost her whole property. The orphan's trust-money had never been invested at all.

Every day lawyers, magistrates' clerks, bailiffs, came to the house. They sealed each box and closet; they did not ask the ladies for permission to visit them; unannounced they bounced in at any hour of the day, ransacked the rooms, and gave vent to reproaches and curses on the dead man, so loud that the mourning women could not but hear them. All they found in the house was taken out in turn and appraised, down to the pictures, with and without their frames; even the wedding-dress, without a bride, did not escape this fate. And then they decided on the date, and had it posted on the door, on which everything was to be sold by auction—everything, not excepting the embroidered dress. The last lot would be the house itself; and when it was sold the former owners could go their way wheresoever they chose, and the beautiful Athalie might look up to Heaven and ask where she was henceforth to lay her haughty head. Where indeed?—she, the orphaned daughter of a fraudulent bankrupt, to whom not even her good name was left, whom no one wanted, not even herself. Of all the treasures she possessed, only two valuable souvenirs remained which she had hidden from the bailiffs—an onyx box and the returned engagement-ring. The box she had concealed in her pocket; and when alone at night, she drew it out and looked at its precious contents. There were all sorts of poison in it. By some odd freak, Athalie had bought it in one of her Italian journeys, and while it was in her possession she thought she could defy the world. She imagined herself able to destroy her own life at any moment, and this idea made her feel as a despot to her parents and her lover. If they do not do all she wishes, the box is there; she need only choose the swiftest poison, and in the morning they would find her a corpse. Now a great temptation assailed her; life lay before her as a desolate waste; the father had made his child a beggar, and the bridegroom had forsaken his bride.

Athalie rose from her bed: she looked into the open box, and sought among the various poisons.

Then she suddenly discovered that she was afraid of death! She had not strength to cast life away; she gazed at herself in the glass—was all that beauty to be annihilated?

She shut the box and put it away. Then she brought out the other jewel, the ring. There is a poison in that too, and of a yet more deadly sort, for it kills the soul. But she has the courage to swallow it—to intoxicate herself with it. She had loved the man who gave her this ring—not only so, but she was still madly in love with him. The poison-box gives bad advice—the ring even worse. Athalie begins to dress; there is no one to help her—the servants have all left the house, Frau Sophie and Timéa are sleeping in the maids' room; the official seal has been attached to the doors of the public apartments. Athalie does not wake the sleepers, but dresses alone. How far the night has passed she can not tell; no one winds up the splendid clocks, now that they are to pass under the hammer. One points to eight o'clock, another to three, but it does not matter. Athalie finds the key of the street-door, and creeps out, leaving all open behind her. Who is likely to be robbed? and besides, who would, like her, venture alone in the dark streets?

At that time the streets of Komorn were decidedly dark at night. One lamp at the Trinity pillar, one at the town-hall, and a third at the main guard—no others anywhere. Athalie takes the road to the Promenade, the so-called Anglia. It is a region of evil reputation. A dark lane between the town and the fort, in which at night fallen women with painted faces and disheveled hair loiter, when they are driven from their haunts on the "little square." Athalie is sure to meet such creatures if she goes by the Anglia. But she is not afraid. The poison she sucked out of the golden ring has taken away from her fear of these impure forms. One only shrinks from the gutter as long as one has kept clear of it.

At the corner stands a sentry: she must try to creep past him without being seen and challenged.

The corner house has a colonnade leading to the square. Here in the day-time the bread-sellers have their stand. Athalie chooses her path through this arcade, as it hides her from the sentry's eyes.

In walking quickly she stumbled over something. It was a ragged woman, quite drunk, lying across the threshold. The half-human creature whom her foot touched gave vent to filthy curses. Athalie took no notice, but stepped aside from the obstacle; she felt easier when she turned the corner toward the Promenade. The light of the main-guard lamp had now disappeared, and she found herself under the gloom of the trees. Through the juniper-bushes shone a ray from a lighted window. Athalie followed that guiding star. There lay the dwelling of the engineer officer. She seized the lion-headed knocker at the little door, over which was painted the double eagle; her hand trembled as she raised it in order to knock gently, and at the sound the soldier-servant came out and opened to her.

"Is the captain in?" asked Athalie.

The fellow nodded, grinning. Yes—he was at home. He had often seen Athalie, and many a pretty bright coin had rolled into his hand from her delicate fingers, when he carried the beautiful lady flowers or choice fruit from his master.

The captain was up and at work; his room was simply furnished, without any luxury. On the walls hung maps and surveying instruments; the strictest military simplicity surprise the in-comer, as well as a penetrating smell of tobacco, which adhered to the books and furniture, and was perceptible even when no one was smoking. Athalie had never seen the captain's room. The house to which he was to have taken her on their marriage-day was very different, but it had been taken possession of by the creditors with all its contents on that very morning. She had only looked in at the window when she walked with her mother on the Promenade in the afternoon to hear the band play.

Herr Katschuka started up in alarm. He was not prepared for a lady's visit; the three top buttons of his violet tunic were unbuttoned, contrary to regulations, and he had laid aside his horsehair cravat. Athalie remained standing at the door with hanging arms and her head down: the captain hastened to her.

"In God's name, fraülein, what are you doing here? What are you here for?" She could not speak—she sunk on his breast and sobbed wildly. He did not embrace her. "Sit down, fraülein," said he, leading her to the plain leather sofa, and then his first care was to put on his cravat again. He drew a chair near the divan and sat down opposite Athalie. "What do you want,

171

fraülein?"

She dried her tears and looked with her radiant eyes long at the captain, as if thus to tell him why she came. Will he not understand?

No, he understood nothing. When she was obliged to break silence, she began to tremble as if with ague.

"Sir," she said, with a quivering voice, "as long as I was prosperous, you were very devoted to me. Is nothing left of that affection?"

"Fraülein," answered Katschuka, with cold politeness, "I shall always be your devoted friend. The blow which fell on you struck me too—we have both lost our all. I am in despair, for I see no means of resuscitating my hopes reduced to ashes. My profession imposes conditions on me which I can not fulfill: it is not allowed to those of us who have no private means to marry."

"I know it," said Athalie, "and it was not that which I wished to suggest to you. We are now very poor, but there may be some favorable turn in our lot. My father has a rich uncle in Belgrade whose heirs we are; at his death we shall be rich again. I will wait for you—do you wait for me. Take back your ring—take me to your mother, and let me stay with her as your betrothed. I will wait for you till you fetch me away, and will be a good daughter to your mother."

Herr Katschuka sighed so deeply that he nearly blew out the light which stood before him. "Alas, fraülein," said he, taking up the golden circle from the table, "that is, unhappily, quite impossible. You little know my mother. She is an ambitious woman—an inaccessible nature. She lives on a small pension, and loves no one. You have no idea what struggles I have had with my mother about my *affaires du cœur*. She is a baroness by birth, and has never consented to this union. She would not come to our marriage. I could not take you to her, fraülein—on your account I have quarreled with her."

Athalie's breast heaved feverishly, her face glowed; she seized with both her hands that of her faithless bridegroom, on which the ring was wanting, and whispered, while tears ran down her cheeks, so low that even the deaf walls could not hear, "You—you have braved your mother for me: I will defy the whole world for you!"

Katschuka dared not meet the speaking eyes of the lovely woman. He

172

drew geometrical figures on the table with the golden circle he still held, as if he would decipher from their angles of incidence the difference between love and madness.

The girl continued in a whisper, "I am already so deeply humiliated that no shame can bring me lower; I have no more to lose in this world. If you were not here, I should have already killed myself. I belong not to myself, but to you—say, what shall I be to you? I have lost my senses, and all is the same to me; kill me, if you choose—I will not stir."

Herr Katschuka, during this passionate speech, had worked out the problem of what he was to answer. "Fraülein Athalie, I will speak frankly—you know I am an honest man."

Athalie had not asked him about that.

"An honest and chivalrous man would be ashamed to take advantage of the misfortune of a woman for the satisfaction of his lowest passions. I will give you good advice as a well-meaning friend, as one who has a boundless respect for you. You tell me you have an uncle in Belgrade: go to him. He is your blood relation, and must receive you in a friendly way. I give you my word of honor that I will not marry, and if we meet again I shall always bring you the same feelings which for years I have experienced toward you."

He told no lie when he gave this promise. But from what his face showed at this moment, Athalie could read what he did not say—that the captain neither now nor for years past had loved her, that he loved another, and if this other was poor and made a beggar, he had good reason to promise on his word of honor that he would not marry. This it was which Athalie read in the cool expressions of her faithless bridegroom. And then something flashed through her brain like lightning. Her eyes flashed too.

"Will you come to-morrow," she asked him, "to escort me to my uncle in Belgrade?"

"I will come," Katschuka hastened to reply. "But now go home. Did any one come with you?"

"I came quite alone."

"What imprudence! Who is to take you back?"

"You need not," she said, bitterly. "If at this hour any one saw us together, what a scandal it would be—for you. I can walk alone. I am not afraid. I have no longer anything worth stealing."

"My servant shall follow you."

"He shall do nothing of the sort. The patrol might arrest the poor devil. After the last post he must not be seen in the streets. I will find my way alone. So then—to-morrow—"

"I will be with you by eight o'clock."

Athalie wrapped herself in her black cloak, and hurried away before Katschuka had time to open the door for her. It seemed to her as if the captain was putting on his sword almost before she had left his door. Is he perhaps going to follow her in the distance?

She stopped at the corner of the Anglia, but no one was following. She ran home in the darkness, and as she hastened through the deep night she concocted a plan in her head. If only the captain once sits by her in the carriage, if he goes with her to Belgrade, he will see that no power on earth can deliver him from her. As she passed through the long market-hall, she stumbled again over the same female figure as it lay on the stones. This time it did not awake nor curse her. What sound sleep these wretches enjoy! But when Athalie got to the door of her home, a thought sunk like lead into her mind. What if the captain was only so ready with his promise of escorting her to Belgrade in order to get rid of her? What if he does not come to-morrow, either at eight or later? A torturing jealousy excited her nerves. When she reached the anteroom, she felt about on the table for the candle and matches she had left there. Instead of these her hand touched a knife—a sharp cook's knife with a heavy handle. This also sheds light on darkness. She grasped the knife and walked up and down. Her teeth chattered: the thought was working in her, how if she were to drive this knife into the heart of that girl with the white face, who sleeps beside her? That would be an end of them both. They would convict her of the murder, and so she would get out of the world.

But Timéa is not sleeping there now.

Athalie only remembered when she had gone to the bed in which Timéa usually slept, that she was sleeping with Frau Sophie to-night. The knife fell from her hand, and then she was frightened. She began to feel how lonely she was, how dark was all around her, dark too in her own soul.

The roll of a drum awoke Athalie out of a distressing dream. She dreamed of a young lady who had murdered her rival, and was led to the place of execution. Already she knelt on the scaffold, the headsman with his naked sword stood behind her, the judge read the sentence and said, "With God there is pardon." The drum beat, then Athalie awoke.

It was the auctioneer's drum. The bidding had begun; but that drum is even more dreadful than the one which gives the signal of death. To listen, when the voice which penetrates even to the street calls out the well-known old favorite things which only yesterday were our own! "Once, twice; any advance?" and then "thrice!" and the drum rolls and the hammer falls. Then it begins again, "Once, twice; any advance?"

Athalie put on her mourning-dress, the only one left to her, and went to find some one. There were only her mother and Timéa to look for. They would probably be in the kitchen.

Both had long been up and dressed. Frau Sophie was as round as a tub. Knowing well enough that no one would search her, she had put on a dozen dresses one over the other, and hidden a few napkins and silver spoons in her pockets. She could hardly move. Timéa was in her simple black every-day dress, and was preparing warm milk and coffee. At the sight of Athalie, Frau Sophie broke into loud sobs, and hung on her neck. "Oh, my dear, darling, pretty daughter! What have we come to, and what will become of us? Oh, that we had not lived to see this day! This dreadful drum woke you, I suppose?"

"Is it not yet eight o'clock?" asked Athalie. The kitchen clock was still going.

"Not eight? Why, the auction began at nine. Can you not hear it?"

"Has no one been to see us?"

"Silly idea! Why, who should visit us at such a time?"

Athalie said no more, but sat down on the bench—the same little seat on which Frau Sophie had described to Timéa the splendid wedding ceremony.

Timéa prepared the breakfast, toasted the bread, and laid the kitchen table for the two ladies. Athalie did not heed the invitation, however much pressed by Frau Sophie. "Drink, my dear, my own pretty! Who knows where

175

we shall get coffee to-morrow? The whole world is against us, and every one abuses and curses us. What will become of us?" But that did not hinder her from gulping down her cup of coffee. Athalie was thinking of the journey to Belgrade, and of her expected traveling companion.

Frau Sophie's mind was much occupied with original notions on easy modes of death. "If there were only a pin in the coffee that it might stick in my throat and choke me." Then the wish arose that the flat-iron would fall down from the shelf as she passed and crush her skull. She would be glad, too, if one of the earthquakes which occasionally occur in Komorn would happen now, and bury the house and all in it. As, however, none of these ways of dying came to pass, and Athalie would not speak, there was nothing left but to vent her wrath on Timéa. "She takes it easily, the ungrateful creature! She is not even crying; indeed it is easy for her to laugh—she can go to service, or work with a milliner and keep herself; she will be glad to be quit of us, and live on her own hook. You just wait, you will soon have to remember us. You'll be sorry—before a year is over you'll repent fast enough." Timéa had done nothing to repent of, but Frau Sophie saw it in the future, and her anger was only surpassed by the grief she felt about Athalie. "What will become of you, you sweet and only darling? Who will take care of you? What will become of your pretty white hands?"

"There, go and leave me in peace," said Athalie, shaking her lamenting mother off her neck. "Go and look out of the window and see if any one is coming up to us."

"Nobody, nobody!—who should be coming?"

Time went on; drum and bid succeeded each other; whenever the kitchen clock struck, Athalie started up, and then let her head fall into her hands again and stared before her. The roses on her cheeks took a violet shade, her lips were blue, an olive shadow darkened her exquisite face; her staring eyes, with deep marks below them, her swollen lips, her painfully contracted eyebrows, turned the ideal beauty into an image of horror. She sat like a fallen angel driven from heaven. It was already noon, and he for whom she waited never came. The noise of the sale came nearer and nearer. The auctioneer went from room to room; they had begun in the outer rooms, now they were coming to the reception-rooms, at whose far end was the kitchen.

Frau Sophie, in spite of her despair, had her senses about her enough to notice that the bidding was very quick. Hardly was anything put up before the drum beat, and "any advance?" was cried. The buyers standing in groups complained, "No one has a chance—the man is mad. Who can this fool be?"

Now only the kitchen department is left, but no one enters it. Outside, the drum is heard, "No one will give more?" It has been bought as a whole, unseen—by some fool.

It struck Frau Sophie, too, that people did not hasten to fetch the lots they bought out of the rooms, as usual at an auction; here nothing is touched. Now comes the principal lot, and every one goes down to the yard, for the house itself is being put up. The buyers press round the table of the official auctioneer; the upset price is named. Then some one makes an offer in a low voice. Among the crowd arises a confused noise, tones of astonishment, laughter, hissing; the people scatter, and again one hears, "He must be a fool." Grumbling and angry, all go away. "Once, twice, thrice!" the hammer falls. The house has found a purchaser.

"Now it's time to go, my sweet darling daughter. We will look out for the last time. If only the tower of St. John's Church would fall and crush us all together!" But Athalie sat on the bench, waiting and waiting, and looking at the clock. It points to two. One little ray of hope still shone through the Egyptian darkness—perhaps it was the dread of pushing through the crowd of bidders which had kept the captain from coming; perhaps he will appear as soon as the yard is clear.

"Don't you hear some one coming?"

"No, my beauty, I hear nothing."

"Yes, mother, I hear some one creeping upstairs gently, on tiptoe."

In truth soft steps approach. Some one knocks at the kitchen door, like a polite visitor who begs permission to enter, and waits till it is given him; and then the door opens gently, and in comes, with hat off, and courteous bow—Michael Timar Levetinczy. He remained standing near the door after saluting the ladies. Athalie rose with an expression of disappointment and hatred; Frau Sophie wrung her hands, and looked up with a mixture of hope and fear; Timéa met his gaze with gentle calmness.

177

"I," began Timar, sending his "I" in advance like a pope in his bull—"I have had this house and all its saleable contents knocked down to me at the auction. I did not buy it for myself, but for the one person in it who is not to be bought, and yet is the only treasure on earth in my sight. . . . Fraülein Timéa, from this day forward you are the mistress of this house. Everything in it belongs to you—the clothes, the jewels in the wardrobes, the horses in the stable, the securities in the safe—all is inscribed in your name, and the creditors are satisfied. You are the owner of the house—accept it from me; and if there is a corner in it where there is room for a quiet fellow who would only impose on you his respect and admiration, and if this corner could be given to me—if there was a little shelter for me in your heart, and you did not refuse my hand—then I should be only too happy, and would swear that the whole aim of my life would be to make you as happy as you made me."

Timéa's face beamed at these words with maidenly pride. A mixture of inexpressible pain, noble gratitude, and holy sacrifice lighted up her countenance. "Thrice, thrice," her lips stammered, but without a sound, only her sympathetic nerves heard what she wanted to utter. This man had so often saved her; he was always so good to her; he had never made sport of her, nor flattered her, and now he gives her all her heart could desire. All? No, all but one thing, and that is gone; it belongs to another.

Timar waited quietly for an answer. Timéa remained silent.

"Do not answer hastily, Fraülein Timéa," he said. "I will await your decision. I will come to-morrow, or in a week, or whenever you like to give me an answer. You are mistress of all I have handed over to you; I attach no conditions to it; it is all registered in your name. If you do not wish to see me here again, it only costs you one word; take a week or a month or a year to consider what you will answer."

Timéa stepped forward with decision from behind the stove where the other two women had pushed her, and approached Michael.

In her manner lay a precocious gravity, which lent to her face a womanly dignity. Since that eventful wedding-day she had ceased to be a child; she had become serious and silent. She looked calmly into Michael's face, and said, "I have already decided."

Frau Sophie listened with envious malice for Timéa's answer. If only she would say to Timar, "I don't want you—go away!" Anything is possible from such an idiot of a girl, who has had another man put in her head. And if Timar, just to revenge himself, were to say, "Well then, stay as you are; you shall have neither the house nor my hand, I will offer both to Fraülein Athalie"—and if he were to marry Athalie! As if cases had not been heard of in which an honest lover was refused by some stuck-up girl, and then out of pique offered his hand to the governess, or proposed to the housemaid on the spot! This hope of Frau Sophie's, however, was not destined to be fulfilled.

Timéa gave her hand to Timar, and said in a low but firm voice, "I accept you as my husband."

Michael grasped the offered hand—not with the fire of a passionate lover, but with the homage of a man, and looked long into the unearthly beauty of the girl's eyes.

And the girl allowed him to read her soul. She repeated her words: "I accept you as my husband, and will be a faithful and obedient wife; I only ask one favor—you will not refuse me?"

Happiness made Michael forget that a merchant should never sign his name to a blank sheet of paper. "Oh, speak! what you desire is already done."

"My request is," said Timéa, "if you take me to wife, and this house becomes yours again, and I the mistress in your house, that you should allow my adopted mother who received me, an orphan, and my adopted sister with whom I have grown up, to remain here with me. Regard them as my mother and sister, and treat them as kindly."

An involuntary tear fell from Timar's eye. Timéa noticed it, seized his right hand with hers, and made a new attack on his heart. "You will, I know you will do as I ask you; and you will give back to Athalie all that was hers?—her nice clothes and jewels; and she will stay with us, and you will be the same to her as if she were my own sister; and you will treat Mamma Sophie as I do, and call her mother?"

Frau Sophie, hearing this, began to sob aloud. She sunk on her knees before Timéa, and covered her hands, her dress, even her feet with unceasing kisses, while she murmured broken and inaudible words.

179

In the next moment Timar was himself again, and the far-seeing vision came to his aid, which at any critical time raised him above his rivals. His quick invention whispered to him what must be done to provide against future complications. He took Timéa's little hands in his. "You are a noble creature, Timéa. You will permit me henceforward to call you by your name? and I will not disgrace your good heart. Stand up, Mamma Sophie; do not cry; tell Athalie she might come nearer to me. I will do more than Timéa asked, for love of her, and for you two; I will provide for Athalie not only a place of refuge, but a happy home of her own; I will pay the deposit for her bridegroom, and give her the dowry which her father had promised to her. May they be happy together."

Timar had foreseen things still below the horizon, and thought that no sacrifice would be too great to get the two women out of the house and away from Timéa, and to manage that the handsome captain should be married to the lovely Athalie.

But now it was his turn to be overwhelmed with kisses and gratitude by Frau Sophie. "Oh, Herr von Levetinczy! Oh, dear, generous Herr von Levetinczy! let me kiss your hand, your feet, your clever head." And she did as set forth in her programme, and kissed besides his shoulders, coat-collar, and his back, at last embracing both Timar and Timéa in her arms, and bestowing her valuable blessing upon them. "Be happy together!"

It was impossible to help laughing at the way the poor woman expressed her joy. But Athalie poisoned all their pleasure.

Proud as a fallen angel who is asked to return, and who prefers damnation to humbling her pride, she turned away from Timar, and said in a voice choked with passion, "I thank you, sir. But I never wish to hear of Herr Katschuka again, either in this world or the next! I will never be his wife; I will remain here with Timéa—as her servant."

180

BOOK THIRD.—THE OWNERLESS ISLAND.

CHAPTER I.
THE MARRIAGE OF THE MARBLE STATUE.

Timar was intensely happy at being engaged to Timéa.

The unearthly beauty of the girl had captivated his heart at first sight. He admired her then, and afterward the sweet nature which he learned to appreciate won his respect. The shameful trick played on her in the house of Brazovics awoke in him a chivalrous sympathy. The airy courtship of the captain aroused his jealousy; all these were symptoms of love, and at last he had reached the goal of his wishes: the lovely maiden was his, and would be his wife.

And a great burden was lifted from his soul—self-reproach; for from the day when Timar found the treasures of Ali Tschorbadschi in the sunken ship, his peace was gone. After each brilliant success of any of his undertakings, the voice of the accuser rose in his breast "This does not belong to you—it was the property of an orphan which you usurped. You a lucky man? You a man of gold? It is not true! Benefactor of the poor? Not true! Not true! You are a thief!"

Now the suit is decided. The inward judge acquits him. The defrauded orphan receives back her property, and in double measure, for whatever belongs to her husband is hers too. She will never know that the foundation of this great fortune was once hers; she only knows it is hers now—thus fate is reconciled.

But is it really reconciled? Timar forgot the sophism that he offered Timéa something besides the treasures which were hers—himself—and in exchange demanded the girl's heart, and that this was a deception, and like taking her by force.

He wished to hasten the wedding. There was no need of delay on account of the trousseau, for he had bought everything in Vienna. Timéa's wedding-dress was made by the best Parisian house, and the bride was not obliged to work at it herself for six weeks, as at that other. That double unlucky dress was buried in a closet which no one ever opened; it would never be brought out again.

But other hinderances of an ecclesiastical nature presented themselves—Timéa was still unbaptized. It was only natural that Timar should wish Timéa, when she left the Moslem faith for Christianity, to enter at once the Protestant Church to which he belonged, so that they might worship together after their marriage. But then the Protestant minister announced it as an indispensable condition of conversion that neophytes should be instructed in the creed of that church into which they were to be received. Here a great difficulty arose. The Mohammedan religion has nothing to say to women in its dogmas. To a Moslem a woman is no more than a flower which fades and falls, whose soul is its fragrance, which the wind carries away, and it is gone. Timéa had no creed.

The very reverend gentleman found his task by no means easy when he tried to convince Timéa of the superiority of the Christian religion. He had converted Jews and Papists, but he had never tried it with a Turkish girl.

On the first day, when the minister was explaining the splendors of the other world, and declaring that there all who in this world had loved each other would be reunited, the girl put this question to him—"Would those meet who had loved each other, or only those whom the minister had united?" This was a ticklish question; but the reverend gentleman answered, from his own puritanical point of view, that only those could possibly love each other who were united by the church, and that it was of course impossible for those who were thus united *not* to love each other. But he was careful not to repeat this question to Herr Timar.

The next day Timéa asked him whether her father, Ali Tschorbadschi, would also arrive in that world to which she was going?

To this delicate question the minister was unable to give a satisfactory reply.

"But is it not the case that I shall there still be the wife of Herr Levetinczy?" asked Timéa, with lively curiosity. To this the Herr Pastor was glad to reply, with gracious readiness, that that would certainly be the case.

"Well, then, I shall ask Herr Levetinczy, when we both go to heaven, to keep a little place for my father, that he may be with us; and surely he will not refuse me?"

The reverend gentleman scratched his ear violently, and thought he had better lay this difficult point before the church synod.

The third day he said to Timar that it would be best to baptize and marry the young lady at once: then her husband could give her instruction in the other dogmas.

The next Sunday the sacred rite was celebrated. Timéa then for the first time entered a Protestant church. The simple building, with its whitewashed walls and unornamented chancel, made a very different impression on her mind from that other church, out of which the naughty boys had chased her when she peeped in. There were golden altars, great wax tapers burning in silver candelabra, pictures, incense filling the air, mysterious chants, and people sinking on their knees at the sound of a bell. Here sat long rows of men and women apart, each with their book before them, and after the precentor had set the tune, all the congregation joined in unison. Then silence, and the minister mounted the high pulpit and began to preach without any ceremony. He did not sing, nor drink from the chalice, nor show any holy relics—only talk, talk on.

Timéa sat in the first row with her sponsors, who led her to the font, where another long sermon was preached. At last it was over; the neophyte bowed her head over the basin, and the minister baptized her, in the name of the Trinity, "Susanna." She wondered why she should be called Susanna, as she was quite satisfied with her own name.

Then they all sat down again and sung the eighty-third psalm, "Oh, God of Israel," which awoke in Timéa a slight doubt as to whether she had not been turned into a Jewess.

All her doubts vanished, however, when another minister arose, and read from the chancel a document which set forth that the noble Herr Michael Timar von Levetinczy, of the Swiss Protestant Church, had betrothed himself to Fraülein Timéa Susanna von Tschorbadschi, also of the Swiss Protestant religion.

Two more weeks must pass before the marriage. Michael spent every day with Timéa. The girl always received him with frank cordiality, and he was happy in his anticipations of the future. He generally found Athalie with his bride, but she made some pretext for leaving the room, and her mother took her place.

184

Mamma Sophie entertained Michael with praises of his bride—what a dear girl she was, and how often she spoke of her kind, good Michael, who had taken such care of her on board the "St. Barbara." Sophie had heard every little detail, which only Timéa could have known, and Michael was delighted to find that she remembered so well.

"If you only knew, dear Levetinczy, how fond the girl is of you!" And Timéa was not confused when she heard Frau Sophie say this. She affected no modest contradiction, but did not strengthen the assurance by any shy blushes. She allowed Timar to hold her hand in his and look into her eyes, and when he came and went she smiled at him.

At last the wedding-day arrived. Troops of guests streamed in from all parts, a long row of carriages stood in the street, as on that other ill-omened day; but this time no misfortune occurred.

The bridegroom fetched the bride out of the house of Brazovics, which was now her own, and took her to the church, but the wedding banquet was in the bridegroom's house. Frau Sophie would not be denied the task of arranging everything. Athalie remained at home and looked from behind the curtain, through the same window at which she had awaited the arrival of her own bridegroom, while the long row of carriages was set in motion.

And there she waited till they all went past again after the marriage, bride and bridegroom now in the same carriage, and looked after them. And if during this time the whole congregation had prayed for the young couple, we may be sure that she also sent a—prayer—after them.

Timéa had not found the ceremony as impressive as Frau Sophie had described it to her. The clergyman did not wear a golden robe or miter himself, nor did he bring out any silver crowns to crown them as lord or lady to each other. The bridegroom wore a velvet coat, as nobles did then, with agraffes and fur on it. He looked a fine man, but he held his head down; he was not yet used to carry it proudly, as beseems the gala suit of a noble. There was no veil wound round the two, no drinking from the same cup, no procession round the altar and holy kiss, not even any altar at all; only a black-robed minister, who said wise things no doubt, but which had not the mysterious charm of the "Gospodi Pomiluj." The Protestant marriage,

185

deprived of all ceremony, leaves the Oriental fancy, with its desire for excitement, quite cold. And Timéa only understood the external ceremony as yet.

The brilliant banquet came to an end; the guests went away, the bride remained in the bridegroom's house.

When Timar was alone with Timéa, when he sat by her side and took her hand, he felt his heart beat and its pulsation spread through his whole frame. . . . The unspeakable treasure which was the goal of all his desires is in his possession. He has only to stretch out his arm and draw her to his breast. He dares not do it—he is as if bound by a spell. The wife, the baroness, does not shrink at his approach. She does not tremble or glow. If only she would cast her eyes down in alarm when Michael's hand touched her shoulder! If only the warm reflex of a shy blush passed over her pale face, the spell would be broken. But she remains as calm and cold and passionless as a somnambulist. Michael sees before him the same figure which he awoke from death on that eventful night—the same which lay on the bed before him like an altar-picture which radiates cold to the spectator, and whose face never changed when her night-dress slipped from her shoulders, nor even when told that her father was dead—not even when Timar whispered into her ear, "Beloved!"

She is a marble statue—a statue which bows, dresses itself, submits, but is not alive. She sees, but her glance neither encourages nor alarms. He can do what he likes with her. She allows him to let down her lovely bright hair, and spread the locks over her shoulders; she allows his lips to approach her white face, and his hot breath to touch her cheek: but it kindles no responsive warmth in her. Michael thinks if he were to press the icy form to his breast, the charm would be broken; but in the act of doing it, an even greater emotion overcomes him. He starts back as if he was about to commit a crime against which nature, his guardian angel, every sensitive nerve in him protested. "Timéa," he whispered to her in caressing murmurs, "do you know that you are my wife?"

Timéa looked at him and answered, "Yes, I know it."

"Do you love me?"

Then she opened wide her large dark eyes, and as he looked into them it seemed to him as if he were granted a glimpse into all the mysteries of the starry heavens. Then she veils them again with her silky lashes.

"Do you feel no love for me?" entreats the husband with a yearning sigh.

That look again, and the pale woman asks, "What is love?"

What is love? All the wise men in the world could not explain it to one who does not feel it. But it requires no explanation for those who have it within them.

"Oh, you child!" sighed Timar, and rose from his wife's side.

Timéa rose also. "No, sir, I am no longer a child. I know what I am—your wife. I have sworn it to you, and God has heard my vow. I will be a faithful and obedient wife to you—it is appointed to me by fate. You have shown me so much kindness, that I owe you a lifelong gratitude. You are my lord and master, and I will always do what you wish and order."

Michael turned away and covered his face. This look of self-sacrifice and abnegation froze all desire in his veins. Who would have the courage to press a martyr to his heart, the statue of a saint, with palm-branches and crown of thorns?

"I will do what you command."

Michael now first began to guess what a hollow victory he had won. He had married a marble statue.

CHAPTER II.
THE GUARDIAN DEVIL.

It has often happened that a man has found his wife's heart to be devoid of all inclination toward him.

And no doubt many have looked for a cure in course of time. What can one do in winter, except look forward to spring? As the daughter of Mohammedan parents, Timéa had been brought up not to see the face of the man who was to be her husband until the wedding-day. There no one asks, "Do you, or do you not, love him?" neither her parents, the priest, nor the man himself. The husband will be good to her, and if he should find her out in infidelity, he will kill her. The principal thing is that she should have a pretty face, bright eyes, fine hair, and a sweet breath—no one asks about her heart. But Timéa had learned in a different school in the house of Brazovics. There she learned that among the Christians love was allowed, and every opportunity given for it; but that any one who did fall in love was not cured like a sick person, but punished like a criminal. She had expiated her crime.

When Timéa became Timar's wife, she had schooled herself strictly, and forbidden every drop of her blood to speak to her of anything except her duties as a wife; for if she had allowed them to talk of her secret fancies, then each drop of blood would have persuaded her to go the same road on which that other girl had twice, in the darkness of the night, stumbled over the body of the sleeping woman, and that stumble would have killed her soul. She crushed and buried the feeling, and gave her hand to a man whom she respected, to whom she owed gratitude, and whose life-companion she was to remain.

This story is repeated every day. And those who meet with it console themselves with the idea that soon the spring will come and the ice will melt.

Michael went with his young wife to travel, and visited Italy and Switzerland. They returned as they went. Neither the romantic Alpine valleys nor the fragrant orange-groves brought balm to his heart. He overwhelmed his wife with all that women like, dress and jewels; he introduced her to the gayeties of great cities. All in vain: moonlight gives no heat, even through a

188

burning glass. His wife was gentle, attentive, grateful, obedient; but her heart was never open to him, neither at home nor abroad, neither in joy nor sorrow. Her heart was buried.

Timar had married a corpse.

With this knowledge he returned from his travels. At one time he thought of leaving Komorn and settling in Vienna. Perhaps a new life might begin there. But then he thought of another plan: he decided to remain in Komorn and move into the Brazovics' house. There he would live with his wife, and arrange his own house as an office, so that business people might have nothing to do with the house his wife lived in. In this way he could be absent from home all day, without its being noticed that he left his wife alone.

In public they always appeared together. She went into society with him, reminded him when it was time to leave, and departed leaning on his arm. Every one envied his lot; a lucky man to have such a lovely and faithful wife! If she were not so true and good! If he could only hate her! But no scandal could touch her.

This spring brings no melting of her ice-bound heart. The glaciers grow every day. Michael cursed his fate. With all his treasures he can not buy his wife's love. It is all the worse for him that he is rich; splendor and great wealth widen the rift between them. Poverty binds close within its four walls those who belong to each other; laborers and fishermen, who have only one room and one bed, are more fortunate than he. The woodman, whose wife holds the other end of the saw when he is at work, is an enviable man: when they have finished they sit down on the ground, eat their bean-porridge out of one bowl, and kiss each other afterward.

Let us become poor people!

Timar began to hate his riches, and tried to get rid of them. If he was unfortunate and became poor, he would get nearer to his wife, he thought.

He could not succeed in impoverishing himself. Fortune pursues those who despise it. Everything he touched, which with another would certainly have failed, became a brilliant success. In his hands the impossible turned to reality—the die always threw six; if he tried to lose his money by gambling, he broke the bank—gold streamed in upon him; if he ran away or hid, it rolled after him and found him out.

And all this he would have joyfully given for a kiss from his wife's sweet lips.

And yet they say money is almighty. Everything is to be had for money. Yes—false; lying love, bright smiles on the charming lips of such as feel it not—forbidden, sinful love, which must be concealed—but not the love of one who can love truly and faithfully.

Timar almost wished he could hate his wife. He would have liked to believe that she loved another, that she was faithless and forgot her wifely duty; but he could not find any cause for hatred. No one saw his wife anywhere but on her husband's arm. In society she knew how to preserve a bearing which compelled respect, and kept bold advances at a distance. She did not dance at balls, and gave as a reason that when a girl she had not been taught to dance, and as a woman she no longer wished to learn. She sought the company of older women. If her husband went on a journey, she never left the house. But what did she at home? For reception-rooms in society are transparent, but not the walls of one's house. To this question Michael had a most convincing reply.

In this house Athalie lived with Timéa.

Athalie was—not the guardian angel but the guardian devil of Timéa's honor. Every step, every word, every thought of his wife, every sigh she uttered, every tear she shed, even the unconscious mutterings of her dreams, were spied upon by another woman, who hated him as well as his wife, and certainly would hasten to make both miserable, if a shadow of guilt could be found on the walls of the house.

If Timéa, at the moment when she begged Michael to allow Athalie and Frau Sophie to continue living in the same house, had listened to anything but the voice of her kind and feeling heart, she could not have invented a better protection for herself than keeping with her the girl who had once been the bride of the man she ought never to meet again.

These pitiless and malicious eyes follow her everywhere; as long as the guardian devil is silent, Timéa is not condemned even by God. Athalie is silent.

Athalie was a real dragon to Timéa, in small things as well as great. No circumstance, ever so trifling, escaped her attention if it afforded her a chance of playing Timéa a trick. She pretended that Timéa wished to show her generosity by treating the quondam young lady of the house as a sister, or like a lady visitor, which was enough to make Athalie behave in company as if she were a servant. Every day Timéa took the broom out of her hand by force when she came in to clean the room; she constantly caught her cleaning "her mistress's" clothes, and if visitors came to dinner, she could not be induced to leave the kitchen. Athalie had received back from Timéa her whole arsenal of ornaments and toilet necessaries. She had wardrobes full of silk and merino dresses; but she chose to wear her shabbiest and dirtiest gowns, which formerly she had put on only when the hairdresser was busy with her coiffure; and she was glad if she could burn a hole in her dress in the kitchen, or drop oil on it when she trimmed the lamp. She knew how much this hurt Timéa. All her jewels too, worth thousands, had been restored to her: she did not wear them, but bought herself a paste brooch for ten kreutzers, and put it on. Timéa took the brooch away quietly, and had a real opal put into it; the faded old dresses she burned, and had others made for Athalie of the stuff she was herself wearing.

191

Oh, yes, one could grieve Timéa, but not make her angry.

Even in her way of speaking, Athalie made a parade of an insufferable humility, although, or rather because, she knew it hurt Timéa. If the latter asked for anything, Athalie rushed to fetch it with an alacrity like that of a black slave who fears the whip. She never spoke in a natural tone, but annoyed Timéa by always lowering her voice to the thin whining sound which gives an impression of servility; she stammered with affected weakness, and could not pronounce the letter *s*.

She never let herself be surprised into forgetfulness or familiarity; but her most refined cruelty consisted in her unseasonable praises of the husband and wife to each other.

When she was alone with Timéa she sighed, "Oh, how happy you are, Timéa, in having such a good husband who loves you so much!" If Timar came home, she received him with naïve reproaches. "Is it right to stay away so long? Timéa is quite desperate, she awaits you with such longing; go in gently and surprise your wife. Hold your hands over her eyes, and make her guess who it is."

Both had to bear the derision which, under the mask of a tender, flattering sympathy, wounded their hearts. Athalie knew only too well that neither of them was happy.

But when she was alone, how completely she threw off the mask with which she tormented the others, and gave vent to her suppressed rage. If alone in her room she threw the broom Timéa had tried to take away furiously on the ground; then again beat the chairs and sofas with the handle, in order, as she said, to shake the dust out, but really to work off her anger on them. If in going out or in her dress caught in the door, or the sleeve on the handle, she wrenched it away with her teeth clinched, so that either the dress was torn or the handle dragged off, and then she was satisfied.

Broken crockery, chipped glasses, mutilated furniture, bore witness in quantities to the disastrous hours they passed in her company. Poor Mamma Sophie avoided her own daughter, and was afraid to be left alone with her. She was the only person in the house who ever heard Athalie's natural voice, and to whom she showed the bottomless depths of the gulf her hatred had dug. Frau Sophie was frightened of sleeping in the same room with her, and in a confidential moment showed her faithful cook the black bruises which her daughter's hand had left on her arms. When Athalie came into her mother's room in the evening, she would pinch her, and scream in her ear, "Why did you ever give me birth?"

And when at last she went to bed, after finishing her day's work with pretended gentleness and hidden fury, she required no one to help her. She tore off her clothes, dragged the knotted strings asunder, ill-treated her hair with hands and comb as if it was some one's else; then stamped on her clothes, blew out the candle, leaving a long wick to smolder and fill the room with its evil odor, and threw herself on her bed; there she bit the pillow, and tore at it with her teeth while she brooded over the torture she had to endure. Sleep only came to her after she had heard a door shut—the door of the lonely chamber of the master; then she was glad—then she could sleep.

It could be no secret to her that the young husband and wife were not happy. She waited with malicious joy to see what mischief could be developed from it.

Neither of them seemed to notice it. No quarrel ever took place; no complaint, not even an involuntary sigh, ever escaped either of them. Timéa remained unchanged, only the husband grew more gloomy every day. He sat for hours by his wife, often holding her hands in his, but he did not look into her eyes, and rose to go away without a word. Men can not keep a secret as women can. Timar got into the habit of going away and fixing the day of his return, and then returning sooner than he was expected. Another time he surprised his wife at a moment when he was not looked for; he pretended a chance had brought him home, and would not say what he wanted. But suspicion was written on his brow. Jealousy left him no peace.

One day Michael said at home that he had to go to Levetinczy, and could hardly get back in less than a month. All his preparations were made for a long absence. When the married couple took leave of each other with a kiss—a cool, conventional kiss—Athalie was present.

Athalie smiled. Another would hardly have noticed the smile, or at any rate would not, like Michael, have marked the derision which lay in it—the malicious mockery at one who little knows what goes on behind his back. It was as if she said, "When you are once gone, you fool—!"

193

Michael took the sting of this spiteful smile with him on his journey. He carried it on his heart half-way to Levetinczy; then he made his carriage turn round, and by midnight he was back in Komorn. In his house there were two extra entrances to his room, whose keys he always carried about with him, so that he could get in without any one knowing of his return. From his room he could reach Timéa's through the several anterooms. His wife was not in the habit of locking her bedroom door. She was accustomed to read in bed, and the maid generally had to come and see whether she had not fallen asleep without putting out the light. On the other side, the room in which Athalie and her mother slept adjoined his wife's bedroom. Michael approached the door noiselessly and opened it cautiously. All was still; every one slept. The room was dimly lighted by the shaded light of a night-lamp.

Michael drew the curtain aside: the same statue of a sleeping saint lay before him which he had once aroused to life in the cabin of the "St. Barbara." She seemed to be fast asleep; she did not feel his neighborhood; she did not see him through her downcast lashes. But a slumbering woman can see the man she loves even in her sleep, and with closed eyes. Michael bent over her breast and counted her heart-beats. Her heart beat with its normal calm. No suspicious symptom to be found—nothing to feed the hungry monster which seeks a victim.

He stood long and gazed on the slumbering form. Then suddenly he started. Athalie stood before him, dressed, and with a candle in her hand. Again that insulting smile of mockery lay on her lips. "Have you forgotten something?" she asked in a whisper.

Michael trembled like a thief caught in the act.

"Hush!" said he, pointing to the sleeper, and hurried away from the bed. "I forgot my papers."

"Shall I wake Timéa that she may get them out?"

Timar was angry at being detected for the first time in his life in a direct lie.

His papers were not kept by Timéa, but in his own room.

"No, do not wake my wife; the papers are in my room—I only wanted the key."

"And you have already found it?" asked Athalie, seriously, who then lighted the candles and officiously conducted Michael to his room.

Here she put down the candle and did not go away. Michael turned over his papers with confusion; he could not find what he sought—naturally—for he knew not what to look for. At last he shut his desk without taking anything out. Again he was met by the hateful smile which from time to time played round Athalie's lips. "Do you wish for anything?" said Athalie, in answer to his inquiring looks.

Michael remained silent.

"Do you wish me to speak?"

Michael felt at these words as if the world was falling on him. He dared not answer.

"Shall I tell you of Timéa?" whispered Athalie, bending nearer to him, and holding the stupefied man under the spell of her beautiful serpent-eyes.

"What do you know?" asked Michael, hotly.

"Everything—do you wish me to tell you?"

Michael was undecided.

"But I can tell you beforehand that you will be very unhappy when you learn what I know."

"Speak!"

"Very well—listen. I know as well as you do that Timéa does not love you. But one thing I know which you do not—namely, that Timéa is as true to you as an angel."

Timar started violently.

"You did not expect that from me? It would have been welcome news to hear from me that your wife deserved your contempt, so that you might be able to hate and reject her. No, sir; the marble statue you have taken to wife does not love you, but does not deceive you. This I only know, but with absolute certainty—oh, your honor is well guarded. If you had engaged the hundred-eyed Argus of the legend as a watchman, she could not be better guarded than by me. Nothing of what she does, says, thinks, escapes me: in the deepest recesses of her heart she can have no feeling hidden from me. You acted wisely in the interests of your honor when you took me into your house. You will not drive me out of it, though you hate me; for you know well that as long as I am here, the man whom you fear can never approach

195

your sanctuary. I am the diamond lock of your house. You shall know all: when you leave town, your house is a cloister while you are absent; no visitors are received, neither man nor woman; the letters which come to your wife, you will find unopened on your writing-table; you can give them to her to read or throw them into the fire, just as you choose. Your wife never sets foot in the streets, she only drives out with me; her only walk is on the island, and I am always with her; I see her suffer, but I never hear her complain. How could she complain to me, who suffer the same torment, and on her account? For from the time when that ghostly face appeared in the house my misery began; till then I was happy and beloved. Do not be afraid of my bursting into tears; I love no longer—now I only hate, and with my whole soul. You can trust your house to me; you can ride through the world in peace; you leave me at home, and as long as you find your wife alive on your return you may be sure that she is faithful to you. For know, sir, that if she ever exchanges a friendly word with that man, or responds to his smile, or reads a letter from him, I would not wait for you, I would kill her myself, and you would only come home to her funeral. Now you know what you leave behind—the polished dagger which the madness of jealousy holds aimed at your wife's heart; and under the shadow of that dagger you will daily lay your head down to sleep, and although I inspire you with loathing, you will be forced to cling to me with desperation."

Timar felt all his mental energy crippled under this outburst of demoniac passion.

"I have told you all I know about Timéa, about you and myself; I repeat once more, you have taken to wife a girl who loves another, and this other was once mine. It was you who took this house from me; under your hand my father and my property sunk into dust; and then you made Timéa the mistress of this house. You see now what you did. Your wife is not a woman, but a martyr. It is not enough that you should suffer; you must also acquire the certainty that you have made her, for whose possession you strove, miserable, and that there can be no happiness for Timéa as long as you live. With this sting in your breast you may leave your house, Herr Levetinczy, and you will nowhere find a balm for your smarting wound, and I rejoice at it with all my heart!"

196

With glowing cheeks, gnashing teeth, and glaring eyes, Athalie bowed to Timar, who sunk exhausted into a chair. But the girl clinched her fist as if to thrust an invisible dagger into his heart.

"And now—turn me out of your house if you dare!" All womanhood was quenched in the girl's face. Instead of a hypocritical submission, it was dominated by the fury of unbridled passion. "Drive me away from here if you dare!"

And proud as a triumphant demon she left Michael's room. She had taken the lighted candle which was on the table away with her, and left the wretched husband in darkness. She had told him that she was not the humble servant, but the guardian devil of the house. As Timar saw the girl with the light in her hand go toward the door of Timéa's bedroom, something whispered to him to spring up, seize Athalie's arm, and setting his foot before the threshold, to cry to her, "Remain then yourself in this accursed house, as I am bound by the promise I gave; but not with us!"

And then to rush into Timéa's room, as on the eventful night when the ship went down, to lift her in his arms from the bed, and with the cry, "This house is falling in, let us save ourselves!" to fly from it with her, and take her to some place where no one spies on her . . . this thought darted through his head . . . that was what he ought to have done.

The door of the bedroom opened, and Athalie looked back once more; then she went in, the door shut, and Michael remained alone in the darkness.

Oh, in what darkness!

Then he heard the key turn twice in the lock. His fate was sealed; he arose and felt round in the dark for his traveling-bag. He kindled no light, made no noise, so that no one should awake and report that he had been here. When he had collected all his things, he crept softly to the door, shut it gently behind him, and left his own house cautiously and noiselessly, like a thief, like a fugitive. That girl had driven him away from it.

Out in the street he was met by a snow shower. That is good weather for one who does not wish to be seen. The wind whistled through the streets, and drove the snowflakes into his face; Michael Timar, however, went on his way in an open carriage, in weather in which one would not turn a dog into the street.

CHAPTER III.
SPRING MEADOWS.

As far as the Lower Danube, the traveler took with him rough and wintery skies; here and there fresh snow covered the fields, and the woods stood bare. The stormy cold suited the thoughts with which Timar was occupied. That cruel girl was right—not only the husband but the wife was wretched. The man doubly so; for he was the author of their mutual misery.

These bitter, disconsolate thoughts followed Michael to Baja, where he had an office, and where, when he traveled into the flax districts of Hungary, he had his letters sent. A whole bundle awaited him; he opened one after another with indifference; what did he care whether the rape had been frost-bitten or not, that the duties in England were raised, or that exchange was higher? But among the letters he found two which were not uninteresting—one from his Viennese, the other from his Stamboul agent. The contents greatly rejoiced him. He put them both away, and from that moment the apathy began to disperse which had hitherto possessed him. He gave his orders to his agents with his usual quickness and energy, carefully noted their reports, and when he had finished with them, proceeded on his way in haste.

Now his journey had an object—no great or important one, but still an object. It was to give a pleasure to two poor people—but a real joy.

The weather had changed; the sky had cleared, and the sun shone warmly down below. In Hungary, where summer follows immediately on winter, these swift changes are common. Below Baja the face of the country, too, was changed. While Michael rushed southward with frequent changes of horses, it was as if nature had in one day advanced by many weeks. At Mohacs he was received by woods decked in new green; about Zambor the fields were spread with a verdant carpet; at Neusatz the meadows were already dressed with flowers; and in the plains of Pancsova golden stretches of rape smiled at him, and the hills looked as though covered with rosy snow—the almonds and cherry-trees were in blossom. The two days' journey was like a dream-picture. The day before yesterday snow-covered fields in

199

Komorn, and to-day on the Lower Danube hedges in bloom!

Michael alighted at the Levetinczy castle to spend the night. He gave his instructions to the bailiff on the day of his arrival; the next morning he got up early, entered the carriage, and drove to the Danube to inspect his cargo ships. Everything was in order. Our Herr Johann Fabula had been appointed overseer of the whole flotilla: there was nothing for him to do. "Our gracious master can go and shoot ducks."

And Herr von Levetinczy followed this good advice of Herr Fabula. He had a boat brought, and ordered provisions for a week, his gun, and plenty of ammunition to be put in it. No one will be surprised if he does not return from the reed-bed, now full of prime water-fowl, before a week has elapsed. It storms with duck, snipe, and herons, the last only valued for their feathers; even pelicans are to be met with, and an Egyptian ibis has been shot there. It is said a flamingo was once seen. When an ardent sportsman once gets into those marshes, you may wait till he comes out! And Timar loved sport, like all sailors. This time Michael did not load his gun. He let his boat float down with the stream till he reached the point of the Ostrova Island—there he seized the sculls and crossed the Danube obliquely. When he got round the island he soon saw where he was. From the southern reed-beds rose the tops of the well-known poplars—thither he went. There was already a channel broken through the rushes, across and along as required, if you only understood it. Where Michael had once been, he could find his way in the dark. What would Almira and Narcissa be doing? What should they be doing in such lovely weather but gratifying their passion for sport? Only, however, within certain limits: the field-mouse must be pursued at night, and that is easy for Narcissa, but she is strictly forbidden to chase birds. To Almira the marmots which came across the ice and settled in the island are positively interdicted. Aquatic prey still remain, and that is good sport too. Almira wades into the pure, clear water among the heaps of great stones at the bottom, and cautiously puts her fore-paw into a hole, out of which something dark is peeping. Suddenly she makes a great jump, draws her foot back, limps whining out of the water on three legs, and on the fourth paw hangs a large black crab, which has caught hold with its claws. Almira hobbles along in despair till, on reaching the bank, she succeeds in shaking off the dangerous monster; it is then carefully inspected by both Almira and Narcissa, to see at what price it can be induced to allow its body to be deprived of the shell. The crab naturally does not quite see the fun of this, and retires with all speed backward to the water. The two sportsmen, however, shove the reactionary party forward with their paws, until at one shove it is turned on its back, and now all three are in doubt what to do next—Almira, Narcissa, and the crab.

Almira's attention is suddenly attracted by another object. She hears a noise and scents something. A friend approaches by water; she does not bark at him, but utters a low growl. This is her way of laughing, like some cheery old gentleman. She recognizes the man in the boat. Michael springs out, fastens the boat to a willow stump, pats Almira's head, and asks her, "Well, then, how is it all? is it all well?" The dog replied many things, but in the Newfoundland-dog language. To judge by the tone, the answer is satisfactory.

Then all at once a pitiful cry disturbs the pleasant greeting. The catastrophe which might have been foreseen has occurred. Narcissa came near enough to the upset and sprawling crab for it to catch her ear with its nippers, and then to bury all its six claws in her fur. Timar rushed to the scene of misfortune, and with great presence of mind, seeing the magnitude of the danger, seized the mailed criminal in a place where its weapons could not reach him, pressed its head between his strong fingers, and obliged it to let go its prey; then he dashed it with such force on to a stone that it was shattered, and gave up its black ghost. Narcissa, to show her gratitude, sprung on to the shoulder of her chivalrous deliverer, and snorted from there at her dead enemy.

After this introductory deed of heroism, Timar busied himself in disembarking what he had brought with him. All are packed into a knapsack, which he can easily throw over his shoulder. But the gun, the gun! Almira can not abide him with a gun in his hand, but he can not leave it here, for it might easily be stolen by some one. What to do? The idea struck Timar to give it into Almira's charge, who then, in her leonine jaws, carried the weapon proudly before him as a poodle bears its master's cane. Narcissa sat on his shoulder and purred in his ear. Michael allowed Almira to go on before and show him the way.

201

Timar felt transformed when he trod the turfy paths of the island. Here was holy rest and deepest solitude. The fruit-trees of this paradise are in bloom; between their white and rosy flower-pyramids wild roses arch their sprays; the golden sunbeams coax the flowers' fragrance into the air; the breeze is laden with it—with every breath one inhales gold and love. The forest of blossom is full of the hum of the bees, and in that mysterious sound, from all these flower-eyes, God speaks, God looks: it is a temple of the Lord. And that church music may not be wanting, the nightingale flutes his psalm of lament, and the lark trills his song of praise—only better than King David. At a spot where the purple lilacs parted, and the little island-home was visible, Michael stood spell-bound. The little house seemed to swim in a flaming sea, but not of water, only of roses. It was covered with rose-wreaths climbing to the roof, and for five acres round it only roses were visible—thousands of bushes, and six-foot rose-trees, forming pyramids, hedges, and arcades. It was a rose-forest, a rose-mountain, a rose-labyrinth, whose splendor dazzled the eye and spread afar a scent which surrounded one like a supernatural atmosphere.

Hardly had Michael entered on the winding path through this wilderness of roses, before a melodious cry of joy was heard. His name was called. "Ah, Herr Timar!"

And she who had uttered his name came running toward him. Timar had already recognized her by her voice: it was Noémi—little Noémi, whom he had not seen for nearly three years. How she had grown since then—how changed, how developed she was! Her dress was no longer neglected, but neat, though simple. In her rich golden hair a rose-bud was fastened.

"Ah, Herr Timar!" cried the girl, and stretched out her hand to him from afar, greeting him with frank delight, and a warm shake of the hand.

Michael returned it, and remained lost in gazing at the girl. Here then, at last, is a face that beams with joy at the sight of him. "How long it is since we saw you!" said the girl.

"And how pretty you have grown!" exclaimed he.

Sympathy shone in every line of Noémi's face. "So you remember me still?" asked Timar, holding the little hand fast in his own.

"We have often thought of you."

"Is Madame Therese well?"

"There she comes."

When she saw Michael she hastened her steps; from a distance she had recognized the former ship's captain, who now again, in his gray coat and with his knapsack, approached her hut. "God greet you! you have kept us waiting a long time!" exclaimed the woman to her visitor. "So you have thought of us at last?" And she embraced Michael without ceremony; then his well-filled knapsack caught her eye. "Almira," she said to the dog, "take this bag and carry it in."

"There are a brace of birds in it," said Michael.

"Indeed! then take care, Almira, that Narcissa does not get at it."

Noémi was affronted. "Narcissa is not so badly educated as that."

To make it up, Frau Therese kissed her daughter, and Noémi was reconciled.

"Now let us go in," said Therese, taking Michael's arm familiarly. "Come, Noémi."

A huge boat-shaped basket made of white osier-twigs stood in the way, and its heaped-up contents were covered with a cloth. Noémi began to lift it by both handles; Michael sprung to help her, and Noémi burst into a childish shriek of laughter, and drew off the cloth. The basket was heaped with rose-leaves. Michael took one handle, and so they carried it together with its sweet cargo along the lavender-bordered path.

"Do you make rose-water?" asked Timar.

Therese threw a glance at Noémi. "See how he finds out everything!"

"With us in Komorn much rose-water is made. Many poor women live by it."

"Indeed? Then elsewhere also the rose is a blessing of the Lord—the exquisite flower which alone would make man love this world! And it not only rejoices his heart, but gives him bread. Look you—last year was a bad season; the late frost spoiled the fruit and the vintage; the wet, cold summer destroyed the bees, and the poultry died of disease: we should have had to fall back on our stores if it had not been for the roses, which helped us in our need. They bloom every year, and are always faithful to us. We made three hundred gallons of rose-water, which we sold in Servia, and got grain in exchange. Oh, you dear roses—you life-saving flowers!"

The little settlement had been enlarged since Timar was last there. There was a kiln and a kitchen for the preparation of the rose-water. Here was an open fire with the copper retort, from which the first essence dropped slowly; near the hearth stood a great tub with the crushed rose leaves, and on a broad bench lay the fresh ones which required drying.

Michael helped Noémi to empty the basket on to the bench; that was a scent, a perfume, in which one could revel and intoxicate one's self!

Noémi laid her little head on the soft hill of rose leaves, and said, "It would be delicious to sleep on such a bed of roses."

"Foolish child," Therese chided her. "You would never awake from that slumber; the odor would kill you."

"That would be a lovely death!"

"Then you want to die?" Frau Therese said, reproachfully; "you want to leave me here alone, you naughty child?"

"No, no!" cried Noémi, embracing her mother with eager kisses. "I leave you, my dear, darling, only little mother!"

"Why do you make such silly jests then? Don't you think, Herr Timar, it is not right for a young girl to allow herself these jokes with her mother—for a little girl who was playing with a doll only yesterday?" Michael quite agreed with Frau Therese that it was inexcusable under any pretense for a young lady to tell her mother that she thought any kind of death would be delightful. "Now just stop here and see that the essence does not boil, while I go to the kitchen to get a good dinner ready for our guest. You'll stay all day, of course?"

"I will stay to-day and to-morrow too, if you will give me something to do for you. As long as you find me work I will remain."

"Oh, then, you can stop the whole week," Noémi interrupted, "for I can find you plenty to do."

"What work would you give Herr Timar, you little simpleton?" laughed the mother.

"Why, of course, to crush the rose leaves!"

"But perhaps he does not know how."

"How should I not know all about it?" said Timar. "I have often enough helped my mother with it at home."

"Your mother was a very good woman, I am sure."

"Very good."

"And you loved her very much?"

"Very much."

"Is she still living?"

"She has long been dead."

"So now you have no one in the world belonging to you?"

Timar thought a moment, and bowed his head sadly—"No one." . . .
He had spoken the truth.

Michael noticed that Therese still stood at the door, doubtful whether
to go or not. "Do you know, good mother," said he, suddenly remembering,
"you need not go to the kitchen to cook anything for me. I have all sorts of
provisions with me; there is only the table to spread—we shall all have
enough."

"Then who has looked after you and provided you so well with
traveling comforts?" asked Noémi.

"Who but our Herr Johann Fabula?"

"Oh, the honest steersman!—is he here too?"

"He is loading the ship on the other bank."

Therese guessed Timar's thought, but she would not be behind him
in delicate tact. She wished to show him that she had no scruple about
leaving him alone with Noémi. "No, I have thought of something else; I will
manage both here and in the kitchen. You, Noémi, can meanwhile take Herr
Timar over the island and show him all the changes since he was here."

Noémi was an obedient daughter; she did without question what her
mother told her. She tied her Turkish handkerchief round her head, which
framed her face charmingly. Timar recognized the scarf he had left as a
present to her.

"Au revoir, darling!" "Au revoir," said the mother and daughter with a
kiss. They seemed to take leave of each other every time they parted, as if
going on a long journey; and when they met again in an hour, they embraced
as if they had been separated for years: the poor things had only each other in
this world.

Noémi threw one more inquiring look, and Therese answered with a nod which meant, "Yes, go!"

Noémi and Timar now wandered on through the whole island. The path was so narrow that they were forced to walk close together, but Almira had the sense to push her great head between them and form a natural barrier. In the last three years cultivation had made great strides on the little island. A practicable road had been cut through the bushes; the old poplars had been uprooted, the wild crabs grafted; a skillful hand had formed neat fences from the broken branches; and where the orchard ceased, hedges divided the island, and hemmed in fields which supplied pasture for lambs and goats. One little lamb had a red ribbon round its neck, and this was Noémi's pet. When the flock saw her they ran to her and bleated a greeting which she understood; then they followed her and Timar to the border of the field where the fence stopped them.

Behind these was to be seen a plantation of fine walnuts, with widespread shady heads and thick trunks, whose bark was smooth as silk. "Look," said Noémi, "those are my mother's pride; they are fifteen years old—just a year younger than I am," she said quite simply.

On the right was the marsh, as Timar well remembered when he first came to the island and made his way through it. Now it was covered with water-plants; yellow lilies and white bell flowers were spread over the surface of the morass, and in the midst stood quietly two storks.

Timar opened the little gate; it was a pleasant reminder to see this wilderness once more, and yet it seemed to him as if his guide was afraid and uncomfortable.

"Are you still all alone here?" asked Michael.

"We are alone. At market-times people come to barter with us, and in winter wood-cutters come and help us to hew the trees and root them up: the wood serves to pay them. We do the rest ourselves."

"But fruit-gathering is very troublesome, especially on account of the wasps."

"Oh, that is not hard work; our friends singing there on the trees help us with the wasp-killing. Do you see all the nests? Our laborers live there; here no one troubles them, and they do us good service. Just listen!"

The wilderness resounded indeed with a heavenly concert. In the evening every bird hastens home, and then they are at their best. The cuckoo, the clock of the woods, has enough to do in striking the hours, and the thrush whistles in Greek strophes.

Then suddenly Noémi screamed aloud, grew pale, and started back with her trembling hand on her heart, so that Timar felt it his duty to seize her by the hand that she might not fall. "What is it?" Noémi held her hand before her eyes and said, half laughing and half crying, in a tone of mingled fear and disgust, "Look, look! there he comes."

"Who?"

"There, that one!"

He saw a large, wrinkled, fat frog, which was creeping quietly in the grass, keeping an eye on the new-comers, and ready for a spring, in case of danger, into the nearest water-course.

Noémi was so paralyzed with fright that she had not the strength to run away.

"Are you afraid of frogs?" asked Timar.

"I have a horror of them; I should be frightened to death if it jumped on me."

"How like a girl! They love cats because they coax and flatter, but they can not bear frogs because they are ugly; and yet, do you know, the frogs are just as good friends to us as the birds: this common, despised animal is the best assistant to the gardener. You know there are moths and beetles and grubs which only come out at night; birds are asleep then, but the detested frog comes out of his hole and attacks our enemies in the dark; he feeds on the night-moths and their grubs, the caterpillars and the slugs, and even the vipers. It is splendid the war he makes on noxious insects. Keep quiet, just look—the ugly, wrinkled frog is not creeping there to frighten you—he is not thinking about it. He is a gentle beast, conscious of no sin, and does not regard you as an enemy. Do you see a blue beetle fanning with his wings? That is one of the worst insects, a wood-borer, of which one grub suffices to spoil a whole young plantation; and our little friend has fixed on him as a prey. Don't disturb him; look, he is drawing himself up for a spring—wait. There! now he has made his leap, and darts out his long tongue like lightning:

the beetle is swallowed. You see that our good frog is not such a disgusting creature, in spite of his shabby coat."

Noémi clasped her hands, quite pleased, and already felt less dislike to frogs. She let Michael lead her to a seat, and tell her what sensible creatures they are, what funny tricks they play, and what curious games exist among them. He told her of the sky-blue frog of Surinam, of which one specimen cost the King of Prussia four thousand five hundred thalers; then of the fire-frog, which sheds a clear light around in the darkness, creeps into houses, hides in the beams, and croaks unmercifully at night. In Brazil sometimes you can not hear the singers in the opera-house for the chorus set up by the frogs which live in the building. Now Noémi was laughing at this awful enemy, and the laugh is half-way from hatred to love.

"If only they would not make such an ugly noise!"

"But you see in these tones they express their tender affection for their little wives, for among frogs only the little husband has a voice—the lady is dumb. The frog exclaims all night to his wife, 'How lovely, how charming you are!' Can there be a more affectionate creature than a frog?"

Noémi was beginning to look at it from the sentimental side.

"Then, too, the frog is a learned animal. You must know that the true frog is a weather-prophet: when it is going to rain he knows it, comes out of the water and croaks his prophecy; when dry weather is coming he goes back to the water."

"Ah!" began Noémi, getting interested.

"I will catch one," said Timar; "I hear one among the bushes."

He soon came back with a tree-frog between his palms. Noémi trembled and got excited. She was red and pale by turns.

"Now look," said Timar to her, opening his hands a little. "Is it not a pretty little thing? It is as lovely a green as the young grass, and its tiny foot is like a miniature human hand. How its little heart beats! How it looks at us with its beautiful wise black eyes with a golden ring round them! It is not afraid of us!"

Noémi, wavering between fear and curiosity, stretched out a timid hand, but drew it quickly back.

"Take it, touch it—it is the most harmless creature on God's earth."

She stretched out her hand again, frightened and yet laughing, but looked into Timar's eyes instead of at the frog, and started when the cold body came in contact with her reluctant nerves; but then suddenly she laughed with pleasure, like a child which would not go into the cold water, and then is glad to be there.

"Now look, he does not move in your hand; he is quite comfortable. We will take him home and find a glass, put water in, and then place a small ladder in it which I can cut out of wood. The frog shall be imprisoned in it, and when he knows that rain is coming he will climb up the ladder. Give it to me; I will carry it."

"No, no; I will keep him, and carry him home myself."

"Then you must hold your hand shut, or he will jump out; but not too tight so as to press him. And now let us go, for the dew is falling, and the grass is wet."

They turned homeward, and Noémi ran on, calling from afar to Therese, "Mother, mother, see what we have caught! a beautiful bird."

Mamma Therese prepared to scold her daughter severely.

"Don't you know that it is forbidden to catch birds?"

"But such a bird! Herr Timar caught it, and gave it to me. Just peep into my hand."

Frau Therese threw up her hands when she saw the green tree-frog there.

"Look how it blinks at me with its beautiful eyes!" cried Noémi, beaming with delight. "We are going to put him in a glass, catch flies for him, and he will foretell the weather for us. Oh, the dear little thing!" And she held the frog caressingly to her cheek.

Therese turned to Timar in astonishment. "Sir, you are a magician! Only yesterday you could have driven this girl out of her senses with such a creature as that."

But Noémi was quite enthusiastic about the frog. While she laid the table on the veranda for supper, she delivered a complete batrachian lecture to her mother on what she had heard from Timar: how useful, as well as wise, amusing, and interesting frogs were. It was not true that they spat venom, as people said, that they crept into sleepers' mouths, sucked the milk

209

of cows, nor that they burst with poison if you held a spider to them—all this was pure calumny and stupid superstition. They are our best friends, which guard us at night; those little soft foot-prints which are visible on the smooth sand round the house, are the consoling sign of their nightly patrol: it would be ungrateful to fear them. Timar had meanwhile prepared a small ladder of willow-twigs for the little meteorologist. He put it in a wide-mouthed bottle, which he half filled with water, and covered with a pierced paper, through which the imprisoned prophet was to receive its provision of flies. It of course went down to the bottom, and declined either to eat or to talk. Noémi welcomed this as a sign that the weather would remain fine.

"Yes, sir," said Frau Therese, as she brought out the supper to the little table at which they all sat down; "you have not only worked a miracle on Noémi, but have really done her a great benefit. Our island would have been a paradise if Noémi had not been so afraid of frogs. As soon as ever she saw one she grew quite white and got a fit of shivering. No human power would have induced her to go across the fence to where the innumerable frogs croak in the marsh. You have made a new creature of her, and reconciled her with her home."

"A sweet home!" sighed Timar. Therese sighed aloud.

"Why do you sigh?" Noémi asked.

"You know well enough."

And Timar too knew to whom the sigh was due.

Noémi tried to give a cheerful turn to the conversation. "I took my aversion to frogs from the time when a naughty boy played me a trick, and threw a great big toad, as brown as a crust, at me. He said it was a bull-frog, and that if he struck it with a nettle it would roar like a bull. He did strike the poor thing, and then it began to moan piteously, so that I can never forget it, as if it would call for vengeance against our whole race; and its body was covered with white froth. The bad boy laughed when he heard the uncanny voice of the poor beast."

"Who was that wicked boy?" asked Michael.

Noémi was silent, and only made an expressively contemptuous movement of the hand. Timar guessed the name; he looked at Frau Therese, and she nodded assent—already they can guess each other's thoughts.

"Has he never been here since?"

"Oh, yes; he comes every year, and never ceases tormenting us. He has found a new way of laying us under contribution. He brings a large boat with him, and as I can not give him any money, he loads it with honey, wax, and wool, which he sells. I give him what he wants, that he may leave us in peace."

"He has not been here lately," said Noémi.

"Oh, nothing has happened to him, I expect his arrival any day."

"If only he would come now!" said the girl.

"Why, you little goose?"

Noémi grew crimson. "Only because I should prefer it."

Timar, however, thought to himself how happy he could make these two people with a single word. But he gloated over the thought, like a child which had some sweets given to it, and begins by eating the crumbs first. He felt an inward impulse to share the joys and sorrows of these islanders.

Supper was over, the sun had set, and a splendid, still, warm night sunk on to the fields; the whole sky looked like a transparent silver veil—no leaf stirred on the trees. The two women went with their visitor to the top of the great bowlder; from there one had a wide view over the trees and the reed-beds far across the Danube. The island lay at their feet like an enchanted lake with variegated waves. The apple-trees swam in a rosy, and the pomegranates in a dark-red, sea of blossom; the poplars looked golden-yellow, and the pear-trees white with snowy bloom, and the waving tips of the plum-trees were radiant in brazen green. In the midst rose the rock like a lighted cupola, wreathed with fiery roses, on whose top old lavender bushes formed a thicket.

"Superb!" cried Timar, enchanted with the landscape outspread before him.

"You should see the rock in summer, when the yellow stonecrop is in bloom," exclaimed Noémi, eagerly; "it looks as if it had on a golden robe. The lavender blossom makes a great blue crown for its head."

"I will come and see it," said Timar.

"Really?" The girl stretched out her hand to him joyously, and Michael fell a warm pressure such as no woman's hand had ever given him in

211

his life. And then Noémi leaned her head on Therese's shoulder, and threw her arm round her mother's neck. All nature was under the spell of deep repose undisturbed by any human sound. Only the monotonous chorus of the frogs enlivened the deep shadows of the night. The sky offered a curious spectacle; half was blue, and the other opal green. There are two sides even to happiness.

"Do you hear what the frogs are saying?" whispered Noémi to her mother—"'Oh, how dear you are, how sweet!' They say that all night long—'Oh, you darling, you sweet!'" and she kissed Therese at every word.

Michael, forgetful of himself and of the whole world, stood on the rock with folded arms. The young crescent glittered between the quivering foliage of the poplars, now shining like pure silver; a wonderful new feeling crept into the man's breast. Was it fear or longing?—memory aroused or dawning hope?—awakening joy or dying grief?—instinct or warning?—madness, or that breath of spring which seizes on tree and grass, and every cold or warm-blooded animal?

Just so had he gazed at the waning moon, which threw its long reflection on the waves as far as the sinking ship. His involuntary thoughts talked with the ghostly magnetic rays, and they with him.

"Do you not understand? I will return to-morrow, and then you will know."

212

CHAPTER IV.
A SPIDER AMONG THE ROSES.

People who live by their labor have no time to admire the moonlight from mountain-tops, or to waste in observation on the beauties of nature: the flocks of sheep and goats already waited to be relieved of their milky tribute by their mistress. Milking was the office of Frau Therese, and it was Noémi's duty to cut grass enough for the herd. Timar continued the conversation meanwhile with his back leaning against the stable-door, and lighting his pipe just as the countryman does when he is courting the peasant girl.

The great boiler must be refilled with fresh rose-infusion, and then they can all go to bed. Timar begged for the bee-house to sleep in, where Frau Therese spread him a couch of fresh hay, and Noémi arranged his pillow. Very little was needed to woo him to slumber. Hardly had he lain down before sleep closed his eyes; he dreamed all night that he had become a gardener's boy, and was making endless rose-water.

When he awoke the sun was already high in the heavens. The bees buzzed round him busily; he had overslept himself. That some one had already been here he guessed, because near his couch lay all the toilet necessaries he had brought in his knapsack. A poor traveler who is used to shaving every day feels very uncomfortable when unable to go through that operation; his mind is as much disturbed by that confounded stubble as if it were a prick of conscience. When he was ready, the women already awaited him at breakfast, which consisted of bread and milk, and then they went to the day's work of rose-gathering.

Michael was, as he desired, set to rose-crushing. Noémi picked off the petals, and Frau Therese was busy with the boiler. Timar told Noémi all about roses. Not that they were like her cheeks, at which she would have burst out laughing, but he imparted to her what he had learned about them in his travels: learned things which Noémi listened to with attention, and which instilled into her a still greater respect for Timar. With young and innocent maidens a clever, intelligent man has a great advantage.

"In Turkey they use rose-water in eating and drinking. There, too,

213

whole groves of roses are planted; there beads are made of roses pressed into the form of balls and strung together: that is why they are called rosaries. In the East there is one lovely kind of rose from which attar is made; it is the balsam rose, and grows on trees of ten feet high, whose branches are bent to the ground by their snow-white burden. Their scent surpasses that of any other kind; if you throw the petals into water and set them in the sun, in a very short time the surface is rainbow-colored with the oil that the petals exude. It is the same with the evergreen rose, which does not shed its leaves in winter. The Ceylon and Rio roses dye the hair and beard light, and so fast that they do not lose their color for years; for this purpose alone there is a considerable trade in them. The leaves of the Moggor rose stupefy; you are intoxicated by their scent as if with beer. The Vilmorin rose has the property that, it if is bitten by a certain insect which is obnoxious to it, it throws out great tubers, which are said to send a crying child to sleep if put under its pillow."

"Have you been everywhere where roses grow?" asked Noémi.

"Well, I have been a good deal about in the world. I have been to Vienna, Paris, and Constantinople."

"Is that far from here?"

"If one traveled on foot one would get to Vienna in thirty days from here, and to Constantinople in forty days."

"But you went in a ship."

"That takes longer still; for I should have to take in cargo on the way."

"For whom?"

"For the owner I was traveling for."

"Is Herr Brazovics still your principal?"

"Who told you about him?"

"The steersman who came with you."

"No longer now—Herr Brazovics is dead."

"Dead! so he is dead? And his wife and daughter?" interrupted Frau Therese, quickly.

"They have lost everything by his death."

"Ah, just God! Thy avenging hand has reached them!"

214

"Mother, good mother!" cried Noémi, with gentle entreaty.

"Sir, there is one more thing you ought to know. When that blow fell on us, when I had implored Brazovics on my knees not to drive us to beggary, it struck me that this man had a wife and child. I determined to find out his wife and tell her my misery—she would help me and take pity on us. I took my child in my arms and traveled in the hottest part of the summer to Komorn. I sought her out in her fine large house, and waited at the door, for they would not let me in. At last Frau Brazovics came out with her five-year-old daughter. I fell on my knees, and begged her for God's sake to take compassion on us, and be our mediator with her husband. The woman seized my arm and thrust me down the step; I tried, in falling, to protect my child with both arms, that it might not be hurt, and struck my head against one of the two pillars which support the balcony. Here is the scar still visible. The little girl laughed aloud when she saw me limping away and heard my baby cry. That is why I sing 'Hosanna,' and blessed be the hand which thrust her away from the steps down which she cast us."

"Oh, mother, don't talk so!"

"So they have come to misery? Have they become beggars themselves—the haughty, purse-proud people? Do they wear rags, and beg in vain at the doors of their former friends?"

"No, dear lady," said Michael; "some one has been found to take care of them."

"Madman!" cried Therese, with passionate force. "Why should he put a spoke in fate's wheel? How can he dare to receive into his home the curse which will ruin him?"

Noémi ran to her mother and covered her mouth with both hands; then she fell on her neck and sealed her lips with kisses. "Dearest mother, do not say such things. Do not utter curses; I can not bear to hear them—take them back. Let me kiss away the dreadful words from your lips."

Therese recovered herself under her daughter's caresses. "Do not be afraid, silly child," she said, shaking her head. "Curses fall idly on the air. They are only a bad, superstitious habit of us old women. God never thinks of noticing the curses of such worms as we are, and keeping them till the day of judgment. My curses will take effect on no one."

"It is already fulfilled on me," thought Timar. "I am the madman who received them into his house."

Noémi tried to bring the subject of roses back. "Tell me, Herr Timar, how could you get such a Moggor rose whose scent stupefies?"

"If you wish, I will bring you one."

"Where do they grow?"

"In Brazil."

"Is that far?"

"The other side of the world."

"Must you go by sea?"

"Two months continuously at sea."

"And why would you go?"

"On business—and to fetch you a Moggor rose."

"Then do not bring me any."

Noémi left the kitchen, and Michael noticed that tears were in her eyes. She only returned to the distillery when she had filled her basket with rose leaves, and shook them out on to the rush-matting, where they made a large hill.

The boiling of yesterday's rose-essence lasted till midday, and after breakfast Frau Therese said to her guest that there was not much work for to-day, and that they could go for a walk in the island. One who was so great a traveler might be able to give good advice to the islanders, as to what vegetables they might usefully and profitably introduce into their little Eden. Frau Therese said to the dog, "Stop here and watch the house! Lie down in the veranda and don't stir!" Almira understood and obeyed.

Michael disappeared with his companions among the plantations.

Hardly had they vanished into the wood before Almira began to prick her ears uneasily and to growl angrily. She scented something. She shook her head, rose from time to time, but lay down again. A man's voice became audible, which sung a German song, whose refrain was, "She wears, if I can trust my eyes, a jet-black camisole." The person coming from the shore sings, of course, on purpose to attract the attention of the inhabitants. He is afraid of the great dog—but it does not bark.

The new arrival appears from among the shadows of the rose-arbor.

216

It is Theodor Krisstyan.

This time he is attired like a fashionable dandy, in a dark-blue tunic with golden buttons; and his overcoat hangs on his arm. Almira does not stir at his approach. She is a philosopher, and reasons, if I fly at this man, the end of it will be that I shall be tied up and not he. I shall do better to keep my opinion of him to myself, and to look on in armed neutrality at what he does. Theodor drew near confidently, and whistling to his huge black enemy. "Your servant, Almira. Come, Almirakin, you dear old dog—where are your ladies? Bark a bit to please me. Where is our dear Mamma Therese?" Almira could not be induced to answer.

"Look, then, little doggie, what I have got for you—a piece of meat; there, eat it. What? Don't you want it? You fancy it's poisoned, you fool? Gobble it up, you beauty!" But Almira would not even sniff at the piece of meat, until Narcissa (it is well known that cats have no decision of character) crept up to it, which made Almira angry, and she began to scratch a large hole in the ground; there she buried the meat, like a careful dog which makes provision for a day of necessity.

"Well, what a distrustful beast it is," murmured Theodor to himself. "Am I to be allowed to go in?"

But that was not allowed. Almira did not say so in words, but she curled her lip to let him see the beautiful white teeth underneath.

"Stupid creature, you don't mean to bite me? Where can the women be? Perhaps in the distillery?"

Theodor went in and looked round—he found no one. He washed his face and hands in the steaming rose-water, and it gave him especial pleasure to think that so he had spoiled the work of a whole day.

When he wanted to come out of the distillery, he found the entrance barred by the dog. Almira had laid herself down across the threshold and showed him her white teeth. "Indeed, so now you won't let me come out, you churl? Very well, I can wait here till the women return. I can find a little place to rest on." And so saying he threw himself on the heap of rose leaves Noémi had turned out. "Ah, what a good bed—a Lucullan couch! Ha! ha!"

The women came back with Michael from their walk through the island. Therese saw with uneasiness that Almira was not lying in the veranda, but was guarding the door of the distillery.

When Theodor heard Therese's voice, he thought of a good trick to play. He buried himself in the rose leaves, so that nothing was to be seen of him; and when Noémi, with the words, "What have you here, Almira?" looked in at the door, he put his head out and grinned at her: "Your own beloved bridegroom is here, lovely Noémi!"

Noémi, starting back, screamed aloud.

"What is it?" asked the mother, hastening up.

"There, among the roses . . ." stammered the girl.

"Well, what among the roses? A spider?"

"Yes . . . a spider . . ."

Theodor sprung laughing from his bed of roses, and like one who has surprised his dear ones with a capital joke, rushed with shouts of laughter to Mamma Therese, embraced her, without noticing her angry looks or Noémi's disgusted face, and kissed her several times.

"Ha! ha! Did I take you by surprise? You sweet dear mamma, be happy: your dear son-in-law is here; he has risen like a fairy from the roses. He! he!" Then he turned toward Noémi, but she slipped away from his embrace, and then first Theodor Krisstyan was aware of the presence of a third person—Michael Timar.

This discovery damped his joviality, which indeed was only put on, and for this reason it was disagreeable to see some one with whom most unpleasant recollections were connected.

"Your servant, Mr. Supercargo!" he addressed Timar. "We meet here again? You have not any more Turkish pashas in your ship? He! he! Don't be afraid, Mr. Supercargo."

Timar shrugged his shoulders and said nothing. Then Theodor turned to Noémi, and put his arm caressingly round the girl's waist, who in answer to it pushed him away and turned her face from him.

"Leave the girl alone!" said Therese shortly, in a severe tone. "What do you want now?"

"There, there—don't turn me out of the house before I have got in. Is it not permissible to embrace my little bride? Noémi won't break if I look at her? What are you so afraid of me for?"

218

"We have good reason," said Therese, sullenly.

"Don't be angry, little mother. This time I have not come to get anything from you: I bring you something—a great, great deal of money. Ho! ho! a heap of money! So much that you could buy back your fine house that you once had, and the fields and gardens on the Ostrova Island—in short, all that you have lost. You shall have it all again. I know that I, as a son, owe you the duty of making good all that you lost by my poor father's fault."

By this time Theodor had become so sentimental that he was shedding tears, but it left the spectators unmoved: they believed as little in his tears as in his laughter.

"Let us go in, into the room," said he, "for what I have to say is not for every ear."

"Don't talk such nonsense," Frau Therese said, angrily. "What do you mean by 'every ear' here on this lonely island? You can say anything before Timar: he is an old friend—but go on. I know you are hungry, and that's what it all means."

"Ah, you dear good mother! how well you know your Theodor's little weakness of always having a splendid appetite. And you do so thoroughly understand the exquisite Greek *cuisine*, at sight of which one would wish to be all stomach. There is no such housekeeper in the world as you are. I have dined with the Sultan of Turkey, but he has no cook who can compare with you."

Frau Therese had the weakness of being sensitive to praise of her housekeeping. She never grudged good things to any guest, and even her deadly enemy she could not send away empty.

Theodor wore a so-called Figaro hat, which was then in fashion, and managed that the low door-way of the little cottage should knock it off his head, in order to be able to say, "Oh, these confounded new-fangled hats! but that's sure to happen when one is used to high door-ways. In my new house they are all folding-doors, and such a splendid view over the sea from my rooms."

"Have you then really a home anywhere?" asked Therese as she laid the table.

"I should think so! At Trieste, and in the finest palace in the town. I

219

am agent to the principal shipbuilder."

"At Trieste?" interrupted Timar. "What's his name?"

"He turns out sea-going vessels," said Theodor, casting a contemptuous look at Timar. "He is not merely a barge-builder—and for that matter his name is Signor Scaramelli."

Timar was silent. He did not care to let out that he himself was having a large vessel built for the ocean trade by Scaramelli.

"I am just rolling in money!" bragged Theodor. "Millions and millions pass through my hands. If I were not such an honest man, I could save thousands for myself. I have bought something for my dear little Noémi, which I once promised her. What did I promise? A ring. What sort of a stone? A ruby, an emerald? Well, it is a brilliant, a four-carat brilliant: it shall be our betrothal ring. Here it is." Theodor felt in his breeches-pocket, fumbled a long time, made at last a terrible grimace, and stared on the ground. "It is lost!" groaned he, turning his pocket out, and showing the treacherous hole through which the valuable engagement-ring with the four-carat diamond had escaped. Noémi broke into a hearty laugh. She had such a lovely ringing voice when she laughed, and one seldom had a chance of hearing it.

"But it is not lost!" cried Theodor; "you may spare your laughter, fair lady!" and he began to draw off his boot—and there really was the ring, which fell out of the turned-over top of the boot on to the tray.

"There it is! A good horse does not run away. My little Noémi's engagement-ring has never left me. Look now, Mamma Therese—your future son-in-law has brought this for his bride; there, what do you say to that? And you, Mr. Underwriter, if you understand these things, what do you value this diamond at?"

Timar looked at the stone and said, "Paste. In the trade it is worth about five groschen."

"Hold your tongue, Supercargo! What do you know about it? You understand hay and maize, and perhaps never saw a diamond in your life."

And so saying, he placed the despised ring, which Noémi would on no account wear, on his little finger, and was busy all through the meal in showing it off. The young gentleman had a fine appetite. During dinner he

220

talked very big about what a gigantic establishment this shipbuilder's was, and how many million square feet of wood were required every year. There were hardly any trees left in the neighborhood fit for building ships. They had to be brought from America. There were only a few left in Sclavonia. Only after he had dined well, he came out with the principal affair.

"And now, my dear lady, I will tell you what I have come about."

Therese looked at him with anxious distrust.

"Now I will make you all happy—you, as well as Noémi and myself. And besides, I can do Signor Scaramelli a good turn. That's enough for me. Says Scaramelli to me one day, 'Friend Krisstyan, I say, you will have to go off to Brazil.'"

"If only you were there now!" sighed Therese.

Theodor understood and smiled. "You must know that from there comes the best wood for shipbuilding. The makaya and the murmuru tree, used for the keel; the poripont and patanova, from which the ribs are made; the royoc and grasgal-trees, which do not decay in water; the 'mort-aux-rats'-tree, the iron-wood for rudder shafts, and sour-gum-tree for paddle-floats; also the teak and mahogany for ship's fittings, and—"

"Pray, stop with your ridiculous Indian names," interrupted Therese; "you think you will turn my head by reeling out a whole botanical catalogue, so that I sha'n't see the wood for the trees. Tell me why—if there are such incomparable trees in Brazil—why you are not there already?"

"Yes, but that's just where my grand idea comes in. Why, said I to Signor Scaramelli, should I travel to Brazil when we have plenty of wood close by even better than that of Brazil? I know an island in the middle of the Danube which is provided with a virgin forest, and where grow splendid trees, which can compete with those of South America."

"I thought so," murmured Therese to herself.

"The poplars take the place of the patanovas; the nut-trees far surpass mahogany, and those we have in hundreds on our island."

"My nut-trees!"

"The wood of the apple-tree is much better than that of the jaskarilla-tree."

"Indeed; so you have already disposed of my apple-trees!"

"Plum-tree wood need not fear comparison with the best teak."

"And those too you would cut down and sell to Signor Scaramelli?" asked Frau Therese, quietly.

"We shall get a mint of money for them; at least ten gulden for each tree. Signor Scaramelli has given me *carte blanche*. He has left me free to make a contract with you. I have it in my pocket; you have only to sign and our fortune is made. And when once the useless trees here are cut down, we will not stay here, but go and live in Trieste. We will plant the whole island with 'Prunus mehaleb'—you know they make Turkish pipe-stems from it. This tree requires no care; we need only keep one man here; he would sell the yearly crop of tubular stems to the merchants, and we should receive five hundred ducats for every rood—for ten roods five thousand ducats."

Timar could not suppress a smile. Speculations of such rashness had not occurred even to him.

"Well, what is there to laugh at?" Theodor said, in a lordly manner. "I know all about these things."

"And I understand, too," said Therese, "what you want. As often as my unlucky star brings you here, you appear like a bird of prey, and I may be sure you have some malicious scheme against me. You know that you will not find any money with me, but you help yourself. Once before you came with a boat and carried off what we had saved for our own use, and turned it into money. Now you are no longer satisfied with the fruit of which you took tithes more jealously than any usurious pasha. You want to sell the trees, too, over my head—those trees, my treasures, my only friends in the world, which I have planted and nurtured, which keep me, and under which I can rest. Fy! for shame! to tell me such stories of getting money for these trees, to build ships of them. For certain, you would only cut them down to sell them for a trifle to the nearest charcoal-burner—that is your splendid plan. Who are you going to take in? Not me, who know your cunning. I tell you, have done with your foolish tricks, or you may yet learn what is the use of Turkish pipe-stems!"

"No, no, Mamma Therese, I am not thinking of joking; you may be sure I did not come here for nothing: remember what day it is. It is my *fête*-day, and the day of my little darling Noémi's birth. You know my poor father and hers betrothed us to each other when we were little; they settled that as soon as Noémi was seventeen we should be united. I should have come from the ends of the earth for such a day as this. Here I am, with all the warmth of my loving heart; but people can not live on love alone. It is true I get good pay from Signor Scaramelli, but that goes to the splendid furniture of my house in Trieste. You must give me something with Noémi, so that she may make an appearance consistent with her rank. The bride can not enter the bridegroom's house with empty hands; she is your only daughter, and has a right to require of you that you should provide for her handsomely."

Noémi had sat down sulkily in a corner of the room, and remained with her back to the company and her head against the wall.

"Yes," continued Theodor. "You must give Noémi a dowry. Do not be so selfish. Keep half your trees, for all I care, and leave the other half to me; where and how I sell them is my affair. Give Noémi the nut-trees for a dowry: for those I have, really, a certain purchaser."

Therese had come to the end of her patience. "Listen, Theodor. I do not know whether to-day is your *fête* or not, but one thing I do know, that it is not Noémi's birthday. And yet more surely I know that Noémi will not marry you, if you were the only man on God's earth."

"Ha! ha! leave that to me—I am not afraid."

"Just as you like; but now, once for all, you shall never have my splendid nut-trees, if Noah's ark was to be built of them. One single tree I will give you, and that you can use for the end you will come to sooner or later. You say to-day is your *fête*-day, and that would be a good day to do it."

At these words Theodor rose, but not to go on his way—only to turn the chair he had been sitting on, and place himself astride on it, with his elbows on its back, and looking into Therese's eyes he said with provoking coolness—

"I must say you are very kind, Mamma Therese; you seem to have forgotten that if I say one word—"

"Say it then! You can speak freely before this gentleman: he knows everything."

"And that this island does not belong to you?"

"Yes."

"And that it would only cost me one word, either at Vienna or Constantinople—"

"To make us homeless and shelterless and beggars."

"Yes; I can do that!" cried Theodor Krisstyan, who, now showing his true colors, looked with greedy eyes at Therese and drew a paper from his pocket, which he held toward her. "Here is the agreement, and here is the date. You know what I can do, and I will do it, if you do not sign this contract immediately." Therese trembled.

"No, sir," said Timar, laying his hand gently on Theodor's shoulder.

224

"You can not do that."

"What?" asked he, throwing his head back defiantly.

"Lay information anywhere of the existence of this island, and of its unauthorized occupation."

"Why should I not do it?"

"Because another has already done it."

"You!" cried Theodor, raising his fist to Michael.

"You!" exclaimed Therese, pressing her hands to her brow.

"Yes; I," said Timar, steadily and calmly. "I have given information both at Vienna and in Constantinople, that here close to the Ostrova Island a nameless and uninhabited islet has been formed in the course of the last fifty years. Then I begged of the Vienna Government as well as of the Sublime Porte to leave me the usufruct of the islet for ninety years: as an acknowledgement of ownership, the Hungarian Government is to receive every year a sack of nuts, and the Sublime Porte a box of dried fruit. The patent in question and the imperial firman are already in my hands." Timar drew the two deeds out of the envelope he had received at his Baja office, and which had, so much pleased him. When he became a great man, he had determined to procure comfort and peace for this poor storm-driven family. That sack of nuts and box of fruit had cost him large sums. "But," he concluded, "I hastened to transfer the rights thus obtained to the present inhabitants and colonists. Here is the official deed of settlement."

Therese fell speechless at Michael's feet. She could only sob and kiss the hands of the man who had freed her from this incarnate curse, and driven away the phantom which oppressed her heart by day and night.

Noémi held her two hands on her heart, as if afraid that it would cry aloud, and betray what her lips suppressed.

"You see then, Herr Theodor Krisstyan," said Michael, "that you have nothing to get on this island for the next ninety years."

Pale with rage, Theodor screamed, foaming at the mouth, "And who are you who dare to meddle in the affairs of this family? What gives you a right to do it?"

"My love!" cried Noémi suddenly, with all the strength of overpowering passion, while she fell on Michael's breast, and threw her arms round his neck.

Theodor said not a word more. He shook his fist in silent rage at Timar, and rushed out of the room. In his look lay that hatred which does not hesitate to use a dagger or to mix poison. But even when he was gone, the girl still held Timar's neck in her embrace.

CHAPTER V.
OUT OF THE WORLD.

What induced Noémi to throw herself on Timar's breast and acknowledge openly that she loved him? Did she wish thus to banish forever the man whose presence was hateful to her, and make it impossible for him any longer to desire her as his wife? Had this child of solitude no idea of the etiquette which demands that such feelings should be concealed in a maiden's breast? Or did she confuse love with the gratitude she could not help feeling toward the man who had freed her and her mother from anxiety, and won for their lifelong enjoyment the possession of this little paradise? Perhaps she was alarmed when she saw her tormentor feeling for a weapon, and had instinctively thrown herself on her benefactor's breast to protect him from attack. She might have thought that this poor ship's captain, whose mother was as poor as her mother, had said that he had "no one" in the world; why should she not be "some one" to him? Would he have returned here if something had not attracted him, and if he cared for her why should she not love him?

No, no; no explanation, no reason, no excuse was needed; here was nothing but pure, unselfish love.

She did not know why, she asked for no reason—she only loved. She loved without inquiring whether it was allowed by God and man, whether it would bring her joy or sorrow. She did not long to be happy or great, her lord's liege lady, crowned with the silver crown, and blessed by the Triune God—she only loved. She never thought of humiliation with bent head, she asked neither the protection of a husband nor the pity and forgiveness of God—she only loved. Such was Noémi.

Poor Noémi! what you must suffer for this! . . . Michael had for the first time in his life heard it said that some one loved him. From real inclination, as a poor ship's captain in another man's service, without selfish interest, for his own sake alone. A miraculous warmth overflowed his heart, the warmth which will awake the dead from their long sleep at the resurrection. He raised his hands timidly and trembling to the shoulders of

227

the girl, and asked, with softly whispering voice, "And that is really true?"

The maiden moved the head which lay on his heart and nodded to him. "Yes; it is true."

Michael looked at Therese. She came toward them, and laid her hand on Noémi's head, as if to say, "Well, then, love him!" It was a solemn and silent scene, in which each could hear the heart-beats of the other.

Therese broke the silence first. "If only you knew," she said to Timar, "how many tears the girl has shed for you. If you had seen her go daily up the rock, and look for hours over the quiet landscape, where you vanished from her sight. If you had heard her whisper your name in her dreams!"

Noémi made a deprecating gesture with her hand, as if to entreat her mother to betray no more. But Michael only noticed it by drawing her closer to himself. See, here at last is one being in the wide world who knows how to love him; who in the "Man of Gold" loves the man and not the gold. And it seemed to him as if he had been in banishment, as long as he had walked through the world, and only now had found a new earth and new heaven, and in them a new life. He bent to kiss the girl's brow, and felt her heart throb against his.

And around him were only springing flowers, fragrant shrubs, humming bees, and singing birds, which all proclaimed "Thou shalt love!" Speechless bliss led them out into the air, and when they looked into each other's eyes, both thought, "How wonderful! thine eyes are the same color as mine." The brilliant sky and the fragrant earth had agreed to inthrall them—their own inclination completed the spell. When a child who has never loved, and a man who has never been loved, meet each other, how is it likely to be with them?

The day drew to a close, but they had not yet been satisfied with joy. The evening fell, the moon rose. Noémi led Michael to the top of the rock, whence she had once looked after the departing guest with tears. There Timar sat down among the sweet lavender; Noémi placed herself beside him, and leaned her curly golden head on the arm of the man, whose enraptured face was raised to the sky. Therese stood behind them and looked down smiling. The silver moon shone radiant from the golden-dusky vault, and the tempting phantom spoke, "Behold this treasure! it belongs to you. You found it; it gave itself to you and is yours. You had obtained all except love, only that was wanting, and now you have found that too. Take, enjoy to the dregs the cup which the Almighty has given you. You will become a new man! The man whom a woman loves becomes a demi-god. You are happy; you are beloved." . . . Only the inner voice whispered, "You are a thief!"

With the first kiss a new world had arisen for Michael; a wonderful change had taken place in his soul. The first feeling which overpowered him was a secret dread, a fear of happiness; should he submit to it or fly from it? Does a blessing or a curse rest on it? does it bring life or death? what follows on it? What deity will answer these questions? The flower is answered when it unfolds its cup, the butterfly when it opens its wings, the bird when it builds its nest; but not the man when he asks, "Is it good or evil to follow the call of my heart?"

And his heart said, "Look in her eyes!" It is not sinful to be transported by a glance of the eye, and this intoxication lasts. Michael forgot the whole world when he looked in her eyes; a new creation arose for him, full of bliss and joy and earthly happiness. The exquisite presentiment stupefied him.

Since his youth no one had loved him. He had once hoped for affection, struggled for it with might and main, and when he thought he was at the goal, his joy was turned to ashes by crushing disappointment. And here to his face he is told that he is beloved. Everything tells him so; the animals which lick his hand, the lips which betray the heart's secret, the blush and the glance which tell more than the mouth. Even she who ought to guard the secret jealousy, the mother of the loving girl, even she betrays it—"She loves so passionately that it will be her death!"

No; that it shall not be. . . .

Timar passed on the island one of those days which outweigh an eternity. A day full of endless feeling—a day of self-forgetfulness and waking dreams, when what a man has longed for in visions of the night actually stands before him.

But when on the third night, after a season of ideally rapturous intercourse, he returned from the moonlit world of enchantment to his solitary dark bedroom, the inward accuser, who would not be silenced or lulled to sleep, called him to account.

This voice would not let him sleep. He was restless all night, and dawn found him out under the trees; his decision was made—he would go away and not come back for a long time, till he was forgotten. Till he also had forgotten that he had lived three days in Elysium, that he had been permitted to know happiness.

When the sun rose, he had been round the whole island, and when he got back he found Frau Therese and her daughter busy preparing breakfast.

"I must go away to-day," said Michael to Therese.

"So soon," whispered Noémi.

"He has a great deal to do," said Therese to her daughter.

This was only natural enough. A captain is only a servant who must look after his affairs, and not waste the time for which he must account to his employer.

He was not pressed to stay—it was quite right that he should leave. He will come back, and they have plenty of time to wait for him—one year, two years, till the hour of death, till eternity. But Noémi did not touch her glass of new milk: she could not have swallowed a drop. He must not be detained; if he has business he must go and attend to it. Therese herself brought out his gun and knapsack, and said to Noémi, "You carry the gun, that Almira may not hurt it. Go with him to the boat."

Timar walked silently beside Noémi; the girl's hand rested in his; suddenly she stood still. Michael did so too, and looked in her eyes. "You want to ask me something?" he said. The girl thought awhile, then she said, "No; nothing." Timar had learned to read her eyes; he guessed her thoughts. Noémi wanted to ask him, "Tell me, my beloved, my all; what has become of the white-faced girl who once came with you to the island, and was called Timéa?"

But she said nothing, only walked on silently with his hand in hers.

Michael's heart was heavy when they said good-bye. When Noémi gave him his gun she whispered to him, "Take care of yourself, that no harm may come to you;" and when she pressed his hand, she looked at him once more with those heavenly blue and soulful eyes, and said, with a voice of entreaty, "You will return?"

Michael was fascinated by the entreating voice. He pressed the child to him and murmured—"Why don't you say 'Wilt not *thou* return?' Why am I never to hear *thou*?"

The girl cast down her eyes and gently shook her head. "Do say 'thou,'" he begged once more. She hid her face on Michael's breast, but would not do his will.

"So you can not, or will not, call me 'thou?'—one single word—are you afraid?" The maiden covered her face with both hands, and was silent. "Noémi, I beg of thee say that one little word and make me happy. Do not let me go without it."

But she shook her head silently and could not utter it.

"Then farewell to you, dear Noémi," faltered Michael, and sprung into his boat. The rushes of the marsh soon hid the island from his gaze. But as long as he could distinguish its woods, he still saw the girl leaning on an acacia-tree, sadly gazing out with her head on her hand; but she did not call after him the desired word.

CHAPTER VI.
THE TROPIC OF CAPRICORN.

After Michael had rowed across to the other side, he gave over the boat to a fisherman to keep till he came back. But would he ever come back?

He wished to go on foot as far as the wharf, where Fabula was busy with the lading of his ships. It is hard work to row against the stream, and in Timar's present frame of mind he was in no mood for muscular exertion; there was in his heart a stronger current, to contend against which he needed all his strength.

The district through which he had to pass was a widespread alluvial deposit of the Danube, like those found in the lower reaches of the river. The capricious stream has burst some dam, and altered its course. Every year it tears portions from one bank and carries them over to the other. On this deposit the trees uprooted with it form a new growth, and through this dark natural forest wind lonely paths—the roads of the osier-cutters and fisher-folk. Here and there you come to a forsaken hut with a shingle roof whose walls are covered with creepers. These sometimes shelter a snipe-shooter, conceal a robber, or form the lair of a wolf and her cubs.

Michael, deep in thought, strode silently on through this desert: he had thrown his gun over his shoulder.

"You can never return here," said Timar to himself. "If it is difficult to carry through one lie with consistency, how can you manage two?—two contradictory lies? If you accept Noémi's love, you will be inseparably bound to her, and must live henceforth two lives, both full of deceit. . . . You are no boy, to be passion's tool, and perhaps it is not passion which you feel, possibly merely a passing desire or only gratified vanity.

"Then the rejected bridegroom—how is he to be got rid of? He would kill you, or you him—a delightful relationship indeed to end on the scaffold!"

He took off his hat and wiped the sweat from his brow; it soothed his burning temples to let the breeze fan them.

"Am I never to be happy?" he sighed. "All these years I have worked

232

early and late for other people; why should I be so wretched? I adored my wife, and her coldness has brought me to despair; but Noémi loves me. That can no longer be altered, and in the island, outside the world, the laws of society and religion have no power. . . . I could easily pay off that fellow who comes between us, and then I could live here in peace for half the year. Timéa would only suppose that I was away on business."

The wind of spring rustled through the young poplar stems. Here, where the path turned, stood a hut made of interwoven osier-twigs, whose entrance was concealed by brambles. Timar stood still and put on his hat. At that moment two shots rattled close to him, the two balls whistling over his head with that unpleasant sound which resembles the buzz of an approaching wasp or the clang of an æolian harp. Michael's hat, pierced by two balls, flew from his head into the bushes. Both shots came from the ruined hut. For the first instant the shock paralyzed his limbs; they came like two answers to his secret thoughts. A shudder ran through his whole body: the next moment rising fury took the place of fear; he lowered his gun, cocked both barrels, and rushed angrily toward the hut, from which the smoke of the discharged weapon poured through the crevices.

Before the muzzle of his gun stood a trembling man—Theodor Krisstyan. His discharged pistol was still in his hand, he held it now as a protection to his head, and shook so that every limb quivered.

"It is you—you!" cried Michael.

"Mercy!" stammered the trembling wretch, throwing away his pistol, and stretching both hands entreatingly to Michael: his knees knocked together, and he could hardly keep his feet; his face was pale as death, his eyes dull, he was more dead than alive. Timar recovered his composure: fear and anger had left him—he lowered his gun. "Come nearer," he said to the assassin.

"I dare not," faltered he, clinging to the wood-work. "You will kill me."

"Don't be afraid; I don't want your life. There"—he discharged his gun in the air—"now I am unarmed, and you have no cause to fear." Theodor crept out. "You wanted to kill me," said Michael. "You wretched creature! I pity you!"

233

The young rascal dared not look at him.

"Theodor Krisstyan, so young, and already a murderer!—but you could not do it. Examine yourself; you are not naturally bad, but your soul has been envenomed: I know your history, and I make excuses. You have good capacities, and use them badly—you are a vagabond and a swindler; does such a life content you? Impossible!—begin afresh—shall I help you to a post in which you can, with your education, honestly support yourself? I have many connections: it is in my power: there is my hand on it."

The murderer fell on his knees before the man he would have killed, seized the offered hand with both his own, and covered it, sobbing, with kisses.

"Oh, sir, you are the first man who has ever spoken thus to me; let me kneel at your feet! From boyhood I have been chased from every door like a dog without a master; I had to steal or beg every morsel I eat; no one gave me a hand but those who were worse than myself, and who led me further astray. I have led a shameful, miserable life, full of deceit and treachery, and I tremble before any one who knows me; and you hold out a hand to me—you, for whom I have been lying in wait like a brigand, you will save me from myself! Let me kneel before you, and thus receive your commands!"

"Stand up! I am no friend to sentiment; tears make me suspicious."

"You are right," said Theodor, "and especially with such a well-known actor as I am, who if you say to him 'Take that groschen and cry,' could at once break into floods of tears. Now people don't believe me if I really weep; I will suppress my tears."

"All the more because I do not intend to address a moral lecture to you, but only to speak of very dry business matters. You spoke of your connection with Scaramelli, and a business journey to Brazil."

"All lies, sir."

"So I thought. You have no connection with Scaramelli?"

"I had, but it was broken off."

"Did you run away, or were you dismissed?"

"The former."

"With trust-money?"

234

"With three or four hundred gulden."

"Say five hundred. Would you not be glad to return them to the firm? I have relations with their house."

"I do not want to remain there."

"And what connection has this with the Brazilian journey?"

"There is not a word of truth in it; no ship-wood comes from there."

"Not even those you mentioned, among which were dye and chemical woods?"

Theodor smiled. "The truth is that I wanted to sell the trees of the ownerless island to a charcoal-burner to get a little money; Therese guessed at once my real object."

"Then you did not come to the island for Noémi's sake?"

"Oh, I have as many wives as the countries I have visited."

"H'm—I know of a very good situation for you in Brazil, an agency for a lately commenced enterprise, where a knowledge of the Hungarian, German, Italian, English, and Spanish languages is necessary."

"I speak and write all these languages."

"I know it—and also Greek, Turkish, Polish, and Russian: you are a clever fellow. I will procure for you this situation, in which you can make use of your talents. The agency of which I speak carries with it a salary of three thousand dollars and a percentage of the profits, the amount of which will depend on yourself."

Theodor could hardly believe his ears. But he was so accustomed to pretense that when he was overcome by real gratitude he had not the courage to give it expression, lest it should be taken for acting.

"Is this your real meaning, sir?"

"What motive should I have at this moment for jesting with you? You attempted my life, and I must secure myself. I can not send you out of the world—my conscience forbids it—so I must try to make an honest man of you in the interest of my own safety. If you are in good circumstances, I shall have nothing to fear. Now you can understand my course of action. As a proof that my offer is in earnest, take my pocket-book. You will find in it the necessary journey expenses to Trieste, and probably as much as what you owe to Scaramelli. At Trieste you will find a letter which gives you further directions. And now we will part—one to the right, and the other to the left."

Theodor's hand shook as he received the pocket-book. Michael lifted his pierced hat from the ground. "And you can look on these shots just as you like. If they were the attack of an assassin, you have every reason not to approach me in any region within reach of the law; but if they were the shots of an insulted gentleman, you know that at our next meeting it is my turn to shoot."

Theodor Krisstyan bared his breast, and exclaimed passionately, "Shoot me if ever I come in sight of you again! Shoot me like a mad dog!" He raised the discharged pistol, and pressed it into Timar's hand. "Shoot me with my own pistol it you ever meet me in this world! Do not ask, say not a word, but kill me!"

He insisted on Michael's taking the pistol, and putting it in his pocket.

"Farewell!" said Timar, and then he left him and went on his way.

Theodor stood still looking after him. Then he ran, and caught him up. "Sir, one word—you have made a new man of me—allow me, if ever I write to you, to begin with the words, 'My Father.' In those words once lay for me shame and horror; let me find in them henceforth a fountain of trust and happiness—my father, my father!"

He kissed Michael's hand with impassioned warmth, rushed away, threw himself down on the grass behind the first bush that hid him from Timar's eyes, and wept—real, true tears.

Poor little Noémi stood for an hour under the acacia-tree where she had taken leave of Michael. Therese, as she stayed out so long, had gone to seek her, and now sat beside her daughter on the grass. Not to be idle, she had brought out her knitting.

Suddenly Noémi exclaimed, "Mother, did you hear?—two shots on the other shore!"

They listened. There was deep stillness in the drowsy air.

"Two more shots! Mother, what is it?"

Therese tried to calm her. "They must be sportsmen, child, who are shooting there."

Noémi's cheeks lost their color, and she looked as pale as the acacia blossoms over her head. She pressed her hands vehemently to her breast and

236

faltered, "Oh, no, no! he will never come back!"

It grieved her to the heart that she had not said the little word "thou" to him when he begged so hard.

"Master Fabula," said Timar to his faithful steward, "this year we will not send the crop either to Raab or Komorn."

"What shall we do with it, then?"

"We will grind it here. I have two windmills on my property, and we can hire thirty water-mills; those will suffice."

"Then we must open a huge warehouse, where we can sell such a quantity."

"That will not be wanting. We will load the flour into small ships, which can go up to Karlstadt; thence we will transfer it in barrels to Brazil."

"To Brazil!" screamed Fabula, quite frightened. "I can't go there with it."

"I was not thinking of sending you there, Master Fabula; your department is the grinding and the transport to Trieste. I will give the agents and millers their orders to-day, and you can scold and manage in my absence just as if I were there."

"Many thanks," said Master Fabula, and shook his head violently as Herr von Levetinczy left the office. "That will be a gigantic folly," he grumbled to himself. "To begin with, the flour will be musty before it arrives; then no one will buy it; thirdly, nobody will ever see the color of money which has to come from Brazil. How could he claim it? there is no fiscal authority there, or even a vice-consul. In short, it is just another of those colossal, everlasting pieces of folly of our Herr Levetinczy, but it will turn out well, to every one's surprise, as every stupid thing does that our master undertakes. And I don't doubt that our flour-ships will come back laden with gold-dust from Brazil; but for all that it is a great folly."

Our Herr Fabula was perfectly right. Timar was of the same opinion. He ran a risk in this speculation of losing at least a hundred thousand gulden. But this idea was not of to-day. It had long been in his mind whether a Hungarian merchant might not make better profits than in grain contracts and the chartering of cargo-ships. Would it not be possible for those goods which have to struggle with foreign competition to find their own place in

237

the great bazaar of the world's market?

The export trade in flour was an old plan of his. To prepare for its execution he had completed his mills, and built a large vessel at Trieste. But the reason of his hasty determination to begin work at once was only on Noémi's account; and his meeting with Theodor had brought this decision to a head.

This business was only a pretext; the principal thing was to put a hemisphere between himself and that man. Those who saw in what ceaseless labor Timar spent the next weeks—how he hurried from one mill to another, and from there to his ships; how he dispatched them the moment they were laden, and personally superintended the transport—all said, "What a pattern of a merchant! He is tremendously rich; he has directors, agents, captains, stewards, overseers, foremen, and yet he sees to all himself like a common contractor. He understands business." (If only they had known what depended on this business!)

Three weeks passed before the first ship laden with barrels of Hungarian flour lay ready to weigh anchor in the harbor of Trieste. The ship was called "Pannonia;" it was a beautiful three-masted galliot. Even Master Fabula was loud in its praise; for he was present at the loading of the flour. But Timar himself never saw it; he had not once come to Trieste to see it before it started. During those weeks he remained in Levetinczy or Pancsova. The whole enterprise was in Scaramelli's name; Timar had his reasons for keeping his own name out of it; and he only communicated in writing with the fully empowered firm of Scaramelli.

One day he received a letter from Theodor Krisstyan. When he opened it he was surprised to find money in it—a hundred gulden note. The contents of the letter ran thus—

"My Father,—When you read these lines I shall be afloat on board the splendid ship 'Pannonia,' as Brazilian agent of the house of Scaramelli.

"Accept my warmest thanks for your kind recommendation. The bank has advanced me two months' salary, of which I inclose a hundred gulden, with the request that you would be good enough to pay it over to the landlord of The White Ship at Pancsova. I am in debt to that amount to that poor man, and am thankful to be able to pay this sum. Heaven bless you for all your goodness to me!"

Timar breathed freely. "The man has already improved; he remembers his old debts and pays them with his savings. What a sweet thought to have brought a lost sheep back to the fold—to be the savior of an enemy who attempted one's life—to give back to him life, the world, honor, and bring to light a pearl purified of the mire in which it lay! Is not this a truly Christian act? You have a generous soul. If only the inward accuser would not reply, 'You are a murderer!'

"You do not rejoice to have saved a man, but rather at getting rid of him. If you received news that a tornado had caught your ship and sunk it with every soul on board, what joy it would give you! You are not thinking of the flour-trade with its profits and losses, but that every year in the swamps of La Plata and the river Amazon that fearful specter walks—the yellow fever—which, like the tiger, lies in ambush for the new-comer. Of every hundred, sixty fall victims to it. It is that of which the prospect gives you pleasure. You are a murderer!"

Timar felt the satisfaction of a man who has succeeded in putting an enemy out of the way—a joy with which bitter self-condemnation and anxious forebodings were mingled.

From henceforward Timar was transformed. He was hardly to be recognized. The usually cold-blooded man betrayed in everything a singular restlessness; he gave contradictory orders, and forgot an hour after what he had said. If he started on a journey, he turned back half-way; he began to avoid business, and seemed indifferent to the most important affairs; then again he grew so excitable that the smallest neglect enraged him. He might be seen wandering on the shore for half a day at a time, with his head down like one who is nearly mad, and begins by running away from home. Another time he shut himself into his room and would not let any one in; the letters which came to him from all parts lay unopened in a heap on his table. This shrewd, clever man could think of nothing but the golden-haired girl whom he had seen for the last time leaning on a tree by the island shore, with her head supported on her arm. One day he determined to return to her, and the next to drive the remembrance of her from his breast. He began to be superstitious; he waited for signs from Heaven, and visions to decide what he should do. Dreams always brought the same face, happy or sad, submissive or inconsolable, and he was more crazy than ever. But Heaven sent him no sign.

One day he decided to be reasonable and attend to his business affairs; that might perhaps steady his brain. He sat down before the heap of letters and began to open them all in turn. All that came of it was that he had forgotten at the end of a letter what he had read at the beginning. He only cared to read what was written in those blue eyes. But his heart began to beat fast when a letter fell into his hands which was heavier than the rest; he knew the handwriting of the address; it was Timéa's.

His blood ran cold. This was the sign from Heaven, this will decide the conflict in his soul.

Timéa writes to him—the angelic creature, the spotless wife. A single tender word from her will exercise an influence on her husband like a cry of "danger" to a drunken man. These well-known characters will call up the saintly face before his mind's eye, and lead him back to the right path.

In the letter is a small object; it must be a loving surprise, a little souvenir. Yes! to-morrow is her husband's birthday. This will be a charming letter, a sweet remembrance. Michael opened the envelope very carefully, after cutting round the seal. The first thing that surprised him was a key which fell out—the key of his writing-table.

But in the letter were these words: "My dear Sir,—You left the key of your writing-table in the lock. That you may not be uneasy about it, I send it to you. God keep you!—Timéa."

Nothing further. Timar had forgotten to take out the key that night when he came home secretly, when the conversation with Athalie had so disturbed his mind.

Nothing but the key and a couple of frigid lines. Timar put down the letter in vexation.

Suddenly a dreadful idea flashed through his mind. If Timéa found this key in his writing-table lock, perhaps she looked through the desk. Women are curious, and do such things. But if she did search in it, she must have found something she would recognize. When Timar disposed of Ali Tchorbadschi's treasures, he had been careful not to part with some objects,

240

which, if they came into the trade, might have led to discovery, but had, for the most part, only sold the separate diamonds. Among the precious objects was a medallion framed in brilliants, which contained a miniature portrait of a young lady, whose features bore a striking likeness to those of Timéa. It must be the picture of her mother, who had been a Greek. If Timéa found this medallion, she must know all; she would at once recognize her mother's portrait, and conclude that this jewel had belonged to her father. This would lead her to the further conclusion that her mother's valuables had fallen into Timar's hands, and thus she would arrive at the knowledge of how he had become rich, and that he had married her at the price of her own money. If Timéa was curious, she now knows all, and then she must despise her husband.

And do not the words of the letter betray this? Does not the wife wish her husband to understand, by the forwarding of the key, that she had discovered his secrets?

This thought was decisive to Michael as to whether his path was to lead up or down! Down!

"It is all one," thought he. "I am unmasked before the woman. I can no longer play the honest man, the true-hearted, generous benefactor. I am found out. I can only sink lower still!"

He was determined to return to the island. But he would not retreat like a defeated foe. He wrote to Timéa, and begged her to open all the letters which should come during his absence, to inform his agents of their contents, and, where a decision was necessary, to dispose, in the name of her husband, of all as she chose. At the same time he sent the key back, that it might be at hand if any documents were wanted.

That was his trump card. With the feeling that his secret was near discovery he hastened to lead up to it, and possibly that very thing might prevent its revelation. He left orders to his agents that all letters concerning his affairs were to be directed to his wife. He was going away for a long time, but he did not say where to.

Late in the afternoon he started in a hired carriage. He hoped his track would be lost, and did not take his own horses. A couple of days ago he had been superstitious, and awaited signs from Heaven, from the elements,

241

to show him the way. Now he noticed them no longer. He was determined to return to the island. But the sky and the elements tried to frighten him by evil omens, and even to detain him by force. Toward evening, when the long lines of poplars on the Danube shore were already in sight, suddenly a reddish-brown cloud appeared in the sky, approaching with great rapidity. The peasant driver began to pray and sigh, but when the smoke-like cloud drew nigh, his prayers changed to curses. The Galambocz gnats are coming!

They are creations of the Evil One, trillions in number, and living in the holes of the Galambocz rocks: suddenly they come out in swarms, forming a thick cloud, and if they descend into the plain, woe to the cattle they find in the open!

The flight of gnats covered the plain through which Timar had to drive; the tiny stinging plague swarmed over the bodies of the horses, creeping into their eyes, ears, and nostrils. The terrified animals could no longer be controlled—they turned round suddenly with the carriage, and bolted in a north-westerly direction. Timar ventured on a jump from the carriage; he leaped cleverly and safely without injury; the horses flew off and away. If he had attended to omens, this might have been sufficient to turn him also aside. But he was now obstinate. He was going on a road where man no longer asks for help from God. He was going where Noémi drew him and Timéa drove him. North pole and south pole, desire and his own will, pressed him on.

When he jumped from the carriage, he continued his journey on foot, keeping along the wooded river-bank. His gun had remained in the carriage, he had come with empty hands: he cut himself a walking-stick, and that was his only weapon: provided with this, he tried to make his way through the thicket. There he lost himself; night surprised him, and the more he wandered the less he found an outlet. At last he came on a hut built of osier-twigs, and decided to spend the night there.

He made a fire out of the dry branches lying near: fortunately he was carrying his game-bag when he jumped from the carriage, and in it were bread and ham; he broiled the ham over the fire and ate it with the bread.

He found also something else in the bag, the pistol with which Theodor had attacked him from the hut; perhaps from this very hut—quite

242

possible that it was the same. He could make no use of the pistol, for he had left his powder-horn in the carriage; but it did him a service by strengthening him in his fatalism: a man who had escaped so many dangers must still have some work to do in the world. And indeed he required some encouragement, for after nightfall it began to be uncanny here in the desert. Not far away wolves were howling, and through the bushes Timar saw the shining green eyes: one and another old Sir Isegrim came up to the back wall of the hut and executed a fearful howl. Timar dared not let the fire out all night, for it alone kept away the wild beasts. When he went inside, the uncomfortable hiss with which snakes receive human beings struck his ear, and a sluggish mass moved under his foot; perhaps he had trodden on a tortoise. Timar kept up the fire all night, and drew fantastic figures in the air with the glowing end of the fire-stick—perhaps the hieroglyphics of his own thoughts.

What a miserable night! He who has a home provided with every luxury, and a comfortable bed; in whose house rules a lovely young woman whom he can call his wife—spends a lonely night in a damp, fungus-grown hut: wolves howl round him, and over his head adders creep slowly through the rush-woven roof. And to-day is his birthday; a happy family festival indeed—in such surroundings! But they suit him—he wants nothing else.

Michael had a pious mind. From childhood he had been used night and morning to put up a silent prayer. He had never lost the habit, and in every danger or trouble of his eventful life, he had taken refuge in prayer. He believed in God; God was his deliverer, and whatever he undertook succeeded. But in this dreadful night he dared not pray; he would not speak with God.

"Do not Thou look where I go." From this birthday he gave up prayer. He defied fate.

When the day dawned, the nocturnal beasts of prey slunk back to their lairs. Timar left his inhospitable refuge, and soon found the path which led direct to the shore of the Danube: here a new horror awaited him. The Danube was enormously swollen, and had overflowed its banks. It was the season of the spring floods after the melting of the snow; the foaming yellow stream was filled with uprooted reeds and tree-trunks. The fisherman's hut which he sought, and which stood on the point of a hill, was in the water up to the threshold, and the boat he had left there was tied to a tree close by.

He found not a creature there. It is impossible to fish in such a flood, and the people had removed all their nets. If he wanted a sign from heaven, a direction from God's finger—here he had it. The swollen river barred his way with its whole majestic strength; at such times no one ventures on the river; the warning was there, the elements commanded him to return.

"Too late," said Timar. "I can not go back; I must go on."

The door of the hut was locked, and he broke it open to get his oars, as he saw through a chink that they were kept there. Then he got into the boat, tied himself in, loosed the boat, and pushed off. The current seized him at once, and rushed on with him. The Danube was at that time a powerful master, and uprooted forests in its rage; a mortal venturing on its surface was like a worm floating on a straw, and yet this worm defied it. He alone managed the two oars, which also served to steer with. On the rapid waves his skiff danced like a nutshell, but the wind was contrary, and tried to drive him back to the shore he came from. But Timar succumbed neither to wind nor water.

He had thrown his hat to the bottom of the boat; his hair, wet with perspiration, fluttered in the wind, and the waves splashing over the side threw their icy spray in his face—but they did not cool him. The thought was hot within him that Noémi might be in danger on the island. But the idea did not paralyze his arms. The Danube and the wind are two mighty powers—but stronger still are the passions and the will of man. Timar felt this. What activity in his mind, what muscle in his arm! It was a superhuman task in which he succeeded, to cross the current at the head of the Ostrova Island. Here he rested awhile.

The island of Ostrova was overflowed, the water was rushing among the trees. Here it was easier to get on by pushing his oars against the trunks; at the back of Ostrova he must let himself float down-stream to arrive at the ownerless island. When he had reached the right spot, and came out from among the trees, a new and surprising spectacle lay before him. The ownerless island was usually hidden behind a thick bed of osiers, over which only the tree-tops were visible; now none of the reeds was to be seen, and the island lay out in mid-stream. The flood had covered the reeds, the trees of the island stood in the water, and only at one place the rock raised its head above the surface.

With feverish impatience he let his boat float down. Every stroke brought him nearer to the erratic bowlder, whose crown was blue with lavender flowers, while the sides were shining gold with climbing nasturtium which clung to the stone; and the nearer he came the greater was his impatience. He could already see the orchard, whose trees stood in the water half-way up their trunk; but the rose-garden was dry, and there the lambs and kids had taken refuge. Now Almira's joyful bark fell on his ear; the black creature came running to the shore, rushed back, came on again, leaped into the water, and swam toward the new arrival and back again.

Does Michael see that rosy face there at the base of a blooming jasmine-bush, hurrying toward him to the very edge of the rushing water? One more stroke, and the boat has reached the shore. Michael springs out and the waves carry off the boat; he no longer wants it, and no one thinks of drawing it ashore.

Each only saw the other. Around them the paradise of the first man!—fruit-laden trees, blossoming fields, tame animals, surrounded by a watery ring, and therein—Adam and Eve.

The maiden stands pale and trembling before the new-comer, and as he rushes toward her, when she sees him before her, she throws herself with a burst of passion on his breast, and cries, in the self-forgetfulness of ecstasy, "Thou hast returned! Thou, thou!" and even when her lips are closed they still say, "Thou, thou!"

Around them is Eden. The jasmine-bush sends down on them its silvery flower-crown, and the choir of nightingales and blackbirds sing "Gospodi pomiluj."

CHAPTER VII.
SWEET HOME.

The waves carried off Michael's boat. That of the islanders, which had brought them here, had long rotted away, and they had never had another. The new-comer could not leave the island before the first fruit-dealers arrived. Before that time weeks and months must elapse.

Happy weeks, happy moons! Uncounted days of unbroken joy! The ownerless island was Timar's home. There he found work and rest. After the flood had passed away, the work of getting rid of the water left in the hollows gave him plenty to do. The whole day he was busy digging canals to carry it away; his hands looked like a laborer's from the blisters with which they were covered. When he threw spade and pick over his shoulder in the evening, and came back to the little cottage, he was met afar off, and lovingly welcomed. And when he had finished his canal and drawn off the marshy water, he looked upon his work as proudly as if it was the only one in all his life which could lay claim to be called a good action, and which he could confidently submit to his inward judge. The day of the opening of this canal was a festival on the little island. They had no church festivals and did not count Sundays: their saints' days were those on which God gave them some special joy.

These islanders were sparing of words. What the holy David said in one hundred and fifty psalms, was by them expressed in a sign, and what the poets have sung of love in all their verses, one glance of the eye was sufficient to tell; they learned to read each other's thoughts on the brow, they learned to think together.

Michael admired Noémi more every day. She was a faithful, grateful creature; she knew no care nor anxiety for the future; happy herself, she diffused happiness around. She never asked him, "What will become of me when you go? Will you leave me or take me? Is it good for me to love you? What church has given you its priestly blessing? Ought you to be mine? Has no other a right to you? What are you out there in the world? What sort of world do you live in?" Even in her face, her eyes, he never read a disquieting doubt—ever and only the one question "Lovest thou me?"

246

Frau Therese reminded Michael one day that he was tarrying long here; but he assured her that Master Fabula was looking after everything, and when Therese looked at Noémi, whose soft blue eyes ever turned like the sunflowers to the sun of Michael's face, she could only sigh, "Oh, how she loves him!"

Timar found it very necessary to dig all day, to drive piles, and bind fascines, in order by hard bodily labor to calm his even more heavily tasked mind. What is going on in the world? Thirty of his ships float on the Danube, and a fleet on the sea: his whole wealth, a property of more than a million, all lies in the hands of a woman. And if this woman in some giddy mood squanders the whole and scatters it to the winds, ruining her husband and his house, could he reproach any one? Was it not by his own will? He was happy here at home, and yet would have liked to know what was going on over there. His spirit lived in two places, was torn in two parts: there, his money, his honor, his position in the world; here, his love held him fast. In truth he could have got away. The Danube is not a sea; he was a good swimmer, and could at any time have reached the opposite shore; no one would have detained him. They knew he had work to do out in the world. But when he was with Noémi he forgot again everything outside her arms; he was sunk in love, bliss, and wonder.

"Oh, do not love me so much!" whispered the girl to him.

And so day after day passed by. The time of fruit-ripening drew near, and the branches were weighed down by their sweet burden. It was a pleasure to watch the daily progress of the fruit, how every day it developed more. Pears and apples began to put on their distinctive colors; the green is tanned to a leathery yellow, or receives gold and red streaks. The brown tone colors purple on the sunny side. In the golden tint mingle carmine splashes, and in the carmine greenish specks; the scented fruit smiles at one like a merry childish face. Timar helped the women to gather it. They filled great baskets with this blessing of heaven. He counted every apple he threw into the basket, how many hundreds, how many thousands. What a treasure! Real gold!

One afternoon, when he was helping Noémi to carry a full basket to the apple-room, he saw strangers arrive at the cottage: the fruit-buyers had come, the first visitors for many months past, bringing tidings from the outer world.

They negotiated about the fruit with Therese—the usual system of barter. Frau Therese wanted as usual to have grain in exchange, but the peddlers would not give her as much as before. They said wheat had become very dear. The corn-merchants of Komorn had made large purchases and driven up the prices; they ground it themselves, and sent it over the seas. Therese would not believe this—it was only gossip of the fruit-hawkers; but Timar paid great attention to it. That was his idea; what had come of it since then? Now he had no more rest for thinking of business and the cares of property. This news was to him what the bugle call is to an old soldier, who at the sound wishes himself back in the battle-field, even from the arms of his beloved.

The islanders thought it quite natural that Michael should make preparations to leave them. His business called him; and then he would return the following spring. Noémi only begged him not to throw away the clothes she had spun and woven for him, and which he had worn while with her. He will preserve them like a jewel.

And then he must often think of his poor Noémi. To that he could not answer in words.

He bribed the fruit-women to stay a day longer. And all that day he did nothing but visit, arm in arm with Noémi, all the places which had been witnesses of his tranquil happiness; here he plucked from a tree, and there from a flowery cluster, some leaflet to keep as a memorial. On every leaf and petal whole romances were written which only two people could read.

The last day passed so quickly! The boatmen wanted to leave in the evening, so as to row while it was cool. Michael must say farewell. Noémi was sensible, and did not cry; she knew he would return, and was more occupied in making provision to fill his knapsack.

"It will be dark when you get to the other side," she said, with tender anxiety. "Have you any arms?"

"No. No one will hurt me."

"But yet—here is a pistol in your haversack," said Noémi, and drew it out; and then her check paled, for she recognized Theodor's pistol, with

248

which he had often, when he came to the island, bragged and threatened that he would shoot Almira. "This is *his* weapon!" Timar was struck by the expression of her face.

"When you left here," said the girl, who was all excitement, "he watched for you on the other side, and shot at you with this pistol."

"What makes you think such a thing?"

"I heard two shots, and then yours. So it was this pistol that you took from him?" Timar was surprised that love can see what the eye can not reach. He could not tell a lie. "Did you kill him?" asked the girl.

"No."

"What has become of him?"

"You need fear him no longer. He is gone to Brazil; a hemisphere lies between us and him."

"I wish there were only three feet of earth between us!" cried Noémi, impetuously, seizing Michael's hand.

Michael looked in her face surprised. "You! you! with such murderous thoughts—you, who can not bear to see a chicken killed, who can not bring yourself to tread on a spider or to stick a butterfly on a pin!"

"But any one who would tear you from me, I could kill, were he a man, a devil, or an angel—!"

And she pressed the dearly beloved man to her breast in a passionate embrace. He trembled and glowed.

On reaching the other side, Michael again visited the fisherman's hut.

Two things occupied his mind: the slender figure among the evening mists on the flower-crowned rock, waving to him its tender farewells; and then that other figure conjured up by his imagination as it looks at home in Komorn. Well, he will have time to picture this image to himself on the long journey from the Lower Danube up to Komorn.

When the old fisherman saw Michael, he began to sigh (fishing-folk do not swear). "Just think, my lord, some rascal of a thief has stolen your boat during the floods: he broke into the hut and carried off the oars. What thieves there are in the world, to be sure!"

It did Timar good that at last some one should call him a thief to his face; that was what he was—and if he had stolen nothing more than a boat!

"We must not condemn the man," said he to the fisherman. "Who knows what danger he was in, or how much he needed a boat. We will get another. But now, my friend, we will get into your boat and try to arrive at the ferry to-night."

The fisherman was persuaded by a promise of liberal payment to undertake this, and by daylight they had reached the ferry where the ships generally took in their cargo. There were post-carriages at the inn on the bank, of which Timar engaged one to take him to Levetinczy. He thought he would there receive reports from the agent of what had passed during the last five months, so that when he got home to Komorn nothing new or surprising should greet him.

There was a one-storied residence on the estate at Levetinczy. In one wing lived the steward and his wife, while the other was given up to Timar. A staircase from this wing led to the park, and by this means he could gain access to the room which he had chosen as an office. Michael must pay attention to the trivial details if he wished to carry out his wearisome deceit consistently. He has been absent for five months, and has, of course, been a long way; but that hardly agrees with his arrival without luggage. In his knapsack there is only the suit of striped linen made for him by Noémi, for the suit in which he had gone to the island was intended for the cold season, and that, by now, was torn and worn out; his boots were patched. It would be difficult to account for his appearance. If he could get through the garden and by the outside steps into his office, the key of which he carries with him, he could there change his clothes quickly, get out his trunk, and when to all appearances he looked as though just come from a long journey, he could call in the steward.

All began well. Timar arrived without being seen, by the garden steps, at the door of his office.

But when he was going to open it with his private key, he made the disquieting discovery that another key was already in the lock. Some one was in the room! But his papers and ledgers were all there, and no one had any business inside. Who could the intruder be? He pulled the door open angrily and went in, and now it was his turn to be startled.

At his writing-table sat the last person he expected to find there. It

250

was Timéa. Before her lay the great ledger, in which she was at work.

A storm of mingled feelings burst over Michael—alarm because the first person he met after his secret journey was his own wife, pleasure at finding her alone, and astonishment that this woman was at work here.

Timéa raised her eyes in surprise when she saw Michael enter; then hastening toward him, she offered him her hand in silence. This white face was still an unsolved enigma to her husband. He could not read in it whether she knew all—whether she guessed something or not. What lay under this cold indifference? restrained contempt or concealed love? Or was the whole only the indolence of a lymphatic race? He had nothing to say to Timéa.

His wife seemed not to remark that his clothes were torn—women can see without looking. "I am glad you have come," said she gently. "I expected you any day. You will find your clothes in the next room; when you have dressed, will you please come back here? I shall have finished by that time." And then she put her pen in her mouth.

Michael kissed Timéa's hand. The pen between her teeth did not invite him to kiss her lips. He went into the adjoining room; there he found a basin of water, a clean shirt, and his clothes and house-shoes as at home. As Timéa could not know the day of his arrival, he must take for granted that she had made ready for him every day—and who knows for how long? But how comes this woman here, and what is she doing? He dressed quickly, hiding his cast-off clothes in a corner of his wardrobe. Some one might ask him what caused these holes in the coat-sleeves, which are quite through at the elbows. And this linen suit with the colored embroidery, would not a woman's eye decipher something from it?—women understand the mysteries of needle-work. He must hide the clothes. He and the soap had hard work to wash his hands clean. Would he not be asked what he had done to make them so black and horny?

When he was ready he went back to the office, where Timéa was waiting for him at the door, and putting her hand on his arm, said, "Let us go to breakfast."

From the office they passed through the dressing-room to get to the dining-room. Another surprise awaited Michael there; the round table was laid with three places—for whom were they intended? Timéa made a signal,

251

and through one door came the servant, through the other Athalie. The third place was for her.

On Athalie's face an unconcealed anger shone when she saw Timar. "Ah, Herr von Levetinczy, you have come home at last! It was a kind thought of yours to write to your wife, 'Take my keys and books, and be so good, dear wife, as to do all my work for me,' and then to leave us five months without news of your whereabouts."

"Athalie!" said Timéa, sternly.

Michael sat down in silence at his place, which he recognized by his own silver drinking-cup. He had been daily awaited here, and the table laid for him. Athalie said no more, but whenever she looked at Timar he could read her vexation in her eyes. This was a satisfactory sign.

When they rose from table Timéa asked her husband to go with her to the office. Michael began to think what he could invent when she should ask him about his journey. But she never referred to it even remotely. She placed two chairs at the desk, and laid her hand on the open day-book. "Here, sir, is the account of your business since the time when you gave over its direction to me."

"Have you carried it on yourself?"

"I understood that you desired me to do so. I found by your papers that you had undertaken a new and wholesale enterprise—the export of Hungarian flour. I saw that here not only your money, but also your credit and your mercantile honor, were at stake, and that on the good result of this affair hung the foundation of an important branch of trade. I did not understand this business, but I thought that it depended more on conscientious and faithful stewardship than on knowledge of affairs. I trusted this to no third person. Directly I received your letter I started for Levetinczy, and took, as you desired, the conduct of business into my own hands. I studied book-keeping and learned to deal with figures. I think you will find everything in order—the books and the cash balance." Timar looked with admiration at this woman, who knew how to apply the millions passing through her hands with such calm good sense, to their right object, to receive and expend moneys, and with a skillful hand to withdraw endangered funds; and who knew even more than that. "Fortune has favored us this year," continued Timéa, "and made up for my inexperience. The five months' income amounted to five hundred thousand gulden. This sum has not lain idle. Taking advantage of the powers intrusted to me, I have made investments."

What sort of investments are they likely to be which occur to a woman?

"Your first experiment with the export of flour succeeded entirely. Hungarian flour became at one stroke an article in request for the South American markets. So your agents write from Rio Janeiro, where all with one accord praise the ability and uprightness of your chief agent, Theodor Krisstyan." Timar thought to himself, "Even when I do evil good comes of it, and the greatest folly I commit turns into wisdom—when will this end?" "After receiving this intelligence I began to consider what you would have done. One must seize an opportunity and occupy with all speed the newly opened markets. I hired immediately many mills, chartered more ships, had them laden, and at this moment a new cargo is on its way to South America, which will defy competition."

Michael was astonished. In this woman there was more courage than in any man. Another woman would have locked up the money that it might not run away, and this one ventures to carry on her husband's enterprise, only in tenfold measure. "I thought you would have acted thus," said Timéa.

"Yes, indeed," muttered Timar.

"My expectations, moreover, were justified by the fact that, as soon as we threw ourselves more openly into this undertaking, a whole herd of competitors appeared, who are grinding away for dear life, and packing off their good in barrels to America. But this need not cause you any anxiety—we shall beat them all. Not one of them knows the secret of the superiority of the Hungarian flour."

"How is that?"

"If one of them asked his wife, perhaps she would have known—that is how I discovered it. Among all the samples of American wheat, I can find none as heavy as ours. We must, therefore, make flour of our heaviest kinds, so as to carry off the prize from the Americans. I selected our heaviest grain; our rivals here use lighter corn, and they will find their mistake, while we shall maintain our position."

Michael kissed Timéa's hand with the sacred awe with which we kiss our beloved dead, who no longer belong to us, but to the ground, and who can not feel our caress. Whenever during his life of happy forgetfulness on the island he had thought of Timéa at all, it was as amusing herself, traveling, going to watering-places, having plenty of money, and wasting it as she chose. Now he saw in what her amusement had consisted—keeping books, sitting at a desk, conducting a correspondence, and learning foreign idioms without the help of a master—and all this because her husband had desired it.

His wife gave him a report of all branches of his extensive business. It was now all as familiar to her as if she had known it from childhood, and everything was in perfect order. While Timar ran over the accounts, he acquired the conviction that if he himself had had to do it all in those few months, he would have been hard at work all day. What labor this must have cost a young woman who had to learn everything by experience! Indeed she must have had but little time for sleep.

"But, Timéa, this is a tremendous task which you have accomplished in my stead!"

"It is true, and at first I found it very difficult, but by degrees I got used to it, and then it was easy enough. Work is wholesome."

What a sad reproach!—a young wife who finds consolation in work. Michael drew Timéa's hand to him. Deep sadness clouded his brow, his heart was heavy. If only he knew what Timéa was thinking.

The key of the desk was constantly in Timar's mind. If Timéa had discovered his secret, then her present conduct to her husband was only a fearful judgment held over him, to mark the difference between the accuser and the accused.

"Have you never been in Komorn since?" he asked Timéa.

"Only once, when I had to look in your desk for the contract with Scaramelli."

Timar felt his blood run cold. Timéa's face betrayed nothing.

"But now we will go back to Komorn," said Timar; "the flour is in full swing; we must wait for news of the fate of the cargoes now at sea, and they will not arrive before the winter. Or would you rather make a tour in Switzerland and Italy? This is the best season for it."

"No, Michael; we have been long enough apart, we will remain at home together."

But no pressure of the hand explains why she would like to remain at home with him. Michael had not the courage to say a tender word to her. Should he lie to her? He would have to live a lie in her presence from morning to evening. His silence even was a falsehood.

Looking through all the papers took the whole time until late dinner, and to this meal two guests were invited—the bailiff and the reverend dean. The latter had begged to be at once informed of Herr von Levetinczy's return, that he might call upon him immediately. As soon as he received the news he hastened to the castle, and of course put on his new decoration. The moment he entered he let off some oratorical fireworks, in which he lauded Timar as the benefactor of the place. He compared him to Noah who built the Ark, to Joseph who saved his people from famine, and to Moses who made manna fall from heaven. The flour trade which he had set on foot was pronounced the greatest enterprise Europe had ever seen. Long live the Columbus of flour export!

Timar had to answer this address of welcome. He stammered and talked great nonsense. He had to control himself that he might not laugh aloud, and say to the worthy preacher, "Ha, ha! do not fancy that I had this idea in order to make your fortune; it was only to get a young rascal out of reach of a certain pretty girl, and if any good came of it, it is only by means of this woman here near me. Laugh then, good people!"

At table good-humor reigned. The dean and the steward were neither of them despisers of the bottle. The wit and anecdotes of the two old men made Timar laugh too; but whenever he cast a glance on Timéa's icy face, the laugh died on his lips. She had left her merriment elsewhere in pledge.

It was evening before they rose. The two old gentlemen reminded each other jocosely that it was quite time to leave, for the husband had returned to his young wife after a long absence, and they would have much to say to each other.

"Indeed you will do wisely to go soon," whispered Athalie to Timar.

"Timéa has such dreadful headaches every evening, that she can not sleep before midnight. See how pale she is!"

"Timéa, you are unwell?" asked Timar, tenderly.

"There is nothing the matter with me," answered she.

"Don't believe her; ever since we came to Levetinczy she has suffered from headache. It is neuralgia, which she contracted by overtaxing her brain, and by the bad air here. I found a white hair in her head the other day. But she conceals her suffering till she breaks down, and even then she never complains."

Timar experienced in spirit the tortures of a criminal stretched on the rack. And he had not the courage to say to his wife, "If you are suffering, let me sleep in your room and take care of you." No; he was afraid of uttering Noémi's name in his sleep, and that his wife might hear it, as she was kept awake by pain half the night. He must shun his marriage-bed.

The next day they started for Komorn, and traveled by post, Michael sitting opposite the two ladies. It was a tedious journey: in the whole Banat the harvest was over; only the maize was still standing, otherwise they saw nothing but monotonous fields of stubble. None of them spoke; all three found it hard to keep awake. In the afternoon Timar could no longer endure the silent looks, the enigmatical expression of his wife; under pretense of wanting to smoke he took a seat by the driver in the open *coupé*, and remained there. When they got out at a post-house, Athalie grumbled at the bad roads, the dreadful heat, the annoying flies, the stifling dust, and all the rest of a traveler's trials. The inns are dirty, the food disgusting, the beds hard, the wine sour, the water impure, and the countenances of all the people frightful. She feels so ill all through the journey, she is quite knocked up, she has fever, and her head will burst: what must Timéa be suffering, who is so nervous?

Timar had to listen to these lamentations all the way, but Timéa never uttered a complaint.

When they arrived at Komorn, Frau Sophie informed them that she had turned gray with loneliness. Gray indeed! She had been very happy—being able to go about all day from house to house to gossip to her heart's content. Timar felt a painful anxiety. Home is either a heaven or a hell. Now at last he would know what lay behind the marble coldness of this silent face.

As he entered the room with his wife, she handed him the key of his desk. Michael knew she had opened it to get out the contract.

This writing-desk was an old and elaborate piece of furniture, whose upper part was closed by a rolled falling cover, under which were drawers of various sizes. In the large drawer lay the contracts, in the small ones notes and valuables; the lock was a puzzle one, which you might vainly turn if you did not know its secret.

Timéa was in the secret, and could have access to all the drawers. With an uneasily beating heart Timar drew out the drawer where those jewels were kept which it had been unadvisable to place on the market. These gems have their own experts, who recognize by certain marks where this stone or that gem came from; and then follows the question, how did he get it? Only the third generation from the finder can venture to show it, as to him it is all one in what way his grandfather came into its possession.

If Timéa had been inquisitive enough to open that drawer she must have seen these gems. And if so, one among them, the diamond locket with the portrait which is so like her, must have been recognized by her. It is her mother's picture, and then she must know all. She knows that Timar has received her father's treasures; it is hard to believe he came by them honestly. And by that dark, perhaps criminal road, they would lead to the fabulous riches which gained her hand for Timar, while he played the generous friend to her whom he had robbed. She may even think worse things of him than are true. Her father's mysterious death, his secret burial, might awake in her the suspicion that Timar had a hand in it.

These doubts were unbearable. Timar must set them at rest, and call yet one more falsehood to his aid. He took out the medallion and went with it to Timéa. "Dear Timéa," he said, sitting down beside his wife, "I have been living a long time in Turkey. What I did there you will learn later on. When I was in Scutari an Armenian jeweler offered me a diamond-framed picture, which is very like you. I bought it, and have brought you the ornament."

When Timéa saw the portrait her face changed in an instant. An emotion which could neither be assumed nor concealed was visible in her sculptured features; she seized the picture with both hands and pressed it eagerly to her lips; her eyes filled with tears. This was true feeling; Timéa's face began to live.

Michael was saved. The girl, overpowered by her long-suppressed feelings, began to sob violently. Athalie heard and came in; she was surprised—she had never known Timéa to sob. But when she saw Athalie she ran toward her like a child, and cried, in a tone of mingled laughter and tears, "See, see! my mother! It is my mother's picture. . . . He has brought it to me!"

And then she hastened back to Michael, put both her arms round his neck, and whispered in a broken voice, "Thanks, oh, a thousand thanks!"

It seemed to Timar as if the time had come to kiss these grateful lips, and to kiss them on and on.

But alas! his heart said, "Thou shalt not steal." Now a kiss on these lips would be a theft, after all that had passed on the ownerless island.

Another thought struck him. He went back to his room, and fetched all the hidden jewels which remained in the drawer.

A wonderful woman this, who, though she had the key in her hands, left the secret drawers untouched and only took out the one paper she required! Then he packed all the ornaments into the bag he had over his shoulder when he came home, and went back to his wife. "I have not told you all," he said to Timéa. "Where I found the picture I discovered also these jewels, and bought them for you. Take them as a present from me."

And then he laid the dazzling gems one after another in Timéa's lap, until the sparkling heap quite covered her embroidered apron. It was like some magical gift from the thousand and one nights.

Athalie stood there pale with envy, with angrily clinched teeth. Perhaps these might all have been hers! But Timéa's face darkened and grew marble-like again. She looked with indifference at the heap of jewels in her lap. The fire of diamonds and rubies could not warm her.

BOOK FOURTH.—NOÉMI.

CHAPTER I.
A NEW GUEST.

What rich bankers call business filled up the winter season, and Levetinczy began to enjoy his position. Riches bring pleasant dreams. He went often to Vienna and took part in the amusements of the commercial world, where many good examples were presented to him. A man who owns a million can allow himself the luxury, when he goes to the jeweler to buy New Year's gifts, of buying two of everything to please two hearts at once.

One for his wife, who sits at home and receives guests or looks after the household—the other for another lady, who either dances or sings, but in any case requires an elegant hotel, jewels, and laces. Timar was so fortunate as to be invited to the parties given at home by his friends, where the lady of the house makes tea—as well as to those differently organized *soirées*, where a very unceremonious set of ladies preferred champagne, and where Timar was constantly attacked by the question whether he had no little friend at the opera yet.

"The pattern of a faithful husband," declared his admirers.

"An unbearable prig," was the verdict of his critics.

But he says nothing, and thinks of—Noémi. What an eternity to have been separated from her—six months; to think of her every day, and not dare to confide his thoughts to a single soul!

He often caught himself on the point of betraying his thoughts; once as he sat at table the words all but escaped him, "Look! those are the same apples which grow on Noémi's island." "When Noémi had a headache, it went away if I laid my hand on her forehead." And if he looked at Timéa's pet white cat, the exclamation hovered on his lips, "Narcissa, where did you leave your mistress, eh?"

He had every reason to be on his guard, for there was a being in the house who watched him as well as Timéa with Argus eyes.

Athalie could not but remark that since his return he was no longer so melancholy as before; every one noticed how well he looked; there must be some mystery in it. And Athalie could not bear any one in this house to be happy. Where did he steal his contentment? Why does he not suffer as he ought to do?

Business prospered. In the first month of the new year news came from the other side of the sea. The flour exported had arrived safely, and its success was complete. Hungarian flour had won such renown in South America, that now people tried to sell the native product under that name. The Austrian consul in Brazil hastened to inform his government of this important result, by which the export trade was increased in a marked degree. The consequence was that Timar was made a privy councilor, and received the minor order of St. Stephen, as an acknowledgment of the services rendered by him to his native land in the fields of commerce and philanthropy.

How the mocking demon in his breast laughed when they fastened the order on to his coat and called him "the right honorable!" "You have to thank two women for this—Noémi and Timéa." Be it so. The discovery of the purple dye had its origin in the eating of a purple snail by the little dog of a shepherd's mistress; but yet purple has become a royal color.

Herr von Levetinczy now first began to rise in the estimation of the people of Komorn. When a man is a privy councilor, one can not deny him a proper portion of respect. Every one hastened to congratulate him, and he received them all with a gracious condescension. Our Johann Fabula came too to wish him joy in the name of the fisher-folk. He was in the gala clothes of his class. On his short dolman of dark-blue cloth shone three rows of shell-shaped silver buttons, as large as nuts, and from one shoulder to the other hung a broad silver chain with a large medallion for a clasp, on which the Komorn silversmith had stamped the head of Julius Cæsar. The other members of the deputation were equally splendid. Silver buttons and chains were at that time still worn by the mariners of Komorn. It was the custom to keep the visitors to dinner, and this honor fell to Fabula. He was a very frank person, who spoke with complete unreserve. When wine had loosened his tongue, he could not forbear to tell the gracious lady that when he first saw her as a girl he would never have thought that she would have become such a good housewife and be the wife of Herr von Levetinczy. Yes, indeed; he was afraid of her then, and now see how wonderful are the ways of God's providence, and how short-sighted are men; how everything has been ordered for the best: what happiness reigns in this house! If only a kind Providence would hear the prayers of those who entreat that a new blessing may be sent down from heaven to the good lord of Levetinczy, in the shape of a little angel.

Timar covered his glass with his hand; a thought started through his mind—"Such a wish might have an unlooked-for result."

But Herr Fabula was not content with good wishes, he thought he must add some good advice. "But his honor rushes about too much. In good truth I would not leave such a sweet, pretty lady alone. But it can't be helped if the master must see to everything himself, for that's why it succeeds. Who would have thought of sending our flour across the sea? To tell the truth, when I heard it—excuse me for making so free—I thought to myself the master must have gone silly; before that flour gets there it will all be musty, while loaves grow out there on the trees and roll on the bushes. And now just see what credit we have all got by it. But it is the master's eye that feeds the horse—"

This was to Michael an unwelcome irony, which he could not leave without contradiction. "My good Johann, if that was the secret of our success, you must bestow all your praises on my wife, for it was she who looked after everything."

"Yes, indeed; all honor to the merits of our noble lady!" said Fabula; "but, with his honor's permission, I know what I know. I know where his honor spent the whole summer."

Michael felt as if his hair stood on end with horror. Could this man know where he had been? It would be awful if he did.

Michael winked with one eye over his glass at his guest, but in vain.

"Well, shall I tell our gracious lady where the master spent the summer? Shall I let it out?"

Michael felt every limb paralyzed by terror. Athalie kept her eyes fixed on his face; he durst not betray by a gesture that the gossip of the tipsy chatterer confused him. "Well, tell us then, Johann, where I was," he said, with enforced calmness.

"I will complain of you to the gracious lady; I will tell her," cried

Fabula, putting down his glass. "His honor ran away without saying a word to any one. He went quietly on board a ship and sailed away to Brazil; he was over there in America and settled everything himself, and that's why it all went so smoothly."

Timar looked at the two women. On Timéa's face was reflected pure surprise, Athalie was vexed. She believed as fully in the truth of Fabula's tale as he did himself, and he would have staked his head on it.

Timar also smiled mysteriously at the story; now he was the one who lied, not Johann Fabula. The man of gold must go on lying.

The story was very useful to Timar. He had now a sufficient excuse for his mysterious disappearances, and it was possible for him to give such an air of probability to the story of his Brazilian voyage that even Athalie believed it. Indeed, she was the easiest to deceive. She knew what Timéa was feeling, and that she was glad to distract herself by absence and work from the thought of him on whose account her heart ached. If a wife can do so, why not the husband? It was even simpler for him to fly from his sorrows to another hemisphere, and in the pursuit of wealth to forget what his heart coveted. How should Athalie have guessed that it was the husband who had already found a cure for his mortal sickness, and who was happy away from home? What would she have given to him who should have revealed the truth? But the rushes round the ownerless island did not chatter like the reeds to which King Midas's barber trusted his secret. Athalie was consumed with envy, while she vainly sought for a key to the riddle. At home and in public, Timar and Timéa presented the exemplary picture of a happy marriage. He heaped on his wife expensive jewels, and Timéa loaded herself with them when they went into society; she wished to shine by this means.

What could better prove the affection of the husband than the diamonds of the wife? Could Timar and Timéa really be a couple whose love consisted in giving and receiving diamonds, or are there people in this world who can be happy without love?

Athalie still suspected Timéa and not Timar. But Timar could hardly wait till the winter was over and spring had come: of course, because then the mills can begin to grind again—what else could a man of business have in his mind?

This year Michael persuaded Timéa not to try her health by the management of business; he would give it over to his agents, and she should go during the summer to some sea-bathing place, to get rid of her neuralgia.

No one asked him where he was going. It was taken for granted that he would again travel to South America, and pretend he had been in Egypt or Italy.

But he hurried away to the Lower Danube. When the poplars grew green, he could not stay at home: the alluring picture filled his dreams and took captive all his thoughts. He never stopped at Levetinczy, but only gave general instructions to his agent and his steward to do their best; then he went on to Golovacz, where he stayed a night with the dean; thence he had only a half-day's journey to get to Noémi. He had not seen her for six long months; his mind was filled with the picture of the meeting. Awake and asleep he was full of longing, and could hardly wait for dawn. Before sunrise he was up, put on his knapsack, threw his gun over his shoulder, and without waiting for the appearance of his host, he left the presbytery and hastened to the wooded river-bank.

The Danube does a good work in widening the limits of the wood every year by retreating from its banks, for in this way the watch-houses built twenty-five years ago on the shore have now taken up a position much further inland. And he who wishes to cross the river without a passport finds in the young brushwood an entirely neutral territory.

Timar had sent a new boat to the hut, where he went on foot; he found it ready, and started as usual alone on the way to the reed-beds. The skiff floated like a fish on the water, and that it traveled so swiftly was not owing to itself alone. The year had grown to April, it was spring, and the trees at Ostrova were already in blossom. So much the more astonished was he at the sight which met his eyes on the other side. The ownerless island did not look green; it seemed to have been burned. As he approached he saw the reason; all the trees on the northern side were quite brown. The boat traversed the rushes quickly; when it touched the bank, Michael saw plainly that a whole long row of trees, Frau Therese's favorite walnuts, were dead—every one of them. Michael felt quite downcast at the sight. At this season he was generally greeted by green branches and rosebuds. Now a dead

265

forest welcomed him—a bad omen.

He pressed forward and listened for the bark of greeting: not a sound to be heard. He walked on anxiously; the paths were neglected, covered by dry autumn leaves, and it seemed to him as if even the birds were silent. When he drew near the hut, a dreadful feeling overcame him—where were the inhabitants? They might be dead and not buried; he had been busied about other things for half a year—with affairs of state, with showing off his young wife, and making money. And meanwhile Heaven had watched over the islanders—if it chose.

As he entered the veranda, a door opened and Therese came out. She looked serious, as if something had frightened her; and then a bitter smile appeared on her face. "Ah! you have come!" said she, and came to press his hand. And then it was she who asked him why he came looking so grave. "No misfortune has happened?" Timar asked, hastily.

"Misfortune? No," said Therese, with a melancholy smile.

"My heart was sore when I saw the dead trees," said Michael, to excuse his serious looks.

"The flood last summer did that," answered Therese; "walnut-trees can not stand wet."

"And how are you both?" asked Timar, uneasily.

Therese answered gently, "We are pretty well, I and the other two."

"What do you mean? the other two?"

She smiled and sighed, and smiled again; then she laid her hand on Michael's shoulder and said, "The wife of a poor smuggler fell ill here: the woman died, the child remained here. Now you know who the other two are."

Timar rushed into the house: at the far end of the room stood a cradle woven of osiers, and near it, on one side, was Almira, on the other Noémi. Noémi rocked the cradle and waited till Timar came to her. In it lay a little baby, with chubby cheeks, which pressed the cherry lips into a soft pout; its eyes were only half shut, and the tiny fists lay over its face. Michael stood spell-bound before the cradle. He looked at Noémi as if to seek the answer to the riddle in her face, on which a sweet ray of heavenly light seemed to shine, in which modesty and love were combined. She smiled and cast her eyes down. Michael thought he would lose his senses.

Therese laid her hand on his arm, "Then are you angry that we have adopted the orphan child of the poor smuggler's wife? God sent it to us."

Angry? He had fallen on his knees, and held the cradle in his embrace, pressing it and its inhabitant to his breast; then he began to sob violently, like one who has kept a whole ocean of sorrow in his heart, which suddenly overflows its bounds.

Timar kissed the little messenger from God wherever he could—its little hands and feet, the hem of its robe, its rosy cheeks. The baby made grimaces under the kisses, but did not wake. At last it opened its eyes, its great blue eyes, and looked at the strange man with astonishment, as if to say, "Does this man want anything of me?" and then it laughed, as if it thought, "I don't care what he wants," and after that it shut its eyes and slumbered on, still smiling and undisturbed by the flood of kisses.

Therese said, smiling, "You poor orphan! you never dreamed of this, did you?" and turned away to hide her tears.

"And am I to have no greeting?" said Noémi, with charming anger. Michael turned to her, still on his knees. He spoke not a word, only pressed her hand to his lips and hid his face silently in her lap. He was dumb as long as the child slept. When the little creature awoke, it began to talk in its own language—which we call crying. It is lucky there are those who understand it. The baby was hungry.

Noémi said to Michael that he must now leave the room, for he was not to know what the poor little orphan was fed upon.

Michael went outside; he was in a transport. It seemed as if he was on a new star, from which one could look down on the earth as on a foreign body. All he had called his own on the terrestrial ball was left behind, and he no longer felt its attraction drawing him thither. The circle in which he had spent his former life was trodden under foot, and he had attained a new center of gravity. A new object, a new life, stood before him; only one uncertainty remained—how could he contrive to vanish from the world? To pass into another sphere without leaving this mortal life behind; to live on two different planets at once, to mount from earth to heaven, to pass again from heaven to earth, there to entertain angels, and here to live for money—alas! this was no task for human nerves. He would lose his reason in the attempt.

Not without reason are little children called angels, or "messengers:" children are indeed messengers from the other world, whose mysterious influence is visible in their eyes, to those who receive them as gifts of God. A wonderful look often meets us in the eye of an infant, which is lost when the lips learn speech. How often Michael gazed for hours at this blue ray from heaven in the baby's eyes, when it lay on a lambskin out on the grass, and he stretched himself beside it, and plucked the flowers it wanted—"There, then, here it is." He had his work cut out to get it away, for the little thing put everything in its mouth. He studied its first attempts at language, he let it drag at his beard, and sung lullabies to put it to sleep.

His feeling for Noémi was quite different now; it was not desire, but bliss—the glow of passion had given place to a sweet contented calm, and he felt like one convalescent from a fever. Noémi, too, had altered since they last met; on her face lay an expression of submissive tenderness, and in all her conduct was a consistent gentleness, which could not have been assumed—a quiet dignity combined with chaste reserve, which surrounds a woman with a halo, compelling respect. Timar could not get used to his happiness: he required many days to be convinced that it was not a dream—that this little hut, half wood, half clay, and the smiling woman with the babbling babe at her breast, were reality and not a vision.

And then he thought, what will become of them?

He strode about the island and brooded on the future.

"What can I give this child? Much money? They know nought of money here. Great estates? This island suffices. Shall I take him with me and make him into a great and wealthy man? But the women could not part with him. Shall I take them too? But even if they consented, I could not do it; they would learn what I am, and would despise me. They can only be happy here: only here can this child hold up its head, where none can ask its name."

The women had called it Adeodatus (Gift of God). It had no other name. What other could it have?

One day when he was wandering aimlessly, deep in thought, about the island, striding through the bushes and weeds, Timar came suddenly to a

268

part where the dry twigs crackled under his feet. He looked round; he was in the melancholy little plantation of dead walnut-trees. The beautiful trees were all dried up: spring had not clothed them with fresh green foliage, and the dead leaves covered the ground.

An idea struck Michael in this vegetable cemetery. He hastened back to the hut. "Therese, have you still the tools you used in building your house?"

"There they are on the shelf."

"Give them here. I have an idea; I will fell the dead walnuts and build of them a little house for Dodi."

Therese clasped her hands in astonishment. But Noémi's answer was to kiss her little Dodi and say to him, "Dost thou hear?"

Michael interpreted the wonder on Therese's face as incredulity. "Yes, yes," he persisted, "I will build the house myself without any help—a little house like a jewel-case, like those the Wallachians build, lined with beautiful oak; mine shall be of walnut, and fit for a prince. I will drive every nail myself, and it shall be Dodi's house when he gets bigger."

Therese only smiled. "That will be fine, Michael. I too built my nest as the swallows do; I formed the walls of clay, and thatched my roof with rushes. But carpentry is not one man's work; the old saw has two handles, and one can not manage it alone."

"But are we not two?" cried Noémi, eagerly. "Can't I help him? Do you fancy my arm is not strong enough?" and she turned her sleeve up to her shoulder to show off her arm. It was beautifully formed, yet muscular, fit for Diana. Michael covered it with kisses from the shoulder down to the finger-tips, and then said, "Be it so."

"Oh, we will work together," cried Noémi, whose lively fancy had seized on Michael's suggestion with lightning speed. "We will both go out into the wood; we will make a hammock for Dodi and sling it from the branches. Mother shall bring us out our meals, and we will sit on the planks we have sawn, and take our dinner out of the same plate: how good it will taste!"

And so it did. Michael took the ax and went out to the walnut-grove, where he set to work. Before he had felled and topped one tree his hands were blistered. Noémi told him women's hands never got sore. When three trees were cut down, so that one trunk could be laid across the other two, Michael wanted Noémi's help. She was quite in earnest, and attacked the task bravely. In her slender form lay stores of strength and endurance. She handled the great saw as cleverly as if she had been taught to do it.

Michael gradually got used to the dressing of the walnut planks; the ax, too, did good service, and Noémi admired him greatly. "Tell me, Michael," she asked him one day, "have you never been a carpenter?"

"Oh, yes," he answered, "a ship's carpenter."

"And tell me, how did you become such a rich man that you can stay away a whole summer from your work, and spend your time elsewhere? You are your own master, I suppose? You take orders from no one?"

"I must tell you all about it some day," said Michael; and yet he never told her how he became rich, so as to be able to spend weeks on the island sawing wood. He often related to Noémi stories of his adventurous journeys through all lands, but in his romantic tales he never said anything about himself. He escaped inquisitive pressure by working hard all day; and when he lay down at night, it was not the time to tease him with questions, though many wives take advantage of the opportunity.

During the long time Timar spent in the ownerless island, he had gradually become convinced that it was by no means so concealed as to be unknown: its existence was known to a large class of visitors. But they never revealed it to the outer world. Smuggling, on the banks of this wooded river, was a regular profession, with its own constitution, its own schools, its secret laws, forming a state within a state. It often surprised Timar to find among the willow-copses of the island a canoe or a boat, watched by no one. If he came back a few hours later, it was no longer there. Another time he stumbled on great bales of goods, which also had disappeared when he returned. All the mysterious people who used the island as a resting-place seemed purposely to avoid the neighborhood of the hut; they went and came without leaving a footmark on the turf. There were cases, however, in which they visited the hut; and then it was always Therese who received their visit. When Almira gave the signal that strangers were coming, Timar left his work and retired into the inner room; he must not be seen by any stranger. It is

270

true the beard he had grown had altered him considerably, but yet some one might come who had seen him elsewhere. The wild people always came to Therese if they had been hurt; they often frequented places where they were likely to be wounded. Sometimes they had deep, dangerous gunshot wounds, which they could not show to the regimental surgeon, for the result would be a court-martial; but the island lady knew of healing salves, could reduce fractures, bind up wounds, and prescribe medicines for fevers. She was sought by sick people who kept secret their abode, for they knew the physicians would never endure this quack-doctoring. She reconciled enemies who dared not go to law, and consoled criminals who repented of their sins, with the hope of God's mercy. Often some fugitive, tired and exhausted with hunger and thirst, came to her threshold. She asked not, "Whence do you come or whither do you go?" She took him in, and let him go when restored and refreshed, after filling his pouch with food.

Many know her whose religion is silence, and there is no bond which binds master and disciple so closely as this. Every one knows that no money is to be found here; even avarice has no reason to wish her ill.

Timar could be certain of having found a place over which centuries might pass before the history of its inhabitants should be drawn into that chaos we call the world. He could go on with his carpentry without fearing that the news would leak out that Michael Timar Levetinczy, privy councilor, landowner, banker, had turned into a woodcutter in an unknown island; and that, when he rested from his hard labor, he cut willow branches to shelter a poor orphan child which had neither parents nor a name of its own. What joys he knew here! how he listened for the first word the child could speak! The little man had such trouble to shape his unskillful lips to the words. "Papa," of course, was the first; what else could it be? The child learns also to understand the sorrowful side of life; when a new tooth comes, what pain and sleepless nights must be endured! Noémi remains at home with it, and Michael runs back from his work to see how little Dodi is. He takes the child from Noémi and carries him about, singing lullabies to him. If he succeeds in putting Dodi to sleep and soothing his pain, how triumphant he is! He sings—

"For all the gold the world could hold, I would not give my Dodi's curl."

271

One day Michael suddenly found that he had grubbed up and cut down all the timber. So far the work had prospered; but now he found he could not get on. House-carpentry is a trade like any other, and must be learned, and he had not spoken the truth when he said he understood it.

Autumn drew near. Therese and Noémi were already used to think it quite natural for Timar to leave them at this season; he must of course earn his bread. His business is of a sort which gets on by itself in the summer, but in winter he must give himself up to it. They knew that from other tradespeople. But in another house the same idea reigned. Timéa believed Michael had business which obliged him to spend the summer away from home: at that season the management of his estates, of his building and export contracts, demanded all his attention.

From autumn to spring he deceived Timéa, from spring to autumn he deceived Noémi. He could not be called inconsistent.

This time he left the island earlier than in other years. He hastened back to Komorn, where all his affairs had progressed in his absence beyond his expectations. Even in the government lottery the first prize must needs fall to him; the long-forgotten ticket lay buried somewhere in a drawer under other papers, and not till three months after the drawing did he bring it out, and claim the unhoped-for hundred thousand gulden, like one who hardly cares for such a trifle. The world admired him all the more. He had so much money, people said, that he wished for no more.

What could he do with it?

He began by sending for celebrated cabinet-makers from Szekler and Zarand, who understand the building of those splendid wooden houses which last for centuries—real palaces of hard wood. The Roumanian nobility live in such houses as these, which are full of beautiful carving inside. The house and its furniture, tables, chairs, and wardrobes, are all the work of one hand. Everything in it is of wood—not a single bit of iron is used.

CHAPTER II.
THE WOOD-CARVER.

On his return home, Michael found Timéa somewhat unwell. This induced him to call in two celebrated doctors from Vienna in order to consult them about his wife's health. They agreed that a change of climate was necessary, and advised a winter sojourn in Meran; so Michael accompanied thither his wife and Athalie. In the sheltered valley, he chose for Timéa a villa in whose garden stood a pavilion built like a Swiss *châlet*. He knew that Timéa would like it. In the course of the winter he often visited her, generally in the company of an elderly man, and found that, as he expected, the *châlet* was her favorite resort.

When he returned to Komorn he set to work to build just such another *châlet* as the one at Meran. The cabinet-maker he had brought with him was a master of his art. He copied the *châlet* and its furniture in the minutest detail; then he installed a large workshop in Timar's one-storied house in the Servian Street, and there set to work. No one was to know anything about it—it was to be a surprise. But the architect required an apprentice to help him, and it was difficult to find one who could hold his tongue. There was nothing for it but to turn Timar himself into an apprentice, and he now vied with his master from morning to night with chisel and gimlet, in carving, planing, polishing, and turning. But as to the cabinet-maker himself, if you had closed his mouth with Solomon's seal, you could not have made him discreet enough to refrain from letting out the secret to his Sunday evening boon companions, of the surprise Herr von Levetinczy was preparing for his wife. First they made the different parts and fitted them together: then the whole, as fast as it was ready, was set up in the beautiful park on the Monostor. He himself, a regular Crœsus, does not shrink from working all day like a laborer, and is as good at the tools as if he were a foreman. He does not trouble about his own affairs, he leaves them to his agents, and saws and carves the whole day long in the workshop. But they must not let it go further, for the gracious lady was to have a surprise when she came home. Naturally the whole town heard of it, and so did Frau

273

Sophie, who wrote to Athalie, who told Timéa, so that Timéa knew beforehand that Michael, when she came home in the spring, would drive with her some fine day to the Monostor hill, where they had a large orchard: there, on the side overlooking the Danube, she would find her dear Meran pavilion exactly copied, her work-basket at the window, her favorite books on the birchwood shelves, her cane chair on the veranda. All this to surprise her; and she must smile as if much pleased, and when she praised the maker, she would hear from him, "You must not compliment me, gracious lady, but my apprentice." "Who executed the best carvings, who made the footstool, these elegant balustrades, these columns and capitals?" "My apprentice." "And who was he?" "The noble lord of Levetinczy himself. All this is his work, gracious lady."

And then Timéa would smile and try to find words to express her thanks. Only words: for he may heap treasures on his wife, or give her black bread that he had earned by his labor; he can not purchase her affection.

And so it was. In the spring Timéa came back. The Monostor surprise was skillfully planned, with a splendid banquet and a troop of guests. On Timéa's face hovered a melancholy smile; on Timar's, reserved kindness, and on those of the guests, envious congratulation. The ladies said no woman was worthy of such a husband as Timar, he was an ideal husband; but the men said it was not a good sign when a husband tried to win his wife's favor by presents and attentions.

Only Athalie said nothing: she sought a clew to the mystery and found none. What had come to Timar? His countenance betrayed something like happiness; what was he concealing under his care for Timéa? In company he was bright and cheerful, unconstrained and at ease with Athalie, sometimes even taking her for a turn in the cotillon. Was he really happy, or was he indifferent? It was vain for him to try and win Timéa's heart; Athalie knew that by her own experience. She had found plenty of wooers, but refused them all—all men were alike to her; she had only loved one, whom now she hated. She alone understood Timéa.

But Michael she could not fathom. He was a man of pure gold, without a speck of rust upon him.

When spring came, Timar again called in the physicians to pronounce

274

on Timéa's health. This time she was advised to try the sea-bathing at Biarritz. Michael took her there, arranged her apartments, took care that she should be able to compete in dress and equipages with English peeresses and Russian princesses, and left a heavy purse with her, begging her to bring it back empty. He was generous to Athalie, put her down as Timéa's cousin in the visitor's list, and she too was to change her dress five times a day, like Timéa. Could any one better fulfill the duties of the head of a family?

Then he hurried away, not homeward, but to Vienna; there he bought the whole furniture of a workshop, and had it sent in chests to Pancsova.

Here he had to invent some pretense to get the boxes over to the island. Caution was most necessary. The fishermen, who often saw him go round the Ostrova Island in a boat, and not return for months, had puzzled their heads as to who he was and what brought him here. When the cases arrived, he had them conveyed to the poplar-groves of the left bank of the Danube, and there unloaded. Then he called in the fishermen, and said they must get them over to the lonely island—they contained arms.

That one word was enough to sink the secret to the bottom of the sea. Henceforward he could go backward and forward by day or night, no one would ever mention his name. They all knew now that he was an agent of the Servian and Montenegrin heroes of the insurrection, and the rack would not have extorted information from them. He became a sacred personage in their eyes. In this way, in order to hide himself in darkness, he deceived every one with whom he exchanged a word. The fishermen ferried over the cases at night, and Timar with them; they looked out for a place on the shore where the thickest bushes grew, and carried the boxes there, and when Michael would have paid them, they would not accept a groschen from him, only grasping his hand.

He remained on the island, and the fishermen left him. It was a splendid moonlight night; the nightingale sung on its nest. Michael went along the bank till he came to the path, and passed the place where he had left off his work last year; the trunks were carefully covered with rushes to keep the wet off.

He approached the little dwelling on tiptoe. It was a good sign that he heard no noise. Almira does not bark, because she is sleeping in the kitchen so as not to wake the child. All is well in the house.

How should he announce himself, and surprise Noémi? He stood before the little window, half covered by climbing roses, and began to sing—
  "For all the gold the world could hold, I would not give my Dodi's curl."

He was not disappointed; a moment later the window opened, and Noémi looked out with a face radiant with joy. "My Michael," whispered the poor child.

"Yes, thy Michael," he murmured, clasping the dear head in both arms. "And Dodi?"

"He is asleep; hush, we must not wake him." And still the lips murmured tenderly, "Come in."

"He might wake and cry."

"Oh, he is no longer a crying child. Just think, he is a year old."

"What! a year already! He is quite a big fellow."

"He can say your name already."

"Does he really talk?"

"And he is learning to walk."

"Just fancy!"

"He eats anything now."

"Impossible; that is too soon."

"What do you know about it? wait till you see him."

"Push the curtain aside that I may see him by the moonlight."

"No; that would not do. If the moon shines on a sleeping child it makes it ill."

"Nonsense!"

"There are all sorts of wonderful things about children, and one must have plenty of faith; that is why women have charge of children, because they believe everything. Come in and look at him."

"I will not go in as long as he is asleep—I might wake him; you come out."

"I can not do that; he would wake if I left him, and mother is asleep."

"Well, then, you go back to him, and I will remain outside."

"Won't you lie down?"

"It is almost day-break. Go back to him, and leave the window open."

276

And he remained standing by the window, looking into the little room, on whose floor the moon painted silver patterns, and trying to distinguish the tones which came from the quiet chamber—a little whimper of an awakened child, then a low song like a dreamy lullaby, "For all the gold . . ." Then the sound of a kiss, which a good baby gets as a reward for going to sleep. With his elbows on the window-sill, and listening to the breaths of the sleepers, Timar awaited the dawn, which filled the little house with light. The red sunrise awoke the child, and there was no more sleep for the others. The baby crowed and babbled; what it said only those two understood—itself and Noémi.

When at last Michael got it into his arms he said, "I shall stay here, Dodi, till I have finished your house."

The child said something which Noémi interpreted to mean, "That is just what I wish."

These were the happiest days of Timar's dual life. Nothing troubled the serenity of his happiness, except the thought of that other life to which he must return. If he could find ways and means to sever himself from that, he might live on here in peace. Nothing would be easier; he simply had to stay here. He would be sought for during the first year, for two or three more he would be remembered from time to time; then the world would forget him and he it, and Noémi would remain to him. And what a jewel she was! Whatever was lovable in woman was combined in her, and every feminine defect was wanting. Her beauty was not of the kind which satiates by its monotony: with every change of expression arose a new charm. Tenderness, gentleness, and fire were united in her disposition. The virgin, the fairy, the woman were harmoniously blended in her. Her love was never selfish; her whole being went out to him whom she loved: his sorrows and joys were hers, she knew no others. At home she thought of every trivial detail which could conduce to his comfort; she helped him in his work with an untiring hand. Ever bright and fresh, if she felt unwell a kiss from him drove away the pain. She was submissive to him, who worshiped her. And when she took the child on her lap, it was a sight to drive the man mad who had made her his own—and yet not really his.

But Timar had not yet made up his mind. He still played with Fate.

The price was too high even for such a treasure as a lovely woman with a smiling child in her arms.

The cost was—a whole world! a property amounting to millions; his position in society; his rank and noble friends; the enterprise of world-wide influence, on whose result hung the future of a great national branch of trade! and besides—Timéa. He might have reconciled himself to the idea of treading his riches under foot: they came from the submarine depths, and might return thither.

But his vanity refused to contemplate the notion that that woman with the white face, which no glow from her husband could animate, might be happy in this life—with another man. Perhaps he hardly knew himself what a fiend was hidden in his breast. The woman who could not love him was fading away before his eyes, while he could live through happy days where he was well beloved. And during this time the house-building made rapid progress, and was already being put together by the workman's skillful hand; the roof was on, and covered with wide planks formed like fish-scales to overlap each other. The carpentry was done, and now came the cabinet-work. Michael completed it without any assistance, and might be seen from morn to eve in the workshop he had arranged in the new house, where he sung all day as he planed and sawed. Like the steadiest of day-laborers, he never left off his work before dark; then he returned to the hut where an appetizing supper awaited him. After the meal he sat down on the bench outside the house, and lighted his clay pipe. Noémi sat by him and took Dodi on her knees, who was now expected to exhibit what he had learned during the day. A new word! And is not this one word a greater acquirement than all the wisdom of the world? "What would you sell Dodi for?" Noémi asked him once in jest. "For the whole earth full of diamonds?"

"Not for the whole heaven full of angels."

Little Dodi happened that day to be full of spirits. In a mischievous mood he caught hold with his little hand of the pipe Michael had in his mouth, and pulled till he got it out of his hold, when he at once threw it on the ground; as it was made of clay, of course it was broken into atoms. Timar was rather hasty in his exercise of justice, and bestowed a little tap on the child's hand as a punishment for the damage done. The boy looked at him, then hid his head in his mother's breast, and began to cry.

"See now," said Noémi, sadly, "you would give him away for a pipe, and this one was only of clay."

Michael was very sorry to have slapped Dodi's hand. He tried to make it up by coaxing words, and kissed the little hand, but the child was shy of him, and crept under Noémi's shawl. All night he was restless, wakeful, and crying. Timar got angry, and said the child was of a willful nature, his obstinacy must be overcome. Noémi cast a gently reproachful glance on him.

The next day Timar left his bed earlier than usual, and went to his work, but he was never heard to sing all day. He left off early in the afternoon, and when he came home he could see by Noémi's face that she was quite alarmed at his appearance. His complexion was quite altered. "I am not well," he said to Noémi, "my head is so heavy, my feet will hardly carry me, and I have pain in all my limbs. I must lie down."

Noémi hastened to make up a bed for him in the inner room, and helped him to undress. With anxiety she noticed that Michael's hands were cold and his breath burning. Frau Therese felt his forehead, and advised him to cover himself well, for he was going to have ague. But Michael had the sensation that something worse was at hand. In this district typhus was raging, for the spring floods had swelled the Danube in an unusual degree, and left malaria behind them. When he laid his head on the pillow he was still sensible enough to think of what would happen if a serious illness attacked him; no doctor was near to help. He might die here, and no one would know what had become of him. What would become of Timéa, and above all, of Noémi? Who would care for the forsaken one, a widow without being a wife? Who would bring up Dodi, and what fate awaited him when he should be grown up, and Michael underground? Two women's lives would be wrecked by his death!

And then he began to think of the revelations of his delirium before the two women who would be with him day and night—of his stewards, his palaces, and of his pale wife—of how he would see Timéa before him, call her by name, and speak of her as his wife—and Noémi knows that name.

Besides his bodily pain, another thing tormented him—that he had struck Dodi yesterday. This trifle lay heavy as a crime on his soul. After he was in bed he wanted the child brought to him that he might kiss it, and whispered "Noémi," with hot breath.

"What is it?" she answered.

But already he know not what he had asked. Directly he was in bed the fever broke out with full force. He was a strong man, and such are the first to succumb to this "aid-de-camp" of death, and suffer the most from it. Thenceforward he wandered continually; and Noémi heard every word he spoke. The sick man knew no one, not even himself. He who spoke through his lips was a stranger—a man who had no secrets, and told all he knew. The visions are akin to the delusions of madness; they turn on one fixed idea, and however the detail may change, the central figure returns ever and again to the surface.

In Timar's wandering there was one of these dominating figures—a woman. Not Timéa, but Noémi—of her he continually spoke. Timéa's name never passed his lips—she did not fill his soul.

For Noémi it was horror and rapture combined to listen to this unconscious babble—horror, because it spoke of such strange things, and took her with him to such unknown regions, that she trembled at a fever which compelled him to look on at such marvels—and yet it was bliss to hear him, for he always talked of her, and her only.

Once he was in a princely palace and talking with some great man. "To whom should his excellency give this decoration? I know a girl on the ownerless island—no one is more worthy of it than she. Give her the order. She is called Noémi; her other name? Do queens have another name? The first. Noémi the first, by the grace of God queen of the ownerless island and the rose-forest."

He carried his idea further. "If I become king of the ownerless island, I shall form a ministry. Almira will be inspector of meat, and Narcissa will be appointed to the dairy department. I shall demand security from them, and name them as confidential advisers." Then he talked of his palaces. "How do you like these saloons, Noémi? Does the gilding of this ceiling please you? Those children dancing on the golden background are like Dodi—are they not like him? A pity they are so high up. Are you cold in these great halls? So am I—come, let us go away. It is better by the fire in our little hut. I do not love these high palaces; and this town is often visited by earthquakes—I fear the vault may fall in on us. There! behind that little door some one is spying on us—an envious woman. Do not look, Noémi! Her malicious glance might do you harm. This house once belonged to her, and now she wanders through it like a ghost. See, she has a dagger in her hand, and wants to murder you; let us run away!"

But there was a hinderance in the way of escape—the frightful mass of gold. "I can not stand up, the gold drags me down. It is all on my breast; take it away! Oh, I am drowning in gold! The roof has fallen in, and gold is rolling down on me. I am suffocating. Noémi, give me your hand; pull me from under this horrible mountain of gold."

His hand lay in Noémi's all the time, and she thought, trembling, what a fearful power it was which tortured a poor sailor with such dreams of money. Then he began again: "You don't care for diamonds, Noémi? You little fool! Do you think their fire burns? Don't be afraid. Ha! you are right, it does burn—I did not know that—it is hell-fire. Even the names are alike—Diamond, Demon. We will throw them into the water—throw them from you. I know where they came from, and I will throw them back into the water. Don't be afraid, I will not remain long under water. Hold your breath and pray. As long as you can stay without taking breath I shall be down below; I am only going to dive into the cabin of the sunken ship. Ah! who is lying on this bed?"

Such a shudder seized him that he sprung from his couch and would have rushed away. Noćmi was hardly able to get him back to bed. "Some one is lying there, but I must not say the name. See how the red moon shines in at the window. Shut the light out. I will not have it on my face. How near it is coming! Draw the curtain across!"

But the curtains were drawn, and besides, it was pitch-dark outside. When the fever-fit passed, he murmured, "Oh, how lovely you are without diamonds, Noémi!"

Then a fantasy seized him. "That man stands at our antipodes on the other side of the earth. If the earth were of glass he could look down upon us. But he can see me just as well as I see him. What is he doing? He is catching rattlesnakes, and when he comes back he will let them loose on the

281

island. Don't let him land; don't let him come back! Almira! Almira! At him! tear him! Aha! now a giant snake has got him; it is strangling him. How frightful his face is! If only I need not see the snake swallow him! Will he look at me? Now there is only his head out, and he keeps looking at me. Oh, Noémi, cover my face that I may not see him!"

Again the dream-scene changes. "A whole fleet floats on the sea. What are the ships laden with? With flour. Now comes a whirlwind, a tornado seizes the ships, carries them into the clouds and tears them into splinters. The flour is all spilled: the whole world is white with it, white is the sea, white the heavens, and white the air. The moon peeps from the clouds, and only look how the wind covers its face with flour! It looks like some red-nosed old toper who has powdered his face. Laugh then, Noémi!" But she wrung her hands and shuddered. The poor creature was by his bed day and night. By day she sat on a chair at his side; by night she pulled her bed close to his and slept beside him: careless of the infection, she laid her head on Michael's pillow, pressed his perspiring brow to her cheek, and kissed away the burning fever-breaths from his parched lips.

Frau Therese tried by harmless remedies to reduce the fever, and took out the glass casements that the fresh air—the best medicine in fever cases—might freely penetrate the little room. She said to Noémi, that by her calculation the crisis would set in on the thirteenth day, when the illness would either take a turn for the better or terminate fatally.

How long Noémi knelt during these days by the sick man's bed and prayed to God, who had tried her so heavily, to have mercy on her poor heart! If only He would give Michael back to life—and then if the grave must have a sacrifice, there was she ready to die in his stead.

Providence delights in what one might call the irony of fate—Noémi offered to cruel death the whole world and her own self, in exchange for Michael's life. She fancied she had to do with a good fellow who might be bargained with. The destroying angel accepted her challenge.

On the thirteenth day the fever and delirium ceased: the previous nervous excitement gave place to intense exhaustion, which is a symptom of improvement, and permits a hope that with the greatest care the patient may be given back to life, if his mind is kept calm and he is preserved from anxiety or emotion: sick people are so easily excited at this stage of convalescence. His recovery hung on perfect tranquillity; any violent excitement would kill him. Noémi stayed all night by Timar's sick-bed: she never even went out once to see little Dodi; he slept in the outer room with Frau Therese. On the morning of the fourteenth day, while Michael lay sound asleep, Therese whispered in Noémi's ear, "Little Dodi is very ill." The child now! Poor Noémi! Her little Dodi had the croup, the most dangerous of all childish maladies, against which all the skill of the physician is often powerless.

Mortally terrified, Noémi rushed to her child. The face of the innocent creature was quite changed. It was not crying—this disease has no characteristic cry, but so much the more dreadful is the suffering. How terrible, a child who can not complain, whom men can not help! Noémi looked blankly at her mother as if to ask, "And have you no cure for this?" Therese could hardly bear this look. "So many miserable sick and dying people have been helped by you, and for this one you know of no remedy!"

"None!" Noémi knelt down beside the child's little bed, pressed her lips on his, and murmured softly, "What is it, my darling, my little one, my angel? Look at me with thy pretty eyes."

But the little one would not lift up the pretty eyes, and when at last, after many kisses and entreaties, it opened the heavy lids, its expression was terrible—the look of a child which has already learned to fear death. "Oh, don't look so! not so!" The child never cried, but only gave utterance to a hoarse cough.

If only the other invalid in there does not hear it! Noémi held her child trembling in her arms, and listened to hear if the sleeper close by was yet awake. When she heard his voice she left the child and went to Michael. He was suffering from great exhaustion, irritable and peevish.

"Where had you gone?" he questioned Noémi. "The window is open; a rat might get in while I was asleep. Don't you see a rat about?" It is a constant delusion of typhus patients to see rats everywhere.

"They can't get in, my darling; there is a grating over the window."

"Ah! and where is the cold water?" Noémi gave him some to drink. But he was very angry with it. "That is not fresh cold water, it is quite warm.

283

Do you want me to die of thirst?"

Noémi bore his crossness patiently. And when Michael fell asleep again, she ran out to Dodi. The two women replaced each other, so that as long as Michael slept, Therese sat by him, and when he awoke she gave Noémi a sign to leave her sick child and take her place by Michael's bed. And this went on through the long night. Noémi passed constantly from one sick-bed to the other, and she had to keep excuses always ready for her husband if he should ask where she had been.

The child grew worse. Therese could do nothing, and Noémi dared not weep for fear of Michael seeing her tearful eyes and asking the reason. The next morning Timar felt easier, and wished for some soup. Noémi hastened out to fetch it, as it was kept ready. The invalid swallowed it, and said he felt the better for it. Noémi seemed delighted at the good news.

"Well, and what is Dodi doing?" asked Michael.

Noémi trembled lest he should see the throbs of her heart at the question.

"He is asleep," she replied, gently.

"Asleep? But why asleep now? He is not ill?"

"Oh, no; he is all right."

"And why do you not bring him to me when he is awake?"

"Because then you are asleep."

"That is true; but when we are both awake together, you must bring him in and let me see him."

"I will do so, Michael."

The child sunk gradually. Noémi had to conceal from Timar that Dodi was ill, and constantly to invent stories about him, for his father constantly asked for him. "Does Dodi play with his little man?"

"Oh, yes, he is always playing with him" (. . . with that fearful skeleton!).

"Does he talk of me?"

"He loves to talk of you" (. . . he will do so soon when he is with the good God).

"Take him this kiss from me;" and Noémi bore to her child the parting kiss of his father.

Another day dawned. The awakening invalid found himself alone in the room. Noémi had watched all night by her child: she had looked on his death-struggle, and pressed her tears back into her heart; why had it not burst? When she went in to Michael she smiled again.

"Were you with Dodi?" asked the sick man.

"Yes, I have been with him."

"Is he asleep now?"

"Yes, he is asleep."

"Not really?"

"Truly, he sleeps well."

Noémi has just closed his eyes—for his last sleep. And she dared not betray her agony. She must show a smiling face. In the afternoon Michael was much excited again: as the day drew on, his nervous irritation increased. He called to Noémi, who was in the next room; she hastened in and looked lovingly at him. The invalid was peevish and suspicious. He noticed that a needle was sticking in Noémi's dress, with a thread of silk in it.

"Ah, you are beginning to work again! Have you time for that? What finery are you making?"

Noémi looked at him silently, and thought, "I am making Dodi's shroud;" and then aloud, "I am making myself a collar."

"Vanity, thy name is woman!" sighed Michael.

Noémi found a smile for him, and answered, "You are quite right."

Again the morning broke. Michael now suffered from sleeplessness; he could not close his eyes. And the thought troubled him as to what Dodi was doing. He sent Noémi out often to see if he wanted anything. And whenever she did so she kissed the little dead child on the bier, and spoke caressing words for Michael to hear: "My little Dodi! my darling sweet, asleep again! Tell mother you love her;" and then she came back to say that Dodi wanted for nothing.

"The boy sleeps too much," said Michael; "why don't you wake him?"

"I must wake him soon," said Noémi, gently.

Michael dozed a little, only a few minutes, and woke with a start. He did not know he had been asleep. "Noémi," he cried, "Dodi was singing; I heard him: how sweetly he sings!"

285

Noémi pressed both her hands to her heart, and drove back the outward expression of her agony with superhuman courage. Yes, he is already singing in heaven, amidst the angelic choir—among the innumerable seraphim! that was the song he joined in.

Toward evening Michael sent Noémi out. "Go and put Dodi to bed, and give him a kiss for me."

She did so. "What did Dodi say?" he asked her. Noémi could not speak; she bent over Michael and pressed a kiss on his lips.

"That was his message, the treasure!" cried Michael, and the kiss sent him to sleep. The child sent it to him from his own slumber.

The next morning he asked again about the boy. "Take Dodi out into the air; it is bad for him to be in the house; carry him into the garden."

They were about to do so. Therese had dug a grave during the night at the foot of a weeping-willow.

"You go too; and stay out there with him. I shall doze, I think, I feel so much better," Michael told Noémi.

Noémi left the sick-room and turned the key: then they carried God's recovered angel out, and committed him to the care of the universal mother—earth. Noémi would not have a mound raised over him; Michael would be so sad when he saw it, and it would retard his recovery. They made a flower-bed there, and planted in its midst a rose-tree—one of those Timar had grafted—with white flowers, whose purity was unstained. Then she went back to the sick man.

His first words were, "Where have you left Dodi?"

"Out in the garden."

"What has he on?"

"His white frock and blue ribbons."

"That suits him so well. Is he well wrapped up?"

"Oh, yes, very well" (with three feet of earth).

"Bring him in when you go out again."

At this Noémi could not stop in the room; she went out and threw herself on Therese's breast, but even then she could not shed a tear. She must not. Then she tottered on into the garden, went to the willow, broke off a bud from the rose-tree, and went back to Michael.

"Well, where's Dodi?" he said, impatiently.

But Noémi knelt down by his bed and held out to him—the white rose. Michael took it and smelled it. "How curious!" he said; "this flower has no scent—as if it had grown on a grave."

She rose and went out. "What is the matter?" asked Timar, turning to Therese.

"Don't be angry," said she in a gentle, soothing tone. "You were so dangerously ill. Thank Heaven, you are getting over it. But this illness is infectious, and particularly during convalescence. I told Noémi that until you were quite well she must not bring the child near you. Perhaps I was wrong, but I meant it for the best."

Michael pressed her hand. "You did quite right. Stupid that I was, not to have thought of it myself. Perhaps he is not even in the next room?"

"No. We have made him a little house out in the garden." Poor thing, she told the truth.

"You are very good, Therese. Go to Dodi and send Noémi to me. I will not ask her again to bring him to me. Poor Noémi! But as soon as I can get up and go out, you will let me go to him, won't you?"

"Yes, Michael." By this pious fraud it was possible to satisfy him till he was out of bed and on the road to recovery. He was still very weak, and could hardly walk. Noémi helped him to dress. Leaning on her shoulder, he left his room, and she led him to the little seat before the house, sat beside him, put her arm in his, and supported his head on her shoulder. It was a lovely warm summer afternoon. Michael felt as if the murmuring trees were whispering in his ears, as if the humming bees brought him a message, and the grass made music at his feet. His head swam.

One thought grew on him. When he looked at Noémi, a painful suspicion awoke in his breast. There was something in her expression which he could not understand; he must know it. "Noémi."

"What is it, my Michael?"

"Darling Noémi, look at me." She raised her eyes to his. "Where is little Dodi?"

The poor creature could no longer hide her grief. She raised her martyr face to heaven, stretched up both hands, and faltered, "There! . . .

there!"

"He is dead!" Michael could hardly utter the words. Noémi sunk on his breast. Her tears were no longer to be controlled; she sobbed violently.

He put his arm round her and let her weep on. It would have been sacrilege not to let these tears have free course.

He had no tears—no. He was all wonder; he was amazed at the greatness of soul which raised the poor despised creature so far above himself. That she should have been able to conceal her sorrow so long out of tender consideration for him whom she loved! How great that love must be! When the paroxysm was over she looked smiling at Timar, like the sun through the rainbow.

"And you could keep this from me?"

"I feared for your life."

"You dared not weep lest I should see traces of tears."

"I waited for the time when I might weep."

"When you were not with me, you nursed the sick child, and I was angry with you."

"You were never unkind, Michael."

"When you took my kiss to him you knew it was a farewell; when I reproached you with your vanity you were sewing his shroud; when you showed me a cheerful face your heart was pierced with the seven wounds of the Blessed Virgin! Oh, Noémi, I worship you!"

But the poor thing only asked him to love her. Michael drew her on to his knee. The leaves, the grass, the bees, whispered now so clearly that he began to understand the swimming in his head.

After a long and gloomy silence he spoke again. "Where have you laid him? Take me to him, Noémi."

"Not to-day," said Noémi. "It is too far for you—to-morrow."

But neither to-morrow nor the next day would she take him there.

"You would sit by the grave and make yourself ill again: that is why I have made no mound over him, nor raised a cross, that you may not go there and grieve."

Timar, however, was sad at this. When he was strong enough to walk alone, he went about seeking for what they would not show him.

288

One day he came back to the house with a cheerful face. In his hand he held a half-blown rosebud, one of those white ones which have no scent. "Is it this?" he asked Noémi.

She nodded: it could no longer be concealed. The white rose had put him on the track, and he noticed that it had been newly transplanted. And then he was tranquil, like one who has done with all that had given an object to life. He sat all day on the little bench near the house, drew on the gravel with his stick, and muttered to himself, "You would not exchange him for the whole earth full of diamonds, nor the whole heaven full of angels; . . . but for a miserable pipe you could strike his hand."

The beautiful walnut-wood house stood half finished, and the great convolvulus had crept over its four walls. Michael never set foot in it.

The only thing that kept up his half-recovered strength and his broken spirit was Noémi's love.

CHAPTER III.
MELANCHOLY.

One bud after another opened on the rose-tree. Timar did nothing but watch the development and blossoming of these rosebuds. When one of them opened he broke it off, put it in his pocket-book, and dried it there on his breast. This was a melancholy task. All the tenderness lavished on him by Noémi could not cure his sadness. The woman's sweet caresses were burdensome to him. And yet Noémi could have comforted him at the cost of a single word; but modest reserve kept back that word, and it never occurred to Michael to question her.

It is characteristic of those whose mind is diseased to occupy themselves only with the past.

At last Noémi said to Timar, "Michael, it would be good for you to go away from here—out into the world. Everything here arouses mournful memories in you; you must go away to get well. I have done your packing, and the fruit-dealers will fetch you away to-morrow."

Michael did not answer, but expressed his assent by a nod. The dangerous illness he had passed through had affected his nerves; and the situation he had brought upon himself, the blow which had struck him, had worked on those nerves so painfully, that he was forced to acknowledge that a longer stay would lead to madness or suicide.

Suicide? There is no easier road out of a difficult position: failure, despair, mental conflict, blasted hopes, heart-pangs, fantastic bugbears, the memory of losses, phantoms of the beloved dead—all these are parts of a bad dream. One touch on the trigger of the pistol, and one awakes. Those who remain behind can go on with the dream.

On the last evening, Michael, Noémi, and Therese sat all three after supper on the little bench outside, and Michael remembered that they had once been four together there.

"What can that moon really be?" asked Noémi.

Michael's hand, which Noémi held in hers, was clinched with sudden violence.

"My evil star," he thought to himself. "Oh, if I had never seen it, that red crescent!"

Therese answered her daughter's question: "It is a burned-out and chilled world, on which neither trees, flowers, nor animals, no air or water, no sounds or colors exist. When I was a girl at school, we used often to look through a telescope at the moon; it is full of mountains, and we were told they were the craters of extinct volcanoes. No telescope is powerful enough to show people on it, but learned men know with certainty that neither air nor water exists there. Without air and water nothing can live that has a human body, so no mortal can possibly be there."

"But what if something did really live in it?"

"What could do so?"

"I will tell you what I think. Often in the old times, when I was still alone, I could not rid myself of one engrossing thought—especially when I sat by myself on the beach, and looked into the water. I felt as if something were drawing me into it, and calling to me that it was good to be down below there, and that there all was peace. Then I said to myself—Good! the body would rest at the bottom of the Danube; but where would the soul go?—it must find a dwelling somewhere. Then the thought arose that the soul which wrenched itself so forcibly and by its own will from its mortal shell could only soar to the moon. I believe that now even more firmly. If neither trees nor flowers, neither water nor air, neither colors nor sounds, can there exist—well, it is all the better fitted for those who did not wish to be encumbered with a body: there they will find a world where there is nothing to trouble them, nor anything to give them pleasure."

Therese and Michael both rose with a start from beside Noémi, who could not understand what had moved them. She did not know that her own father was a suicide, and that he whose hand she held was ready to become one. Michael said the night was cool, they had better go in. One more haunting thought was now linked with the sight of the moon. The first he inherited from Timéa, the other from Noémi. What a fearful penalty—that the man should continually see before him in the heavens that shining witness, eternally recalling him to his first sin, the first fateful error of his ruined life!

The next day Michael left the island: he passed by the unfinished walnut-wood house without even glancing at it.

"You will return with the spring flowers," whispered Noémi tenderly in his ear. The poor thing thought it quite natural that for half of the year Michael should not belong to her. "But to whom does he then belong?" That question never occurred to her.

When Michael arrived at Komorn, the long journey had still more exhausted him. Timéa was frightened when she saw him, and could hardly recognize him; even Athalie was alarmed, and with good reason.

"You have been ill?" said Timéa, leaning on her husband's breast.

"Very ill, for many weeks."

"On your journey?"

"Yes," answered Timar, to whom this seemed like a cross-examination. He must be on his guard at every question.

"Good God! and had you anyone to nurse you there among those strangers?"

The words had almost escaped him, "Oh, yes, an angel!" but he caught himself up and answered, "You can get anything for money." Timéa did not know how to show her sympathy, and so Michael could detect no change in the always apathetic face. She was always the same, and the frigid kiss of welcome drew them no closer together.

Athalie whispered in his ear, "For God's sake, sir, take care of your life!"

Timar felt the poisoned sting hidden beneath this tender consideration. He must live that Timéa might suffer; for if she became a widow, nothing would stand in the way of her happiness. And that would be a hell to Athalie.

It seemed to Timar as if the demon who hated both him and his wife was now praying for the prolongation of his detested life, so that their mutual suffering might last the longer. Every one remarked the great change which had taken place in him. In the spring he was a strong man in the prime of life; now he was like a feeble, voiceless shadow.

He withdrew to his office as soon as he arrived, and spent the whole day there. His secretary found the ledger lying on the desk just as he had opened it; he had not even looked at it. His agents were informed of his return, and hastened to present yards of reports. He said to them all, "Very good," and signed what they required, sometimes in the wrong place, sometimes twice over. At last he shut himself up from every one in his room, under pretense of requiring sleep. But his servants heard him walking up and down for hours together.

When he went to the ladies to dine in their company, he looked so gloomy and stern that no one had the courage to address him. He hardly touched food, and never tasted wine. But an hour after dinner he rang for the servant, and asked angrily whether they were ever going to get the meal ready—he had forgotten that it was over. In the evening he could not sit up, so tired was he; when he sat down he dozed off at once; as soon, however, as he was undressed and in bed, slumber fled suddenly from his eyes. "Oh, how cold this bed is—everything in the house is cold!" Every piece of furniture, the pictures on the walls, even the old frescoes on the ceiling, seemed to cry to him, "What have you come here for? This is not your home! You are a stranger here!" How cold is this bed!

The man who came to call him to supper found him already in bed. On hearing this, Timéa came to him and asked whether he would have something.

"Nothing—no, nothing at all," answered Timar. "I am only overtired by the journey."

"Shall I send for the doctor?"

"Pray don't. I am not ill."

Timéa wished him good-night, and went away after again feeling his forehead with her hand. But Timar was not in a condition to sleep. He heard every noise in the house; he heard them whispering and creeping on tiptoe past his door, so as not to disturb him. He was thinking where a man could best flee from himself. Into the realm of dreams? That would be good, indeed, if only one could find the way there as easily as into the kingdom of death. But one can not force one's self to dream. Opium? That is one way—the suicide of sleep. Gradually he noticed that it was growing darker in the room: the shades of night veiled closely every object, the light grew dim. At last he was surrounded by a darkness like that of a thick, motionless mist, like subterranean gloom, or the night of the blind: such an obscurity one "sees" even in sleep. Michael knew he was asleep, and the blindness lying over his eyes was that of slumber. Yes, he now had full consciousness of his position. He was lying in his own bed in his Komorn house—a table beside him with an antique bronze lamp-stand, and a painted lamp-shade with Chinese figures on it; over his head hung a large clock with a chime; the silken curtains were let down. The curious old bed had a sort of drawer below it, which could be drawn out and used as a second bed. It was beautifully made—one of those beds only found in fine old houses, in which a whole family might find room to sleep. Timar knew that he had not bolted his door; any one could come in who chose. How if some one came to murder him? And what difference would there be between sleep and death? This puzzled him in his dreams.

Once he dreamed that the door opened softly and some one entered: a woman's steps. The curtain rustled, and something leaned over him: a woman's face. "Is it you, Noémi?" Michael thought in his dream, and started. "How came you here? If some one saw you?" It was dark, he could see nothing; but he heard the person sit down by his bed and listen to his breathing. Thus had Noémi done many a night in the little hut. "Oh, Noémi, will you watch again all through the night? When will you sleep?"

The female figure, as if in answer, knelt down and drew out the shelf below the bed. Michael felt a mixture of fear and rapture in his breast. "You will lie down beside me; oh, how I love you, but I tremble for you!" and then the figure prepared a bed on the shelf and lay down. The dreamer in the bed longed to bend over her, to embrace and kiss her, and would have called again to her, "Go, hasten away from here, you will be seen;" but he could move neither limbs nor tongue, they were heavy as lead; and then the woman slept too. Michael sunk deeper into dreamland. His fancy flew through past and future, soared into the region of the impossible, and returned to the sleeping woman. He dreamed that he was awake, and yet the phantom was beside him.

At last it began to dawn, and the sun shone through the window with more wonderful radiance than ever before. "Awake, awake!" whispered Michael in his dream. "Go home—the daylight must not find you here. Leave me now!" He struggled with the dream. "But you are not really here—it is only a delusion!"

He forced himself to sever the bonds in which sleep held him, and awoke completely. It was really morning, the sunlight streamed through the curtains, and on the shelf below the bed lay a sleeping woman with her head on her arm.

"Noémi!" cried Michael. The slumbering form awoke at the call and looked up. It was Timéa—

"Do you want anything?" asked the woman, rising hastily from her couch. She had heard the tone but not the name. Her husband was still under the influence of his dream. "Timéa!" he stammered sleepily, astonished at the metamorphosis of Noémi into Timéa.

"Here I am," said she, laying her hand on the bed.

"How is it possible?" cried he, drawing up the quilt to his chin as if afraid of the face leaning over him.

"I was anxious about you, I was afraid you might have some attack in the night, and I wanted to be near you." In the tone of her voice, in her look, lay such sincere and natural tenderness as could not be assumed: a woman's instinct is fidelity.

Michael collected himself. His first feeling was alarm, his second self-reproach. This poor woman lying by his bed was the widow of a living man. She had never known a joy in common with her husband; now when he was in pain, she came to share it with him; and then followed the eternal falsehood—he must not accept this tenderness, he must repulse it.

Michael said with forced composure, "Timéa, I beg you not to do this again; do not come into my room. I have been suffering from an infectious illness; I caught the plague on my journey, and I tremble for your life if you approach me. Keep far from me, I adjure you; I wish to be alone, both by day and night. There is nothing the matter with me now, but I feel that I must, for prudence' sake, avoid all those belonging to me; so I beg you earnestly not to do this again, never again." Timéa sighed deeply, cast down her eyes, and left the room. She had not even undressed, but had only lain down in her clothes at her husband's feet.

When she was gone, Michael got up and dressed; his mind was much disturbed. The longer he continued this dual life, the more he felt the conflict of the double duties he had taken on himself. He was responsible for the fate of two noble, self-sacrificing souls. He had made both miserable, and himself more unhappy than either.

What outlet could he find? If only one or other were an every-day creature, so that he could hate and despise her or buy her off! But both were equally nobly gifted: the fate of both was so heavy a charge against the author of it, that no excuse existed. How could he tell Timéa who Noémi was, or Noémi about Timéa? Suppose he were to divide all his wealth between the two, or if he gave his money to one and his heart to the other? But either was alike impossible, for neither was faithless or gave him a right to reject them.

Living at home made Michael yet more ill.

He never left his room all day, spoke to no one, and sat till evening in one place, without doing anything. At last Timéa resorted to a physician. The result of the consultation was that Michael was ordered to the seaside, that the water might restore to him what the land had taken from him. To this advice he replied, "I will not go where there is company." Then they suggested that he should choose some place where the season was over and the visitors gone; there he would find solitude. The cold baths were the important point. He now remembered that in one of the valleys near the Platten See he had a summer villa, which he had bought years ago when he hired the fishing of the Balaton lake, and he had only been there two or three times since. There, said he, would he spend the end of the autumn.

The doctors approved his choice. The districts of Zala and Vessprimer on the banks of the lake are like the Vale of Tempe. Fourteen miles of unbroken garden-land form a charming chain of landscapes, with country-seats strewn here and there. The splendid lake is a sea in miniature, full of loveliness and romance; here is soft Italian air, the people are kind and cordial, the mineral springs curative; nothing could be better for a depressed invalid than to spend the autumn here. So the doctors sent Michael to the Platten See. But they had forgotten that toward the end of the summer hail-storms had laid waste the whole district; and nothing is more depressing than a place ruined by hail. The vineyards, which usually resound during the vintage with joyous cries, now stand deserted: the leaves of the fruit-trees are

296

coppery-green or rusty brown; they take their leave until the coming spring: all is silent and sad; even the roads are overgrown with moss, for no one uses them. In the cornfields, instead of the sheaves of grain, ineradicable weeds abound, and instead of the golden heads, thistles, burdock, and nightshade are rampant, for no one comes to cut them down.

At such a season Michael arrived at his villa on the Balaton. It was an ancient pile. Some noble family had built it as a summer residence, because the view had pleased them and they had money enough to afford themselves this luxury. It had but one low story within massive walls, a veranda looking over the lake, and trellises with large fig-trees. The heirs of the first owners had got rid of the lonely château for a nominal price, as it had no value except to a person bitten with the misanthropic desire to live there in solitude.

No human dwelling is to be found within two miles of it, and even beyond that distance most of the houses are uninhabited. The presses and cellars are not open on account of the failure of the vintage. At Fured all the blinds are down and the last invalid has left; even the steamers no longer ply; the pump-room at the baths stands empty, and on the promenade the fallen leaves rustle round the feet of the passer-by—no one thinks it worth while to sweep them away. Not a man nor even a stork is left in the place—only the majestic Balaton murmurs mysteriously as it tosses its waves, and no one knows why it is angry. In its midst rises a bare rock, on whose top stands a convent with two towers, in which live seven monks—a crypt full of princely bones from top to bottom.

And here Timar came to seek for health.

Michael only brought one servant with him, and after a few days sent him back under pretense that the people of the house sufficed for his service. But there was only one old man, and he quite deaf.

Round the villa no human voice was heard, not even the sound of a bell, only the haunting murmur of the great lake.

Timar sat all day on the shore, and listened to the voices of the water. Often, when there was not a breath of air stirring, the lake began to roar, then the color of its surface changed to an emerald green as far as the eye could see: over the dark mirror of the waves not one sail, not a single ship, barge, or boat was visible; it might have been the Dead Sea.

This lake possesses the double quality of strengthening the body and depressing the mind. The chest expands, the appetite increases, but the mind is inclined to a melancholy and sentimental state which carries one back to fairyland.

Timar floated for hours on the gently rocking waves; he wandered whole days on the shore, and could hardly tear himself away when night fell. He sought no distraction from shooting or fishing. Once he took out his gun, and forgot it somewhere by the trunk of a tree: another time he caught a pike, but let it get away with his fly. He could fix his attention on nothing.

He had taken a powerful retracting telescope with him, through which he gazed at the starry heavens during the long nights; at the planets with their moons and rings, on which in winter white spots are visible, while in summer a red light surrounds them; and then at that great enigma of the firmament, the moon, which when looked at through the glass appears like a shining ball of lava, with its transparent ridges, its deep craters, bright plains and dark shadows. It is a world of emptiness. Nothing is there except the souls of those who violently separated themselves from their body to get rid of its load. There they are at peace; they feel nothing, do nothing, know neither sorrow nor joy, gain nor loss; there is neither air nor water, winds nor storms, no flowers or living creatures, no war, no kisses, no heart-throbs—neither birth nor death; only "nothing," and perhaps memory.

That would be worse than hell, to live in the moon as a disembodied soul in the realm of nothingness, and to remember the earth, where are green grass and red blood, where the air echoes with the roll of the thunder and the kisses of lovers, where life and death exist. And yet something whispered to Michael that he must take refuge among the exiles to that region of annihilation. There was no other way of escape from his miserable existence.

The nights of autumn grew longer and the days shorter, and with the waning daylight the water in the lake grew colder and colder. But Timar enjoyed bathing in it even more. His frame had regained its former elasticity, all traces of his illness had vanished, nerves and muscles were as steel; but his mental agony increased.

The nights were always clear and the skies thickly sown with stars:

298

Timar sat by his open window and studied the shining points in boundless space through his glass, but never until the moon had set. He detested the moon, as we grow to hate a place we know too well, and with whose inhabitants we have quarreled.

During his observations of the starry heavens he had the exceptional good fortune to witness one of those celestial phenomena which are all but unique in the annals of astronomy. A comet returning after centuries of absence appeared in the sky. Timar said to himself, "This is my star; it is as lost as my soul; its coming and going are as aimless as mine, and its whole existence as empty and vain a show as is my life." Jupiter and his four moons were moving in the same direction as the comet; their orbits must cross. When the comet approached the great planet, its tail seemed to divide; the attraction of Jupiter began to take effect. The great star was trying to rob its lord, the sun, of this vaporous body. The next night the comet's tail was split in two. Then the largest and most distant of Jupiter's moons drew rapidly near.

"What has become of my star?" asked Timar.

The third night the nucleus of the comet had grown dull and began to disperse, and Jupiter's moon was close to it. The fourth night the comet had been divided into two parts; there were two heads and two tails, and both the starry phantoms began in separate parabolic curves their aimless flight through space. So "this" occurs in the heavens as well as on earth?

Timar followed this marvelous phenomenon with his telescope till it was lost in impenetrable space. This sight made the deepest impression on his mind; now he had done with the world. There are hundreds of motives for suicide, but the most urgent are to be found among those who give themselves up to scientific research.

Keep a watchful eye on those who seek to fathom the secrets of nature without a technical education. Hide away the knife and the pistol every night, and search their pockets lest they carry poison about them.

Yes, Timar was determined to kill himself. This idea does not come to strong characters all at once, but it ripens in them by degrees. They grow used to it as the years go by, and carefully provide for its execution. The thought had now ripened in Timar, and he went systematically to work.

When the severe weather set in, he left the Platten See and returned to Komorn. He made his will. His whole property he left to Timéa and the poor, and with such careful foresight that he provided a separate fund out of which Timéa, in case she married again, or her heirs if they stood in need of it, would receive a pension of a hundred thousand gulden.

The following was his plan. As soon as the season permitted he would go away, ostensibly to Egypt, but really to the ownerless island. There he would die.

If he could induce Noémi to die with him, then in death they would be united. Oh, Noémi would consent! What would she do in this world without Michael? What worth would the world have for such a one as she?

Both there by Dodi's side.

Timar spent the winter partly in Komorn, partly in Raab and Vienna; everywhere his life was a burden to him. He thought he read in every face, "This man is melancholy mad." He noticed people whispering and making signs when he appeared—women were shy of him, and men tried to look unconscious; and he fancied that in his distraction he did and said things which gave evidence of his mental disease, and wondered people did not laugh. Perhaps they were afraid of laughing.

But they had no reason to fear. He was not lively to throw pepper in the eyes of the people near him, though odd fancies did now and then occur to him; as, for instance, when Johann Fabula came to make him an oration as curator of the church, and stood as stiff before him as if he had swallowed the spit, an impulse seized Timar, almost irresistibly, to put both hands on the curator's shoulders and turn a somersault over his head.

Something lay in Michael's expression which made the blood run cold.

Athalie met this glance; often, as they sat at meals, Timar's eyes were fixed on her. She was a wonderfully beautiful woman; Michael's eyes rested on her lovely snowy neck, so that she felt uneasy at this silent homage to her charms.

Michael was thinking—"If only I had you in my power for once, you lovely white throat, so as to crush the life out of you with my iron hand!" This was what he longed for when he admired the splendid Bacchante form of Athalie.

Only Timéa was not afraid of him—she had nothing to fear. At last it seemed impossible to Timar to wait for the tardy spring. What does he want with the springing flowers who will soon be at rest under the turf?

The day before his departure he gave a great banquet, and invited every one, including even slight acquaintances. The house was crowded with guests. Before sitting down he said to Fabula, "My brother, sit near me, and if I get drunk toward morning and lose my senses, see that I am carried into my traveling-chaise, and put me on the seat; then harness the horses and send me off." He wished to leave his house and home while unconscious.

But when the guests toward morning had sunk one here and another there under the table, our Herr Johann Fabula was snoring comfortably in his arm-chair, and only Timar had kept his head. Mad people are like King Mithridates and the poison—wine does not affect them. So he had to get his carriage himself and start on his journey. In his head reality and dreams, imagination, memory, and hallucination were in a whirl. It seemed to him as if he had stood by the couch of a sleeping saint with a marble face, and as if he had kissed the lips of the white statue, and it had not awoke under his kiss. Perhaps it was only a vision. Then he thought he remembered that behind the door of a dark recess, as he passed, a lovely Mænad's head looked out, framed in rich tresses. She had sparkling eyes and red lips, between which shone two rows of pearls, as she held the candle and asked the sleep-walker, "Where are you going, sir?"

And he had whispered in the witch's ear, "I am going to make Timéa happy."

Then the ideal face had turned to a Medusa head, and the curls to snakes. Perhaps this was hallucination too.

Timar awoke toward noon in his carriage, when the post-horses were changed. He was already far from Komorn, and his intention was unchanged. Late at night he arrived on the Danube shore, where the little boat he had ordered awaited him; he went over in the night to the island.

A thought came into his head. "How if Noémi were dead already?" Why should not this be possible? What a burden it would free him from—that of persuading her to the dreadful step. He who has one fixed idea

301

expects of fate that everything should happen as he has planned.

Near the white rose-bush no doubt a second already stands, which will bloom red in spring—on Noémi's grave. Soon there will be a third with yellow blossoms, the flower of the man of gold.

Occupied with these thoughts, he landed on the island shore. It was still night and the moon shone. The unfinished house stood like a tomb on the grass-grown field; the windows and door-ways were hung with matting to keep out snow and rain. Michael hastened to the old dwelling. Almira met him and licked his hand; she did not bark, but took a corner of his cloak in her teeth and drew him to the window. The moon shone through the lattice, and Michael looked into the little room, which was quite light.

He could clearly perceive that only one bed was in the room, the other was gone. On this bed slept Therese; it was as he had thought—Noémi was already at rest under the rose-bush. It is well.

He knocked at the window. "It is I, Therese." At this the woman came out on the veranda. "Are you sleeping alone, Therese?" said Timar.

"Yes."

"Has Noémi gone up to Dodi?"

"Not so. Dodi has come down to Noémi."

Timar looked inquiringly in her face. Then the woman grasped his hand, and led him with a smile to the back of the house, where the window of the other little room looked out. This room was light, for a night-lamp was burning there. Timar looked in and saw Noémi on the white bed, with her arm round a golden-haired cherub which lay on her breast. "What is this?" Timar faltered out.

Therese smiled gently. "Do you not see? Little Dodi longed to come back to us; it was better here, he thought, than up in heaven. He said to the dear Lord, 'Thou hast angels enough; let me return to those who had only me'—and the Lord allowed it."

"How can it be?"

"H'm! h'm! The old story. A poor woman again who died, and we have adopted the poor orphan. You are not angry?" Timar trembled in every limb as if with ague. "Pray do not wake the sleepers before morning," said Therese, "It is bad for babies to be waked: children's lives are so precarious.

You will be patient, won't you?"

It never occurred to Timar to protest. He threw off his cap and cloak, drew off his coat, and turned up his shirt-sleeves. Therese thought he was mad. And why not? He ran out to the walnut-house, tore the mattings down, drew out his carpenter's bench, placed the unfinished door-panel on it, took his chisel and began to work.

It was just growing light. Noémi dreamed that some one was at work in the new house; the plane grated over the hard wood, and the busy workman sung—

"For all the gold the world could hold, I would not give my Dodi's curl."

And when she opened her eyes she still heard the plane and the song.

CHAPTER IV.
THERESE.

Timar had succeeded in robbing every one.

From Timéa he stole first her father's million, then the manly ideal of her heart, and kept for himself her wifely troth. From Noémi he stole her loving heart, her womanly tenderness, her whole being. Therese he robbed of her trust, the last belief of her misanthropic mind in the possible goodness of a man; then he took the island, in order to restore it to her, and so to obtain her gratitude. Theodor Krisstyan he defrauded of half a world—for he exiled him to another hemisphere. From Athalie he took father, mother, home, and bridegroom, her whole present and future happiness. He robbed his friend Katschuka of the hope of a blissful life. The respect shown to him by the world, the tears of the poor, the thanks of the orphan, the decorations bestowed by his king, were they not all thefts? By deceit he obtained from the smugglers, the fidelity with which they guarded his secret—a thief who steals from other thieves! He even robbed the good God of a little angel. His soul was not his; he had pledged it to the moon, and had not kept his promise: he had not paid what he owed. The poison was ready which was to transport him to that distant star of night—the devils were already rejoicing and stretching out their claws to receive the poor soul. He took them in too; he did not kill himself, but defrauded even death. He laid hands on a paradise in the midst of the world, and took the forbidden fruit from the tree while the watching archangel turned his back, and in that hidden Eden he defied all human law: the clergy, the king, the judge, the general, the tax-collector, the police—all were deceived and defrauded by him.

And everything succeeded with him. How long would he go unpunished?

He could deceive every one but himself. He was always sad, even when he outwardly smiled. He knew what he ought to be called, and would gladly have shown himself in his true character.

But that was impossible. The boundless, universal respect—the rapturous love—if only one of these were really due to his true self! Honor, humanity, self-sacrifice were the original principles of his character, the atmosphere of his being. Unheard-of temptations had drawn him in the opposite direction; and now he was a man whom every one loved, honored, and respected, and who was only hated and despised by himself. Fate had blessed him since his last illness with such iron strength that now nothing hurt him, and instead of aging he seemed to renew his youth.

He was busy all through the summer with manual labor. The little house he had erected the year before he now had to finish, and to add the carver's and turner's work to it. He borrowed from the Muses their creative genius: a great artist was lost in Timar. Every pillar in the little house was of a different design: one was formed of two intwining snakes, whose heads made the capital; another, of a palm-tree with creepers climbing up it; the third showed a vine with squirrels and woodpeckers half hidden in its branches; and the fourth a clump of bulrushes rising from their leaves. The internal panels of the walls were a fanciful mosaic of carving; every table and chair was a work of art, and exquisitely inlaid with light-colored woods to make a pleasant contrast with the dark walnut. Each door and window betrayed some original invention; some disappeared in the wall, some slid up into the roof, and all were opened and shut by curious wooden bolts—for as Timar had declared that no nail should be put into the whole house which was not made by himself, not a morsel of iron was used in it.

What delight when the house was ready and he conducted his dear ones into it, and could say, "See, all this is my handiwork! A king could not give his queen such a present."

But it had taken years to complete it, and four winters had Timar spent in Komorn and four summers in the island, before Dodi the second had his house ready for him.

Then Michael had another task before him; he must teach Dodi to read. Dodi was a lively, healthy, good-tempered boy, and Timar said he would teach him everything himself—reading, writing, swimming, also gardening and mason's and carpenter's work. He who knows these trades can always earn his bread. Timar fancied things would always go on thus, and he could live this life to the end of his days. But suddenly fate cried "Halt!"

Or rather not fate, but Therese. Eight years had passed since Timar

305

had found his way to the little island. Then Noémi and Timéa were both children: now Noémi was twenty-two, Timéa twenty-one, Athalie would soon be twenty-five; but Therese was over forty-five, Timar himself nearly forty, and little Dodi was in his fifth year.

One of them must prepare to go hence, for her time was come, and her cup of suffering was full enough for a long life: that one was Therese.

One summer afternoon when her daughter was out with the child, she said to Timar, "Michael, I have something to tell you—this autumn will be my last. I know that death is near. For twenty years I have suffered from the disease which will kill me; it is heart complaint. Do not look on this as a figure of speech; it is a fatal disease, but I have always concealed it, and never complained. I have kept it under by patience, and you have helped me by the love you showed and the joys you prepared for me. If you had not done so, I should long have lain beneath the sod. But I can bear it no longer. For a year past sleep has fled from my eyes, and I hear my heart beat all day. It throbs quickly three or four times, as if frightened, then comes a sort of half-beat; then it stops entirely for a few moments, till it begins pulsating again rapidly after one or two slow throbs, followed by short beats and long pauses. This must soon come to an end. I often turn faint, and only keep up by an effort of will; this will not last through the summer—and I am content it should be so. Noémi has now another object for her affection. I will not trouble you, Michael, with questions, nor require of you any promise; spoken words are vain and empty—only what we feel is true. You feel what you are to Noémi, and she to you. What is there to disquiet me? I can die without even troubling the merciful God with my feeble prayers. He has given me all I could have asked of Him. Is it not so, Michael?"

Michael's head sunk. This had often of late destroyed his sleep. It had not escaped him that Therese's health was failing rapidly, and he had thought with trembling that she might be suddenly overtaken by death. What would then become of Noémi? How could he leave the delicate creature here alone the whole winter with her little child? Who would help and protect her? He had often put the question aside, but now it confronted him, and must be considered.

Therese was right. The same afternoon a friendly fruit-woman came to the island, and while Therese was counting out her baskets of peaches, she suddenly fell down in a swoon. She recovered quickly, and three days later the woman came again, Therese was determined to serve her, and fainted once more. The fruit-dealer sighed heavily; the next time she came Noémi and Michael would not let her go in to Therese, but served her themselves. The woman remarked that the good lady would do well to see the priest, as she seemed so seriously ill.

Noémi did not yet know that her mother was dangerously ill; her frequent fainting-fits were put down to the hot weather. Therese said that many women suffered in the same way as they grew older. Timar was very attentive to her; he would not let her be troubled with household work, took care that she should rest, and made the child be quiet if he was noisy, but Therese's sleeplessness could not be cured.

One day all four sat together at dinner in the outer room, when Almira's barks announced the approach of strangers. Therese looked out, and said in great alarm, "Go inside quickly, that no one may see you."

Timar looked out, and he too saw that it would not be advisable for him to meet the new-comer, for it was none other than his Reverence Herr Sandorovics, the dean who had received the order, who would not fail to recognize Herr von Levetinczy, and would have some pleasant things to say to him. "Push the table away and leave me alone," said Frau Therese, making Noémi and Dodi rise too. And as if all her strength had returned, she helped to carry the table into the next room, so that when his reverence knocked at the door she was alone, and had drawn her bedstead across the door-way so as to prevent access to the inner apartment.

The dean's beard was longer and grayer since we last saw him; but his cheeks were rosy, and his figure that of a Samson. His deacon and acolyte, who had come with him, had remained in the veranda, and were trying to make friends with the great dog.

The reverend gentleman came in alone, with his hand out as if to give any one a chance of kissing it. As Therese showed no inclination to avail herself of the opportunity, the visitor was at once in a bad temper. "Well, don't you know me again, you sinful woman?"

"Oh, I know you well enough, sir, and I know I am a sinner—what brings you here?"

"What brings me, you old gossip? You ask me that, you God-forsaken heathen! It is clear you don't know me."

"I told you before that I knew you. You are the priest who would not bury my poor husband."

"No—because he left the world in an unauthorized way, without confession or absolution. Therefore it befell him to be put under ground like a dog. If you don't wish to be buried like a dog too, look to it: repent and confess while there is yet time. Your last hour may come to-day or to-morrow. Pious women brought me the news of your being near death, and begged me to come here and give you absolution—you have to thank them for my presence."

"Speak low, sir; my daughter is in the next room, and she would be alarmed."

"Indeed! your daughter? and a man and a child too?"

"Certainly."

"And the man is your daughter's husband?"

"Yes."

"Who married them?"

"He who married Adam and Eve—God."

"Foolish woman! That was when there were no priests nor altars. But now things are not managed so easily, and there is a law to govern them."

"I know it: the law drove me to this island; but that law has no jurisdiction here."

"So you are an absolute heathen?"

"I wish to live and die in peace."

"And you have permitted your daughter to live in shame?"

"What is shame?"

"Shame? The contempt of all respectable people."

"Does that make me warm or cold?"

"Unfeeling clod! You only care for your bodily weal. You never think of the salvation of your soul. I come to show you the way to heaven, and you prefer the road to hell! Do you believe in the resurrection, or in eternal life?"

"Hardly—at any rate, I am not longing for it. I do not want to awake to another life; I want to sleep peacefully under the trees. I shall fall into dust, and the roots will feed on it, and leaves will grow from it: and I want no other life. I shall live in the sap of the green trees I planted with my own hands. I do not believe in your cruel God who makes His wretched creatures live on to suffer beyond the grave. Mine is a merciful God, who gives rest to animals, trees, and men when they are dead."

"Could there be a more obstinate sinner! You will go to hell-fire—to the tortures of the damned!"

"Show me where the Bible says that God created hell, and I will believe you."

"Oh, you pagan! You will be denying the existence of the devil next," cried the priest in a rage.

"I do deny that God ever created such a devil as you believe in: you invented one for yourselves, and did that badly, for your devil has horns and cloven feet, and such creatures as that eat grass and not men."

"The earth will open and swallow you up like Dathan and Abiram. Do you bring up the little child in this belief?"

"He is taught by the man who has adopted him."

"Who?"

"He whom the child calls father."

"And what is his name?"

"Michael."

"What is his surname?"

"I never asked him."

"What! you never asked his name? What do you know of him?"

"I know he is an honest man, and loves Noémi."

"But what is he? A gentleman, a peasant, a workman, a sailor, or a smuggler?"

"He is a poor man, suited to us."

"And what else? I must know, for it is part of my duty. What faith does he confess? Is he Papist, Calvinist, Lutheran, Socinian, or perhaps a Jew?"

"I have not troubled myself about it."

"Do you keep the fasts of the Church?"

309

"Once for two years I never touched meat—because I had none."

"Who baptized the child?"

"God—with a shower of rain, while He sat on high on His rainbow throne."

"Oh, you heathen!"

"Why heathen?" asked Therese, bitterly. "God's hand was heavy on me; from the height of bliss I fell into the deepest misery. One day made me a widow and a beggar. I did not deny God, nor cast His gift of life away. I came to this desert, sought God and found Him here. My God requires no sacrifice of song and bell, only a devout heart. I do my penance, not by telling my beads, but by work. Men left me nothing in the world, and I formed a blooming garden from a desert wilderness. All deceived, robbed, and scorned me; the tribunal condemned me, my friends defrauded me, the Church despised me, and yet I did not hate my kind. I am the refuge of the stranger and the destitute; I feed and heal those who come to me for aid, and sleep with open doors winter and summer; I fear no one. Oh, sir, I am no heathen!"

"What sort of rubbish you talk, you chattering woman! I never asked you all that, but I ask you about the man who lives in this hut, whether he is a Christian or a heretic, and why the child is not baptized? It is impossible that you should not know his name."

"Be it so; I will not tell a lie. I know his name, but nothing more. His life may have secrets in it, as mine had: he may have good reasons for hiding himself. But I know him only as a kind good man, and harbor no suspicions of him. Those were 'friends' who took my all from me, noblemen of high station, who left me nothing but my weeping child. I brought up the little child, and when she was my only treasure, my life, my all, I gave her to a man of whom I knew only that he loved her and she loved him. Is not that to have faith in God?"

"Don't talk to me of faith. For such a belief as that, witches in the good old time were brought to the stake and burned, all over the Christian world."

"It is lucky that I possess this island by right of a Turkish firman."

"A Turkish firman!" cried the dean, in astonishment. "And who procured it for you?"

"The man whose name you want to know."

"And I will know it on the spot, and in a summary way. I shall call the sacristan and the acolyte in, make them push away the bed, and go in at that door, which I see has no lock."

Timar heard every word in the next room. The blood rushed to his head at the thought that the ecclesiastical dignitary would walk in and exclaim, "Aha! it is you, Herr Privy Councilor Michael von Levetinczy!"

The dean opened the outer door, and called in his two sturdy companions. Therese, in her extremity, drew the bright Turkish quilt over her up to the chin. "Sir," she said in an imploring tone to the dean, "listen to just one word which will convince you of the strength of my faith, and show you that I am no heathen. Look, this woolen quilt I have over me came from Broussa. A traveling peddler gave it to me. See now, so great is my trust in God that I cover myself with it every night; and yet it is well known that the oriental plague has been raging in Broussa this month past. Which of you has faith enough to dare to touch this bed?"

When she looked round, no one was there to answer. At the discovery that this quilt came from the plague-infected districts round Broussa, all had rushed away, leaving the lonely island and its death-stricken inhabitants as a prey to all the devils of hell. The accursed island was now the richer by one more evil report, which would keep away people who valued their lives.

Therese let out the refugees. Timar kissed her hand and called her "Mother!"

"My son!" whispered Therese, and looked steadily into his eyes. With that look she said to him, "Remember what you have heard. And now it is time to get ready for the journey." Therese spoke of her approaching death as of a journey.

Leaning on Timar and Noémi, she was led out to the green field, and chose the place for her grave.

"Here in the middle," she said to Timar, taking his spade from his hand and marking out the oblong square. "You made a house for Dodi; make mine here. And build no mound over my grave, and plant no cross upon it;

plant there neither tree nor shrub; cover it all with fresh turf, so that it may be like the rest. I wish it; so that no one, when in a cheerful mood, may stumble over my grave and be saddened by it."

One evening she fell asleep, to awake no more. And they buried her as she desired. They wrapped her in fine linen, and spread for her a bed of aromatic walnut leaves. And then they made the grave look like the rest, and covered it with turf, so that it was the same as before. When on the next morning Timar and Noémi, leading little Dodi by the hand, went into the field, no sign could be seen on the smooth surface. The autumn spiders had covered it with a silvery pall, and on the glistening veil the dewdrops sparkled in the sun like myriads of diamonds.

But yet they found the spot in this silver-broidered green plain. Almira went in front; at one place she lay down and put her head on the ground: that was the spot.

BOOK FIFTH.—ATHALIE.

CHAPTER I.
THE BROKEN SWORD.

Timar remained on the island till frost covered the green grass—till the leaves fell, and the nightingales and thrushes were silent. Then he made up his mind to return to the world, the world of reality; and he left Noémi behind, alone with her little child on the ownerless island. "But I shall come back this winter"—and with those words he left her.

Noémi did not know what those words betokened at Michael's home. Round the island the Danube was never entirely frozen in the severest winter; the glass never fell much below freezing-point; ivy and laurels could stand the cold with ease. But Michael had severe weather for his journey. On the upper Danube snow had already fallen, and he took a whole week to reach Komorn. He had to wait a whole day before he could cross the river—there was so much ice that it was unsafe to launch a boat. Once he had ventured alone in a small boat across the river in flood; but then Noémi was waiting for him. Now he was going to Timéa—to get a divorce from her.

His decision was taken—they must have a divorce. Noémi could not live alone on that desert island. The woman must have justice in return for her fidelity and love: accursed would he be who could find it in his heart to abandon her who had given herself to him body and soul. And then, too, Timéa would be happy.

That thought gnawed him—that Timéa would be happy. If only he could hate her, if he had a single accusation to bring against her, so as to put her away as one he could despise and forget!

He had to leave his carriage at Uj-Szöny, for wheels could not yet pass the ice, so he arrived on foot at home. When he went in, it seemed to him as if Timéa were afraid of him; as if the hand she gave him trembled, and her voice too, when she greeted him. This time she did not offer him her white cheek to be kissed.

Timar hastened to his room, on pretense of laying aside his wraps. If only there was some reason for this embarrassment! And another sign had not escaped him—Athalie's expression. In her eyes shone the fire of a diabolical triumph, the light of a malicious joy. How if Athalie knew something?

At table he met the two women again. They all three sat silently together, watching each other. Timéa only said to Michael, "This time you have stayed away very long."

Timar would not say, "I shall soon leave you altogether," but he thought it. He had to consult his lawyer first as to a possible ground for a separation. It was impossible to think of one. Only "unconquerable mutual aversion" could be put forward.

But would the wife consent? All depended on her. Timar pondered this question all the afternoon, and told the servants not to tell any one of his return, as he could not see visitors.

Toward evening some one opened the door. Athalie stood before him, with the same spiteful satisfaction shining from her eyes, the same triumphant smile playing round her lips. Michael drew back before her repellent glance.

"What brings you here, Athalie?" he asked, with confusion.

"Well, Herr von Levetinczy, what do you think? Do you not want to know anything from me?"

"What?" he whispered eagerly, shutting the door, and staring at Athalie with wide-opened eyes.

"What do you want to know?" said the beautiful woman, still smiling. "Indeed that is hard to guess. I have been in your house these six years; every year I have seen you return home, and every year with a different expression on your face. At first tormenting jealousy, then easy good humor, afterward assumed tranquillity, and absorption in business. I studied all these phases. Last year I thought the tragedy was over—you looked like a man who is ready for the grave. But you may be sure that on all this round world there is no one who prays for your life as I do."

Michael frowned, and possibly Athalie understood him.

"No, sir," she repeated, passionately; "for if there is anyone in the world who loves you, they can not possibly wish that you may live long as heartily as I do. Now I see the same look on your face as last year—that is the true one: you would like to hear about Timéa?"

315

"Do you know anything?" asked Timar, eagerly, putting his back against the door as if to keep Athalie a prisoner.

She laughed scornfully; not she but Michael was the prisoner.

"I know much—all," she replied; "enough to bring us all to perdition. Myself and the other, and you too."

Michael's blood froze in his veins. "Tell me all."

"That is what I came for. But listen quietly to the end, that I may tell you things which lead to madness, if not death."

"One word first, is Timéa unfaithful?"

"She is, and you will be absolutely convinced of it."

In Timar's heart a nobler feeling arose to protest against this suspicion. "Take care what you say!"

"Your saintly picture, then, came down out of its altar-frame to listen to a report which said that the noble major had fought on her account with some strange officer, and wounded him so badly that his own sword broke in two over the head of his adversary. The picture heard this rumor. Frau Sophie told her, and the eyes of the saintly image shed tears. Perhaps you are a heretic, and do not believe in miraculous tears. But it is true; and Frau Sophie told the noble major next day. Frau Sophie loves to be a go-between; she loves flattery and intrigue. The reported tears had the result that Frau Sophie brought back a box and a letter from the major. In the box were the half-broken blade and the handle of the sword with which the major had fought. It was a souvenir."

"Well, there is nothing wrong in that," said Michael, with affected calm.

"Ah, yes, but the letter!"

"Did you read it?"

"No; but I know what it contained."

"How can you know that?"

"Because the saint replied, and Frau Sophie was the messenger."

"Go on," said Timar.

"Yes, for the story is not nearly finished. The letter was not a scented pink note; it was written on your own desk, sealed with your own seal, and its contents might have been to repulse the major's advances forever and ever.

316

But that was not what it said."

"Who knows?"

"Frau Sophie and I, and you will be a third directly. How unexpectedly you returned to-day!—how can people come at such an inconvenient time? The Danube is full of ice, the ice-flakes lie in heaps, and no living creature can cross. One would think that on such a day the town would be so safely shut off that even a jealous husband, if he were outside, could not get in. How could you come to-day?"

"Do not torture me, Athalie."

"Did you not notice the confusion on your picture's face when surprised by your arrival? Did not her hand tremble in yours? You managed your arrival so badly; Frau Sophie had to go out again to the smart major with the short message—'It can not be to-day.'"

Timar's face was disfigured with rage. Then he sunk back in his chair and said, "I don't believe you."

"You need not do so," said Athalie, with a shrug. "I will only advise you to trust your own eyes. It can not be to-day, because you have come home; but it might be to-morrow. Suppose you went away? You often go in winter to the Platten See, when it is frozen and they begin to fish under the ice. It is capital sport. You might say to-morrow, 'While this cold lasts, I will be off to Fured to see how the *fogasch* get on,' and then you might shut yourself up in your other house here, and wait till some one taps at your window and says 'Now.' Then you would come back here."

"And I should do that?" exclaimed Timar, shuddering.

Athalie looked him up and down contemptuously. "You are a coward!" and with that she turned to go.

But Michael sprung after her and seized her by the arm.

"Stop! I will take your advice and do what you tell me."

"Then listen to me," said Athalie, and pressed so close to his face that he felt her burning breath.

"When Herr Brazovics built this house, the room in which Timéa sleeps was the parlor. Who were his usual guests? Business people, boon companions, merchants, dealers. This room has a hiding-place in the wall above the staircase, where the steps turn, and the inner side makes an angle.

317

Into this hole in the wall it is possible to gain access from outside. There is a closet where old rubbish is kept, which is seldom opened. But even if it stood open it would hardly occur to any one to try the screws of the ventilator one after another. The center screw on the right-hand side is movable. But even if any one drew it out it would tell nothing—it is only a simple peg. But whoever is in possession of a peculiar key, which can be inserted in place of the peg, only requires to press the top of the key, from which wards instantly appear, and by a single turn of the key the cupboard is noiselessly pushed aside. From thence one can enter the hiding-place, which receives light and air from a slit in the roof. This hollow in the wall goes as far as Timéa's bedroom, where in former times Herr Brazovics' guests used to pass the night. The concealed passage ends in a glass door which is hidden from the room by a picture. This picture is a mother-of-pearl mosaic representing St. George and the dragon, and appears to be a votive image built into the wall. It has often been proposed to take the picture away, but Timéa never would allow it. One of the pieces of mosaic can be slipped aside, and through the blank space everything that passes in the room can be seen and heard."

"What did your father want with such a hiding-place?"

"I think it had to do with his business. He had many affairs with contractors and officials. There was good living to be had at his house, and when he had got his visitors into a good temper, he left them to themselves, slipped into the secret room and listened from thence to their conversation. In this way he obtained much important business information, from which he derived considerable advantage. Once when he had himself taken rather too much at table, he sent me to listen in the passage, and in this way I learned the secret. The key is in my possession. When all Herr Brazovics' property was seized by judicial decree, I could, if I had chosen, have conveyed all his valuables out of the house by this means. But I was too proud to steal."

"And can you get into the bedroom from this hiding-place?"

"The picture of St. George is on hinges, and can be opened like a door."

"So that you can at any time enter Timéa's room from that passage?" asked Michael, with an uncontrollable shudder.

318

Athalie smiled proudly. "I never needed to creep in to her by secret routes. Timéa sleeps with open doors, and you know that I can always pass freely through her room. She sleeps so soundly too."

"Give me the key."

Athalie took the puzzle key from her pocket. The lower end was shaped like a screw, only on pressing the handle a key appeared. She showed Timar how to manage it. A voice in his heart—perhaps that of his guardian angel—whispered to Timar to throw this key into the deep well in the yard. But he took no heed of the voice; he only listened to Athalie's whisper in his ear.

"If you leave home to-morrow and come back at the signal, go straight to the hiding-place, and you will learn all you want to know. Will you come?"

"I shall be there."

"Do you generally carry arms?—a pistol or a dagger?—one can never tell what may happen. The picture of St. George opens to the right when you press on a button-shaped handle, and when open it just covers Timéa's bed. Do you understand?"

She pressed Michael's hand violently, looking with flaming eyes of rage into his, and added something, but not audibly. Only her lips moved, her teeth chattered, and her eyes rolled—they were soundless words. What could she have said? Timar stared in a dazed way like a sleep-walker, then suddenly raised his head to ask Athalie something. He was alone—only the key grasped in his hand showed that it was no dream.

Never had Timar suffered such torture as in the long hours till the evening of the next day. He followed Athalie's advice, and remained at home till noon. After dinner he said he must go to the Platten See and look after the fishery he had hired.

As he had crossed the ice-floes of the Danube on foot to get to Komorn, he could easily go over again without luggage in the same way. His carriage too was waiting on that side, for it had not yet been able to get across: a road would have to be prepared. Without any interview with his agents, without a glance at his books, he thrust a pile of bank-notes, uncounted, into his pocket, and left the house. At the threshold he met the

319

postman, who brought a registered letter, and demanded a receipt. Michael was in too great haste to go back to his room; he carried pen and ink with him, and laying the receipt on the broad back of the postman, he signed his name to it. Then he looked at the letter. It was from his agent at Rio Janeiro; but without opening it, he put it in his pocket. What did he care for all the flour trade in the world? He kept one room in his house in the Servian Street always heated in winter. This room was entered by a separate staircase, which was kept locked, and was divided by several empty rooms from the offices. Timar reached it unobserved; there he sat down by the window and waited.

The cold north wind outside drew lovely ice-flowers on the window-panes, so that no one could see in or out.

Now he would get what he wanted—the proof of Timéa's infidelity. And yet—yet, the thought hurt him so deeply! While his fancy pictured this first private rendezvous between that woman and that man, every drop of blood seemed to rush to the surface and darken the light of his mind.

Shame, jealousy, thirst for vengeance consumed him.

It is hard to endure humiliation, even if some advantage is to be derived from it. He now began to feel what a treasure he possessed in Timéa. He had been ready enough to abandon this treasure, or even voluntarily to give it back, but to allow himself to be robbed of it!—the thought enraged him. He struggled with himself as to what he should do. If Athalie's instilled poison had reached his heart, he would have kept to the idea of a murderous rush with a dagger in his hand from behind the picture, so as to kill the faithless wife amidst the hottest caresses of her lover. Athalie panted for Timéa's blood; but a husband's revenge seeks a different object—he must have the man's life. Not like an assassin, but face to face—each with a sword in his hand, and then a struggle for life or death. Then, again, cold-blooded calculating reason comes uppermost, and says, "Why shed blood? you want scandal, not revenge; you should rush from your hiding-place, call in the servants, and drive the guilty woman and her seducer from your house. So a reasonable being would act. You are no soldier to seek satisfaction at the point of the sword. Here is the judge, and here the law."

But still he could not forbear from keeping stiletto and pistol ready on the table as Athalie had advised. Who knows what may happen? The moment will decide which gets the upper hand—whether the vengeful assassin, the dishonored husband, or the prudent man of business who would reckon an open scandal to his credit side, as facilitating the desired divorce.

Meanwhile evening had come. One lamp after another was lighted: Herr von Levetinczy paid for the lighting of this street out of his own pocket. The shadows of the passers-by flitted across the frozen panes.

One such figure stopped before the window, and a low knock was heard. It seemed to Timar as if the ice-flowers detached from the glass by the tap were the rustling leaves of a fairy forest, which whispered to him, "Do not go." He hesitated. The tap was repeated.

"I am coming!" he called in a low voice, took pistol and dagger, and crept out of the house.

The whole way he never met a human creature; the streets were already deserted. He only saw a dark shadow flitting on before him, vanishing in the darkness now and then, and at last slipping round the corner. He followed, and found all the doors open; some helping hand had opened the wicket, the house-door, and even the closet in the wall. He could enter without any noise; at the point described he found the movable screw, and put the key in its place; the secret door flew open, and shut behind him.

Timar found himself in the concealed passage—a spy in his own house.

Yes! A spy too! What meanness was there he had not committed? and all this "because a poor fellow remains always only a clerk, and it is the rich for whom life is worth living." Now he has riches and splendor.

Stumbling and feeling about, he groped along the wall, till he came to a part where a feeble light was perceptible. There was the picture of St. George: the light of the lamp shone through the crevices of the mosaic. He found the movable piece of mother-of-pearl, in whose place was a thick sheet of glass. He looked into the room; on the table stood a lamp with a ground glass shade. Timéa walked up and down.

An embroidered white dress floated from her waist; her folded hands hung down. The door of the antechamber opened, and Frau Sophie came in; she said something low to Timéa, but Timar could hear every whisper. This hole in the wall was like the ear of Dionysius, it caught every sound. "Can he

321

come?" asked Frau Sophie.

"I am waiting for him," said Timéa.

Then Frau Sophie went out again. Timéa drew from her wardrobe a drawer, and took out a box; she carried it to the table and stood opposite Timar, so that the lamp threw its whole light on her face; the listener could detect the slightest change of expression. Timéa opened the box. In it lay a sword-hilt and a broken blade. At first glance the woman started, and her contracted brows betokened horror. Then her face cleared, and took once more, with its meeting eyebrows, the look of a saint's picture, with a black halo round its brow. Tenderness dawned in her melancholy features; she lifted the box and held the sword so near her lips that Timar began to tremble lest she should kiss it. Even the sword was his rival.

The longer Timéa looked at it, the brighter grew her eyes. At last she plucked up courage to grasp the hilt; she took it out and made passes in the air with it. . . . If she had known that there was some one near her to whom every stroke was torture—

There was a tap at the door. Timéa put down the broken sword hastily, and stammered out a faint "Come in!" But first she pulled down the lace of her sleeves, which had fallen back from her wrist. The major entered. He was a fine man, with a handsome, soldierly face. Timéa did not go to meet him, but stood by the lamp; Timar's eyes never left her. Damnation!—what did he see? As the major entered Timéa blushed. Yes, the marble statue could glow with sunrise tints, the saint's image could move, and the virginal snow-white adorned itself with roses. The white face had found some one who could set it on fire. Was further proof, were words wanting?

Timar was near bursting from the picture, and, like the dragon before St. George killed it, would have thrown himself between the two before Timéa's lips could speak what her face betrayed.

But no. Perhaps he had only dreamed it—Timéa's face was colorless as ever. With calm dignity she signed to the major to take a chair; she sat down on a distant sofa, and her look was severe and cold. The major held his shako in one hand, and in the other his sword with its golden knot, and sat as stiff as if he had been in his general's presence. They looked at each other in silence—both struggling with painful thoughts. Timéa broke the silence. "Sir

322

you sent me a curious letter in company with a yet more singular present. It was a broken sword." She opened the box and took out a letter. "Your letter runs thus: 'Gracious lady, I have fought a duel to-day, and my adversary owes it only to the chance that my sword broke that he was not killed on the spot. This duel is intimately connected with most extraordinary circumstances, which concern you, and still more *your husband.* Allow me a few minutes' interview, that I may tell you what you ought to know.' In this letter the words 'your husband' are twice underlined, and this it was which decided me to give you the opportunity of speaking to me. Speak! In what does your duel concern the private affairs of Herr von Levetinczy? I will listen to you as long as what you have to say treats of him: if you enter on any other subject I will leave you."

The major bowed with grateful fervor. "I will begin then, madame, by telling you that an unknown man has been about in the town, who wears the uniform of a naval officer, and therefore has an *entrée* to military society. He seems to be a man of the world, and is an entertaining companion. Who he may be I know not, for it is not my way to be inquisitive. This man has spent some weeks among us, and seems to have plenty of money. He gave as a reason for being here that he was waiting for Herr von Levetinczy, with whom he had important private affairs to settle. At last he began to annoy us, and looked so mysterious as he asked every day about Herr von Levetinczy, that we fancied he must be an adventurer, and one day we drove him into a corner. We wished to know what manner of man he was, and I undertook the inquiry. When we asked why he did not go to your husband's agents, he said his business was of a very private and delicate nature, which could only be personally discussed. 'Listen,' I said. 'I do not believe that you have any delicate business with Herr von Levetinczy; who you are we do not know, but we do know that he is a man of honor and character, whose position and reputation are above suspicion. He is a man whose private life is blameless, and who can therefore have no reason for private interviews with people of your sort.'"

While the major spoke, Timéa had risen slowly; she now stepped up to him and said, "I thank you."

And again Timar saw on her white cheek that soft rosy glow, never seen by him before, but which now rested there. The woman had flushed at the thought that the man she loved could defend him who, as her husband, stood between their two hearts.

The major continued his narrative, and in order not to confuse Timéa by looking at her, sought some other object in the room on which to fix his eye. He chose the dragon's head in the picture of St. George. But that was the exact spot through which Timar looked into the room, so that it seemed to him as if the major directed his words purposely to him, although it was much too dark where Timar stood for any one to see him.

"On this the man's face changed suddenly; he leaped up like a sleeping dog when one treads on his tail. 'What!' he cried, so that every one could hear. 'You think Levetinczy is a rich man with a great name—a clever man, a happy family man, a faithful subject? I will prove to you that this man, if I can once meet him, will take flight from here next day—that he will leave his lovely wife and his house in the lurch, and fly from Hungary, from Europe, so that you will never hear of him again.'"

Timéa's hand strayed involuntarily to the hilt of the broken sword.

"Instead of answering the man, I struck him in the face."

Timar drew back his head from the peep-hole, as if the blow might reach him.

"I saw at once that the man regretted what he had said. He would gladly have escaped the consequences of the blow, but I would not let him off. I stood in his way and said, 'You are an officer and carry a sword—you know to what such an affair leads among men of honor. There is a ball-room upstairs at the hotel; we will have the candles lighted; then you shall choose two of us as seconds, I also will choose two, and we will fight it out.' We did not leave him time for reflection. The man fought like a pirate: twice he tried to seize my sword with his left hand; then I got angry and gave him such a cut over the head that he fell. Luckily for him, it was with the flat of the blade, which was the reason of my sword breaking. The next day the man, so our surgeon told me, had left the town—his wound can not have been a dangerous one."

Timéa took out the Turkish sword and looked at the hilt; then she laid it on the table and stretched out her hand in silence to the major. He

324

took it gently in both his own, and carried it to his lips; it could hardly be seen whether he kissed it. Timéa did not draw it away.

"I thank you!" whispered the major, so low that Timar could not hear it in his hiding-place, but the eyes said it too. A long pause followed. Timéa sat down again on the sofa and supported her head on her hand.

The major spoke at last. "I did not request an interview, gracious lady, to boast of a deed which in itself must be painful to you, and was really only the duty of a friend, nor to receive the thanks you so kindly offered me by a grasp of the hand. That was a more than sufficient reward. But not on that account did I request you to meet me, but to ask a very important question. Gracious lady, is it possible that there should be any truth in what this man said?"

Timéa started as if struck by lightning. And the bolt struck Timar too; every nerve thrilled at the question.

"What are you thinking of?" cried Timéa, passionately.

"At last it is out," said the major, rising from his chair. "And now I will not go without an answer. I say openly, is it possible that there is truth in this accusation? I have not repeated all that this man said about Levetinczy: he accused him of everything that can be said against a man. Is it conceivable that Timar's life could take such a frightful course as that which the last owner of this unlucky house only escaped by death? For if that is possible, then no respect could restrain me from beseeching you in God's name, dear lady, to delay not a moment in fleeing from this doomed house. I can not leave you to ruin—I can not look on while another drags you into the abyss."

The glowing words found a response in Timéa's bosom. Timar watched in trembling excitement his wife's mental conflict. Timéa remained victorious; she collected all her energy, and answered quietly, "Do not be alarmed, sir. I can assure you that that man, whoever he was, and wherever he came from, told a lie, and his accusations are groundless. I know intimately the position of Herr von Levetinczy; for during his absence I managed his affairs, and am thoroughly acquainted with every detail. His finances are in order, and even if all he has now at stake were lost by some unlucky chance, no pillar of his house would be shaken. I can also tell you with a clear conscience that of all his property there is not a thaler dishonestly come by. Levetinczy is a rich man, who need not blush for his wealth."

Why did Timar's cheeks burn so there in the darkness?

The major sighed. "You have convinced me, gracious lady; I never believed anything against his financial reputation. But this man had much to say about your husband in his character as head of a family. Allow me to ask you one thing: Are you happy?"

Timéa looked at him with inexpressible pathos, and in her eyes lay the words, "You see me, and yet you ask?"

"Riches and luxury surround you," continued the major, boldly; "but if that is true—which on my honor I never asked, and which, when told me, I answered with the lie direct, and a blow in the face—if it is true that you suffer and are unhappy, I should not be a man if I had not the courage to say to you, gracious lady, there is another who suffers like you. Throw far from you these unlucky riches; make an end of this suffering of two people, who in the next world can accuse a third person in the sight of God of being the cause of it: consent to a divorce!"

Timéa pressed both hands to her breast, and looked up like a martyr on her road to the stake: all her anguish was aroused at this moment.

When Timar saw her so, he struck his forehead with his fist, and turned his face from the Judas-hole through which he had been looking. For the next few moments he saw and heard no more. When torturing curiosity drew him again to the spot of light, and he cast a look into the room, he no longer saw a martyr before him. Timéa's face was calm.

"Sir," she said gently to the major, "that I should have heard you to the end is a proof of my respect. Leave me this feeling, and never again ask me what you did to-day. I call the whole world to witness whether I have ever complained by word or tear. Of whom should I complain? Of my husband, who is the noblest and best man in the world? Of him who saved the strange child's life? who thrice defied death in the waters' depths for my sake? When I was a despised and derided creature he protected me; for my sake he visited the house of his deadly enemy, that he might watch over me. When I had become a homeless beggar he gave me—a servant—his hand, his riches, and made me mistress of his house. And when he offered me his hand he meant it; he was not deceiving me." As she spoke, Timéa went to a close

326

and opened the doors. "Look here, sir," she said, as she spread out before the major the train of a dress hanging within. "Do you recognize this dress? It is the one I worked. You saw it for weeks while I worked at it. Every stitch is a buried dream, a sad memory to me. They told me it was to be my wedding-gown; and when it was finished, they said, 'Take it off: it is for another bride.' Ah! sir, that was a mortal stab to my heart: I have been sore from that incurable wound all these years. And now should I separate myself from the good man who never courted me, as a child, with flatteries, to turn my head, but remained respectfully in the distance, and waited till others had trodden me under foot to raise me to himself, and has never ceased, with superhuman, angelic patience, his endeavors to cure my wound and to share my sorrow with me? I should separate from the man who has no one but me to love him, to whom I am a whole world, the only being that ties him to life, or at whose coming his gloomy face is cheered? I should leave a man whom every one honors and loves? Tell him that I hate him—I, who owe everything to him, and who brought him no dowry but a sick and loveless heart?"

The major hid his face at these words of the passionate and excited woman. And that other man behind the picture of St. George—must he not feel like the dragon when the knight thrust his spear into him?

"But, sir," continued Timéa, whose lovely face was illumined by the irresistible charm of womanly dignity, "even if Timar were the exact opposite of all that he is known to be—if he were a ruined man, a beggar—I would not leave him—then least of all. If disgrace covered his name, I would not discard that name; I would share his shame, as I have shared his success. If the whole world despised him, I should still owe him eternal gratitude; if he were exiled, I would follow him into banishment, and live with him in the woods if he were a robber. If he wished to take his life, I would die with him—"

(What is that? Is it the dragon that weeps there in the picture?)

"And, sir, if even the bitterest, cruelest insult of all to a woman were inflicted on me—if I learned that my husband was unfaithful, to me—that he loved another—I would say, 'God bless her who gave him the happiness of which I have robbed him;' and I would not even then divorce him—I would not do it if he wished it. I will never separate from him, for I know what is due to my oath and the salvation of my soul!"

And the major too sobbed—he too.

Timéa stopped to recover her composure. Then in a soft and gentle voice she continued: "And now leave me forever. The stab you gave my heart years ago is healed by this sword-stroke: I keep this broken blade as a remembrance. As often as my eye falls on it, I will think that you are a brave soul, and it will be balm to me. And because for years you have never spoken to me nor approached me, I will forgive your having come and spoken to me now." . . .

When Timar burst through the closet out of the hiding-place, a dark figure stood in his way. Was it a shadow, a phantom, or a spirit? It was Athalie. Timar pushed, the dark figure away, and while he pressed her with one hand against the wall, he whispered in her ear, "I curse you! and accursed be this house and the ashes of him who built it!"

Then he rushed like a madman down the stairs.

CHAPTER II.
THE FIRST LOSS.

Escape! But where? That is the question.

The church clocks in the town struck ten: the barriers were down by now across the wooden bridge over the narrow part of the river to the island, from which the ice formed the only road across the rest of the Danube. It was impossible to get past without alarming the sentries, who had orders from the commandant of the garrison to let no one go on the ice between eight in the evening and seven in the morning—not even the pope himself. It is true that a couple of bank-notes of Herr Levetinczy's might compass what a papal bull could not procure, but then it would be reported next day all over the town that the "man of gold" had fled in haste and alone, at dead of night, across the dangerous ice. That would be a good sequel to the gossip which had arisen from the duel. It would at once be said, "There, you see he is already thinking of escaping to America," and Timéa would hear it too.

Timéa! oh, how hard it is to evade that name; it follows him everywhere. He can do nothing but return home and wait for daylight. As cautiously as a thief he opened his door. At this hour all the other inhabitants were asleep.

When he got to his room, he lighted no lamp, and threw himself on the sofa. But the phantoms which pursued him found him quite as easily in the dark.

How that marble face blushed!

So there is life there under the ice, only the sun is wanting. Marriage is for her eternal winter—a polar winter. The wife is faithful; and the rival is a true friend. He breaks his sword over the skull of him who dared to slander the husband of the beloved woman. And Timéa loves the man, and is as unhappy as he. The misery of both comes from Timar's imputation as an honest man; those who love him idealize him; no one ventures to think of deceiving or robbing or disgracing him—of breaking a splinter from the diamond of his honor: they guard it like a jewel.

Why do they all respect him? Because no one knows him.

If Timéa knew, if she discovered what he really was, would she still say, "I would share the shame of his name, as I have shared its glory!" Yes; she would still say so. Timéa will never leave him: she would say, "You have made me unhappy; now suffer with me." It is an angel's cruelty, and that is Timéa's nature.

But how about Noémi? What is she doing on the lonely island which she can never leave, thanks to Timéa's high principle? Alone during the gloomy monotony of winter, with a helpless child at her knee! What is she thinking of? No one can take her a word of consolation. She may be trembling in that desert for fear of bad men, ghosts, wild beasts! How her heart must sink when she thinks of her absent darling, and wonders where he may be! If she knew! If both those women knew what a thorough scoundrel was the man who had caused them so much sorrow—if any one was found to tell them!

Who can the stranger be who has already said enough to deserve a blow in the face, and a cut of the major's sword? A naval officer. Who can this enemy be? It is impossible to discover; he has disappeared with his wound from the town. Something told Timar it would be wise to fly from this man. Fly! his whole mind was set upon it—there was nothing he dreaded so much as being obliged to remain in one spot. As soon as he left the ownerless island, no place was a home to him. When he stopped for dinner on a journey, he could not wait till the horses were fed, but walked on ahead. Something always drove him onward.

And sleep had fled from his eyes. The clock struck twelve; seven more long hours till morning! He determined at last to kindle a light. For mental anxiety there is a remedy more effectual than opium or digitalis—prosaic work. Whoever has plenty to do, finds no time to dwell on love troubles. Merchants seldom commit suicide for love. Cares of business are a wholesome counter-irritant to draw the blood from the nobler parts.

Michael opened and read his letters in turn: all contained good news. He remembered Polycrates, with whom everything succeeded, and who began at last to be afraid of his luck.

And what was the foundation of this monstrous success? A secret unknown to all but himself. Who had seen Ali Tschorbadschi's treasure

330

spread out in the cabin? Only himself—and the moon. But that is an accomplice, and has seen other things too. It is the "Hypomochlion" of creation, to prevent crimes from coming to light. Michael was too deeply sensitive by nature not to feel that such overwhelming good fortune, springing from so foul a root, must eventually fall into dust—for there is justice under the sun. He would joyfully have looked on at the loss of half his wealth, or even given up all, if so he could have hoped to close his account with Heaven. But he felt that his penance consisted in the fact that his riches, influence, the renown of his name, his supposed home-happiness, were only a cruel irony of fate. They buried him, and he could not extricate himself to live the only happy life, whose center was Noémi—and Dodi. When the first Dodi died, he learned what he had been to him. Now, with the second, he felt it still more; and yet he could not make them his own. He lay buried under a mountain of gold which he could not shake off. What he had seen in the delirium of fever, he now really felt. He lay buried alive in a grave full of gold. Above his head stood on the grave-stone a marble statue which never moved—Timéa. A beggar-woman with a little child came to gather thyme on his tomb—Noémi. And the man buried alive vainly strove to cry out, "Give me your hand, Noémi, and pull me out of this golden tomb!"

Timar went on with his correspondence. One letter was from the Brazilian agents. His favorite scheme—the export of Hungarian flour—had been brilliantly successful. Timar had gained by it honor and wealth. As he ran through the letters, it occurred to him that when he left home in the morning he had received a registered letter with a foreign stamp. He found the letter in his coat pocket. It was from the same correspondent whose favorable report he had just read, and ran thus:

"Sir,—Since my last, a great misfortune has occurred. Your *protégé*, Theodor Krisstyan, has cheated us shamefully and brought disgrace on us. We are blameless in the matter. This man has for years past seemed so trustworthy and active, that we put the most perfect confidence in him; his salary and commission were so large that he could not only live comfortably, but could save money, which he invested in our house. While he left his avowable savings to grow to a small capital in our hands, he robbed us frightfully—intercepted money, forged bills, and made false claims on the firm, which was easy, as he had your power of attorney—so that our loss already amounts to some ten million reis. But what makes it more serious is the discovery that during the last few years he has been mixing the imported flour with some of inferior quality from Louisiana, and by this Yankee trick has seriously impaired the credit of the Hungarian article for years to come—even if we are ever able to restore it."

"This is the first blow," thought Timar; and on the most tender point for a great financier. It touched him in what he was most proud of, and what had obtained for him the rank of a privy councilor. And so falls the brilliant fabric erected by Timéa—Timéa again!

Timar read on hurriedly—

"Bad company has led the young criminal astray: this is a dangerous temptation in this climate. We had him arrested at once, but none of the stolen money was found in his possession. He had lost part at the gambling-table, and got rid of the rest with the help of the Creoles; but it is quite possible that the rogue has managed to conceal considerable sums, in the hope of being able to get at them when again at liberty. However, he must wait some time, for the court here has sentenced him to fifteen years at the galleys."

Timar could read no further. He let the letter fall on the table; then he stood up and began to pace the room restlessly.

Fifteen years at the galleys! Fifteen years chained to the bench, and nothing to look at all that time but sky and sea! Fifteen years to endure the sickening noonday heat, without hope or comfort—to endure life on the ever-restless sea, and curse unmerciful man! He will be an old man before he gets his freedom. And why? In order that Herr Michael Timar, Baron von Levetinczy, may live undisturbed in his forbidden joys on the ownerless island—that no one may betray Noémi to Timéa, nor Timéa to Noémi. You never thought of this when you sent Theodor to Brazil, and yet you did count on the chance of opportunity making him into a thief. You did not lay him dead on the spot with a bullet, as a man kills in a duel him who stands in the way of his love. You pretended to a paternal affection for him, and sent him on a three-thousand miles' voyage; and now you will look on at this slow decay through fifteen horrible years—for you will see him, though all the earth and all her oceans lie between!

The stove had gone out. It was cold in the room, whose windows were covered with frost-flowers. And yet sweat dropped from Timar's brow, as he strode up and down the narrow space. So, then, every one is consecrated to misfortune to whom he gives his hand—on that hand is a curse.

Oh, what an awful night this is! Will it never be day? He felt as if this room were a dungeon or a tomb.

But the terrible letter had a postscript. Timar came back to the table to read it. The postscript was dated a day later, and ran thus: "I have just received a letter from Port-au-Prince, in which we are informed that three slaves have escaped from the galley on which our prisoner was placed. I fear our man is among them."

After the perusal of these lines, Timar was a prey to indescribable anxiety. Though he had been perspiring before, he began to shiver now. Had the fever returned? He looked round fearfully. What was he afraid of? He was alone in the room, and as frightened as a child who has been hearing ghost stories. He could not endure the room any longer. He took out his pocket-pistol and looked to its priming; then he tried his dagger, whether it was loose in its sheath.

Away! It was still night—not yet two o'clock; but he could not await the morning light here. And could he not get across to the Uj-Szöny side without a bridge? Above the island the ice would bear. It only required a man who was less afraid of darkness and danger than of the flickering candle and the outspread letter. He held that over the light and burned it; then he blew out the candle and crept out of the window.

Only when he was in the street did he feel his heart lighter: here he was a man again. Meanwhile fresh snow had fallen, which he heard crackling under his feet while he hurried to the shore, along the whole Servian Street right up to the harbor.

CHAPTER III.
THE ICE.

The Danube was completely frozen over up to Prestburg, and could be crossed anywhere. Still, in order to cross from Komorn to Uj-Szöny, he had to go round a long way by the point of the island, for sand-banks exist there on which in summer the miners wash their gold, and on these mounds the ice often lies in great heaps, forming barricades difficult to surmount. Timar had a plan ready; as soon as he came in sight of the Monostor, where stood his villa, he would strike out in that direction. But something intervened to upset his calculations. He had expected a starry night, but when he reached the Danube a fog came on. At first only thin, transparent mist; but while Timar was seeking a path on the ice, the fog became so thick that you could not see three steps in front of you. If he had given ear to the voice of reason, he would have instantly turned round and tried to find his way back to the bank. But he was in a frame of mind in which a man is inaccessible to reason; by fair means or foul he meant to get across. Apart from the fog, it was a dark night; and above the island the Danube is at its widest, and the passage over the ice-floes the most difficult. Monstrous heaped-up masses of frozen snow form oblique stretches of barricade, and in many places the ice takes the shape of capriciously cleft ridges, from which rise six-foot pinnacles of frozen water instead of fingers of rock. In coasting round these, Timar suddenly found that he had lost himself. He had already been an hour on the river; his repeater struck a quarter to three; he ought long ago to have reached the other side; he must have lost his reckoning.

He listened; no sound in the dark night. It was beyond question that he was not approaching the opposite village, but getting further away from it. Not even a dog could be heard to bark. He fancied that instead of crossing the river he must have been walking along it, and determined to change his course. The Danube was nowhere more than two hundred paces wide; he must reach the shore somewhere if he kept straight on. But in mist and darkness one does not know which way one goes; a barrier of ice which must be avoided takes one, in spite of every care, out of the right road—one walks in zigzags and comes back to the spot where one was before; even if you get into the right path, and would only have to walk on to reach the bank, you think of something else, deviate slightly, and get back into that confounded ice labyrinth again.

Past five. Nearly four hours already had he wandered about. He felt exhausted. He had not slept all night, nor eaten all day, but had struggled with the most enervating mental emotions.

His only hope was, that when day at last dawned he would be able to guess by the sun where the east lay, and then, as an old sailor, could ascertain his position. If he had come across a hole in the ice, the current of the water would have shown him in what direction to go; but the surface was entirely covered, and without an ax it was impossible to make a hole. At last it began to dawn, but the fog hid the sun. Nine o'clock, and he had not yet found the shore, though the fog seemed to grow less and the sun's disk was visible, like a pale, colorless ball, a mere shadow of its glorious self. The air was full of countless glittering particles of ice, which melted into a dazzling vapor. Now he will discover where he is.

The sun was already too high to indicate the true east, but it showed something else. It seemed to Timar, as he peered through the brilliant mist, as if he could distinguish on his right the outline of the roof of a house.

Where there is a house there must be land. He walked straight toward it, and was careful to keep in a direct line; soon he found himself close to it—but the house was a water-mill.

The ice-floes had detached it from its winter refuge, or perhaps had found it belated, still chained to the shore, and carried it off. The shrouds were as neatly sawn asunder by the sharp ice-flakes as if a clever carpenter had done it: the wheels were shattered and the mill-house wedged into a mass of ice, forming a parapet round it.

Timar stood before it in horror. His head swam as if he had seen a ghost. The sunken mill in the Perigrada whirlpool occurred to him. Is not this the ghost of that mill which comes to visit him at the end of his career, or perhaps to take possession of him? A ruined mill amidst the ice! A house so near its downfall! He went in; the door was open, probably from the shocks received amidst the blocks of ice. The machinery was all complete, so that

335

Timar felt at any moment the white miller's ghost might enter and shake the meal into the sacks. On the roof, the beams, on every little ledge sat crows. A couple of them fluttered away when they saw him; the rest sat still and took no notice of him.

Timar was dead beat. For eight hours continuously he had wandered on the ice; the hinderances he had met with had fatigued him yet more; his stomach was empty, his nerves overstrained, his limbs stiff with cold. He sat down exhausted on a post inside the mill.

His eyes closed. And hardly had they done so before he saw himself standing at the bow of the "St. Barbara," with the hatchet in his hand, and near him the girl with the pale face.

"Away from here!" he cried to her; the ship rushed down the cataract. The wave-curl came to meet them. "Into the cabin!" But the girl never stirred. Then the sea struck the ship. Timar fell from his seat: that woke him, and he realized his danger. If he fell asleep there, he would certainly freeze to death. No doubt that is the easiest way to take one's life; but he had work to do in the world—his hour had not struck.

He went out of the mill—the fog was too thick to see anything; it was not day but night. The sighs which might go up to Heaven are swallowed in the dark clouds which will not let them pass. Was there nothing living near to help him in his extremity?

When the mill was carried away by the ice there were mice in it: they waited till the ice had set; then they left the mill and found their way to the shore—on the thin snow-covering their tiny footsteps were visible. Timar followed them. The smallest of all the mammalia in this way conducted the wise and strong human being for a whole half hour till he reached the shore. Thence he easily found the road, and arrived at the inn where he had left the post-chaise. Mist was behind and before him, and no one saw whence he came. In the parlor he devoured salt calves'-feet which had been prepared for the wagoners, drank a glass of wine, had the horses put to, lay down in the carriage, and slept till evening. He dreamed constantly that he was on the ice; and when the carriage shook, he awoke under the impression that the ice had broken under him, and that he was sinking into fathomless depths.

As he had started late from Szöny, he only reached his villa at Fured

336

the next evening. The fog accompanied him the whole way, so thick that he could not see the Platten See. They were preparing for the first catch of the season next day; he gave orders to his steward to have ready plenty of wine and malt brandy.

Galambos, the old fishing overseer, predicted a large haul. One good sign was that the lake had frozen so early. At this time, just before spawning, the fish come up the gulf in shoals. It was a still better omen that Herr von Levetinczy had come himself. He always had luck.

"I—luck!" echoed Timar to himself, sighing heavily.

"I would almost venture to bet that we shall catch the king of the fogasch himself."

"How do you mean, the king?"

"It is an old fogasch which every fisherman on the lake knows, for we have all had him in our nets in turn; but no one can land him, for when he finds he is caught he works a hole at the bottom with his snout, and manages to get out of the net. He is a regular rogue; we have put a price on his head, for he destroys as many young fry as three fishermen. He is a huge beast, and when he swims on the surface, one would think he was a whale; but we'll get him to-morrow."

Timar did not contradict, but sent every one away and lay down. Now he first felt how tired he was; and he slept a long and healthy sleep, undisturbed by dream-faces. When he awoke he was perfectly fresh; even the anxieties which occupied his mind had faded into the background as if they were a year distant. The small span of time between to-day and yesterday seemed like an eternity. It was not yet daylight, but it surprised him that the moon was shining through the frost-covered panes. He got up quickly, bathed as usual in icy water, dressed, and hurried out to see the Balaton.

This presents, when frozen—especially the few first days—a most enchanting sight. The huge lake does not freeze like rivers, on which the ice masses gradually collect: here in one moment of calm the whole surface is covered with a sheet of ice like crystal; and in the morning a smooth unruffled mirror is outspread. Under the moonlight it is a looking-glass in one piece without a flaw—only the tracks are visible upon it, by which the inhabitants of the contiguous villages communicate with each other. They

337

traverse it like measuring-lines on some great glass table—you see the reflection of the mountains of Tihany, with the double tower of the church, as distinctly as if it were real, only the towers are upside down.

Timar stood long absorbed in this fairy picture. The fishermen woke him from his dream; they arrived with nets, poles, and ice-axes, and said the work must begin before sunrise. When all had assembled, they formed a circle, and the old chief intoned a pious hymn, which all repeated after him. Timar walked away; he could not pray. How should he address a psalm to Him who is omniscient, and who can not be deceived by songs and hymns? The music could be heard two miles away over the level surface, and the echoes of the shore repeated the sound. Timar walked a long way over the lake. At last it began to dawn, the moon paled, and the eastern horizon was tinted with rosy red, which caused a wonderful transformation in the color of the giant ice mirror, dividing it into two sharply contrasted halves. One side assumed a coppery-violet hue, while the other looked azure blue against the pink sky.

In proportion to the growing light, the splendor of the sight increased; the purple red, the gold of the sky, were repeated in the pure reflection, and when the glowing ball, radiant with fiery vapor, shot up from the violet mists of the horizon and shone down on the glittering surface, it was a spectacle such as neither sea nor land can show, as if two suns rose at once in two real skies. The moment the sun had passed through the earth-fogs, its glorious rays leaped forth.

The fishing-captain Galambos cried from the distance to Timar, "Now you will hear something. Don't be afraid! Ho! ho!"

"Afraid!" thought Timar, shrugging his shoulders, incredulously. What in the world could frighten him now? He would soon know.

When the sun first shines on the frozen lake, a wonderful sound is heard from the ice, as if thousands of fairy harp-strings were struck. One is reminded of the tones from Memnon's statue, only that it does not last so long. The mysterious cling-clang grows louder, as if the nixies down below struck their harps with all their force: then follows a droning and cracking, almost as loud as a shot, and on every snap follows a glittering fissure in the ice, which till then was clear as glass. In every direction the gigantic mirror is flawed till it is like a huge mosaic, formed of millions of tiny dice, pentagons, and many-sided prisms, and whose surface is of glass. This is what causes the sound. He who hears it for the first time finds his heart beating faster; the whole surface hums, rings, and sings under his feet. Some cracks are like thunder, and are heard miles away. The fishermen, however, proceed quietly with the spreading of their nets on the top of the groaning ice, and in the distance may be seen hay wagons, drawn slowly by four oxen across the surface. Man and beast are used to the ice-voices, which last till sunset.

This remarkable phenomenon made a curious impression on Michael's mind. He was very sensitive to the great life of nature. In his emotional temperament the thought was implanted that everything living has consciousness—wind, storm, and lightning, the earth itself, the moon and stars. But who could understand what the ice under his feet was saying?

Then suddenly was heard a fearful detonation as if a hundred cannon had been fired at once, or a subterranean mine had been exploded—the whole surface trembled and shook. The effect of this thunderous convulsion was fearful—the ice opened in a cleft three thousand yards long, and between the edges of the floes yawned a six-foot chasm. "*A Rianás! a Rianás!*" (the ice-cleft), cried the fishermen, and ran to the place, abandoning their nets.

Timar stood only two paces from it. He had seen it happen. His knees trembled with the frightful shock, which had driven the two ice masses apart; he was stunned with the effect of this natural phenomenon. The arrival of the fishermen roused him; they told him that among the natives this fissure was called *Rianás*, a word unknown elsewhere. It was a great danger for travelers across the lake, for it was not visible far off, and it never froze over, because the water was always moving in it. It was therefore the first care of these good people, wherever a footpath led to the crack, to plant at both edges a pole in the ice with a bundle of straw at the top, so that those who approach might have warning. "But what is even more dangerous," said the fisherman, "is when, under great pressure of wind, the separated floes again unite. Then there is such a grinding and crushing! Very often the power of the wind is sufficient to raise the edges of the two floes, so that there is an empty space between the water and the uplifted ice. God pity those who go over there without knowing it, for the ice which does not touch the water is certain to give way under them!"

It was nearly noon before they could get to work. It is capital sport, this fishing under the ice. In the bay, where the fishermen's experience tells them the shoals of fish will lie, two large holes are made in the ice some fifty fathoms apart, and then a square of smaller holes is formed, so that the two large openings form the opposite angles. The pieces of ice hewn from the holes are piled round their edges, so that passengers may be warned of the danger of falling in. When the sun shines on these white heaps, they look like colossal diamonds. The fishermen sink the huge net sideways into the large hole, spread out its two ends, and fasten them on poles, each three and a half fathoms in length. One man pushes the pole with the net under the ice, while another waits at the next small hole, and when the pole appears there he pushes it on to the third hole, and so on, while the other side of the square is being treated in the same way with the second pole and the other end of the net. Both meet at the opposite large hole. The net, which is sunk to the bottom with lead weights, while its top edge is held up by ropes over the ice, forms an absolute prison for all the fish within the square, which usually swarm at this season. The fogasch and sheath fish leave their miry bed and come up to breathe at the ice-holes; they have their family festivals in the winter, when cold-blooded animals make love. The strong ice-roof protects them from the foreign element, but not from its inhabitants—men.

The ice now only assists in their destruction. When they discover that the net is pressing on them, it is already too late to find an outlet. They can not leap out, because the ice shuts them in, and even the fogasch can not as usual burrow in the mud, to get under the net, for the weight of his splashing companions leaves him no space to work. The fishermen lay hold on the rope and draw steadily. The united exertion of twenty men shows how great is the strain on them; it must be several hundred-weight. The surface of the large hole begins to be alive with the crowd of fishes pressing to the only outlet, there to meet their death. Various forms of fish-mouths peep out of the water—transparent jelly-fish, red tails, blue, green, and silver scales press up, and between them comes up sometimes a great silurian, the shark of the Balaton, a Wels of a hundred pounds' weight, with wide jaws and horse-shoe mustache; but it disappears into the depths again, as if to find safety there.

Three fishermen dip the living crowd out from the top with large landing-nets, and throw the fish on to the ice without more ado, where old and young leap about together: thence they can not escape, for the holes are all surrounded with heaps of ice. It is a regular witches' dance—wide-mouthed carp leaping high in air, the pike in its despair wriggling like a snake among the gasping heaps of perch and bass. One conger after another is hauled out with a hook and thrown on the frozen surface, where, laying down his ugly head, he flaps his fellow-prisoners into pieces with his heavy tail. The space around the hole is all covered with fishes. The carp jump like water-rats, but no one notices—they can not get away. The lazier fishes lie in heaps on both sides.

"I said so," murmured old Galambos; "I knew we should have a good catch. Wherever our gracious master shows himself, luck comes with him. If only we could catch the fogasch-king."

"If I am not mistaken, we've got him in there," said the man who was next him at the rope. "There's some great beast shooting about in the net; I feel it in both my arms."

"Ha! there he is!" cried another, whose landing-net was full of fish, as an enormous head like that of a white crocodile appeared above the water. The whole head was white; in the open mouth were two rows of sharp teeth like those of an alligator, but with four fangs meeting like a tiger's—a formidable head indeed. They may well call him the king of the lake, for there is no other creature in it, even of his own race, able to vie with him.

"There he is!" screamed three others at once, but the next instant the brute had sunk; and now began the struggle.

As if the imprisoned brute had suddenly given the word to his body-guard for a last and decisive combat, a dangerous tumult began inside the net. The skirmishing corps of pike and carp ran their heads against the tightly drawn meshes; the men were obliged to beat down the marine giants with loaded staves. The fishes became furious; the cold-blooded creation showed itself capable of heroic devotion, and rose against the invaders in pitched battle. The struggle ended in the defeat of the fishes. The dog-fish were knocked on the head, the net shook out many beautiful white fogasch and schille; but the fogasch-king would not show himself.

341

"He has got away again," grumbled the old chief.

"No, no; he is in the net still!" said the hauling-men, clinching their teeth. "I feel by my arms how he is pushing and fighting; if only he does not break the net."

The catch was enormous already; there was no room to stand without treading on fishes.

"There goes the net! I heard it crack!" cried the first man. Half the net was still in the water.

"Haul!" growled the old fisherman, and all the men put out their whole strength. With the net came the rest of the fishes, and the fogasch-king was among them—a splendid specimen indeed, more than forty pounds weight, such as is only seen once in twenty years. He had really torn the net with his great head; but he had caught his prickly fins in the meshes, and could not get free. When they got him out he gave one of the men a blow with his tail which knocked him backward on the ice. But that was his last effort; the next moment he was dead. No one has ever held a living fogasch in his hand. It is thought that his lungs burst as he is taken out of water, and he dies instantly.

The delight of the fishermen at the capture of this one was greater than over the whole rich haul. They had been after him for years; and every one knew the cannibal, for he had the bad habit of eating his own kind. That was why he was king. When he was opened they found a large fogasch in his inside, quite recently swallowed; his flesh was overlaid with a thick layer of yellow fat, and white as linen.

"Now, honored sir, we will send him to the gracious lady," said the old fisherman. "We will pack him in ice, and your honor will write a letter and say he is the king of the fogasch. Whoever eats him will eat a king's flesh."

Michael approved the suggestion, and assured the men they should get a reward. When they had finished with the fogasch, the short winter's day had come to a close; but only in the sky, not on the ice—there it was lively enough. From every village came the people with baskets and hampers and wooden kegs; in the kegs was wine, in the hampers pork, but the baskets were meant for the fish. When it came to the division of the spoil, a complete

342

fair formed round the fishermen. After sunset, torches were made of dry osier-twigs, fires were lighted on the ice, and then began the bargaining. Carp and pike, conger and bass, are good enough for poor people. Only the fogasch and schille are sent to Vienna and Pesth, where they fetch high prices; all the rest go for a song—and even so there is room for a large profit, for in one haul they had caught three hundredweight of fish. This Timar is indeed a favorite of fortune! The unsold fish are packed in baskets and put in the ice-house, whence they will be sent to the Vessprimer market.

Timar wanted to give a feast to all the assembled crowd. He had a ten-gallon cask brought on to the ice and the top knocked out; then he begged the captain to prepare a fish-soup, such as he only could concoct. Certain selected fishes, neither rich nor bony, were cut in pieces into a great kettle; then some of the blood, and handfuls of maize and vegetables, were added. The whole art lies in the proper proportions of the mixture, which the uninitiated never understand. Of this delicious mess Herr Timar himself consumed an incredible quantity. Where good wine flows and fish-soup is brewed, be sure there will be gypsies to be found. Almost before they thought of it, a brown band of musicians appeared, who, as soon as the cymbal-player was seated on an upturned basket, began to play popular airs.

Where gypsies and rosy wenches and fiery youths get together, dancing will soon begin. In a twinkling a rustic ball was improvised on the ice, and rose to a frolicsome height. Round the bonfires circled the active couples, shouting, as they leaped, like King David, and before he knew where he was, Timar too, whom a handsome girl had caught by the arm, was drawn into the whirl. Timar danced.

In the clear winter darkness the cheery fires illuminated the ice for many a mile. The fun lasted till midnight. Meanwhile the fishermen had finished carrying the fish into the ice-house. The joyous crowd dispersed on their homeward way, not without cheers for the feast-giver, the generous Baron von Levetinczy.

Timar stayed till Galambos had packed the fogasch-king in a box, between ice and hay, and nailed the lid down. It was put into the chaise which had brought Timar, and the driver was told to get ready to drive for his life to Komorn: there is no time to lose in dispatching fish. He wrote himself to Timéa. The letter was written in an affectionate and cheerful mood. He called her his dear wife, and described the picturesque scene on the frozen lake, and the terrible cleft in the ice. (That he had been so near the *Rianás* he did not mention.) Then he gave a description of the fishing, with all its amusing details, and finished with an account of the night festival. He told her how much he had been entertained, and how he had quite lost his head, and even ventured on a dance with a pretty peasant girl on the ice.

Some men write these amusing letters when they are contemplating suicide. When the letter was ready he took it to the driver. The old fisherman was there too. "Go home now, Galambos," Michael advised. "You must be tired."

"I must go and make up the fire on the ice," said the old man, lighting his pipe, "for the smell of fish brings the foxes and even bears from all the forests round, to fish on their own account: they watch for the fishes, which put their heads out of the holes, and drag them out, and that frightens away the others."

"No, no!" said Michael, "don't keep up the fire. I will keep guard—I often watch all night. I will go out now and then and fire my gun; that will send all the four-footed fishermen to the right-about." This satisfied Galambos, who invoked God's blessing on his master, and trotted away.

The deaf vine-dresser, the only other inhabitant of Timar's house, had long been asleep. To add to his deafness, he had drunk so much good wine that one might be certain his night's rest would be unbroken. Timar too went to his room and stirred up his fire.

He was not sleepy; his excited brain required no rest. But there is another form of repose; or is it not rest to sit near an open window and look out on dumb nature? The moon had not yet risen; only the stars of heaven shone down on the smooth ice. Their reflection was like rubies spread on a blight steel plate, or the lights which flicker over graves on Hallowe'en.

He gazed before him, and did not even think. He sat without any sensation, either of cold or of his own pulses, neither of the outer nor inner world—he only wondered. This was rest.

CHAPTER IV.
THE PHANTOM.

The stars glittered in heaven and sparkled from their frozen mirror: no breath disturbed the silence of the night. Then Michael heard behind him a voice which greeted him with "Good-evening, sir."

At the door of the bedroom stood, between the two lights of the lamp and the fire, a figure, at sight of which Timar's blood ran cold. In the bitter midnight, through the dense fog, he had fled from this specter across the frozen Danube.

The man's dress was that of a naval officer, whose uniform had, however, visibly suffered from storms and weather. The green cloth had altogether faded on the shoulders, and some buttons were gone. The shoes, too, were in sad condition. The soles had worn away at the tip so that the naked toes were visible; over one shoe a piece of carpet was tied. The wearer was suited to his ragged dress. A sunburned face with a neglected beard; in place of the shaven mustache, a few bristly hairs; across the forehead a black handkerchief covering one eye. This was the figure which had wished Timar a good-evening.

"Krisstyan!" said Timar, very low.

"Yes, to be sure; your dear Theodor—your dear adopted son, Theodor Krisstyan! How good of you to recognize me!"

"What do you want?"

"First, I want to have that gun in my own hands, lest it should remind you of the words with which we parted last time—'If I ever appear before you again, shoot me down.' Since then I have changed my mind." So saying he seized Timar's gun, which leaned against the wall, threw himself into a chair by the fire, and laid the gun across his knee. "There, now we can talk quietly. I have come a long way, and I am dreadfully tired. My equipage left me in the lurch, and I had to travel part of the way on foot."

"What do you want here?" said Timar.

"First, a respectable suit, for what I am wearing bears signs of the severity of the weather." Timar went to the closet, took out his pelisse

345

trimmed with astrakhan, and the rest of the suit, laid them on the ground between himself and Krisstyan, and pointed to them in silence. The vagrant held the gun in one hand, keeping his finger on the trigger, lifted the clothes one by one with the other, and looked them over with the air of a connoisseur.

"Very good—but there is something wanting to this coat. What do you think it is? Why, of course, the purse."

Timar took his pocket-book from a drawer, and threw it over. The vagabond caught it with one hand, opened it with the help of his teeth, and counted the notes inside.

"We are getting on," he said, placing the pocket-book in the pocket of the pelisse. "Might I ask for some linen? I have worn mine for a week, and I fear it is hardly fit for company." Timar handed him a shirt out of the wardrobe. "Now, I have got far enough to proceed to the toilet. But first I have a few explanations to make in order to explain one or two things to his honor the privy councilor. But why the devil should we bother with titles! We are old friends, and can talk openly."

Timar sat down speechless by the table.

"So then, my dear fellow," said the fugitive, "you will remember that you sent me some years ago to Brazil. How affected I was! I adopted you as a father, and swore to be an honest man. But you did not send me over there to make an honest man of me, but in order that I might not stand in your way in this hemisphere. You calculated that a worthless youth, without a good fiber in him, is sure to come to grief in that part of the world. He either turns thief, or gets drowned, or somebody shoots him—anyway, he would be got rid of. But you intrusted me with a large sum of money. What was that to you? Only a stalking-horse. You reckoned on my robbing you, so that you might arrest and imprison me; and so it turned out. Once or twice I nearly did you the favor of dying of some native plague, but unluckily for you I pulled through. And then I devoted my whole energy to business; I robbed you of ten million reis. Ha! ha! Spanish thieves reckon in half-kreutzers, so that the sum may sound larger—it is not more than a hundred thousand gulden. If only you knew what lovely necks the women there have, you would not think it too much; and they will only wear real pearls. But your

346

stupid agent, the Spaniard, looked at it from a different point of view; he had me arrested and tried, and the rascal of a judge sentenced me—just for a foolish boyish trick—only think, to fifteen years at the galleys! Now, just say, was it not barbarous?"

Timar shuddered.

"They took off my fine clothes, and in order that they might not lose me, they branded me on the arm with a hot iron." The felon threw off his uniform-coat as he spoke, drew his dirty shirt from his left shoulder, and showed Timar, with a bitter laugh, the mark still fiery red on his arm. "Look you, it was on your account that they branded me like a foal or a calf, lest I should go astray. Don't be afraid—I would not run away from you, even without that."

With morbid curiosity Timar gazed at the burn on the miserable wretch, and could not turn his eyes away.

"After that, they dragged me to the galleys, and riveted one of my feet to the bench with a ten-pound chain." With that he threw his torn shoe from his foot, and showed Timar a deep wound on his raw ankle. "That also I carry as a remembrance of you," sneered the escaped criminal.

Timar's eyes rested as if fascinated on the disfigured foot.

"But just think, comrade, how kind fate can be! The ways of Providence are wonderful by which an unhappy sufferer is led to the arms of his friends. On the same bench where they had been good enough to fasten me, sat a respectable old man with a bushy beard. He was to be my bed-fellow for fifteen years. It is natural to take a good look at a man who is wedded to you for so long a time. I stared at him awhile, and then said in Spanish, 'It seems to me, señor, as if I had met you before.' 'Your eyes do not deceive you—may you be struck blind!' replied the amiable individual. Then I addressed him in Turkish, 'Effendi, have you not been in Turkey?' 'I have been there; what's that to you?' Then I said in Hungarian, 'Were you not originally called Krisstyan?' The old fellow was much surprised, and said, 'Yes.' 'Then, I am your son Theodor, your dear Theodor, your only offspring!' Ha! ha! Thanks to you, friend, I found my father, my long lost father, over there in the New World on the galley-slave's bench. Providence in its wonderful way had united the long-divided father and son! But may I

347

beg you to give me a flask of wine and something to eat, for I am thirsty and hungry, and have many interesting things to tell you, which will amuse you intensely."

Timar did as he asked, and gave him bread and wine. The visitor sat at the table, took the gun between his knees, and began to eat. He devoured like a starved dog, and drank eagerly: at every draught he smacked his lips, like an epicure who has dined well. And then he went on, with his mouth full:

"After we had got over the first joy of the unexpected meeting, my dear papa said, while he thumped me on the head, 'Now tell me, you gallows-bird, how you got here?' Naturally my filial respect had prevented me from addressing the like question to my parent. I told him that I had defrauded a Hungarian gentleman named Timar of ten million reis. 'And where did he steal all that?' was my old man's remark. I explained that he never stole—that he was a rich landowner, merchant, and trader. But that did not alter my father's opinion: 'All the same, whoever has money stole it. He who has much stole much, and he who has little stole little: if he did not steal it himself, his father or grandfather did so. There are a hundred and thirty-three ways of stealing, and only twenty-two of them lead to the galleys.' As I saw it was useless to try and change my old man's opinion, I no longer disputed the point. Then he asked me, 'How the devil did you come in contact with this Timar?'

"I told him the circumstances. 'I knew this Timar when he was a poor skipper, and had to wash his own potatoes in the ship's galley. Once I was sent by the Turkish police to track an escaped pasha who had fled on one of Timar's ships to Hungary.' 'What was his name?' growled my father. 'Ali Tschorbadschi.' 'What!' he exclaimed, striking me on the knee. He leaped up so that I thought he would jump overboard. Ha! ha! he forgot the chain. . . . 'Did you know him too!' Then the old man shook his head and said, 'Go on; what became of Ali Tschorbadschi?' 'I detected him at Ogradina: I hurried on in front of the ship to Pancsova, where every preparation was made to arrest him. But the vessel arrived without the pasha. He had died on the way, and as he was not allowed burial on shore they had thrown the corpse overboard. All this Timar proved by documentary evidence.' 'And Timar was then quite poor?' 'No richer than myself.' 'But now he has millions?' 'Of which I was

348

lucky enough to secure ten million reis.'

"'Now, you fool, you see I was right—he stole his wealth. From whom? he killed the pasha and hid his money. I knew Ali Tschorbadschi—well. He was a thief too, like every other man, especially like every other rich man. He belonged to the 122d and 123d class of thieves. Under those numbers we reckon governors and treasurers. He was in charge of the treasures of another thief—the sultan himself, No. 133.

"'Once I found out that thief No. 132, the grand vizier, wished to twist the treasurer's neck, to get back what he had stolen. I too was then in the Turkish secret police; only a sort of No. 10, simply a fraudulent bankrupt. I had a good idea: now if I could manage to push on into the ranks of the No. 50 thieves! I went to the pasha, and revealed the secret that he was on the list of rich men whom the minister meant to strangle as conspirators, in order to secure their property. What would he give me if I saved both him and his treasures? Ali Tschorbadschi promised me a quarter of his wealth when once we should both be in safety. "Yes," said I, "but I should like to know first how much the whole comes to, for I will do nothing with my eyes shut. I am a family man—I have a son whom I should like to settle in life."' Ha! ha! The old man said it so seriously that it makes me laugh now to think of it. 'You have a son?' said the pasha to my father. 'That is well; if I escape I will give my only daughter to your son, and so the whole property will remain in the family: send me your son that I may know him.' By God! if I had only known then that the lovely lady with the white face and meeting brows was destined for me! Do you hear, comrade?—but I must have another drink, to drown my grief. . . . You will permit me to empty my glass to the health of your spouse, the loveliest of ladies?"

The galley-slave rose with the courtesy of a prince and drank the toast. Then he threw himself back in his chair, and drew breath through his teeth like a man who has dined well. "My father agreed to the bargain. 'We decided,' said he, 'that Ali Tschorbadschi should pack his jewels in a leather bag, which I was to take with me in an English ship, which would convey me as an unsuspected person, with all my luggage, to Malta. There I was to await Ali Tschorbadschi, who was to leave Stamboul as if on a pleasure trip, with his daughter, but without any luggage, make his way to the Piræus, and thence by a Greek trader to Malta. The pasha showed great confidence in me. He left me alone in the treasure-chamber, so that his own visits there should not be noticed, and commissioned me to select the most precious objects and pack them in the leather bag. I could describe now all the jewels I chose. The antique gems, the girdles of pearls, rings, agraffes, a casket full of diamonds—'

"'Could you not hide a few away?' asked I.

"'You ass's head!' he replied, 'why should I take a single diamond and become thief No. 18, when it was in my power to steal them all?'

"Aha! my old father was a clever fellow! 'The devil I was! I was a moon-calf. I ought to have done as you say. I stuffed my bag full, and brought it to the pasha without arousing suspicion. He put a few rouleaux of louis d'or among the jewels in the bag, closed it with a puzzle-lock, and fastened lead seals to the four corners: then he sent me for a *caïque*, that I might get quietly away. I was back in a quarter of an hour. He handed me the bag with the English steel puzzle-lock and the four lead weights. I took it under my cloak and slipped through the garden door to the boat; on the way I handled the bag and felt the agraffes, the casket, and the rouleaux. In an hour I was on board an English ship, the anchor was weighed, and we left the Golden Horn.' 'And you never took me,' said I, with child-like reproach to my papa, 'who was to marry the pasha's lovely daughter?' 'You fool!' cried the old man, 'I didn't want you or your pasha or his lovely daughter; I never meant to wait for you at Malta: with the money given me for the journey I embarked direct for America, and the leather bag went with me. But, confound it! when I got to a safe place I took out my knife and slit the bag, and what do you think fell out of it?—copper buttons, rusty horse-shoes, and instead of the casket full of diamonds, a stone inkstand—in the rouleaux, instead of louis d'or were heavy paras, the sort the corporals use for paying the private soldiers. The rascally thief had robbed me! In all my 133 classes this had never occurred; there was no number for it. While I went for the boat, the thief had prepared another identical bag filled with all sorts of rubbish, and sent me with it across the ocean, while he fled in another direction with the real jewels. But look you, there is justice not only on land but by water, for the great thief ran into the net of a still greater, who robbed and murdered him.' And this tip-top thief, who deprived the other of his property and his life was—you—brother of my heart—Michael Timar Levetinczy, the man of gold!" said the fugitive, as he rose and bowed mockingly.

Timar answered not a word.

"And now we will talk in a different way," said Theodor Krisstyan, "but still at three paces' distance, and without forgetting that the gun is aimed at you."

Timar looked indifferently down the muzzle of the gun. He had himself loaded it with ball.

"This discovery considerably increased the sufferings of my slavery," continued the adventurer. "Instead of living comfortably on Ali's treasure, I had to drag out a miserable existence on the hateful sea. And why? Because Michael Timar had smuggled the treasures which were intended for me from under my nose, and also the girl I should have married, the fair little savage who had grown up for me on the desolate island. Of her too Timar must needs defraud me, for he could not be happy with the wife whose father he had killed; he must needs have a mistress as well. Fy! Herr Timar. So it was for that you sent me to the galleys for fifteen years."

Blow after blow fell on Timar's shame-stricken face. No doubt many of these accusations were false—they were not all true. He had not "killed" Timéa's father, had not "stolen" his treasures; he had not "defrauded" him of Noémi, nor "got rid of" Theodor, but on the whole he could not entirely deny the charges. He had played a false game, and thereby got mixed up in every sort of crime.

The deserter continued: "When we were lying in the Gulf of Rio Grande do Sul, yellow fever broke out on board our ship. My father caught it, and lay in the death agony beside me on the bench—no one removed him. It is not the custom; a galley-slave must die where he is chained. This was a horrible situation for me. The old man shivered with ague the whole day, he swore and gnashed his teeth. He was unbearable with his continual curses on the Blessed Virgin, which he always uttered in Hungarian. Why did he not swear in Spanish? It sounds so fine, and then the rest would have understood; and why should he swear at the Madonna? I could not put up

351

with it—there were plenty of other saints he could have maligned; it is not the thing for an educated man, a gentleman, to speak ill of the ladies. This caused a coolness between me and my old man. Not his deadly fever, which I might catch, merely his insufferable language. Strong as were the ties which united father and son, I decided to sever them, and succeeded in escaping in company with two others. We filed our chains at night, struck down the overseer, who had seen our proceedings, and threw him into the sea; then we launched the small boat and set off. It was very rough and our boat was swamped; one of my companions could not swim, and got drowned; the other could swim, but not so well as the shark which pursued him. I only knew by his shrieks that the sea-devil had caught him and bitten him in two. I swam ashore. How I obtained this naval uniform and the arms and money requisite for my passage, I will tell you some other day over a glass of wine, when we have plenty of time. But now let us conclude our business; for you know we have to settle our account together."

The outcast put his hand up to the handkerchief over his eye. The slowly healing wound seemed to be an unpleasant reminder. The severe cold to which he had been exposed had not done it any good.

"I tried to get to Komorn, where I knew you had your permanent home, and went to visit you. They said in your office that you had not yet come from abroad; what country you were in no one knew. Very well, thought I, then I will wait till he returns. To pass the time, I went to the cafés, and made acquaintance with officers to whom my uniform was an introduction, and then I visited the theaters. There I saw that exquisitely beautiful lady with the marble face and the melancholy eyes—you can guess whom I mean. With her was always another fair lady—oh! what murderous eyes that one has; she is a corsair in petticoats. I began to feel my way. Once I contrived to get a seat close by the wicked angel, and paid her attentions which she received graciously: when I asked leave to wait upon her, she referred to her mistress, on whom everything depended. I spoke admiringly of that awe-inspiring Madonna, and remarked that I had known her family in Turkey, and that she resembled her mother very strongly.

"'What,' said the lovely lady, 'you knew her mother? she died very young.' 'I have only seen her portrait,' said I. 'It portrayed just such a pale, sad

352

face, surrounded with a double row of diamonds of great value.' 'You too have seen the splendid ornament then?' said she. 'My mistress showed it me when Herr Timar von Levetinczy gave it to her.'"

Timar clinched his fists in impotent rage.

"Aha! now we know all about it," continued the adventurer, turning to the tortured man with a cruel smile. "You gave Ali Tschorbadschi's daughter the treasures you stole from her father. In that case the rest of the jewels must have fallen into your hands, for they were with the picture. You can no longer deny it. . . . And now we are on a level: we need not scruple to talk openly."

Timar sat there paralyzed before the man into whose hands fate had delivered him. It was unnecessary to keep his gun from him: Timar had not strength to stand.

"You kept me waiting a long time, my friend, and I began to get anxious about you; besides, my pocket-money was coming to an end. My rich aunt's remittances, the advices from my steward, my bankers, and the admiralty, for which I daily inquired at the post-office, failed to arrive—for excellent reasons. You were highly respected wherever I went: an upright merchant, a great genius, a benefactor to the poor. Your exemplary private life was described; you were the model husband; wives would burn your body when you died and dose their husbands with your ashes. Ha! ha!"

Timar turned away his face.

"But perhaps I weary you? Well, I am coming to business. One day I was in a bad temper, because you would not come home, and when some one mentioned you at the officers' café, I could not refrain from casting a doubt on the possibility of one man's uniting so many good qualities. Then a ruffian replied with a slap in the face: I confess I was not prepared for this; but my cheek deserved it—why had it not kept my tongue quiet? I was as sorry as a dog that I ventured to let fall a disrespectful word, and took the lesson to heart. I will never slander you again. If the box on the ear had been all, I should not so much have cared—I'm used to that; but the insolent fellow forced me to go out with him, because I had attacked your good name. As I soon learned, this madman was a lover of your Madonna when she was a girl, and now he was fighting for the honor of the Madonna's husband.

353

That is a piece of good luck which could only happen to you, you man of gold. But I owe you no thanks for your good fortune; again it was I who had to pay for it: I got a cut over the head right down to the eyebrow. Look!"

He thrust aside the silken bandage, under which was visible a long scar with a dirty plaster over it, the inflamed skin showing that the wound was not healed. Timar looked at it with a shudder.

Krisstyan drew the bandage over it again, and said with cynical humor, "That is *souvenir* number three which your friendship has bestowed on me. Well, there is all the more standing to my credit. I could not remain any longer in Komorn after this; but 'Stay,' said I—'I know where to have him; I know where the foreign country is whither he goes in the interest of his fatherland: it is not in any unknown land—it is none other than the ownerless island. I will follow him there.'"

At this Timar cried furiously, "What! you went to the island?" He trembled with rage and fear.

"Don't jump up, young friend!" said the felon, soothingly. "This gun is loaded; if you move it might go off, and I could not answer for the consequences. Besides, calm yourself. It did you no harm for me to go there, only myself; I always have to pay the piper when you go to the ball—it's as certain as if it were one of the ten commandments—you dance and I pay. You get into my bed, and it's me that they throw out of window. Why did I go to the ownerless island? only to look for you. But when I got there you had left, and I found no one but Noémi and a little brat . . . oh, fy, friend Michael! who would have thought it of you? . . . but hush! we mustn't tell anybody. . . . Dodi he's called, isn't he? A fine, forward boy; but how frightened he was of me, because I had my eye bound up! It is true that Noémi was startled too, for the two were quite alone on the island. It grieved me to hear that good Mamma Therese was dead; she was so kind, she would have received me differently. Just fancy—this Noémi would not even let me come in and sit down: she said she was afraid of me, and Dodi still more so, because they were alone. 'That's just why I have come, that you may have a man in the house to protect you.' By the bye, what potion have you given the girl that she has grown so pretty? Really she has become a splendid creature—it makes one's heart laugh to look at her; I never stopped telling her so. Then she tried to make ugly faces at me; I began to jest with her. 'Is it right,' said I, 'to make grimaces at your bridegroom?' That did not answer; she called me a vagrant, and turned me out. 'All right,' I said, 'I would go and take her with me,' and then I put my arm round her waist." Timar's eyes flashed fire. "Sit still, comrade; *you* need not jump up, but I had to, for the girl fetched me a box on the ear—just about twice as hard as the one I got from the major. To be accurate, I must acknowledge that she chose the other cheek, so as to make it equal."

Timar's face brightened.

"Then I did get angry. I am well known to be an admirer of the fair sex, but this insult demanded satisfaction. 'Well, I will just show you that you will come with me, if you don't allow me to stop here. You will follow me of your own accord'—and with that I took little Dodi's hand to lead him away.

"Devil!" cried Timar.

"Gently, gently, we can't both speak at once; your turn will come, and then you can talk as much as you like—but hear me out. I was not quite right when I said there were only two on the island—there were three; that confounded beast Almira was there. The dog had been lying under the bed, and seemed not to notice me, but when the child began to cry, the great brute flew out at me without being asked. I had my eye on her, drew out my pistol quickly, and shot her through the body."

"Murderer!" groaned Timar.

"Nonsense! If I had no more on my conscience than that dog's blood! and the beast was not even crippled by the ball; she made nothing of it. She only flew at me more furiously than ever, bit me in the arm, threw me down, and held me so that I could not move: in vain I tried to get at my second pistol—she held my arm in her teeth like a tiger. At last I entreated Noémi to set me free; she tried to get the beast away, but the raging fiend only sent her teeth deeper in. Then Noémi said, 'Ask the child—the dog will obey him.' I begged Dodi's help. The boy is kind-hearted; he had pity on me, and put his arms round Almira; then the dog let go, and the child kissed her." A tear ran down Timar's cheek. "So I was provided with another memento," said Theodor Krisstyan, as he pushed his dirty, blood-stained shirt-sleeve down from his shoulder. "Look at the mark of the dog's bite; all three fangs went to the bone: that is memorial number four, for which I have to thank you. I bear on my skin a whole album of wounds which I owe to you: the brand, the chain-sore, the sword-cut, and the dog's bite—all are remembrances of your friendship. And now say, what shall I do to you that our account may be balanced?"

As the escaped prisoner said to Timar, "And now say what shall I do to you?" he stood entirely undressed before him, and Timar had to look at all the horrible wounds with which he was scarred from head to foot . . . and naked, too, the wretch's soul stood there, and it too was full of loathsome wounds inflicted by Timar's hand.

The man knew that Timar had played a bold game with him; and now he was at his mercy: even physically he had not power to cope with him; his limbs were as feeble as those of a man overcome with sleep. The sight of the scarred form had the unnerving effect of an evil spell. The adventurer knew it, and no longer took precautions against him. Rising from his chair, he leaned the gun in the corner and spoke over his shoulder to Timar, "Now, then, for the toilet; while I dress you you can think over your answer to my question, what I shall do with you."

With that he tossed his ragged clothes one after another into the fire, where they flared crackling up, so that the flame rushed up the chimney. Then he began to put on Timar's clothes in a leisurely way. On the mantel-piece he found Timar's watch: this he put in his waistcoat-pocket, and inserted Timar's studs in his shirt-front, finding time to arrange his hair in the glass. When he was quite ready, he threw up his head, and placed himself before the fire with outstretched legs and folded arms. "Well; now then, comrade."

Timar began to speak. "What do you require of me?"

"Aha! at last I have loosed your tongue! How if I were to say an eye for an eye, a tooth for a tooth? go and have a gallows-brand burned on you; wander by land and sea among sharks, Indians, jaguars, rattlesnakes, and secret police; be cut over the head by your wife's lover, be bitten by your mistress's dog—and then we shall begin to share alike. But you see I am not so hard on you; I won't talk about my wounds—a dog's bones soon mend—I will be kinder than you. I must disappear for a time; for I am wanted not only because of your money—my escape from the galleys, and the overseer I threw overboard, are not yet forgiven. Your money will do me no good till I get rid of the burn and the scar on the chin. I shall get rid of the one with vitriol, and for the other mineral baths will be of service. I am not afraid of your putting my pursuers on my track—you are too wise for that; but foresight is the mother of wisdom. In spite of our close friendship, it might happen that some one should give me a knock on the head in the dark, or some convenient brigands might shoot me, or a friendly glass of wine might

357

send me the same road as Ali Tschorbadschi. No, my dear fellow, I would not even venture to ask you to fill me this wine-flask again, not even if you drank first. I shall always be on my guard."

"What do you want then?"

"How formally you talk! my company is too low for you. But first let us ask what the noble lord wants on his side. Probably that I should hold my tongue over all the secrets I have got hold of. The noble lord would perhaps not be disinclined to settle on me in return an income of a hundred thousand francs in government stock."

Timar without hesitation replied, "Yes."

The vagabond laughed. "I require no such heavy sacrifice, your honor. I told you money was no use to me at present. Such a gallows-bird, with so many bad habits, would be arrested anywhere, and then what good should I get of my income? What I want is, as I said, rest, and a place where I can remain hidden for a considerable time, and where I should meanwhile enjoy a comfortable, easy life; that is reasonable enough surely?"

With that he took the gun up again, sat down on the chair, and held the gun before him in both hands, so as to be ready to fire at any moment. "I do not ask the hundred thousand francs at present; I only demand—the ownerless island."

Timar felt as if struck by lightning; these words roused him from his stupor. "What do you want with it?"

"Illustrissimo! See now. The air of the island is excellent, and most necessary to the re-establishment of my health, which suffered much in South America. I have heard from that dear departed saint, Frau Therese, that healing herbs grow there which are good for wounds; in botany books I have read that they will even make boiled flesh sound again. Then, too, I long for a quiet, contemplative life after all my trials; after the sybarite existence I have led, I long for the rustic joys of the golden age. Give me the ownerless island, excellency—serene highness."

The fellow begged so mockingly with the gun in his hand.

"You are a fool," said Timar, whom these jeers enraged, and then he turned his chair round and showed Theodor his back.

"Oh, don't turn your back on me, noble sir—señor, eccelenza, my lord, durchlaucht, mynheer, pan volkompzsnye, monsieur, gospodin, effendi. In what language shall I address you, to persuade you to grant the poor fugitive's request?"

This unseemly mockery did not do the assailant any good, but lessened the effect of the spell which lay on Timar, who began to recover from his stupefaction, and to recollect that he had to deal with a condemned man who was really in mortal danger. He spoke angrily. "Have done! Name any sum—you shall have it! if you want an island, go and buy one in the Greek Archipelago, or in China; if you are afraid of pursuit, go to Rome, Naples, or Switzerland: give yourself out as a marquis, get on terms with the Camorra, and no one will touch you; I will give you money—but you won't get the island."

"Indeed? Your lordship is going to talk to me like that?" cried Krisstyan. "The drowning man has risen again, and is going to swim ashore—now just wait till I push you in again. You think to yourself, 'Very well, booby, tell any one what you know; the first result will be that you will be arrested, clapped into jail, and forgotten there like a dog; you will soon be too dumb to tell anything more—or something else may happen.' I see what you think. But don't mistake the man you have to deal with. Now learn that you are tied hand and foot, and that you lie at my mercy like a miser gagged and bound by robbers, who must bear thorns thrust under his nails, his beard plucked out hair by hair, and boiling oil dropped on his skin, till he tells where his money is hidden. I shall do the same with you; and when you can bear no more, then cry 'enough.'"

Timar listened with the deadly interest of a man on the rack to the words of the galley-slave. "Till now I have told not a soul what I know, on my honor. Except the few words which escaped me at Komorn, I have never spoken of you, and what I said then was neither fish nor flesh; but all I know of you is written down—I have it here in my pocket, and in four different documents, with different addresses. One is a denunciation to the Turkish Government, in which I reveal what Ali Tschorbadschi took from Stamboul, and what, as the confiscated property of a traitor, is due to the sultan. Even the jewels described to me by my father are enumerated there, piece by piece, with the account of their present possessors, and of how they came by them.

359

In the second letter I inform the Viennese authorities of your murder of the pasha, and your theft of his property. My third letter is directed to Frau von Levetinczy at Komorn. I tell her what you did to her father, and how you came into possession of her mother's picture and the other treasures you presented to her. But I have told her something else besides—the place you go to when you are not at home—the secret joys of the ownerless island—the intrigue with another woman—the deceit you practice on her. I tell her about Noémi and little Dodi. Now shall I drive another thorn under your nails?"

Timar's breast heaved with heavy panting sobs.

"Well, as you say nothing, we will proceed," said the cruel torturer. "The fourth letter is to Noémi. I tell her in it all she does not yet know: that you have a lawful wife out in the world—that you are a gentleman who has dishonored her, and can never be her husband; who only sacrificed her to his base lusts, and who is a murderer besides. What! you don't ask for mercy yet? Do you see those two towers? That is Tihany; there live pious monks, for it is a monastery; there I shall deposit the four letters, and beg the prior, if I do not return within a week, to forward them to their addresses. It would be no use for you to put me out of the way, for the letters would still reach their destination, and then you could not stay any longer in this country. You can not go home; for even if your wife forgave you her father's death, she would never forgive you Noémi. Justice would make inquiries, and then you would have to let out how you came by your riches.

"The Turkish Government would bring you to trial, and the Austrian too. The whole world would soon learn to know you, and those who looked on you as a man of gold, would see in you the very scum of humanity. You could not even take refuge in the ownerless island, for there Noémi would shut the door against you; she is a proud woman, and her love would turn to hatred. No, there is nothing left to you but to fly from the world, like me; change your name, like me; slink secretly from town to town, and tremble when steps approach your door, like me. Now, shall I go or stay?"

"Stay!" groaned the sufferer.

"Oho! you give in!" cried the rascal; "then let us sit down again. First, will you give me the ownerless island?"

360

A feeble subterfuge occurred to Timar's heart, which he used to gain time. "But the island belongs to Noémi, not to me."

"A very true observation; but my request is not altered by that fact. The island belongs to Noémi, but Noémi belongs to you."

"What do you mean?" asked Timar, wildly.

"Now don't roll your eyes; don't you know you are fast bound? Let us take it all as it comes. The thing can be arranged. You write a letter to Noémi, which I will carry; meanwhile that fierce black brute will have died, and I can land safely. In the letter you will take leave of her; you will say that you cannot marry her, because unavoidable family complications stand in the way; that you have a wife, the beautiful Timéa, whom Noémi will remember: you will write that you have taken care to provide for her suitably; that you have recalled her former betrothed from the New World, who is a fine handsome fellow, and ready to marry her and shut his eyes to the past. You will promise to provide for them both handsomely in the future, and give them your blessing and good wishes for a happy life together!"

"You want Noémi too?"

"Why, what the devil! Do you think I want your stupid island in order to live there like Robinson Crusoe? I shall want something to sweeten my life in that desert. Over there I have reveled in a surfeit of embraces from black-eyed, sable-tressed women; now, after seeing Noémi's golden locks and blue eyes, I am quite mad about her. And then she struck me in the face, and drove me away; I must have payment for that. Is there a nobler revenge than to give a kiss for a blow? I will be the master of the refractory witch; that is my fancy. And by what right do you deny her to me? Am I not Noémi's betrothed, who would make her my legal wife and bring her to honor, while you can never marry her, and can only make her unhappy?"

The man drops boiling oil on Timar's heart: he wrung his hands in agony.

"Will you write to Noémi, or shall I take these four letters over to the cloister?"

In Timar's torture the words escaped him, "Oh, my little Dodi!"

The fugitive laughed with a knavish grin. "I'll be his father, a very good sort of father—"

At that instant Michael sprung from his seat, threw himself with a leap like a jaguar's on the convict, seized him by both arms before he could use his weapon, dragged him forward, gave him a blow in the back and a shove which sent him flying through the open door on to the landing, tumbling over and over: there he got up with difficulty, still giddy with his fall, stumbled over the first step, and limped groaning and swearing down the stairs. All below was darkness and silence. The only man besides these two in this winter castle was deaf, and sleeping off a carouse.

CHAPTER V.
WHAT HAS THE MOON TO TELL?

Timar could have killed the man—he had him in his power; and Timar felt a madman's strength in his muscles: yet he did not kill him. Timar said to himself, the man is right; destiny must be fulfilled. Michael was not a miscreant who conceals one crime by another, but of that nobler sort which is willing to atone for past sin. He stepped out on to the balcony, and looked on with folded arms while the man left the castle and limped away toward the gate of the court-yard. The moon rose meanwhile over the Somogy hills, and illuminated the front of the castle.

The dark figure on the balcony would be a good mark for any one who wished to aim at it. Theodor Krisstyan walked underneath, and looked up: the half-closed wound on the brow had reopened in his fall, and was bleeding; the blood ran down over his face. Perhaps Timar had gone outside just because he expected the furious man would shoot him out of revenge. But he only stood still in front of him, and began to mutter words without sound—just like Athalie. How well those two would suit! Krisstyan only spoke by movements of the mouth. He limped, for he had hurt one foot in his fall. He struck his left hand on the gun, which he still held, then seemed to say "No," shook his fist at Timar, and threatened him by gestures. This pantomime meant, "Not thus will I destroy you; I have another fate designed for you; just wait!" Timar looked after him as he left the yard, following him with his eyes along the snowy path as far as the ice-covered lake. He gazed after him till he could only see a black speck moving in the direction of the double towers on the high peak.

Storm-clouds were rising over the Zala range. Timar saw them not. Round the Platten See a hurricane often arises in calm weather without the slightest warning; the fishermen who hear from afar the rustling of the leaves have not time to get back to the shore: the bursting storm drives a snow-cloud before it, from which tiny crystals drift down, sharp as needle-points. The cloud only covered half of the great panorama, wrapping the Tihany side, the peninsula with its rocky ridge and its gloomy church, in darkness, while the eastern level lay bright in the moonlight. The storm roared howling through the tall forests of the Aracs valley; the vanes on the ancient castle groaned like the cries of accursed spirits; and as the furious wind swept across the ice, it drew from the frozen floes such an unearthly music that one could fancy one saw the spirits which uttered it chasing each other, and yelling in their flight.

Amidst the ghostly music it seemed to Timar as if he heard through the howling of the tempest an awful scream in the distance, such as only human lips can utter—a cry of anguish, despair, blasphemy, which would rouse the Seven Sleepers and make the stars shudder. After a few seconds it came again, but shorter and more feeble, and then only the music of the storm was audible.

That ceased too. The snow-shower swept across the landscape; the storm held only one snow-cloud; the trees were still; the tones of the wind moaning over the ice-flats faded away in the distance with dying chords; the sky cleared, and all was once more silence. Timar's heart too was at rest; he had finished his career. No road lay open to him. He could go neither forward nor back; he had fled as long as life was possible; and now the abyss yawned in front of him which had no other shore. His whole life passed before him like a dream, and he knew that at last he was about to awake from it. His first desire for the possession of the rich and lovely girl was the origin of all these events; his life hung on it like the enigma of the Sphinx. When the riddle was solved, the Sphinx would fall into the abyss.

How could he live on, unmasked before the world, unmasked before Timéa, and before Noémi? Thrown down from the pedestal on which he had stood for years at home and abroad, under the halo of his sovereign's favor and his compatriots' veneration! How could he ever look again on the woman who had defended him in his rival's presence with such holy sorrow when she learned that he was the very opposite of all she had admired in her husband, and that his whole life was a lie? And how could he meet Noémi when she knew he was Timéa's husband? or dare to take Dodi on his lap? Nowhere, nowhere in the wide world was there a place where he could hide. It was as that man had said: there was nothing for him but to turn his back on the civilized world—like him; to change his name—like him; to sneak like

364

a thief from one town to another—like him; to wander homeless on the face of the earth. . . .

But Timar knew of another place; there is the moon's icy countenance—what did Noémi say? There live those who cast their lives away because they have ceased to know desire; they go where nothing exists: if that man seeks out Noémi on the ownerless island and brings despair on the lonely creature by his news, she will follow him there—to the frozen star.

Timar felt so tranquilized by this reflection that he had the self-control to direct his telescope on to the waning moon, on whose sphere shining spaces alternated with large, crescent-shaped shadows, and there came to choose a monstrous ravine, and say, "That shall be my dwelling; there will I wait for Noémi!"

Then he went back to his room. The adventurer's burned clothes still glowed red on the hearth, the ashes showing the texture of the charred cloth. Timar laid fresh logs on, so that the fire might destroy every remnant. Then he threw on his cloak and left the house. He bent his steps toward the Platten See. The moon lighted the great ice-floes, an icy sun shining over a world of ice. . . . "I come, I come!" cried Timar; "I shall soon know what you have to tell me—if you have called me I shall be there." He went straight to the great chasm. The poles erected by the good fishermen, the sticks with straw bundles on the top, warned every wanderer from afar to keep away—Timar sought them out. When he reached one of these danger-signals he stopped, took off his hat, and looked up to heaven.

Years had passed away since last he prayed. In this dark hour the Great Being came to his mind who teaches the stars their courses and rides on the storm, and who has created only one creature which defies its Maker—man. In this hour he was impelled to uplift his soul to Him. "Eternal Might, I fly from Thee, yet to Thee I come. I come not to ask for mercy: Thou didst lead me, but I fled from Thy ways; Thou didst warn me, yet I would not hear. Now, with blind obedience, I depart for the hereafter: my soul will rest there in cold annihilation. I must atone for making so many miserable who have been mine and have loved me; take them into Thy protection, Thou Eternal Justice! I have sinned, and I give myself up to death and damnation—they are not guilty—I alone. Thou Everlasting Justice, who hast brought me to this, be just also to them. Protect, console these feeble women, the helpless child, and give me alone over to Thine avenging angels—I am judged and I am silent."

He knelt down. Between the edges of the fissure the waves of the Balaton plashed softly. The gloomy lake often moans even in a dead calm, and when its surface is ice-bound it swells up in the clefts and roars like the sea. Timar bent down to kiss the waves, as one kisses his mother before he starts for a long journey—as one kisses the pistol before blowing out one's brains with it.

And as he bent down to the water, a human head rose from the depths in front of him. Over the forehead of the upturned face was a black band covering the right eye; the other eye, bloodshot, glassy, and cold as stone, glared at him; through the open mouth the water ran out and in . . . the phantom sunk again.

Timar sprung, half crazed, from his kneeling position, and stared after the ghostly apparition: it was as if it called on him to follow. Between the frozen margins the living water splashed. And again in the distance resounded the organ-tones which are the precursors of the nocturnal storm: amidst the howling of the approaching gale were heard the shrieks and groans of the miserable spirits, and higher and higher swelled the ghostly song. Again the whole frozen mass gave out the unearthly music, like the strings of myriad harps, until the sound grew into a booming roar, as though the lightning lured an awful, deafening melody from the resounding waves. The voices of the storm bellowed below the surface. With a frightful crash the floes were set in motion, and the tremendous pressure of the atmosphere closed once more the chasm in the ice.

Timar fell trembling on his face upon the still quivering glassy mirror.

CHAPTER VI.
WHO COMES?

The hoar-frost had turned the ownerless island into a silver wood; continuous mists had hung every twig with flowers of rime. Then came bright sunny days; they melted the rime into ice: every branch received a crystal cloak, as if the whole island were of glass. This glistening load bent down the boughs like those of a weeping-willow, and when the wind stirred the wood, the icicles struck together and rang like the silver bells in the fairy stories. Over the thickly frosted paths only one track led from the house, and that went to Therese's resting-place. This was Noémi's daily walk with little Dodi. Now there were only those two to go there; the third, Almira, lay at home at the last gasp: the ball had touched a vital part, and there was no hope of cure.

It was evening. Noémi lighted her lamp, brought out her wheel, and began to spin. Little Dodi sat by her and played at water-mills, holding a straw against the revolving wheel.

"Mother," said the boy suddenly, "bend down a little; I want to whisper that Almira may not hear."

"Say it aloud; she won't understand, Dodi."

"Oh, yes, she understands what we say—she knows everything. Tell me, will Almira die?"

"Yes, my little one."

"And who will take care of us when Almira is dead?"

"God."

"Is God strong?"

"Stronger than all the world."

"More than father?"

"Your father gets his strength from God."

"And the wicked man with his eye bandaged, why does God make him strong? I am so afraid of his coming again; he will take me away."

"Don't be afraid; I won't let you go."

"If he kills us both?"

"Then we shall both go to heaven."

"And Almira too?"

"No; not Almira."

"Why not?"

"Because she is an animal."

"And my little bird?"

"No; not Louise."

"Oh, don't say that; she can fly up to heaven better than we can."

"She can not fly as high as heaven."

"Then there are no animals and no birds there? Well, then, I'd rather stop down here with papa and my little Louise."

"Yes, stay, my sweetheart!"

"If papa were here he would kill the wicked man?"

"The bad man would run away from him."

"But when is father coming back?"

"This winter."

"How do you know?"

"He said so."

"Is everything true that father says? Does he never tell a story?"

"No, my boy; what he says is always true."

"But it is winter now."

"He will soon be here."

"If only Almira does not die before he comes!"

The boy got up from his stool and went to the groaning dog.

"Dear Almira, do not die! Don't leave us alone here! See, now, you can't go with us to heaven; you can only be with us here. Do stay. I will build you a lovely house like the one father built for me, and give you half of all I have. Lay your head on my lap and look at me. Don't be frightened; I won't let the naughty man come and shoot you again. If I hear him coming, I will fasten the door-latch; and if he puts his hand in, I will cut it off with my ax. I will take care of you, Almira."

The wise creature raised its beautiful eyes to the boy, and wagged its tail gently on the ground; then it sighed, as if understanding all that was said. Noémi stopped spinning, leaned her head on her hand, and looked into the flickering lamp.

When that dreadful man went raging away, he had yelled in at the window, "I shall come back and tell you what the man is whom you love." That he should come again was threat enough, but what did he mean? Who can Michael be? Can he be other than he seems? What will that horrid phantom have to tell, which has turned up from the antipodes? Oh, why had Michael not done as Noémi said—if only three feet of earth lay between them!

Noémi was no feeble woman; she had grown up in the desert and learned to trust in herself; the enervating influences of the outer world had never affected her mind. The wolf knows how to defend her lair against the dogs with claws and teeth. Since that fearful visit she always carried Michael's knife in her bosom, and—it is keen and sharp. At night she fastened a beam across the door.

As fate wills. If one comes first, she will be a happy and blessed woman; if the other, she will be a murderess—a child of wrath.

"Almira, what is the matter?"

The poor beast, struggling with death, raised its head painfully from the child's lap, and began to sniff the air with outstretched neck. It whined and growled uneasily, but the sound was more like a hoarse rattle. Whether its tones were of pleasure or anger, it was hard to distinguish. The animal scented the approach of a visitor. Who is it? Is it the good or the bad man? the life-giver or the murderer? Out there in the silence of the night the sound of steps was heard on the frosty grass. Who comes?

Almira gasped heavily, struggling to get up, but fell back. She tried to bark, but could not. Noémi sprung from her seat, felt with her right hand under her shawl, and seized the handle of the knife.

All three listened silently—Noémi, Dodi, and the dog. The steps come quickly nearer. Ah, now all three recognize them!

"Papa!" cried Dodi, laughing.

Noémi hastened to cut the rope which fastened the door-bolt with her sharp knife, and Almira raised herself on her fore-feet and suddenly gave utterance to a bark.

The next moment Michael had Noémi and Dodi in his arms. Almira

369

crawled to her beloved master, raised her head to him once again, licked his hand, then fell back dead.

"Will you never leave us again?" faltered Noémi.

"Don't leave us alone any more," begged little Dodi.

Michael pressed both to his breast, and his tears streamed over his dear ones. "Never—never—never!"

CHAPTER VII.
THE CORPSE.

With the last days of March the hard winter of this year came to an end. Balmy south winds and rain softened the ice of the Platten See, which broke up during a strong north wind, and drove over to the Somogy shore.

Among the floating ice the fishermen found a body. It was already in an advanced stage of decomposition, and the features were unrecognizable; but yet the identity of the individual could be ascertained with the greatest certainty. These were the mortal remains of Michael Timar Levetinczy, who disappeared so suddenly after the memorable capture of the fogasch-king, and for whose return those at home had waited so long. On the body could be recognized clothes belonging to that gentleman—his astrakhan pelisse, his studs, and his initials marked on the shirt. His repeater was in the waistcoat-pocket, with his full name enameled on the case. But the strongest proof was afforded by the pocket-book, which was crammed with bank-notes, whose number could still be deciphered, and on which Timéa's hand had embroidered "Faith, Hope, Charity;" while in the side-pocket were four other letters tied together, but the writing was completely obliterated, as they had been four months exposed to the action of water. About the same time, the fishermen at Fured found Herr von Levetinczy's gun entangled in a net. Now all was explained.

. Old Galambos remembered all about it. The gracious master had said to him that if foxes and wolves came down on to the lake in the night, he would go out with his gun and have a shot at them.

Many others then remembered that on that night a snow-storm had passed across the lake, which only lasted a short time. No doubt, to this was due the accident to the noble lord. The snow blew in his face; he did not notice the ice-rift, fell in, and was sucked under.

When Timéa received the first news of the event, she went at once to Siosok, and was present in person at the judicial inquiry. When she saw her husband's clothes she fainted away, and could only with difficulty he brought back to consciousness; but she held her ground, she was present when the disfigured remains were laid in the leaden coffin, and specially inquired for the ring of betrothal, which, however, was lost—the fingers were gone.

Timéa had the dear relics brought to Komorn, and interred in the splendid family vault, with all the pomp which is permissible by the rites of the Protestant Church, to which the deceased had belonged. On the black velvet coffin, name and age were marked with silver nails. Senators and deputies carried him to the hearse. On the coffin lay his knightly sword, with a laurel crown, and the decorations of the Hungarian Order of St. Stephen, the Italian Order of San Maurizio, and the Brazilian Annunciata star.

The pall-bearers were Hungarian counts, and on each side of the hearse walked the dignitaries of the city. Before it marched the school-children, the guilds with their banners, then the national guard in uniform and with muffled drums: behind came the ladies of the town all in black, and among them the mourning widow, with the white face and with weeping eyes. The celebrities of the country and the capital, the military authorities, even his majesty had sent a representative to the funeral of the venerated man. With them went a countless multitude of people, and amidst the tolling of all the bells the procession moved through the town. And every bell and every tongue proclaimed that a man was gone whose like would never be seen again: a benefactor of the people, a pillar of the nation, a faithful husband, and the founder of many a generous endowment.

The "Man of Gold" was carried to his grave. Women, men, and children followed him through the whole town to the distant cemetery. Athalie too was in the procession. When they bore the coffin down to the open grave, the nearest friends, relations, and admirers of the deeply mourned followed him into the vault.

Among them was Major Katschuka; in the crowd on the narrow steps he came in contact with Timéa and—with Athalie. When they came up again, Athalie threw herself on the bier and prayed to be buried too: luckily Herr Johann Fabula was there, and he raised the beautiful lady from the ground, bore her back in his arms to the daylight, and explained to the astonished crowd how much the young lady had loved the dear deceased, who had been a second father to her.

After the lapse of a few months a splendid monument was erected on

which might be read this inscription in letters of gold:—
HERE LIES THE HIGH AND NOBLE LORD,
MICHAEL TIMAR LEVETINCZY.

Privy Councilor, President of Committees, Knight of the Orders of St. Stephen, St. Maurice, and the Annunciata. The great Patriot, the True Christian, the Exemplary Husband, the Father of the Poor, Guardian of the Orphan, Supporter of Schools, a Pillar of the Church.

Regretted by all who knew him, eternally mourned by his
FAITHFUL WIFE TIMÉA.

On the granite pedestal stands a marble statue of a woman bearing a funeral urn. Every one says this statue is a faithful likeness of Timéa.

And Timéa goes every day to the burial-ground to deck the grass with fresh wreaths, and to water the flowers which smell so sweetly within the railings of the tomb: she waters them with showers of cold water—and burning tears.

Theodor Krisstyan could never have dreamed that he would be so highly honored after his death.

CHAPTER VIII.
DODI'S LETTER.

A year and a half passed away since Michael came home to the ownerless island. He had not left it for a single day.

Great events had occurred during this interval. Dodi had learned to write. What joy when the little dunce made his first attempt with chalk on a board: the letters are dictated to him—"write *l* and *ó*, and then pronounce them both together." He was surprised that that meant *ló* (Hungarian for horse), and yet he had not drawn a horse. A year later he could address a birthday letter to his mother in beautiful copper-plate on white paper—it was a greater achievement than Cleopatra's Needle, covered with hieroglyphics.

When Dodi's first letter was fluttering in Noémi's hand, she said, with a tear in her eye, to Michael, "He will write like you."

"Where have you seen my handwriting?" asked Michael, in surprise.

"In the copies you set Dodi, to begin with; and then too in the contract by which you gave us the island. Have you forgotten?"

"Yes; it is so long ago."

"And do you not write to any one now?"

"No one."

"You have not left the island for a year and a half; have you nothing to do now out in the world?"

"No. And I shall never have anything to do there again."

"What will become of your business then?"

"Would you like to know?"

"Yes, indeed. The thought troubles me that a clever man like you should be shut up here in the narrow bounds of this island, and only because you love us: if you have no other reason for staying here always except your great love for us, it pains me."

"It is well, Noémi. I will tell you then who I was out there in the world, what I did there, and why I stay here. You shall know all: when you have put the boy to bed, come to me on the veranda and I will tell you everything. You will shudder and wonder over what you will hear; but in the

374

end you will forgive me, as God forgave me when He sent me here."

After supper Noémi put Dodi to bed, and then came out to Michael, sat beside him on the bench, and leaned on his breast. The full moon shone down on them between the leaves: it was now no longer the ghostly star, the ice-paradise of suicides, but a kind acquaintance and friend. And then Michael told Noémi all that had befallen him out in the world.

The sudden death of the mysterious passenger, the sinking of the ship and the concealed treasures: how he had married Timéa. He described her sorrow and her suffering; he spoke of Timéa to Noémi as of a saint; and when he described faithfully the nocturnal scene when he had watched Timéa from his hiding-place, and how the woman had defended her husband against evil report, against her own beloved, and against her own heart, how Noémi sobbed and how her tears flowed for Timéa!

And then Michael described to her what he had suffered in the fearful situation from which he could not free himself, having on one side the ties of his worldly position, his riches, and Timéa's fidelity; while his love, his happiness, and every aspiration of his soul drew him in another direction. How sweetly Noémi consoled him with her soft kisses! . . .

When, finally, he told her of the awful night in which the adventurer appeared at his lonely castle, of how despair had led him to the brink of the grave, and how, as he looked down into the waves, instead of his own face mirrored in the water, the dead face of his enemy emerged from the depths, and God's hand suddenly closed before his eyes the opening of the icy tomb—oh! how passionately Noémi pressed him to her breast, as if to hold him back from falling into the grave.

"Now you know what I have left behind in the world, and what I have found here. Can you forgive me for what you have suffered and for all my offenses against you?" Noémi's tears and kisses replied.

The confession had lasted long: the short summer's night was over, and it was daylight when Michael concluded the story of his life.

He was forgiven. "My guilt is obliterated," said Michael. "Timéa had recovered her freedom and her wealth. The vagabond had on my clothes and carried my pocket-book away with him: they will bury his body as if it were mine, and Timéa is a widow. I have given you my soul, and you have accepted it. Now all is equal."

Noémi took Michael's arm and led him into the room where the boy was asleep. He awoke under their kisses, opened his eyes, and when he saw that it was morning, he knelt up in his little bed, and with folded hands offered his morning prayer: "Dear Lord, bless my good father and my dear mother!"

"All is forgiven, Michael! . . . One angel prays for you beside your bed, the other at your grave, that you may be happy."

Noémi dressed little Dodi, and then her eyes rested thoughtfully on Michael. She wanted time to realize all she had heard from him, but women have quick perceptions.

Suddenly Noémi said to her husband, "Michael, you have still one duty to fulfill in the world."

"What duty, and to whom?"

"You owe Timéa the secret that other woman revealed to you."

"What secret?"

"About the door which leads into her room from the secret passage. You must tell her of it. Some one might get in to her when she is asleep and alone."

"But no one knows of this secret passage except Athalie."

"Is that not enough?"

"What do you mean?"

"Michael, you little know us women. You don't know what Athalie is, but I can guess. My tears flowed for Timéa, because she is so wretched because she does not love you, and you are mine; but if she felt for you what she feels for that other man, and if you spurned me for her sake, as that man did Athalie, then may God keep me from ever seeing her asleep and in my power!"

"Noémi, you frighten me."

"That is what women are. Did you never know it. Hasten to reveal this secret to Timéa. I want her to be happy."

Michael kissed Noémi on the brow. "You darling child! I dare not write to Timéa, for she would recognize my writing; and then she could not be my widow, nor I your husband returned from the dead, and ascended into the paradise of your love."

"Then I will write to her."

"No, no, no! I won't allow it. I have heaped gold and diamonds upon her, but she shall not have a word from you; that is one of my own treasures. I brought Noémi nothing of Timéa's, and I will not give Timéa anything of Noémi's. You shall not write her a word."

"Well, then," said Noémi, smiling, "I know another who can write to Timéa. Dodi shall write the letter."

Timar burst out laughing. There was a world of humor, of child-like simplicity, happy pride, and deep emotion in the idea. Little Dodi will write to warn Timéa of her danger. Dodi to Timéa! . . . Timar smiled with tears in his eyes. But Noémi was in earnest; she wrote the copy, and Dodi wrote the important lines on ruled paper, without a mistake. Of course he had no idea what he was writing. Noémi gave him a lovely violet ink, a decoction of marsh-mallow, and sealed the letter with white wax; and as there was no seal in the house, nor even a coin which could serve for one, Dodi caught a pretty golden-green beetle, and stuck it on the wax, instead of a coat of arms. The letter was given to the fruit-dealer to take to the post.

Little Dodi's letter went off to Timéa.

CHAPTER IX.
"YOU STUPID CREATURE!"

The lovely widow was in the deepest mourning. She went nowhere, and received no visitors.

More than a year had passed since her husband's burial.

Timéa had another name in the calendar—Susanna. Her first name came from her mother, who was a Greek; but the second she had received at her baptism. This she used when she had to sign documents, and St. Susanna's day was considered her *fête*.

In provincial towns the *fête*-days are scrupulously kept. Relations and friends come without invitation, as a matter of course, to visit the person whose *fête* it is, and meet with a hospitable reception. Some noble families, however, have adopted the custom of sending invitations to these family-parties, by which it is made evident that those who do not receive cards may keep their congratulations to themselves.

There are two St. Susannas in the year. Timéa chose the one whose *fête* fell in winter, because then her husband used to be at home, and invitations were sent out a week beforehand. Of the other name no notice was taken. Timéa was not in the calendar of Komorn, nor even in the national Pesth calendar, and at that time there were no others in the province; so he who wanted to know Timéa's own *fête*-day must search far and wide.

It fell in the merry month of May. At that season Herr Timar would have been long away on his journeys; nevertheless, Timéa received every May a lovely bouquet of white roses on the day of St. Timéa. Who sent it was not stated; it came by post, packed in a box.

As long as Timar lived, Herr Katschuka had invariably received invitations to the Sunday receptions, which he as regularly answered by depositing his card at the door: he never came to the parties. This year the *fête*-day party had been omitted, as the faithful Susanna was in mourning. On the morning of the lovely May day on which Timéa's beautiful white-rose bouquet usually arrived, a servant in mourning livery brought a letter to Katschuka. On opening the envelope the major found a printed invitation-card inside, which bore the name, not of Susanna, but of Timéa Levetinczy, and had reference to that very day. Herr Katschuka was puzzled. What a curious notion of Timéa! To draw the attention of all Komorn to the fact that Susanna, a good Calvinist, was keeping the day of the Greek saint Timéa, and the more because she only sent out her invitations the same morning! It was an outrageous breach of etiquette. Herr Katschuka felt that this time he must accept. In the evening he took care not to be among the earliest arrivals. The time named was half past eight; he waited till half past nine, and then went. As he laid aside his cloak and sword in the anteroom, he asked the servant whether many visitors had arrived. The servant said no one had come yet. The major was startled. Probably the other guests had taken the shortness of the invitation badly, and decided not to appear; and he was confirmed in this idea when, on entering the saloon, he found the chandeliers lighted and all the rooms brilliantly illuminated—a sign that a large assembly was expected. The servant informed him that his mistress was in the inner room.

"Who is with her?"

"She is alone. Fraülein Athalie has gone with her mamma to Herr Fabula's house—there is a great fish-dinner there."

Herr Katschuka did not know what to think: not only were there no other guests, but even the people of the house had left the mistress alone. Timéa awaited him in her own sitting-room.

And for this grand party, amid all this splendor, Timéa was dressed entirely in black. She celebrated her *fête*-day in mourning: amid the radiance of the golden lusters and the silver candelabra a black mourning-dress, which, however, was not suited to the face of its wearer. On her lips hovered a charming smile, and a soft color lay on her cheeks. She received her single guest most cordially. "Oh, how late you are," she said, as she gave him her hand.

The major pressed upon it a respectful kiss. "On the contrary, I fear I am the first."

"Not at all. All I invited have already arrived."

"Where?" asked the major, in astonishment.

"In the dining-room—they are at table, and only waiting for you."

379

With these words she took the arm of the wondering man, led him to the folding-doors, and threw them open; and then, indeed, the major knew not what to think. The dining-room was brilliantly lighted with wax candles; a long table was spread with places for eleven, and the same number of chairs were placed round it, but no one was there—not a single creature. But as the major threw a glance round he began to comprehend, and the clearer the riddle grew, the more his eyes were dimmed with tears. Before each of nine of the places stood a white-rose bouquet under a glass shade—the last of freshly gathered flowers; the roses of the others were dry, faded, and yellow.

"Look, they are all there which greeted me on Timéa's *fête*-day year after year—these are my birthday guests. There are nine of them. Will you be the tenth? Then all whom I have invited will have assembled."

The major, in speechless delight, pressed the lovely hand to his lips "My poor roses—"

Timéa did not refuse him that privilege—possibly she would have allowed even more; but the widow's cap stood in the way, and Timéa felt it.

"Do you want me to exchange this cap for another?"

"From that day I shall begin to live again."

"Let us set apart for it my own *fête*-day, which every one knows."

"Oh, but that is so far off."

"Don't be alarmed, there is a St. Susanna in the summer; we will keep her day."

"But that is distant too."

"It is not an eternity to wait till then. Have you not learned patience? Remember, I want time to get used to happiness—it does not come all at once; and we can see each other every day till then—at first for a minute, and then for two, and then forever. Is it agreed?"

The major could not refuse, she begged so sweetly.

"And now the banquet is over," whispered Timéa; "the other guests are going to sleep, and you must go home too. But wait a moment—I will give you back a word from your last birthday congratulations." She took from the fresh rose-bouquet one bud, touched it hardly perceptibly with her lips, and placed it in the major's button-hole; but he pressed the rose, this "one word," to his lips and kissed it. . . .

When the major had gone, and looked up from the street at the windows of the Levetinczy house, all was dark. He was the last to leave.

Timéa learned gradually the art of growing used to hope and happiness—she had a good teacher. Thenceforward, Herr Katschuka came every day to the house; but the major did not keep to the prescribed arithmetical progression—first one minute, then two. The wedding was fixed for the day of St. Susanna, in August. Athalie too, it appeared, had resigned herself to her fate. Herr Fabula's wife was dead, and she accepted his hand; it is not unusual for a pretty girl to give herself to a rich widower—one knows how he treats his wife, and one runs less risk in taking him than some young dandy who has not yet sown his wild oats. Heaven bless their union!

Timéa proposed to give Athalie, as a dowry, the sum which Michael had offered her, and which she had refused. Every one thought she was trying to become a suitable wife for Herr Fabula. But Katschuka was not deceived; he saw through her black heart. He knew what he had done to Athalie, and the reckoning she had against Timéa, and destiny never leaves such a score unsettled. Have you forgotten, you lovely white woman, that this other girl was mistress here when you came; that she was a rich and honored bride, wooed by men and envied by women? And from the moment when the water cast you on these shores, misfortune followed her—she was made a beggar, brought to shame, spurned by her betrothed. It was not your fault, but it was owing to you—you brought bad luck; it sat on your forehead, between your meeting eyebrows, and brought the ship to destruction, and the house in which you set foot; it ruins those who injure you, as well as those who set you free. And you are not afraid to sleep under the same roof with Athalie—this roof!

Since Katschuka came to the house, Athalie had controlled herself, and treated even her mother kindly. She made tea for her which Frau Sophie liked, especially with plenty of rum in it—she made it herself; and was very good to the servants too, treating them also to tea, which, for the men-servants, almost might have been called punch; they could not say enough for her. Frau Sophie guessed the reason of all this kindness—those servile natures always look for a reason if they receive a favor, and repay it with suspicion.

"My daughter is currying favor with me, that I may go with her when she marries; she knows nothing of housekeeping—she can't even make milk-soup. That's why I am 'Dear mamma' all over the place, and get tea every night; as if I did not know what is in my daughter Athalie's mind!" She will soon know even more.

Athalie carried her submissiveness to servility, in the presence of Timéa and the major. Neither by look nor manner did she betray her former claims. When he came, she opened the door with a smile, showed him in to Timéa, politely took part in the conversation, and, when she left the room, she might be heard singing next door. She had adopted the manners of a maid-servant.

Once Timéa asked her to play a duet, on which Athalie said modestly, that she had forgotten her music—the only instrument she could play on now was the chopping-board. Since the great catastrophe, Athalie only played the piano when she knew no one could hear.

Do not your nerves shudder when this woman looks you in the face? does not your blood run cold when she stoops to kiss your hand? when she laces your boots, is it not as if a snake wound round your foot? and when she fills your glass, does it not occur to you to look what may be in it? No, no, Timéa has no suspicions; she is so kind, she treats Athalie like a sister; she has prepared a dowry of a hundred thousand gulden, and told Athalie so. She wished to make her happy, and thought she could console her for the loss of her first betrothed. And why should she not think so? Athalie herself refused him. When Timar offered her the money she said, "I will never have anything to do with the man again, either in this world or the next." Timéa did not know of the visit Athalie had paid by night to her betrothed, when she was sent away by him alone and rejected; and Timéa did not know that a woman will give up the man she hates to another woman, even less willingly than the one she loves; that a woman's hate is only love turned to poison, but still remains love. Katschuka, however, well remembered that nocturnal meeting, and therefore he trembled for Timéa, but dared not tell her so.

Only one day was wanting to the *fête* of St. Susanna. Timéa had gradually laid aside her mourning, as if it was hard to separate from it entirely and as if she wished to learn gladness slowly. First she allowed white lace at her neck; then she changed black for dark gray, and silk for wool; then white stripes appeared in the gray; and at last only the cap remained of the mourning for Michael Levetinczy. This also will disappear on the *fête*-day; the beautiful Valenciennes cap of the young wife is already made, and must be tried on.

An unlucky fit of vanity induced Timéa to wait to do this till the major arrived. For a young widow the lace cap is what the orange-blossoms are to a girl. But the major was late because the white-rose bouquet was late in arriving from Vienna: this was the second *fête*-day bouquet in one year. A whole shoal of letters and notes of congratulation had arrived for Timéa, who had many acquaintances far and near. Timéa had not opened a single one; they lay in a heap in a silver basket on the table, many of them directed by children, for Timéa had a hundred and forty god-children in the town among the orphan boys and girls. She would have enjoyed these naïve letters, but her thoughts were otherwise occupied.

"Look what a comical one this is!" said Athalie, taking up one of the letters; "instead of a seal, there is a beetle stuck on the wax."

"And what curious ink it is!" remarked Timéa. "Put it with the others—we will read it to-morrow."

Some secret voice whispered to Timéa that she had better read it to-day. It was Dodi's letter which was put aside.

But see, here comes the major; then all the hundred and forty god-children and their letters were forgotten, and Timéa ran to meet him. Nine years ago the fortunate bridegroom had brought a splendid red-rose bouquet to another bride.

And she too was present; and possibly the great mirror into which Athalie had cast her last glance on her bridal dress was the same which now stood there.

Timéa took the lovely white bouquet from the major's hand, put it in a splendid Sèvres vase, and whispered to him, "Now I will give you something: it will never be yours, but always mine, and yet it is a present for you." The pretty enigma issued from its box—it was the lace cap.

"Oh, how charming!" cried the major, taking it in his hand. "Shall I try it on you?" The major's words died on his lips—he looked at Athalie.

Timéa stood before the glass with childish pleasure, and took off her widow's cap; then she grew grave, put it to her lips and kissed it, while she said low and brokenly, "Poor Michael!"—and so she laid aside the last token of her widowhood.

Herr Katschuka was holding the white cap.

"Give it me that I may try it on."

"Can I help you?"

The hair was then dressed very high, so that Timéa required assistance.

"You don't know how; Athalie will be so good."

Timéa spoke quite simply, but the major shuddered at the pallor which overflowed Athalie's face at the words: he remembered how Athalie had once said to Timéa, "Come and put on my bridal veil!" And perhaps even she had not then thought what venom lay in the words. Athalie came to Timéa to help her with the cap, which required to be fastened with pins on both sides. Athalie's hand trembled—and she pricked Timéa's head with one of the pins.

"Oh, you stupid creature!" cried Timéa, jerking her head aside.

The same words, before the same man!

Timéa did not notice, but Herr Katschuka saw what a flash flew over Athalie's face—a volcanic outburst of diabolical rage, a glow of flaming spite, a dark cloud of purple shame; the muscles quivered as if the face was a nest of snakes stirred up by a rod. What murderous eyes! What compressed lips! What a bottomless depth of passion in that single look. Timéa regretted her hasty word almost before it had passed her lips, and hastened to atone for it. "Don't be angry, dear 'Thaly; I forgot myself," she said, turning to kiss her. "You'll forgive me—you are not angry?"

The next moment Athalie was as humble as a maid who has done some damage, and began in a flattering tone, "Oh, my dear pretty Timéa, don't *you* be angry; I would not hurt your dear little head for the world. How sweet you look in your cap, just like a fairy!" And she kissed Timéa's shoulder.

A shudder ran through the major's nerves.

CHAPTER X.
ATHALIE.

The eve of the *fête*-day was also the eve of the wedding—a night of excitement. The bride and bridegroom were sitting together in Timéa's room—they had so much to talk about.

What do they say? Flowers only can understand flower-speech, the stars the language of the spheres, one pillar of Memnon answers another, the dead comprehend the Walkyrie, sleep-walkers the speech of the moon—lovers only the language of love. And he who has ever known this sacred emotion will not profane it, but guard it like a secret of the confessional. Neither the wise king in his marvelous song, nor Ovid in his love elegies, nor Hafiz in his ardent lays, nor Heine in his poems, nor Petöfi in his "Pearls of Love," can describe it—it remains one of the secrets of eternity.

At the back of the house was a noisy company—all the household. This had been a busy day with preparations for the morrow's feast—a culinary campaign; the press of work had lasted till late at night: then, when all had been roasted and iced according to orders, Frau Sophie found time to show herself liberal. She called together her staff, and bestowed upon them all the good things which had suffered during the heat of the fray—for this was unavoidable: what ought to have risen had sunk into a pancake; what ought to have jellied had melted into soup; here a cake had stuck to the mold and would not turn out whole; there a scrap, a cutting, a ham-bone, a piece of hare, a drumstick of pheasant remained over. All which could not be sent up to table was left as a rare tidbit for the servants, and they could boast of having tasted everything before the gentry were served.

But where was Athalie?

The whispering lovers thought she was with her mother, amusing herself in the kitchen. There, they thought she was of course with the bridal pair, and enjoying the bliss of being a silent witness of their happiness—or perhaps no one thought of her at all. And yet it might have been well if some one had interrupted themselves to ask, "Where is Athalie?"

She sat alone in the room where she had seen Timéa for the first time. The old furniture had long been replaced by new; only one embroidered stool remained as a remembrance. Athalie was sitting on it when Timar entered, in company with the pale maiden. There sat Katschuka, at work on Athalie's portrait, over which, while he gazed at Timéa, his pencil drew a long line. Athalie sat alone there now. The portrait had long ago gone to the lumber-room; but Athalie seems to see it still, and the young lieutenant who begged her with his flattering tongue to smile a little and not to look so haughty.

The room was dark; only the moon shone in, but it would soon go down behind the gable of the tall church of St. Andrew.

Athalie reviewed the horrid dream called life. There were wealth, pride, and happiness in it: flatterers had called her the prettiest girl in Komorn, the queen, and pretended to adore her; then came a child by chance into the house—a ridiculous creature, a lifeless shadow, a cold doll, made to be an object of ridicule, to pass the time away by pushing it about. And only two years later, this vagrant, this white phantom, this reptile, was mistress of the house, and conquered hearts, turning a shipping-clerk, by the magic of her marble face, into his master's powerful enemy, into a millionaire, and causing the betrothed bridegroom to be false to his troth.

What a wedding-day was that! The bride, recovering from her swoon, found herself lying alone on the ground. And when splendor and homage were at an end, she longed still to be loved—loved in secret and in concealment. This too was denied her.

What a memory was that!—the path she had trodden to the house of her former lover and back again, twice in the darkness! her vain expectation next day! how she had counted the strokes of the clock, amidst the noise of the auction! And he never came! Then long years of painful dissimulation, of disguised humiliation! There was only one person who understood her—who knew that the balm of her heart was to see her rival share her passion, and fade away under it.

And the one man who knew to his cost what Athalie really was—the only hinderance to Timéa's happiness, the finder of the philosopher's stone which exercises everywhere a malevolent spell—that one man finds his death

386

by a single false step on the ice!

And then happiness comes back to the house, and no one is miserable but herself. In many a sleepless night the bitter cup had filled drop by drop up to the brim; only one was wanting to make it overflow; and that last drop was the insulting word, "You stupid creature!" To be scolded like a maid, humbled in his presence! Athalie's limbs shook with fever. What was now going on in the house? They were preparing for the morrow's wedding. In the boudoir whispered the betrothed couple; from the kitchen, even through all the doors, came the noise of the merry-making servants.

But Athalie never heard the cheerful din: she heard only the whisper. . . . She had something to do during the night. . . . There was no light in the room; but the moon shone in, and gave light enough to open a box and read the names of the poisons inside it—the unfailing drugs of an Eastern poisoner. Athalie chose among them, and smiled to herself. What a good jest it would be if to-morrow, at the moment of drinking some toast, the words should die on the lips of the feasting guests! if each saw the face of his neighbor turn yellow and green; if they all sprung up crying for help, and began a demoniac dance, fit to make the devil laugh; if the bride's lovely face petrified into real marble, and the proud bridegroom made grimaces like a skull!

Ping! . . . A string gone in the piano! Athalie started so that she dropped what she held, and her hands twitched convulsively. It was only a string, coward! Are you so weak? She put back the poisons in her box, leaving out only one, and that not a deadly poison, only a sleeping-draught. The first idea had not satisfied her; that triumph would not suffice: it would not be sufficient revenge for "You stupid creature!" The tiger cares not for a corpse, he must have warm blood. Some one will have to take poison, but that is only herself—a poison not to be bought at the chemist's: it lies in the eye of St. George's dragon. She slipped noiselessly out to go to the hiding-place whence a view of Timéa's room could be obtained. The sweet murmurs and the caressing looks of the lovers will be the poison she must absorb in order to be fully prepared.

The major was about to take leave, and held Timéa's hand in his. Her cheeks were so rosy! Was any more deadly poison needed? They did not speak of love, and yet no third person had a right to listen. The bridegroom asked questions allowed to no one else. "Do you sleep alone here?" he asked, with tender curiosity, lifting the silken hangings of the bed.

"Yes, since I became a widow."

"(And before too," whispered Athalie, behind the dragon.)

The bridegroom, availing himself of his privileges, pursued his researches in the bride's room.

"Where does this door lead to?"

"Into an anteroom where my lady visitors take off their cloaks; you came that way when you visited me the first time."

"And the other little door?"

"Oh, never mind that—it only leads to my dressing-room."

"Has it no exit?"

"None; the water comes by a pipe from the kitchen, and flows away by a tap to the basement."

"And this third door?"

"You know that is the corridor by which you reach the principal entrance."

"And where are the servants at night?"

"The females sleep near the kitchen, and the men in the basement. Over my bed hang two bell-ropes, of which one goes to the women's room and the other to the men's."

"There is no one in the adjoining room?"

"There Sister Athalie and Mamma Sophie sleep."

"Frau Sophie too?"

"Yes, to be sure. You want to know everything. To-morrow it will all be differently arranged."

("To-morrow?")

"And do you lock the door when you go to bed?"

"Never. Why should I? All my servants love me, and are trustworthy; the front door is barred, and I am safe here."

"Is there nowhere a secret entrance to this room?"

"Ha! ha! You seem to take my house for a mysterious Venetian palace!"

("Is it your house? Did you build it?")

"Do, to please me, lock all your doors before you go to bed."

("He seems to guess what we shall all be dreaming of to-night.")

Timéa smiled, and smoothed away the frown from the bridegroom's grave face.

"Well, then, for your sake I will lock all my doors to-night."

("See that they are secure," whispered the dragon.)

Then followed a tender embrace and a long, long kiss.

"Do you pray, my beloved?"

"No; for the good God in whom I believe watches ever."

("How if He slept to-day?")

"Forgive me, dearest Timéa; skepticism does not become a woman. Her adornment is piety; leave the rest to men. Pray to-night."

"You know I was a Moslem, and was never taught to pray."

"But now you are a Christian, and our prayers are beautiful. Take your prayer-book to-night."

"Yes, for your sake I will learn to pray."

The major found in the book of devotion Timar had once given his wife, the "prayer for brides."

"I will learn it by heart to-night."

"Yes, do so—do so!"

Timéa read it aloud. Athalie felt a diabolical rage in her heart. The man will be discovering the secret in the wall; he will keep Timéa up praying all night. Curses, curses on the prayer-book!

When the major left the anteroom, Athalie was already there. Timéa called from her room to light the major to the door, thinking there would be a servant there as usual; but to-day, as we know, they were engaged in anticipating the morrow's feast. Athalie took the candle which stood outside, and lighted the major along the dark passage. The happy bridegroom had no eyes for any other woman's face—he saw only Timéa, and thought it was the maid-servant who opened the door for him. He wished to be generous, and pressed a silver thaler into Athalie's hand; then he started as he recognized the voice.

"I kiss your hand, kind sir."

"Is it you, fraülein? A thousand pardons! I did not recognize you in the darkness."

"No consequence, Herr Major."

"Pardon my blindness, and give me back the insulting present, I beg."

Athalie drew back with a mocking bow, hiding the hand which held the thaler behind her. "I will give it you back to-morrow—leave it with me till then; I have fairly earned it."

Herr Katschuka swore at his stupidity. The inexplicable load he felt on his spirits seemed to have redoubled in weight. When he reached the street, he felt it impossible to go home, but went toward the main guard and said to the officer on duty, "My friend, I invite you to my wedding to-morrow; be so good as to let me share your watch to-night—let us go the rounds together."

In the servants' hall there was great fun. As the major had rung for the porter when he left, the mistress was known to be alone, and her maid went up to ask for orders. Timéa thought she was the one who had shown the major out, and told her to go to bed—she would undress herself; so the maid went back to the others.

"If only we had a drop of punch now," said the porter, thrusting the door-key into his pocket.

As if by magic, the door opened, and in came Fraülein Athalie, bearing a tray of steaming glasses, which clinked cheerfully together. "Long live our dear young lady!" cried every one. Athalie set the tray on the table with a smile. Among the glasses stood a basin full of sugar well rubbed over

390

with orange rind, which made it yellow and aromatic. Frau Sophie liked her tea made in that way, with plenty of rum and orange-sugar. "Are you not going to join us?" she asked her daughter.

"Thanks; I had my tea with our gracious lady. My head aches, and I shall go to bed." She wished her mother good-night, and told the servants to go to bed in good time, as they must get up early next day. They fell eagerly on the punch, and found it perfectly delicious. Only Frau Sophie did not like it. When she had tasted the first spoonful, she turned up her nose. "This tastes just like the poppy-syrup that bad nurses give the wakeful babies at night." It was so unpleasant to her that she could not take any more, but gave it to the cook's boy, who had never tasted anything so good before. She said she was tired with her day's work, and conjured the household not to oversleep themselves, and to take care no cat got into the larder; then she said good-night, and followed Athalie.

When she entered their bedroom, Athalie was already in bed. The curtains were drawn; she knew Athalie's way of turning her back to the room and putting her head under the clothes. She hastened to get into bed.

But she could not get rid of the taste of that single spoonful of punch, which spoiled her enjoyment of the whole supper. After she had put out the light, she leaned on her elbow and looked toward the figure in the other bed. She looked, till at last her eyes closed and she fell asleep. Her dreams carried her back to the servants' hall. She seemed to see them all asleep there—the coachman stretched on the long bench, the footman with his head on the table, the groom on the ground, using an overturned chair as a pillow, the cook on the settle, the house-maid on the hearth, and the cook's boy under the table. Before each his empty glass; she alone had not drunk hers. She dreamed that Athalie, with bare feet and in her night-dress, crept up behind her and said in her ear, "Why don't you drink your punch, dear mamma? Do you want more sugar?" and filled the glass with sugar up to the brim. But she noticed the repulsive smell. "I don't want it!" she said in her dream. However, Athalie held the steaming glass to her mouth. She turned away, and pushed the glass from her, and with that movement she upset the bottle of water which stood on the table beside her, and all the water poured into the bed. That thoroughly awoke her.

391

And still she seemed to see Athalie before her with threatening looks. "Are you awake, Athalie?" she asked, uneasily; no answer. She listened; the sleeper could not be heard to breathe. Sophie got up and went to Athalie's bed; it was empty. She could not trust her eyes in the dim twilight, and felt with her hands: no one there. "Athalie, where are you?" she murmured, anxiously. Receiving no answer, a nameless horror numbed her limbs. She felt blind and dumb; she could not even scream. She listened, and then fancied she was deaf: neither inside nor out was there the faintest sound. Where could Athalie be?

Athalie was in the secret room—she had been there a long time.

The patience of that woman, to be so long learning the prayer by heart! At last Timéa shut the book and sighed deeply. Then she took the candle and looked to see that all the doors were locked. She looked behind the curtains; her bridegroom's words had implanted fear in her breast, and she looked round carefully to see if any one could get in. Then she went to the dressing-table, took down her plaits, wound her thick hair round and round her head, and put a net over it. She was not free from vanity, this young creature: that her hands and arms might be white, she rubbed them with salve and put on long gloves. Then she undressed, but before she lay down she went behind the bed, opened a closet, and took out a sword-hilt with a broken blade; looking tenderly at it, she pressed it to her breast. Then she put it under her pillow; she always slept with it there. Athalie saw it all. Timéa extinguished the light, and Athalie saw no more; she only heard the clock tick, and had the patience to wait.

She guesses when sleep will close Timéa's eyes—that is the time. A quarter of an hour seems like an eternity; at last the clock strikes one. The picture of St. George with his dragon (which is by no means dead) moves aside, and Athalie comes out, barefoot, so that no sound is heard. It is quite dark in the room—the shutters are shut and curtains drawn; her groping hand finds Timéa's pillow; she feels underneath, and a cold object meets her hand. It is the sword-hilt. What hell-fire runs through her veins from the cold steel! she too presses it to her heart. She draws the edge of the blade through her lips and feels how sharp it is. But it is too dark to see the sleeper—one can not even hear her gentle breathing; the blow must be well aimed, and

Athalie bends her head to listen.

The sleeper moves, and sighs aloud in her dream, "Oh, my God!" Then Athalie strikes in the direction of the sigh. But the blow was not mortal: Timéa had covered her head with her right arm, and the sword only hit that, though the sharp steel cut through the glove and wounded her hand. She started up and rose on her knees in the bed; then a second blow caught her head, but the thick hair blunted it, and the sword only cut the forehead down to the eyebrow.

Now Timéa seized the blade with her left hand. "Murderer!" she screamed, sprung out of bed, and while the sharp edge cut the inside of her left hand, she caught the enemy with her wounded right hand by the hair. She felt it was a woman's, and now knew who was before her.

There are critical moments in which the mind traverses a chain of thought with lightning speed: this is Athalie; her mother is next door; they want to murder her out of revenge and jealousy; it would be vain to call for help, it is a struggle for life. Timéa screamed no more, but collected all her strength in order, with her wounded hand, to draw down her enemy's head and get the murderous weapon from her.

Timéa was strong, and a murderer never puts forth his full strength. They struggled silently in the darkness, the carpet deadening their footfalls. Suddenly a cry sounded from the next room. "Murder!" screamed the voice of Frau Sophie: at the sound Athalie's strength gave way.

Her victim's blood streamed over her face. In the next room was heard the sound of falling glass; through the broken window Frau Sophie's screeching voice was heard resounding down the quiet street, "Murder, murder!"

Athalie let go the sword in terror, and put up both hands to loosen Timéa's fingers from her hair: now she is the one attacked and she the one alarmed. When she got her hair free, she pushed Timéa away, flew to the opening of the hiding-place, and drew the picture gently over the entrance.

Timéa tottered forward a few steps with the sword in her hand, and then fell swooning on the carpet.

At Frau Sophie's cry, double-quick march was heard in the street—the patrol was coming—the major was the first to reach the house.

Frau Sophie knew him and called out, "Quick, quick! they are killing Timéa!" The major tore at the bell, thundered at the door, but no one came; the soldiers tried to burst it in, but it was too strong and would not give way. "Wake the servants," shouted the major. Frau Sophie ran, with the courage born of great fear, through the dark rooms and passages, knocking up against doors and furniture, till she came to the servants' rooms. Her dream had come true. The whole household lay asleep: a burned-down candle flickered on the table, and threw uncanny shadows on the grotesque group.

"There are murderers in the house!" screamed Frau Sophie, in a voice quivering with terror; the only answer was a heavy snore. She shook some of the sleepers, called them by name, but they only sunk back without waking up. Blows could be heard on the house door. The porter too was asleep, but the key was in his pocket; Frau Sophie got it out with great difficulty, and ran through the dark passages, down the dark stairs, and along the dark hall to open the door, while the fearful thought went with her—how if she were to meet the murderer? and an even more frightful doubt pursued her—suppose she should recognize that murderer?

At last she got to the door, found the key-hole, and opened it. A bright light burst in—there was the military patrol and the town-watchmen with their lanterns. The captain of the guard had come, and the nearest army-surgeon, all only half dressed in the first clothes they could find, with a pistol or a naked sword in their hand.

Herr Katschuka rushed up the steps straight to the door which led to Timéa's room—it was locked on the inside: he put his shoulder against it and burst the lock.

Timéa lay before him on the ground, covered with blood, and unconscious. The major raised her and carried her to the bed. The surgeon examined the wounds, and said none of them was dangerous, the lady had only fainted. As soon as his anxiety for his beloved one was relieved, the thirst for vengeance awoke in the major—"Where is the murderer?" "Singular," said the officer; "all the doors were locked inside—how could any one get in, and how could he get out?" Nowhere was there a suspicious mark; even the instrument of murder, the broken sword, a treasure kept by Timéa herself, and generally put away in a velvet box, lay blood-stained on the

394

ground. The official physician now arrived: "Let us examine the servants." They all lay sound asleep, and the doctor found that none of them was shamming: they were all drugged. Who could have done it?

Her mother gazed at him in silence and could not answer. She did not know. The captain opened the door of Athalie's room, and they all went in, Frau Sophie following half fainting; she knew the bed must be empty.

Athalie was in bed and asleep. Her white night-dress was buttoned up to her neck, her hair fastened into an embroidered cap, her lovely hands lay on the quilt. Face and hands were clean, and she slept.

Frau Sophie leaned stupefied against the wall when she saw Athalie. "She too has been drugged," said the doctor.

The army-surgeon came up and felt her pulse: it was calm. No muscle moved on her face, no quiver betrayed her consciousness.

She could deceive every one by her marvelous self-control; all but one—the man whose beloved she had tried to murder.

"Is she really asleep?" asked the major.

"Feel her hand," said the doctor; "it is quite cool and calm."

Athalie felt the major take hold of her hand. "But just look, doctor," said he; "if you look closely you will see under the nails of this beautiful hand—fresh blood!"

At these words Athalie's fingers suddenly clinched, and the major felt as if eagle's claws were running into his hand. She laughed aloud and threw off the bedclothes. Completely dressed, she sprung up, looked the astonished men proudly up and down, cast a triumphant glance at the major, and threw a contemptuous look at her mother.

The poor woman could not bear it, and sunk fainting to the ground.

CHAPTER XI.
THE LAST STAB.

In the archives of the Komorn Court, one of the most interesting trials is that of Athalie Brazovics. The woman's defense was masterly; she denied everything, knew how to disprove everything, and when they thought they had caught her, she managed to throw such mystery over it all, that her judges knew not where to have her. Why should she murder Timéa? She was herself engaged, and had good prospects, while Timéa was her benefactress, and had promised her a rich dowry.

Then, too, no traces of the murder could be found except in Timéa's room. Nowhere was a bloody rag or handkerchief to be found—not even the ashes of anything which could have been burned. Who had drugged the servants could not be ascertained. The household had supped together, and among the various sweets and foreign fruits there might have been something which stupefied them. Not a drop of the suspected punch was to be found; even the glasses which had held it were all washed out when the patrol entered.

Athalie maintained that she also had taken something that evening which tasted peculiar, and that she had fallen so fast asleep that she neither heard her mother's cry nor the noises afterward, and only awoke when the major touched her hand. The one person who had found her bed empty half an hour before was her own mother, who could not give evidence against her. Her strongest point was that Timéa had locked all the doors, and was found insensible. How could a murderer get in and get out again? And if there had been an attempt to murder, why should she be suspected more than the rest?

The major remained with Timéa till late at night; perhaps if he left, some one might creep into the room again. They did not even know whether the assassin was man or woman. The only one who knew, Timéa, did not betray it, but kept to her assertion that she could not remember anything about it; her alarm had been so great that everything had faded from her memory like a dream.

She could not accuse Athalie, and was not even confronted with her.

Timéa was still crippled by her wounds, which healed slowly; but the shock to her nerves was more serious than the bodily injury, and she trembled for Athalie. Since that dreadful night she was never left alone—a doctor and a nurse watched her by turns. By day the major hardly left her side, and the magistrate often visited her in order to cross-examine her; but as soon as Athalie was mentioned, Timéa was silent, and not another word could be extracted from her.

The doctor advised at last that she should hear some amusing reading aloud. Timéa had left her bed, and sat up to receive visitors.

Herr Katschuka proposed to open the birthday letters which had been put aside on that eventful day. That would be as good as anything—the naïve congratulations of the god-children to the miraculously saved lady, which no one had yet read. Timéa's hands were still bandaged. Herr Katschuka opened the letters and read them aloud. The magistrate, too, was present. The patient's face brightened during the reading, which seemed to do her good.

"What a curious seal this is," said the major, as he took up a letter which had a golden beetle stuck on the wax.

"Very odd," said Timéa; "I noticed it too."

The major opened it. After he had read the first line—"Gracious lady, there is in your room a picture of St. George"—the words stuck in his throat, his eyes rolled wildly, and while he read on, his lips turned blue, and cold sweat stood on his brow: suddenly he threw the letter from him, and rushed like a madman to the picture, burst it in with his fist, and tore it and its heavy frame from the wall. There behind it yawned the dark depths of the secret chamber.

The major dashed into the darkness, and returned in a moment with the evidence of the murder—Athalie's bloody night-dress —in his hand. Timéa hid her face in horror. The magistrate picked up the letter, put it in his pocket, and took possession of the proofs.

Other things were found in this hiding-place: the box of poisons, and Athalie's diary, with the frightful confessions which threw light on her soul's dark abysses, as the phosphoric mollusks do in the coral forests of the sea.

What monsters dwell there! Timéa forgets her wounds; with clasped hands she implores the gentlemen, the doctor, the magistrate, and her betrothed too, to tell no one, and keep the whole thing secret. But that would be impossible; the proofs are in the hands of justice, and there is no longer hope for Athalie except in God's mercy. And Timéa can no longer disregard the legal summons: as soon as she can leave her room, she must appear in court and be confronted with Athalie. This was a cruel task. Even now she would only say that she remembered nothing about the murderous attack.

The marriage with the major had to be hurried on, for Timéa was to appear in court as Katschuka's wife. As soon as her health allowed, the wedding took place quite privately, without any festivity, without guests or banquet. Only the clergyman and the witnesses, the magistrate and the doctor, were present. No other visitors were admitted.

Human justice would not spare her the painful scene: once again she had to be brought face to face with her murderess. Athalie had no dread of this meeting, but awaited with impatience the moment when her victim would appear. If with no other weapon, she wished by her eyes to inflict one more stab on Timéa's heart. But she started when the official said—"Call Emerich Katschuka's wife!"

Katschuka's wife! Already married to him! But in spite of that she showed unconcealed satisfaction when Timéa entered, and Athalie saw the face paler than ever, the red line over the marble forehead, the scar from the murderous blow; this memento was from her. Her lovely bosom swelled with joy when Timéa was required to swear in the name of the living God that she would answer truly, and all she said was true, and when Timéa drew off her glove and raised her hand, so that the disfiguring scar of a frightful sword-cut was visible. That, too, was a wedding-present from Athalie. And Timéa swore with that maimed and trembling hand that she had forgotten everything, and could not even remember whether the murderer with whom she had struggled was a man or a woman.

"Fool!" muttered Athalie between her teeth. (Did they not struggle hand to hand?) "What I dared to do, you dare not even accuse me of."

"We are not asking that," said the president. "We only ask you, Did this letter, in a child's writing, and sealed with a beetle, really come to you by post, and on the very day of the attack? Was it then sealed, and did no one know its contents?"

Timéa answered all these questions calmly with Yes or No.

Then the president turned to Athalie—"Now listen, Athalie Brazovics, to the contents of this letter:—

"'Gracious Lady,—There is in your room a picture of St. George on the wall. This picture covers a hiding-place, to which the entrance lies through the lumber-room. Have this hole walled up, and watch over your valuable life. Long and happy may it be.

Dodi.'"

And then the president raised a cloth from the table. Under it lay the accusers of Athalie—the bloody night-dress, the box of poisons, and the diary.

Athalie uttered a scream like a mortally wounded animal, and covered her face with both hands, and when she took them away, that face was no longer pale, but fiery red. She had a narrow black ribbon round her neck; she tore it off now with her two hands, and threw it away, as if to bare the lovely neck for the headsman, or perhaps rather to utter more easily what now burst from her.

"Yes, it is true I tried to kill you, and I am only sorry I did not succeed. You have been the curse of my life, you pale-faced ghost! Through you I have incurred eternal damnation. I tried to kill you—I owed it to myself. See now, there was enough poison to send a whole wedding company into eternity; but I longed for your blood. You are not dead, but my thirst is quenched, and I can die now. But before the executioner's ax severs my head from my body, I will give your heart one more stab, from which it will never be healed, and whose torture shall disturb your sweetest embraces. I swear! hear me, oh, God! hear me, ye saints and angels, and devils! all ye in heaven and earth!—be gracious to me only so far as I speak what is true." And the raving woman sunk on her knees, and threw up her hands, calling heaven and earth to witness. "I swear! I swear that this secret—the secret of the hidden door—was only known to one person besides myself, and that one was Michael Timar Levetinczy. The day after he learned this secret from me he disappeared. If any one has told this, then Michael Timar Levetinczy did no die next day! He lives still, and you can look for your first husband's return So help me God, it is true that Timar lives! He whom we buried in his stead was a thief who had stolen his clothes. And now live on with this stab in your heart."

CHAPTER XII.
THE PENITENT IN "MARIA-NOSTRA."

The court sentenced Athalie to death for attempted murder. The king's mercy commuted this sentence into imprisonment for life in the penitentiary of "Maria-Nostra."

Athalie still lives. Forty years have passed since then, and she must be nearly seventy years old, but her defiant spirit is unbroken; she is obstinate, silent, and unrepentant. When the other prisoners are taken to church on Sundays, she is locked into her cell, because it is feared that she might disturb the devotions of the rest. Once when she was forced to go there, she yelled out to the priest "Liar!" and spat on the altar.

At various times during this period great acts of amnesty have been passed, and on national festivals hundreds of prisoners have been liberated, but this one woman was never recommended to mercy. Those who advised her to repent in order to secure a pardon received the reply, "As soon as I am free I will kill that woman!"

She says it still; but she whom she hates has long fallen into dust, after suffering for many years from that last stab inflicted on her poor sick heart.

After the words "Timar still lives," she never could be happy again: like a cold phantom it overshadowed her joy; her husband's kisses were forever poisoned to her. And when she felt the approach of death, she had herself taken to Levetinczy, that she might not be placed in the tomb where God knows who mouldered away under Timar's name. There she sought out a quiet willow grove on the Danube shore, in the part nearest to where her father, Ali Tschorbadschi, rested at the bottom of the river: as near to the ownerless island as if some secret instinct drew her there. From her grave the island rock was visible.

No blessing rested on the wealth Timar left behind him.

The only son Timéa bore to her second husband was a great spendthrift: in his hands the fabulous wealth vanished as quickly as it had grown, and Timéa's grandson lives on the pension he receives from the fund bequeathed by Timar for the benefit of poor nobles. This is all that is left of his gigantic property.

On the site of his Komorn palace stands another building, and the Levetinczy tomb has been removed on account of the fortifications. Of all the former splendor and riches not a trace remains.

And what is passing meanwhile on the ownerless island?

CHAPTER XIII.
NOBODY.

Since Timar's disappearance from Komorn forty years had passed. I was in the alphabet-class when we schoolboys went to the funeral of the rich lord, of whom people said afterward he was perhaps not dead, only disappeared. Among the people the belief was strong that Timar lived, and would some day reappear; possibly Athalie's words had set this idea afloat—at any rate, public opinion was strongly in favor of it.

The features, too, of the lovely lady came before me, whom every Sunday I admired as she sat near the organ; her seat was the nearest in the pew to the chancel. She was so radiant with beauty and yet so gentle. I well remember the excitement when it was reported that a companion of this beautiful woman had tried to murder her in the night. I saw the condemned prisoner taken to the place of execution in the headsman's cart; it was said that she would be beheaded. She had on a gray gown with black ribbons, and sat with her back to the driver; before her was a priest holding a crucifix. The market-women overwhelmed her with abuse, and spat at her; but she gazed indifferently before her, and noticed nothing.

The people thronged round the cart; curious boys hurried in troops to see the lovely head separated from the neck. I looked on fearfully from a closed window—oh, dear, if she had looked at me by chance! An hour later the crowd returned grumbling; they were disappointed that the beautiful criminal had been respited. She had only been taken up on to the scaffold, and there informed of the pardon.

And then after that I saw that other lovely rich lady every Sunday in church; but now with a red mark across her forehead, and each year with a sadder and paler face. All sorts of stories were told of her; children heard them from their mothers, and repeated them in school.

And, finally, time swept the whole story out of people's memory.

Some years ago, an old friend of mine, a naturalist, who is celebrated as a collector of plants and insects throughout the world, described to me the singular district between Hungary and Turkey, which belongs to neither State, and is not any one's private property.

On this account it offers a veritable California to the ardent naturalist, who finds there the rarest flora and fauna. My old friend used to visit this region every year, and stay there for weeks zealously collecting specimens: he invited me to share his autumn expedition. I am somewhat of a dilettante in this line, and as I had leisure, I accompanied my friend to the Lower Danube.

He led me to the ownerless island. My learned friend had known it for five-and-twenty years past, when it was in great part a wilderness, and all the work in progress.

Apart from the reed-beds, which still surround and conceal the island, it is now a complete model farm. Surrounded by a dike, it is protected from any floods, and is intersected by canals, provided with water by a horse-power pumping-engine.

When an enthusiastic gardener gets here, he can hardly tear himself away; every inch of ground is utilized, or serves to beautify the place. The tobacco grown here has the most exquisite aroma, and, when properly treated, is a first-class product; the bee-hives look from a distance like a small town, with one-storied houses and many-shaped roofs. The rarest fowls are bred in one inclosure, and on the artificial lake swim curious foreign ducks and swans. In the rich meadows graze short-horned cows, angora goats, and llama sheep with long, soft, black hair.

It is easy to see that the owner of the island understands luxury—and yet that owner never has a farthing to call his own; no money ever enters the island. Those, however, who need the exports, know also the requirements of the islanders—such as grain, clothes, tools, etc.—and bring them for barter.

My learned friend used to bring garden seeds and eggs of rare poultry, and received in exchange curious insects and dried plants, which he sold to natural history collections and foreign museums, and made a good profit out of them, for science is not only a passion but a means of sustenance. But what surprised me most agreeably was to hear pure Hungarian spoken by the inhabitants, which is very rare in that neighborhood.

The whole colony consisted of one family, and each was called only by his Christian name. The six sons of the first settler had married women of the district, and the numbers of grandchildren and great-grandchildren already exceeded forty, but the island maintained them all. Poverty was unknown; they lived in luxury: each knew some trade, and if they had been ten times as many, their labor would have supported them. The founders of the family still superintended the work.

The male members of the family learn gardening, carpentry, coopering, preparation of tobacco, and the breeding of cattle; among them are cabinet-makers and millers; the women weave Turkish carpets, prepare honey, make cheese, and distill rose-water; and all these occupations go on so naturally that it is never necessary to give orders; each knows his duty, fulfills it untold, and takes pleasure in its completion. The dwellings of the ever-growing families already form a whole street; each little house is built by division of labor, and the elders help the newly married. Strangers who visit the island are received by the nominal head of the family, whom the others call father. Strangers know him under the name of Deodatus. He is a well-built man of over forty, with handsome features; he it is who arranges the terms of barter and shows visitors over the colony.

When we arrived Deodatus received us with the kind cordiality one exhibits to old friends; the naturalist was a regular annual visitor. The subjects of our discourse were pomology, horticulture, botany, entomology, in all of which Deodatus seemed to be well versed; in everything pertaining to gardens and cattle-breeding he had reached a high standard. I could not conceal my surprise, and asked him where he had learned it.

"From our father," answered Deodatus, with a sigh.

"Who is that?"

"You will see him when we assemble in the evening."

It was the time of apples. All the young people and women were busy gathering the pretty golden-yellow, brown, and crimson fruit. It lay in pyramids on the green turf, like cannon-balls inside a fortress. Joyous cries resounded through the island; when the sun set, a bell gave the signal for the holiday feast. At this signal every one hastened to fill baskets with the remaining fruit, which was then carried into the apple-store.

We also, with Deodatus, bent our steps to the place whence the sound came. The bell was on the top of a small wooden building, which, as well as its little tower, was overgrown with ivy; but one could guess by the fantastic forms of the columns under the veranda, that the architect had carved many a thoughtful dream and wish into his work.

Before this house was a circular space with tables and chairs; there every one met when work was over.

"Here dwell our old people," whispered Deodatus.

They soon came out—a fine pair. The wife might be sixty, the man eighty. The great-grandfather's face had that characteristic look which makes you remember a good picture you have once seen, even if forty years ago. I was quite startled: his head was nearly bald, but the remaining hair and his beard were hardly gray, and on his firm, calm features age seemed to have no hold. A temperate and regular life and a cheerful disposition preserve the features unspoiled.

The great-grandmother was still an attractive woman. Her once golden hair certainly was flecked with silver, but her eyes were still girlish, and her cheeks blushed like a bride's when her husband kissed her.

The faces of both beamed with happiness when they saw their whole large family round them, and they called each to them by name and kissed them. This was their joy, their devotion, their song of praise.

Deodatus, the eldest son, was the last to embrace his parents, and then our turn came. They shook hands with us too, and invited us to supper. The old lady still kept the care of the cooking department in her own hands, and she it was who provided for all the family, though each had full liberty to sit at a separate table with any others he cared for, and take his meal with them; but her husband sat down at a table with us and Deodatus. A tiny golden-haired angel of a child called Noémi climbed on his lap, and had permission to listen, wondering, to our wise talk.

When my name was mentioned to the old man he looked long at me, and a visible color rose in his cheeks. My learned friend asked him whether he had ever heard my name before; the old man was silent. Deodatus hastened to say that his father had for forty years read nothing of what was passing in the world: his whole study was books of farming and gardening. I therefore undertook, as people do who have made a profession of imparting what they know, to bring my wares to market, and I told him what was going on in the world. I informed him that Hungary was now united to Austria by the word "and."

He blew a cloud from his pipe: the smoke said, "My island has nothing to do with that."

I told him of our heavy taxes: the smoke replied, "We have no taxes here."

I described to him the fearful wars which had been waged in our kingdom and all over the world: the smoke answered, "We wage war here with no one."

There was at that time a great panic on the exchanges, the oldest firms failed; and this too I explained to him. Only his pipe's steady puffs seemed to say, "Thank God, we have no money here."

I described to him the bitter struggle of parties, the strife between religion, nationalities, and ambition. The old man shook the ashes out of his pipe—"We have neither bishops, electors, nor ministers here."

And finally, I proved to him how great our country would be when everything we hoped for was fulfilled.

Little Noémi meanwhile had fallen asleep on her great-grandfather's lap, and had to be carried to bed. This was more important than what I was talking of; the sleeping child passed into the great-grandmother's arms. When the old lady left us, the old man asked me, "Where were you born?" I told him.

"What is your profession?"

I told him I was a romance-writer.

"What is that?"

"One who can guess by the end of a story what the whole story was from the beginning."

"Well, then, guess my story," said he, clasping my hand. "There was once a man who left a world in which he was admired, and created a second world in which he was loved."

"May I venture to ask your name?"

The old man seemed to grow a head taller; then raising his trembling hands, he laid them on my head. And at this moment it seemed to me as if once, long, long ago, that hand had rested on my head when childish curls covered it, and as if I had seen that noble face before.

To my question he replied, "My name is Nobody." With that he turned away and spoke no more, but went into his house, and did not appear again during our stay on the island.

This is the present condition of the ownerless island. The privilege granted by two kingdoms, that this speck of ground should be excluded from any map, will last for fifty years more.

Fifty years! Who knows what will have become of the world by then?

THE END.

Made in the USA
Middletown, DE
04 October 2018